GEM OF THE WANDERER

A Novel

BOB MADDUX

BOB MADDUX
For information, contact:
Ezekiel 12 Publications
San Deigo, California
bob.maddux@gmail.com

Printed Worldwide
First Printing 2025
First Edition 2025

10 9 8 7 6 5 4 3 2 1

Interior Book Design by Walt's Book Design
www.waltsbookdesign.com

To Claudia

CHAPTER 1

TRANS DIMENSIONAL PASSAGE

LYNREXS (MID-SUMMER), 5512

The corridor was long. Green vines grew everywhere, obscuring the ceiling with their leaves. Bracken had walked in this place before, yet each time its lushness became more alluring. The verdant growth formed an oval around him as if it had been spun on an organic loom. Ahead, the passage veered to the right and sloped upward. He followed it, his nostrils filling with the wet, pungent scent of moss. Rivulets of water ran between his toes, refreshing his feet with their cool currents. He had shed his boots along with his coat and leather belts before departing. Now he wore only a light shirt and pants and carried a bag over one shoulder.

Just minutes before, he had been in Oak Forest, lifting one of the glowing Mingus stones from its container. The gem's brilliant rays had cast gleaming streaks across his chiseled features as he lifted it to his mouth and swallowed. He had taken one of the most potent gems. He knew it was powerful enough to carry him and his ensemble farther into this realm than he'd ever been before. In fact, farther than most had ever gone.

The effects of the Mingus gem, the substance that had lifted him to this realm, tingled in the tips of his long fingers. Looking down at his arm, he could see the pale outline his com-patch had left on his tan wrist. For some reason, communication devices would not transition between dimensions. Instead, they mysteriously vanished and then reappeared once he returned to his world.

Now he was deep within the stone's spell. Miniature pools of light vibrated in his blue pupils as they widened under the stone's power. His mind responded immediately, carrying him beyond the natural plane. Guided first by his awakened perception, his strong but lanky form had followed, his senses surging with delight. Moments later, his whole body— along with his clothing and bag—had rematerialized in this higher realm.

Tiny creatures chirped in the background, their call a warm, sensual melody. He had often wondered why this link between the dimensions was so inviting. This time, though, he had more important questions concerning the death of his friend Silas.

He often struggled with memories of his friend, standing on the edge of the cliff in Oak Forest just before he jumped. Why hadn't he realized what Silas was about to do? Why hadn't he done more to stop him? Flashes of the scene rushed up at him as if he'd been the one plunging into the canyon.

He remembered how they'd both been drawn into the deception that had destroyed his friend. They were on the deck behind Roon's house, which overlooked Crysar Canyon. A faint single moon was the only witness to their ordeal.

A stream of ethereal fog drifted from the dwelling where the band was playing. The strange substance emanating from the music captivated them both but especially Silas. It surrounded them, finally cascading over the edge of the canyon, forming a large pool of glistening light at the bottom.

Both Silas and Bracken followed the mysterious current as it spilled over the edge of the deck. Bracken wondered if it was real or another surreal effect of the gem's power. Then he thought of Lisha, and he felt a slight tug to be near her, like a tether between them that had become too taught. He went back to find her.

When he returned, Silas was stripping off his clothes and calling to him. "Do you see him, Bracken? Look, he's calling me to join him,"

Bracken had also seen the glowing face, beckoning them from the swirling fog below. But then he doubted. He rejected the call from the shimmering being even as it spoke in his mind. "*I am comfort, I am home.*

Come, I'll help you. You have no need to fear." It pulled at him with a promise of peace.

Silas climbed on top of the deck's railing and declared, "It's beautiful, don't you see it, Bracken? So sparkling … I've got to dive in."

Bracken moved to stop him, but he was too late. His hand caught air instead of his friend's arm. Stretching out toward the glowing face, Silas dove toward the shimmering pond.

For a brief second, he had hung in the air, hovering like a bird in an updraft. But then in a perfect swan dive, he plunged into the pool of light, its wisps of white swirling around his ankles as he disappeared into its vapor.

For a moment, all was quiet as Bracken stared in disbelief. Then the fantasized bubble of beauty popped, the swirling miasma vanished, and the dream was over. Silas screamed just before his body crashed into the rocks below. Instantly the glistening cloud faded and all was silent again.

In shock, Bracken had gazed for a long time at the broken body of his friend until the reality of the moment finally hit him. Why? Why had he jumped? Who had called to them? It tormented him even now. He struggled to come back from the nightmare.

Gathering all his thoughts, he encouraged himself. *I will find the answer. I will know why. I will know what really happened.* He focused until peace returned. Dipping his hands in the moisture at his feet, he lifted them to his head and ran his fingers through his dark hair, pulling back the loose strands that tended to fall across his brows. His deep-blue eyes seemed to brighten as his long lashes brushed aside the drops of water that fell on them from his hair. Refreshed now, he smiled, flashing a row of white teeth, each as straight and sturdy as his fresh conviction. Then he closed his mouth and clenched his jaw, its sharp lines pointing the way forward as he continued his journey.

Dazzling light flooded the passage as Bracken reached the crest of the slope. Light filtering through the open places in the branches above him struck small motes of dust, turning them to brilliant jewels. The air had its own radiance as it sparkled, quivered, and scintillated around him. He breathed in the scent of mint, and then the smell of jasmine met it somewhere in his brain and created a whole new fragrance.

The light increased until it formed one glistening yellow wall. A small emerald door appeared in its center. It opened at his touch, and he walked through.

Another tunnel stretched before him, longer than the previous one. He walked on. Purple flowers bloomed among the ferns and vegetation around him, fluttering in the slight draft. He paused to touch one. Its texture was flesh-like. Each nerve in his hand responded with delight as he stroked its surface.

Then without warning, The Fear came—a foreboding so strong it was painful. He and his friends had called it that: The Fear. Because once it forced its way into your consciousness, the terror could dominate you. You could struggle with it, but it always seemed to come back, stalking, waiting, and silently pursuing you. He sensed only a hint of warning before it overcame him. Pleasure quickly melted into anxiety. Evil crept up on tiptoe and then shouted at him.

Was someone watching him, lurking just beyond his view? He searched the green plants and twisting vines for a clue to his panic. They were still. He listened intently to the clicking he'd heard since beginning his walk. At first it had been pleasant, like the sound of crickets chirping, but now it haunted him. It sounded like unkind laughter. He felt as if someone was secretly scrutinizing him, playing with his mind and mocking him.

He placed his hand on the side of his bag. He could feel the oval forms of the remaining energy eggs Ley Os, the gem dealer, had given him. He could always rely on them if things got desperate. Their explosive power could stop half a dozen assailants if he used them soon enough.

His ears opened wider as he listened … laughter … he concentrated more … chirping … then laughter again.

He forced away dark thoughts with purposeful words. *I won't be distracted. Silas's death must have a reason. I won't let fear keep me back. It's only my imagination.* As he reassured himself, the laughter faded. He continued to gather his courage. *I will find the answer. I will know the truth.* His anxiety eased as he ignored the thought that he was being watched.

Then The Fear was gone. It left as quickly as it had come, and he could once again feel the warmth of the Mingus Effect. It was filling his whole body now. Each pore seemed to breathe the air, which had suddenly become charged.

He pulled his thoughts together and reminded himself of why he had come. He knew he must press on and find the Zyphon level. That's where Os had told him he'd find answers.

Yes, he had to find the Source! Find who or what had drawn Silas to his death. What evil had deceived and seduced him. Memories of his friend's broken and twisted body flashed through his mind again. How long would they haunt him? Would his quest never end? Would he have to live without an answer?

He shook himself and walked on. The world suddenly changed around him. The green vanished. The tunnel became golden. Light radiated from light. He walked, almost skating on liquid brilliance, its radiance so bright that it surged under his feet like an incandescent tide. With each step, he felt waves flowing away from him, swirling, cresting, and pooling again like schools of iridescent water creatures playing in the eddies his footsteps created.

The smell of mint had vanished and was replaced by a scent of cinnamon. It tickled his nostrils and sent explosions of delight surging up through his mind, causing the neurons and axons in his brain to dance around one another.

Then he pulled back, ignoring the pervading pleasure that beckoned him to lose himself. This time it would be different. Not like before, when he had spent hours wandering, merely to fill his senses, his mind, and his emotions with pleasure. "I must find the source," he whispered under his breath. "There's some key beyond this level."

As if cued by his confession, the light ahead faded, but as he came closer, he realized it was only an opening into another room. Entering, he looked up. Crystalline panels rose around him like the walls of a cathedral, their apex somewhere beyond his sight. Abruptly, the light beneath his feet swirled and solidified into a marble-like substance, its glow fading. In the distance a figure materialized, drifting toward him like a gossamer angel. It was the only thing glowing now as darkness closed in around him.

CHAPTER 2

ABOVE TRANS DIMENSIONAL PASSAGE

LYNREXS (MID-SUMMER), 5512

The shadow watcher, known as Strieme, peered down into the corridor, observing as the light creature approached Bracken, and he recalled the words of the one who had ordered him to his task: "One of their kind has penetrated into the upper levels. This is serious, and we must find a way to keep him ignorant. If not, he will uncover the truth. Not just why his friend died but what lies ahead for him if he continues to search."

"I think terror is in order. Shall I bring it?"

"Of course, that would be the most gratifying, but there are other methods. We want him to quit looking for answers and spend his time in pleasure seeking. But there are ways to keep him hoping, ways to create fresh ideals in his mind. That should satisfy him for the moment until we come up with another plan. I will try them first, but if he seems unconvinced then you can act. You're not the only one I've assigned to this task. But follow him closely. Perhaps you will yet have your opportunity for torment. But wait for my signal."

Turning his attention back toward the corridor, he watched as the glowing orb approached Bracken. Hatred expanded in his heart like a poison vapor as he glared at the youth. He was looking forward to tormenting this fragile creature. It would be a delight to order his vassals to attack.

He sent out his command to them through the mind link. Immediately he heard the snarls of his slaves and knew they'd be ready. Their growls were like a delightful song, unharmonious to most but a melody to him. He smiled and continued to stand watch. It would not be long now.

CHAPTER 3

TRANS DIMENSIONAL PASSAGE

LYNREXS (MID-SUMMER), 5512

Bracken felt a chill as the corridor continued to darken. Moments before it had been flooded with light. Now only the strange figure was lit. It stopped just before it reached him, hovering slightly above his head. Bracken held up a hand to shield his eyes as they adjusted to its radiance. Then it spoke, its voice resonating and reassuring. "Welcome to the Zyphon, Bracken, my name is Hiffornak."

As his eyes adjusted to its brightness, he lowered his hand and stared at the being. Internally, though, he raised a defense. *How does this creature know my name? Perhaps it can read my thoughts? Whatever the case, I need it to give me answers.*

He looked boldly into the light and spoke. "Ley told me I might meet you here. He said he'd encountered some of your race near this level." Bracken remembered the Mingus dealer's words. "Lots of strange forces out there, Bracken. Most of them are friendly, though."

The circle of radiance moved closer. "Few of your kind have ever penetrated this far," the stranger continued. "It's good to see one so diligent in his search for knowledge." A soft hum of dissipating energy vibrated as he spoke. "Such hunger will be well rewarded."

The luminous creature's words rippled across Bracken's thoughts, stroking away his doubts. "Thank you for the compliment," Bracken replied, a bit unsure of the creature's intent. "Is it really possible that I'm one of the few who's come this far?"

"Absolutely, we've been monitoring all of your movements in this realm, and yes, you're one of the few."

Bracken briefly entertained a sense of pride, as if he was some sort of celestial mountain climber having crested a previously unconquered peak. "Well, I'm not content merely entertaining myself with pleasure. I've come for answers."

"That's what we thought. It appears you have a level of courage few of your kind possess." The words were reassuring and brought a bit of comfort in this strange realm.

Temporarily forgetting his quest, Bracken began to lose himself in the gentle ripple of this creature's voice. Other, unseen quiet voices seemed to beckon him as well ... *relax, rest, drift ...*

He shook himself and pushed the temptation away. "Yes, I've come looking for answers, answers about my friend's death." Bracken remembered again the shattered body of his companion lying dead on the sharp rocks at the bottom of the Crysar Canyon. The memory helped to jar him from his dream-like state. "And why are you here?" Bracken asked, peering closer, hoping to penetrate the cloud of light.

"I am a representative of Naacan, and I've come to guide you."

As Bracken listened to the gentle tones emanating from the light cloud, he noted the diplomatic grace of the strange being. Still, he felt cautious.

The creature was speaking again, "Our people are from another realm that is linked to yours by this passage."

The words took on a strange dissonance, and the light around him warped and then pixilated momentarily before returning to its former state. Bracken backed away, "And what kind of world is that?"

"Naacan is a simple place, one of happiness. Our history has been timeless and peaceful, interrupted only when others like you have joined us seeking a higher plane of existence."

The shroud of brightness seemed to be revolving in a slow orbit around Hiffornak. Bracken stared beyond him, hoping to see where he had appeared from. Darkness blocked his gaze.

"How did you find your way here, then?"

"All my kind are creatures of light. We move freely through progressive spheres of energy. It's a simple thing for us to pass into this lower realm."

Bracken was growing impatient. "Then why haven't I seen you before?"

"We have chosen to remain hidden from you and the others who have been exploring this dimensional link." The speaker lowered his luminous form until it almost touched the ground. "We weren't sure of your intentions. We don't give away our secrets to just anyone. They're much too valuable to be squandered, and we've discovered that often when we do share them they go unappreciated."

The creature moved closer to Bracken, and its presence seemed to bring a certain comfort in the dim atmosphere. "Many of your kind appear to be like children playing with a new toy, but I am glad to see there are those like you who seek answers, not simply pleasure. This is why I've been sent. I'm to assist you in your quest."

Bracken looked about the darkening room. Stuttering slightly, he turned back to Hiffornak, "I … I am seeking answers, but too often I've run into dead-ends and confusion."

The luminous creature responded with the words of cautious advice. "These levels hold the answers to many mysteries, some more elusive than others. But you must be careful here, for there are other forces that seek to destroy and enslave your kind. Still, we have seen that you're different. You're the type that will not be taken hostage."

The creature's richly toned voice steadied Bracken. The reassuring words filled the hollow place left by his friend's tragic departure. But bitter memories emerged and pushed away any consolation. Bracken looked down, restraining his sense of sorrow. The frozen substance beneath him matched his mood, growing darker each moment.

"Perhaps this is what happened to Silas?" offered Bracken, looking back to Hiffornak. "Everything looked so beautiful just before he died and then suddenly it became a nightmare."

"A fearful possibility in this region," the light creature responded. "Such depths of discovery are not without some misfortunes."

"I've had my share of those lately." It wasn't just Silas's death, but Bracken's grief over Lisha too. Since they had parted in anger, he'd been filled with doubt about how he had handled his jealousy. His heart longed for her again in spite of his efforts to quell it. At lonely moments, visions of her both inspired and taunted him.

Then to add to his troubles, there had been the Pirax, the armed assault force that had been brutalizing The Community. His journey here had allowed him a momentary respite, but he suspected that once he returned to Oak Forest he and his companions would be fleeing the inforcement team.

The light creature's reply interrupted Bracken's thoughts. "We are aware of your Community and the bond you feel for one another. It's certainly regrettable that you have suffered such setbacks. But remember, life is a cycle." Hiffornak's voice took on a philosophic inflection. "If one dies, he will come again. Noble ventures will repeat themselves, eventually finding success. We are all like the passing rays of the sun, vanishing only to beckon the coming of another day. And perhaps that day is beginning here with you."

Bracken eyed Hiffornak. "How can that be? You must know the attitude in the Community, and of the Pirax assaults. Hope is gone! The Fathers have forbidden us to ..." Bracken's mouth filled with a bitter taste at the mention of the leaders of his land. Their actions only proved how narrow, selfish, and oppressive their ideas were. "The Council of Fathers has suppressed any new ideas. They've closed their ears to the words of the edge-poets who sing of a new hope and future for our planet. And of course the power of the Mingus gem is a threat to their hold on power. They've used the 'Rax to contain its spread and crush any dissidence."

The light creature responded gently, clearly sensing Bracken's tone. "Yes, I know. This is why I have been sent, not only to answer your questions, but also to encourage you. You are weary, but soon you will be refreshed. Relax, rest in this moment. Embrace the light."

A soft radiance emanated from the cloud of light that surrounded the creature. It flowed toward Bracken, and as it reached him, a gentle fragrant breeze soothed, caressed, and comforted him until every worry vanished.

Deep within, Bracken sensed that this renewing force was what he needed. Time ceased as peace spun a cocoon of renewal around him. Thoughts slowed to a trickle, and reassuring warmth encased him. Stillness settled over his mind like a silky sheet. All was at peace.

Then, like the newness of dawn, the sage-like voice stirred him and he awoke from the dream. "Now that you have been strengthened, it is time for you to return to your friends. Bring them back here to meet with me. Then I will be able to instruct you further. My kind are here to teach, guide, and protect you. In spite of the battles, you will succeed and overcome every obstacle."

Bracken felt heartened at the Naacanite's words. They began again with a whisper, his voice starting to fade. "Bring them soon …" His voice dimmed, "Follow the surge from the Mingus Effect. It will lead you to me …"

The glow vanished and Bracken found he was alone again. Everything in him wanted to linger, wanted to stay in the warmth of Hiffornak's spell, but a strange chill dampened his bones as he stared into the air where the representative had previously floated.

Why had Hiffornak abandoned him? Had something driven him away? He looked into the darkness where the creature had been moments before and shouted, "You had such encouraging words. You gave me hope and now you're gone. Where are you?"

The bleakness of the murky atmosphere seemed to chase away the promises he'd heard moments before. He cried out again, angry now at the one who moments before had brought him assurance. "Maybe you were just another illusion, another empty dream. In fact, I'm not sure what's real anymore. You spoke such words of promise but I tempted not to believe them."

He peered into the wall of shadows that now rose around him and wondered. Was there some threatening presence nearby? Is that what had driven the glowing one away? Aware of the change in his surroundings, he realized the Mingus pulse was dissipating. The stone's power was fading.

A semi-glow of purple and orange appeared and enveloped him. He turned and walked back, retracing his steps. A vortex of murky fog appeared before him. In its center, an opening formed. His heart seemed to tell him not to enter it, as if something was lying in wait for him there. But there was no time for earlier fears. He had to move now while the effect was still strong.

Shaking off his apprehensions, he thrust through the portal. He emerged to a darkened chamber on the other side, gloomy tunnels running off in various directions.

The return journey through the Mingus realm was usually less brilliant, but it had never before been this obscure, opaque, and sterile. Nonetheless, Bracken stepped forward, taking the first path to his right, letting the Mingus sensations guide him. His perception of the Mingus Effect was growing faint and hard to follow. He struggled to hold on to it for it had always guided him back to his home world. He hoped it would remain until he left the passage.

He sensed a gentle tugging inside, pulling him back to his own dimension. He had to return to the exact place where he had entered this higher realm. If the effect vanished completely before he returned, he might find himself ejected into a less comfortable spot than Oak Forest.

He quickened his pace at the thought. Staring into the darkness, he walked cautiously ahead. His ears pricked as he heard a familiar sound. The chirping had returned, but it soon morphed into haunting laugher once again.

He saw motion farther down the corridor. A dark form retreated into an intercepting passage to his left. The sense of fear returned. It invaded his thoughts like a dagger that pricked, pierced and cut away the peace he had known only moments before.

He wanted to run. He heard someone padding up from behind him. When he turned to look, a louder series of footsteps sounded in front of him. He whirled back, his eyes focusing on two serpentine creatures that materialized before him. Their heads were hideously contoured. One of them opened its mouth, exposing a vicious set of fangs. A low rasp cut into the air.

The creatures stared at him with an evil glint. Like flames of a smoldering fire, the monsters' gaze consumed the dry flax of Bracken's courage.

The Fear returned with crushing terror. A gruesome strength held him, pulling him down, tearing at his hope. "I won't let you take me," he shouted, fleeing down the corridor.

Dark forms moved to stop him. He dodged, momentarily evading his pursuers. He sprinted down a faintly lit hall to his right. Glancing back, he could see more forms chasing him. He ran down the tunnel, gasping for air as his pursuers drew closer. He raced blindly into the semi-darkness. Without warning, he slammed into a dead-end, bruising his head and an arm. Turning back, he saw that the dark beasts were nearly upon him. In desperation, he thought of using the energy egg in his pouch, but by now the range would be too close and there wasn't time to set the specs on the device. The explosion would destroy him along with his stalkers.

Stunned and confused, he turned around and charged back into his pursuers. Hands grabbed him. Feet tripped him. Claws gouged at his flesh. He fell, his body smothered by his hunters. Their hot and rancid breath stung his nostrils. The pain was too much; Bracken felt himself fading.

Then from deep within, it came … a name, a flicker of hope, that which he had ignored before … that which he'd deemed empty and foolish … That Name. He screamed it just as he lost consciousness. In that moment, the creatures lessened their grip and then everything faded into blackness.

Hours later, he awoke. The creatures were gone. He was falling. His body writhed. Every cell in his mind felt as if it was burning. He was alone, his surroundings a blur of color. He shut his eyes and searched for a comforting memory. There was none, only two haunting questions. *Where am I? What strange power rescued me?*

The pain subsided and he opened his eyes. Nev Broc stood over him, shaking him. "Are you all right, Bracken? Maetrek, hey man, wake up." His voice cracked with worry. He shook Bracken again, staring intensely into his face. "You there, Bracken?"

Bracken could barely make out the faint forms of his friends, and he realized he was back in Roon's house in Oak Forest. The soft fur of the bed beneath him beckoned him back into unconsciousness. The light from the molded brass shades above him gave off a relaxing glow and then faded as he closed his eyes.

Nev put his hand under Bracken's head and lifted it, making sure his friend was listening. "We weren't sure if you'd ever come back. We're glad you made it. We couldn't have waited much longer. We must leave now."

Bracken had to force his eyes open, the lids heavy with fatigue. Through the haze that clouded his vision, he could make out Nev's bushy hair and beak-like nose. Inside he felt sleep tugging at him, pulling him back into the shadows. Sleep. Rest. He wanted to shut everything out.

Nev's voice stirred him again. "We've got to leave. The Pirax are closing in."

Bracken began to slip away again. Struggling, he fought against his lethargy. "Where are we going?"

"To Raka. We can hide there. Os and the others have the trans loaded. I've got to remove your com-link. Ley's worried that the 'Rax will try to track us. We're leaving them here. Roon has a safe place to hide them." Nev began to slide the device from Bracken's wrist, where it had reappeared, once he returned from the Mingus realm. Its face glowed blue in the darkened room, confirming that it had reconnected to the planet-wide communication grid.

Bracken managed to mumble, "Help me to the rig." Then he remembered his musical instrument and his long coat. "Please bring my clothes and stam."

"Don't worry, I've already packed them in the rig."

In the background, he could hear equipment being loaded as they struggled toward the large trans-max. Shapes moved back and forth through the fog that still veiled his sight.

When they reached the vehicle, its door opened with a *whoosh*. Someone helped Nev lift him onto a bunk. Soon he heard the drive unit lumber to life. Then the trans-max moved off through the twilight, heading up the long road that led toward the distant desert.

Bracken awoke periodically during the night of travel to hear echoes of a threat. He would stare bleakly about, mumbling, and then fall unconscious again. Finally, he gave up struggling and slept a deep, long sleep.

Descending out of the night sky, Strieme the shadow watcher, kept pace with the accelerating transmax. His eyes gleamed as the force of his stare penetrated the roof of the moving vehicle. Then a rasping whisper flew like a searing dart toward Bracken. "You may have escaped this time, but we will feast on your soul in the end, once you've served your purpose. Fools like you will soon be caught again."

CHAPTER 4

LOWER THRONE ROOM

LYNREXS (MID-SUMMER), 5512

Strieme's body rose up from the granite floor like a marble statue. The muscles of his arms bulged beneath his glistening skin like twisted ropes of hardened bronze, and his massive calves protruded from his legs like gray, steel cylinders. His silver tunic with three vertical strips of purple near his chest signified his high rank.

Standing fully erect, he overshadowed most of his cohorts, who trembled whenever he moved among them. Yet he was trembling now. Deep within his core, a shaft of fear was pointed at his heart. He shivered under its threat as he stood alone, the sounds of tormented voices rising from chambers somewhere deep beneath him.

Gradually his eyes adjusted to the dim, ambient light of the cavernous room. The gloomy gallery provided some comfort, its bleakness masking his ugly but powerful body. He had been beautiful, even angelic, once, but years of wicked indulgence had left him a gnarled shadow of his former glory.

Moments ago, the voice of his master had come into his mind with an overwhelming sense of authority, the words carrying an underlying threat. He had responded immediately, descending until he arrived at this hidden chamber. Shortly before, he'd been in the strata-place, effortlessly moving in and out of dimensions as he monitored the activities of those he'd been assigned to watch. That strata-place had a certain beauty and warmth, but its brightness only enhanced his sense of wretchedness.

Now that his vision was clear, he could see the Shadow Czar seated on a high throne several yards in front of him. Strieme bowed, genuflecting over and over again as he approached the dais. Every movement was calculated to show complete obedience to the one on the throne. He knew that any improper gesture could offend his master and relegate him to a place of torment like those whose suffering cries rose from below.

The voice that had summoned him now spoke in his mind, a low commanding rumble like the grinding of stone against stone. "There is a threat to our protocol," the voice ground out the words reluctantly. "As you know our target has used the … Name." The enthroned one nearly choked as he uttered the last word, almost spitting it from his mouth. "Such boldness must not be tolerated. And to think we almost had this fool trapped. Now I'm afraid he's become a threat."

There was another pause and then the sound of a slow expelling of air between clenched teeth before the voice spoke again. "Somehow he called out, and our grip was broken." The frustration in the voice coming from the throne was like gravel on glass, the words scratched from a larynx scarred from repeated rants. Strieme marveled that his leader was taking such a personal interest in this problem. The Shadow Czar often remained at a distance, allowing his lackeys to carry out his wishes. Apparently he'd chosen to get involved in this matter directly.

The enthroned one had faced many such vexations, often finding his minions failing at what he considered simple tasks. "Your vassals have also blundered. We have a short window open to us. If you fail again, another opportunity is unlikely, and that would be onerous for you."

Strieme could sense the threat in those words, and images of torment flashed in his mind. The speech of his commander roared like a shout even though the actual volume hadn't changed. It carried a much deeper resonance now, one that seemed to smother his soul. He was the slave of evil, and it easily overcame and commanded him.

In the past, he had delighted in wickedness and allowed it to twist around him like a sensuous nest of snakes. Eons before, he had given himself over to its carnal pleasure, joining many of his race that swore allegiance to its rebellion. There had been such promise in their uprising. Their leader had assured them of a quick victory. He declared they would no longer be ruled by another but be free to serve their own desires. Yet their war had failed and they'd been cast down.

Now they were still being ruled, but this time it was by one whose grip was relentless as it choked, compressed, and constricted them until their souls reached a state of asphyxiation, bending finally into complete obeisance. In spite of this oppression, Strieme had found pleasure elsewhere: in the suffering of others.

The evil that commanded him now brought with it a level of torture, murder, and oppression that had crushed countless lives. He'd learned to enjoy each nuanced moment of suffering, constantly crafting new techniques to bring torment to those he brought under his will. Still, like some unyielding addiction, this pleasure carried with it an accompanying authority, holding him with a grasp he knew he could never break. He also found that the one wielding the greatest evil was always the strongest. That strong one was enthroned above him at this very moment, a being whose lust for terror and torture was without equal. Strieme envied his power even as he was repelled by it.

His master's voice interrupted his musings. "I'm choosing to overlook this incident because you've rarely failed me. You are one of the few I can count on. So you have a fresh assignment. You must bring this foolish upstart back under our power." Slowly the speaker's voice changed, becoming alluring and comforting, each word promising pleasure. "If you capture him, I will grant you Theema with one hundred souls. You may indulge your senses on a deeper level than you ever have before."

It was the ultimate incentive, Theema, the torture Strieme would be allowed to inflict on the living beings whose minds would be chained to him. The Night Ruler had the power to open secret portals and connect him to unsuspecting souls. Souls he'd be allowed to torment at will. How far he'd come … epochs ago, he had lived for a different purpose, his pleasure had come from bringing pleasure to others, but now it came from tormenting them.

The commanding voice continued, "I'm assigning several new agents. Instruct them to employ the subtle methods woven in the pleasant-lies.

Promise him truth but appeal to his lust. It has worked for ages, and it will work on him as well. Also create strife between him and his companions. This will increase his confusion and create a depression we can use. Here are his records."

Instantly all the details of the assignment, including the name, facial recognition, and location of his assignee flooded his mind, making an audible as well as graphic display there. He ran through the items some of which he'd seen before, others new—*Name: Bracken Maetrek; Location: Western Nerkush; Possible trajectory: Accad, Demur, Zorek, Rimlex, Shidow; Closest friends: Silas, Lisha; Our available agents: ...* the interface continued to scroll through his thoughts.

As he anticipated the assignment, he thought of his reward, and its promise of pleasure grew in him even now. A sensual tingling began at his core as he thought of the unbearable and mental pain he would bring to his charges. This very thought drove him now, and it would soon consume him with unstoppable passion.

A final word came from the enthroned one, "Your success will bring me great pleasure, as will your failure, because then I'll find a special joy in personally punishing you."

"I will succeed, Master."

"For your sake that must be more than wishful thinking."

With that threat still echoing in his mind, the twisted one ascended, moving quickly through a labyrinth of intersecting corridors until he stood again in the strata-place. From this high position, a series of access points allowed him to move unseen into the path of the one he'd been assigned to, the youth known as Bracken Maetrek. A glint of wicked pleasure smoldered in his dark eyes as they focused on his victim. A slight smile appeared at the edge of his mouth as he savored the thought of his future reward. This simple fool would be like so many others who had fallen to his machinations.

CHAPTER 5

HIGH REALM

LYNREXS (MID-SUMMER), 5512

The guardian and watcher know as Michess walked on stones of sapphire. They stretched as far as he could see. Each time his foot touched the gleaming surface, joyous energy surged into his whole being. This was not his first appearance at this exalted level, but whenever he was summoned here the environment seemed more glorious. That was no surprise. He knew that the One who dwelled here had no end, no margin, no boundary, and therefore there would be no limits here. Wonders kept unfolding, as a scribe unrolling an endless scroll.

So he walked forward, taking in new splendor with each step. He finally stopped before a throne. It rose from the bejeweled plain like a crystal spire. Overwhelmed, he felt his legs give way. He bowed low, and pleasant words emerged in his mind like fragrant flowers. "Michess. What wonders have you seen today?"

He knew that the One who had summoned him already knew the answer to that question. But it was the sincere expression of interest that reassured him. "I've seen many things. Some hard to describe, but wonders nonetheless."

"And have you seen things we must be concerned about?"

Michess knew his master already had the answer to that question as well. "Yes, especially with the one I've been assigned to." The pleasantness changed.

Now there was another moment of wonder exploding in his mind, a new scented blossom opening, one he could not recall. Then he remembered. *No limits here.*

"So what have you done? What are you plans?" his master already knew what had occurred but asks for the purpose of instruction.

"I thought it was wise that I stepped in and I plan to in the future. Surely there will be more trouble ahead for him."

"Yes. There will be trouble. But, remember, there's a right time for everything. I wish now that you hold back for a season."

"But I'm concerned that the enemy might prevail."

The fragrance came again with these thoughts. "He might. But now is the time to trust. Your charge will have to find his way."

"Yes, but what if ...?"

"Such 'ifs' are part of the risks we've chosen to take. He must choose even as you have chosen."

"But what if he chooses wrong?"

"Then all of us will suffer. But we must take that chance."

"Then I take no action?"

"There will be a time to act, but for now you must watch. Watch and whisper to him. Remind him of what he once believed to be true."

"Will that be enough?"

"For now, yes. My words carry a weight with them. They can be ignored for a while, but ultimately they will come back to him and he will see that they are true. The right moment for the revealing of my power will come, and then we will deal with those who oppose him."

"As always, your wise advice is my command."

"I will call again soon, and you will bring me another report at that time."

"May my duty always bring you pleasure."

"It has. Till then."

"Till then."

Rising to his feet and turning, Michess looked around. An ancient phrase whispered in his mind. "Standing in the shadow of brilliance there is no shadow, only degrees of light." Looking into those "shadows," he saw rows of beings, each so powerful that one could shake a planet with its breath. Still they held their great power in check, fully obedient to the one on the throne.

Looking through the veil of brilliance, along the endless row, he seemed to see a faint smile of approval on each face. They cheered him on in silent peace. Walking now to the edge of that which had no edge, he wondered where all this was leading. No doubt a great struggle was ahead. But for now he must remain on his assignment. So he simply spread his wings, flexed his muscles, and sailed off to the watching shaft.

CHAPTER 6

RAKA

TAR-LYNREXS (LATE-SUMMER), 5512

Dawn came to the Valley of Raka as pale sunlight crested the distant mountains. The darkness slowly withdrew to reveal a semi-barren landscape. A collage of sand and rock spread itself across the flatlands, sparsely sprinkled with red and blue foliage. Here and there a series of dunes rose and fell like waves on a yellow sea. Stillness clung to the remaining moments of twilight as the sun crept farther into the morning sky. The preceding day had been long and hot. This one promised to be the same, as the calm air warmed rapidly under the increasing heat of the sun.

Within his small adobe hut, Bracken Maetrek stretched his lanky frame upon his bunk and groaned. It had been days since they had fled from Oak Forest. His body was still sore, but he could sense it gradually healing, even though he'd grown thinner from the basic diet being fed them by their new master, Terresh Shad, the owner of the vinweok farm where they now served basically as slave laborers. It was a miracle he'd survived the attack in the corridor. He wondered what had been the key to his release. Perhaps it was the Name, the one he had called out to in his desperation. No, he couldn't accept that as an answer. It was too simple, too familiar.

Bracken sat up and looked out his window toward the workers' compound. It was quiet. A few sand-devils swirled in the early dawn air. A frisq, one of the wild desert dogs that roamed the wastelands at night, could be heard barking in the distance. The other huts were quiet. No one else had stirred yet.

Beyond the courtyard a massive white building rose above the other mud shacks. Terresh Shad lived there. He owned this part of the desert and everything on it. His mansion-like home gave off a stark glow in the twilight. It reflected its owner's nature, thought Bracken. Shad was a cold, calculating businessman at heart, not a humanitarian running a refugee camp. Bracken and his fellow fugitives had come here to hide, but their sanctuary was turning into a nightmare. There was a cost for living under Shad's protection, and that fee was becoming pricier every day.

Depressed, Bracken lay back down and rolled over in bed. He could smell the stench of the unwashed tunic he now lived most of his days and nights in. His coat, leather pants, and other clothing were stored in the trans-max. There was little need for any of it in this baking climate.

He counted the markings he had made on the wall to record the passing days. They had been here three sevens. Three sevens of slaving on this ranch just so they could hide from the Pirax. He wanted desperately to leave. The smell, the sweat, and the barrenness were more than he could take. If it weren't for the Parax who were hunting for him and his companions, they could leave. But they all knew what awaited them if they were caught. They'd be sentenced for the crime of using the Mingus stones and sent to the Lyten quarries to pay for their lawlessness. They'd be forced to spend years digging the stones for the walls of the new palaces that would house the rulers in Accad, his region's capital.

To him and the others in his group it was no crime to explore the realm of the Mingus stone. Through its influence and the creative gifts it released in them, they'd broken with the narrow way of thinking ingrained by their elders. Through it they had connected with a force that could shift the whole future of their world. They were riders on the clouds of a coming tempest that would bring change to Ebbern, his planet that desperately needed such change. In fact, it needed a revolution, and if that upheaval failed to come soon then he was certain that all of his world would be destroyed.

But for now because of the Pirax and their ruthless crusade to enforce the will of the Fathers, they were marooned out here. This exile only made his questions about Silas more difficult to bear. He could do nothing about them here. Then there was Community in Accad. Would they survive without Os's leadership? As soon as the pressure was off, they had to leave. As their leader, Os must realize that none of them could take much more of this barren existence.

In the meantime, though, Bracken tried to push away the useless frustrations and get a few more moments of sleep, but as he did a faint sound came to his ears from the distant hills. He ignored it at first, but as it grew louder, he sprang up and ran to the door. Staring off toward the southern horizon, he could see three black dots slip over the high ridge. He grabbed a set of sight enhancers that dangled from a worn strap hanging on a peg by his door. He moved out from the shade of his hut and pointed them in the direction of the humming sound he'd heard earlier. He instantly recognized the air ships. The Pirax sky flyers were moving rapidly. They would be overhead in no time.

He hurried into the center of the workers' compound, shouting a warning. Grabbing the leather thong at the bottom of the muster bell, he shook it frantically. The clarion call echoed through the compound, shattering the last quiet moments of dawn.

Rubbing their eyes and squinting in the bright morning light, several people staggered from their shelters. Ley Os, the wiry man who had first introduced Bracken to the stone of power, flung back his front door and yelled out at him, "Why all the noise? The stinking vinweoks will eat soon enough."

Os's once-smooth face was now unshaved, his hair disheveled. The desert life was wearing on all of them. It blasted away at the liquid of their youth, like a drumming desert storm, drying up their civility. Bracken could remember many a night with Os, captivated not only by his rhetoric but also by his handsome features and the smooth texture of his personality. All that was gone now, and Ley's countenance appeared more like the weathered exteriors of their shelters than the youthful moisture of Oak Forest.

Bracken rang the bell again. "It's not vinweoks, Ley. Look!" Bracken pointed toward the approaching craft. "The way they're moving, they'll be here before we have time to hide. We've got to act now."

Suddenly a high-pitched sound from the ancient broadcaster squeaked across the compound. "This is Shad!" The curt voice was tense. "The Pirax must have heard you were here, Os. We don't have much time. If you run, you can make it to the cave where your trans-max is stored before they get a clear visual on us." The ancient broadcast instrument hummed and popped between words. "Hurry, I'll cover for you."

As the drumming of the sky flyers' vertical lifters grew closer, Ley and the others sprinted toward the high rocky hill behind Shad's house. Scrambling over it, they disappeared into the darkened entrance of a cave.

The lumbering rotors of the 'Rax's flyers beat noisily through the dry desert air as they sped toward Shad's ranch. When they finally arrived they stirred a small storm of dust beneath them as they maneuvered to land. Shad looked up to see the faces of the pilots focused on their control systems as they guided their craft. After hovering momentarily above the workers' compound, the three air ships settled to the earth amid a whirl of grit in front of Shad's mansion.

The Pirax guards, their grim faces barely visible through their facemasks, looked determined as they leaped to the ground from the flyers, forming an impenetrable phalanx. Their dark helmets and body armor seemed to absorb the bright sun making them appear almost wraithlike among the sand cloud their vehicles had raised. Standing in stark contrast to their black gear, their polished handheld shields overlapped each other in one long, unbroken line of protection.

The tall Pirax captain, his muscular body apparent even beneath his body armor, stepped from his flyer and strode forcefully toward Os's dwelling. Behind him, his men stood ready, their thrusters covering his approach. He stopped before the gate. "Come out, Shad! The Council has some questions for you." The 'Rax officer's words seemed to bounce off the towering white façade and then slowly fade as if its structure had drained them of their authority. The heavy wooden door at its front opened slowly, complaining loudly on its weathered hinges.

Shad, munching on his mouth drug, ambled out, stopping a few feet from the captain. The old man's gray eyes glared at the Pirax officer. His face that seemed as rough as his tattered work clothes was leathery and worn, but when he spoke, his voice was surprisingly youthful, "What's the Council want with a desert rat like me? I'm just livin', mindin' my own business."

"Not you, Shad, but some rebels from Accad."

The farmer spat on the ground. "You think they're here?"

"Rumor has it that when they left Oak Forest they were headed this way. Leader of the group is a guy called Os."

"Can't recall anyone by that name comin' here," he lied.

Shad's legitimate workers stood quietly in front of their compound's gate warily eyeing the Pirax. Shad pointed toward them. "You're welcome to check through the group, but I don't think you'll find them."

The captain turned to one of his aides. "Take two men and check their identity cards." The three broke away from the others and paced quickly to the compound. The officer turned back to the farmer.

"Shad, you're notorious for hiding rebels. You couldn't keep this ranch going without them." The captain gazed disdainfully at the milling herd of vinweoks. "No one would want to live here unless they were trying to hide."

"Ain't that way with me!" Shad pulled his weathered hat back on his tan forehead. "I find this place most enjoyable. The evenings are especially nice."

"I'm sure they are," sneered the captain, walking around toward the side of the massive building. Shad followed him. "I'll take the sea breeze of Accad to this stench any day."

"Each to his own, sir." Shad chewed again and spat the blue syrup onto the sandy soil. "There's nothing like a desert sunset."

"And being downwind from a herd of vinweoks," the captain snorted. "How can you stand the smell of those beasts?" The ugly creatures milled about several large pens, pressing at the rails.

"It ain't so bad when you consider what their meat sells for on the markets in Accad." Shad took a deep breath, smiling as he exhaled.

"You don't have to remind me of that. I've only had two of their steaks this year." The officer stopped near the edge of Shad's yard and stared off toward the flatlands and rocky mounds in the distance. For a moment, he eyed the surrounding landscape. His aide came running up to confirm that the search of the workers had revealed nothing. Dismissing him with a grunt, the captain gazed out into the desert again. "If they're hiding out there, we might spend ten sevens locating them."

"They ain't out there. Not even a bush bird can live out there without water!"

"Yes, I'm sure you're right," the captain grumbled as he whirled around and walked back toward his flyer. Passing the phalanx, he muttered at them, "Let's go, men! This place reeks!"

The Pirax boarded their craft. In a cloud of dust and sandy grit, the sky flyers lifted off and headed back the way they had come.

CHAPTER 7

RAKA

TAR-LYNREXS (LATE-SUMMER), 5512

S had smiled in triumph as he watched the departing sky flyers move out of range. The smirk on his face quickly dissolved at the bellowing of the impatient vinweoks. He walked to his house and switched on his broadcaster. "They're gone, Os. You can come out. Those toy soldiers could have ruined the herd with their interruption." His amplified voice boomed out across the plain toward the rocky hills where the fugitives were hiding. "And hurry, you slow-bellies! The vinweoks are annoyed! Much more of this and their meat will sour."

Bracken, Os, and the others straggled out from behind the rock and stared off toward the vanishing sky flyers. "How'd they know we were here?" asked Bracken bitterly. He was growing tired of the hiding, tired of the anxiety, tired of the Pirax on their backs. Apparently they could even be a threat here in Raka.

Os motioned for them to start back toward the ranch. "I'm not quite sure how they found us. Perhaps an informer told them. It could have been someone at the Sea Sphere. That place is full of people who know I'm friends with Shad." Os adjusted the bill of his rumpled hat. Tufts of sandy hair jutted out from under its rim. His skin now was ruddy, but his eyes were still a clear steel blue. His stare was penetrating when he was obsessed with an idea. Right now, though, he was squinting under the sun's glare as he walked beside Bracken toward the snorting vinweoks. "I think they're through looking for us for a while. Their trip up here had to be a last resort."

Bracken kicked at a stone in his path. As it rolled over, a pair of sand crawlers scurried away, their four sets of eyes darting back and forth on their small shell-like heads. "Does that mean we can leave this hole soon?"

"We'll have to see what the others think," said Os. "But don't worry. We'll be out of here as soon as possible. I'm as sick of this place as you are. I hope I never see another vinweok again."

Bracken looked off toward the waiting herds with disgust. "They kinda resemble the 'Rax, don't they?" he said with a sneer.

Os removed his tattered work shirt and tied it around his waist. "Yeah, and neither of them seems to want to give us any rest. I'm as tired of looking at those ugly faces as you are, Bracken. We'll be moving on as soon as I'm sure it's safe."

Bracken lagged behind Os. He wanted a few quiet moments with his thoughts before he went to work. As he watched Os trudge along ahead of him, bitterness rose inside him. He still admired his leader, but he'd begun to question the man's motives, his judgment. Why had he led them here? Weren't there better places to hide? What about the Mount Tasken region—couldn't they have lost themselves in its deep forest, lived off the abundant wildlife, and forged for fish in its crystal streams?

Then there'd been the act of betrayal with Lisha. Ley had taken her from Bracken in a moment of confusion and weakness. He knew she had welcomed it, but he still harbored a deep wound and inwardly resented his leader for it. Neither one of them possessed her now, though. What good was his bitterness doing him? He needed the gem dealer's friendship; maybe he should excuse the breach in their relationship for the time being. Besides, there were higher ideals they were both pursuing that would bind them together for the foreseeable future.

The putrid scent of vinweoks brought him out of his contemplation. He could hear Os still muttering to himself. "I'm not planning on staying here forever."

Bracken wrinkled his nose as the beasts' odor wafted toward him. "It already seems like forever," he whispered under his breath. No matter how long he'd been around their sickening smell, he couldn't adjust to it.

A vinweok, Bracken thought, was one of the most repulsive creatures he'd ever seen. Its squat, gray body was covered with matted stripes of hair running in opposite directions with no seeming pattern. Its flat snout was cursed with a grotesque array of breathing receptors. Beneath these, a sagging tusk-filled mouth swaggered from side to side. The plodding creature guided its way by means of two twisted antennae, protruding above its hair-filled ears.

Normally, it fed upon the wild desert shrubs that grew in the Valley of Raka. But since its flesh had been discovered to be a delicacy, it had become profitable to raise them on a more nutritious diet. Each grew fat and content before it was butchered and carted to the populous seaside city of Accad, to tingle the palate of the wealthy.

Shad had grown rich from such shipments and dreamed of raising herds that would fill the entire valley. But this strange breed had one flaw. For all their ugliness, they possessed a strange sensitivity; if they became overly agitated, their bizarre digestive system tended to malfunction, causing its gastric juices to leave a distinctive and fetid taste in their flesh.

As Bracken and the others reached the feeding pens, the milling herds grew excited. Their rank, sweating bodies glistened in the sunlight. The rest of the crew from the compound joined them. Together the group reluctantly lifted their shovels and began heaving the yellow grain into the troughs where the creatures ate. They would feed the beasts in groups with only a slight rest break between shifts.

Great clouds of dust began to rise from the desert floor as the first herd of giant animals advanced, pushing one another in an attempt to reach the feeding pens first. Bracken and his fellow workers labored furiously to keep up with the appetite of the ravenous beasts. The smell of the animals' bodies mixing with the dust was nauseating.

Bracken's eyes burned and watered with bits of grit. By now the sun had risen well into the morning sky. As its rays penetrated the cloud of dust, Bracken and his friends appeared as ghostly figures in an ethereal cloud of sparkling light. But to those coughing and laboring with the bellowing vinweoks, it was more like a hell. Sweat trickled down Bracken's brow and added to the burning in his eyes. It ran in streams from under his arms and down his chest. As the sweat mixed with the rancid air and dust, his body began to itch. But he found little time to relieve it.

The vinweoks must be fed. If they weren't, they could become enraged, and once that began, their meat could quickly sour. One herd had become inedible because of the failure of a feeding crew to appease them in time; so, choking and spitting, Bracken continued to shovel.

A half an hour later, the first herd had been fed. The satiated creatures lumbered off as the rounders brought in the next group of animals. Bracken stopped and tied his bandanna around his face. Next to him, Ley leaned on his shovel. Removing a rag from his pocket he wiped his brow with it.

Bracken was struck with a sudden ache for the comfort and fellowship of his friend Silas. He often remembered his sense of humor and positive attitude. He wished Silas could be with him now to help him face the challenges of desert life that tended to depress him. He repeatedly found himself ending his days thinking of Silas, of home, and dreaming of better times.

He loved to watch the sky fill with hues of purple and gold as the last rays of light painted the clouds clustered against eastern mountains. But then they would fade to gray along with the memories, as another lonely night stretched before him. Sure there were still some great times as he, Chepa, and his band brought out their stams and played music late into the night, warming themselves against the chill by the small fires that Shad allowed them to build from time to time.

On some of those nights he had traded his boredom and loneliness for the embrace of another female member of their group. The young women who adored the musicians were so loyal that they'd been willing to join them even in this barren place. But as intense as the lust and sensuality could be, it often vanished just as quickly as it had come once they moved on to another member of their group.

He longed to connect again with Lisha. But she was far away, and the starkness of his environment made her tenderness all the more haunting. He was lonely and tired. Tired of looking and not finding answers. He was tempted to think that all his searching had been a waste and that his time in the Mingus realm had not been real. Perhaps it had only been a fantasy.

Perhaps Lisha had been a dream too, and that dream was fading with each bitter day here in Raka.

Bracken let his own implement fall to the ground. Exhausted, he sat down in the sand. The other workers had already collapsed in the gritty soil.

Tightening his sagging shirt around his waist, Os walked over and sat down beside Bracken. "I wonder how things are going back in Accad?" he said with a sigh. "I imagine the Pirax hit all my network of Mingus suppliers in the city." Ley took a stick of drug weed from his pocket and began chewing it, spitting the excess syrup into the sand between sentences. "If the High Council has its way, there will be nothing left of the Community soon."

Bracken grimaced. He liked the friendly atmosphere of Accad, where he and others had formed an uncommon community in one of its older neighborhoods, the unique people with their smiles, laughter, and blissful ways. He thought again of the tree-lined streets, the spacious parks filled with frolicking people dancing on the grass as they listened to Chepa's group and the other bands that played there.

Os continued chewing. "Well, I guess we should have expected it. Ever since the Community started, it's been considered a cancer by the High Council."

"That still seems crazy to me," said Bracken in disbelief. "As far as I'm concerned it was the only livable place in all of Accad. People there seem to really love each other whatever their race or culture."

"You know it all started with the edge-poets and musicians years ago in another decaying neighborhood in Accad," recalled Ley. "It was the only place they could afford to live. So they gathered there and began a whole new society."

"Yes, I'd read about that."

"They planted the seeds of their ideals there that grew into the movement that we now call the Community. Those musical sages had great vision. They sang and spoke about a new culture where people of all races and backgrounds could experiment with a new lifestyle. They didn't have the Mingus stones then, but they had the sacred herbs that took them to other realms. But even those were illegal and suppressed by the Pirax."

Bracken drew in the sand with his finger, randomly creating circles and squares. They'd had conversations like this many times before but repeating them seemed to help reinforce their vision. "I recall how the rumors came even as far as Tizra about their different way of life and radical ideas. But it spoke to me, and obviously many like me who came to the Community."

Os took his hat off, brushed the dust from it, and placed it back on his head. "Yes, the idea that there are hidden doors of perception that will give us true insight into the meaning of life can't be handled by The Fathers. They've always seen existence from a mere material viewpoint. Only what they see with their eyes and touch with thier greedy hands must be real."

"And they must be first in line to have it," inserted Bracken.

"Well, that's changing, and I'm determined to see that others understand it whatever the cost to me."

Looking down, Bracken spotted a stinging four-legged insect crawling toward him. It methodically maneuvered its way through the sand. Annoyed, he flicked it away with his finger. "Everyone there was looking for something better, something different. No wonder the Fathers are so set on destroying us. They're threatened by anything that challenges their narrow views." Bracken had made this statement many times, but somehow by voicing it again it brought the contrast between the two cultures into focus once more and gave fresh resolve to their rebellion.

"It's because they're afraid," said Os. "Besides, in their narrow view of reality they still cling to the stiff morals forged by their forefathers. But those don't work anymore. They know it, and they don't really live by them now anyway, so we're a threat."

"Coming down on us hard is their only option."

"Exactly. We've broken free. We're not bound up like them and they're jealous. They're hipocrites. In secret they break the codes they claim we must keep. Besides, so many of them are caught up in all the stuff they can collect, their power and wealth, at the cost of others going without."

"You're right, Ley. We're not in this just because we want change. We actually believe it's time to bring in a new order. It's time that we care about others enough to lay aside our fears, and really love. Hopefully we can keep that vision alive."

Ley took the dregs of the weed from his mouth and tossed them away. "That's my dream. Even though the High Council seeks to destroy anything they think is going to change the present order of things. But even if they do, we'll just start over somewhere else. What we've got between us will work anywhere. It's our ideals, our love, our brotherhood." Ley's steel eyes were beginning to grow intense. "We're part of something they'll never understand. They can't. They're too old, too narrow. The future's ours and they know it." His voice was rising now, his heart and mind stirred by his convictions. "They're trying to hold on to an old dream. It's our turn to dream now, and they're simply not part of it. When we take over, they'll be like we are now, on the outside."

Bracken grew quiet, letting Os drone on. He listened but not with the same assurance he'd shown in the past. He knew what they had spoken was true, but he'd lost some of the inner conviction he'd held before. Os seemed to be changing. Now he was much like the others in the group at Raka, too much like himself, growing more disagreeable every day. His words sounded right, but they felt empty at times like this; it was an emptiness that even the purple weed couldn't assuage.

Bracken remembered a night when they'd first arrived in Raka, when Ley had opened up to him about his past. He'd been surprised to hear Ley had been hurt by his father's emotional distance. Os had shared how he'd grown to hate the way the man used his wealth to manipulate those in power. It made him resent everything his father stood for, and it had been responsible for his search for meaning elsewhere. But underneath all the rhetoric something was growing. He'd loved Ley's conviction that the walls of prejudice, class, and power that separated so many in the current culture had to be pulled down. Those ideals resonated deeply with Bracken. Those were the things that drew him to Ley in the beginning, but now they'd begun to seem empty here in the desert.

The caldron of Raka had put a lot of his ideals to the test. He found character flaws, selfish acts, and even a certain elitism emerging in the ranks of their group. These sorts of attitudes had always been there in the larger Community, but Bracken had chosen to ignore them. But like the heat of the desert, they became oppressive and could no longer be overlooked. It was clearly affecting his relationship with the gem dealer. Their closeness was beginning to evaporate just like moisture in this desolate land. Bitterness had grown in Ley and seemed to act like a toxin slowly spoiling any essense of kindness that had dwelt there before.

Shad had told Bracken how many of the trees in this region had once drawn life from a great subterranean aquifer, but as it dried over the years the soil became poisoned with useless minerals. As the trees drew those noxious substances into their branches they soon became barren and eventually withered. At sunset you could see them standing out against the distant purple of the mountains, stark, lonely, sentinels, black as death, their long and leafless branches twisting toward the sky like some soul in torment. Bracken was sure this was what was happening to Ley. The man had begun with such hope, but his frequent run-ins with the Pirax along with the unresolved issues from his youth had begun to erode his dreams. All of these things were slowly drawing a vein of brackishness into his ideals. Bracken could sense it sometimes in his own heart as well but refused to believe it. He was convinced that his generation would be different even if there were a few like Ley that sought power over others more than power to help others.

As the next herd approached, Os finished his speech. "We'll all be back together soon. Something will work out. You'll see, Bracken."

Bracken stood up, picking his shovel off the ground. "Sure, Ley ... sure it will," he said tersely.

The new group of animals was more ravenous than the first. They rammed up against the feeding troughs struggling with one another. Groaning, the crew went back to work.

Shouts came from near the watering trough as workers directed the previous herd toward it. The nose of the water tower was lowered to release its precious contents into the troughs. The trampling droves collected along the long rows of water receptacles. The snorting beasts drank deeply to wash down their meal. Bracken tried to forget his own thirst. He remembered Shad's rule: No water for the workers until the vinweoks were fed.

Out of the corner of his eye, Bracken saw the rancher standing on the sun deck of the great house, his sinewy frame casting a narrow shadow to the ground below. He was watching the operation through his eyepiece. The air crackled with static from his communicator as he conversed with Rollion, his foreman. Rollion, a tanned, massive man, quickened the pace, shouting orders over the broadcaster he held in his right hand.

The heat increased as the sun rose higher in the sky. A tenseness seemed to pervade the air. The other workers cursed at the beasts and then at each other. Bracken wearily stared down the line of vinweoks. Perhaps only four hundred remained to be fed. They would be through in an hour.

Bracken's muscles ached under the load of his shovel. He continued to choke, spitting from time to time to bring up the particles that lodged in his lungs. His head pounded. A giant burning hammer seemed to be pounding down on his back, pounding down on all of them, pounding out the last bit of life.

The itching had grown almost unbearable. His burning eyes had begun to water and swell. They smarted under the glare of the sun and from the pain of the grit. His dust-caked cheeks were streaked with tears. He comforted himself with the thought that he would be done soon.

Suddenly someone yelled behind him. It was the shrill and familiar voice of Ley. Another fight had started. In these conditions, patience was as rare as water and much thinner. Without warning, Bracken was struck in the back with the blade of a shovel. The blow knocked him beneath the feet of the vinweoks. Drex Stead, one of Ley's friends, stood over him, poised to strike again. He and Bracken had had words earlier when he'd questioned Ley's leadership. Bracken struggled to rise and was hit in the face by feed. Bracken's hands dug deep into the grit beneath him. He came up throwing it at Drex's eyes. Around them, others were brawling too.

"Stop, you fools!" yelled Rollion. He firmly grabbed Stead and Os and shouted again. "Return to your cells! The other crew will finish this shift!" His giant size and force of personality had a sobering effect on all of them. "Bracken, stay and keep order!"

The battle was over as quickly as it had begun. The opponents warily withdrew from each other and walked toward the workers' compound, muttering. Remaining behind, Bracken leaned against his shovel and placed his hand upon the deep rent in his coveralls. He was bleeding where the blade of Drex's shovel had struck him. He stanched the flow of blood with his handkerchief.

As he waited for the next crew, he stared into the feeding trough before him. The noise of the restless waiting vinweoks was deafening.

Why am I here? Why do any of us stay? What strange force still holds us together even though we've begun to despise one another?

It seemed like only yesterday that their whole group was in the heart of Accad enjoying the closeness of the Community. He fondly recalled the days of music and soaring moments of pleasure they shared under the influence of the Mingus stones. The nights lost in the joys of unrestrained sensuality as they put aside the moral restraints of their parents.

They'd written songs about their adventures and together drifted on a tide of what appeared to be a growing understanding of this higher calling to their generation. But a tide of circumstance had washed them ashore on this barren land in the heart of Raka, and it appeared that no new current would carry them back to that now-distant place.

Through his exhaustion, Bracken remembered a better day, an orchard, trees, and his father's voice. That day was years earlier in the small lazy town of Tizra in southern Nerkush. It had been a time of peace and closeness with his father, Kreswen ... a time he had tried to forget as he'd distanced himself from his parents, his home, all of those old and naïve ways. It was so far away now ... just a memory. But something within him seemed to reawaken ... a thread of hope amid his disillusionment.

Could he have been wrong about it all? Was his father really as out of touch as he'd thought? Those were the kind of questions that haunted him here in this barren place.

CHAPTER 8

NEDI FOREST—TIZRA

PAR-SIMTESH (NEW-SEASON), 5498

Kreswen, a handsome man, watched his child Bracken darting through the patchwork of shade cast by the tall trees of Nedi Forest. This brought him great delight for, in spite of his fascination with ancient things, observing the vigor of youth seemed to bring him back to the present. Most of his career as a teacher of the history kept him absorbed in the past, so during these breaks from his job, he enjoyed pondering the future that the youthfulness of his child promised. Presently all his attention was focused just on keeping pace with the boy running ahead of him, periodically plunging into the surrounding woods to return each time with some new discovery in hand.

The child's lanky body reminded Kreswen of his younger self, and for the most part he'd maintained that slim frame to this day. Time had changed some things, though. There were the manly marks of age the sun had branded on his face and a slight sagging here and there in his olive skin.

It was also true that his hair was making a retreat up his forehead, but his blue eyes reflected a clear intellect, and his white teeth stood in an unbroken row, enhancing his frequent smiles. It had become obvious that the boy was blessed with the same mental prowess that had carried his father to a respected place amongst the scholars at Tizra's Advanced Mind-Training Center.

Just past his seventh year, the child had already learned to appreciate the beauty of the deep forest. His mental alertness was matched by an artistic temperament that caused him to revel in the beauty around him.

The forest had become like a home for both father and son. They spent many days here together whenever Kreswen had time away from the pressures and demands of his work at the Center.

Below them, Greenbrook slowly wound its way down toward Tizra. He and Bracken had angled there for hours, catching the gleaming fish and wogs that swam in its clear waters. Now on their way home, he once again marveled at the growing sense of love he felt for his young boy.

The sun winked at them through the high trees as they made their way toward the glen. The grass played about their ankles above their sandaled feet, tickling their bare legs. Already it had begun to yellow with the coming of Yiane, first warmth. Somehow, though, the smell of the deep forest was always the same. The tall trees seemed to filter the air and add their pleasant and fragrant blessing to the atmosphere of the shade beneath them.

He knew that the child sensed this too. He was different than the other youngsters in Tizra. Even though his body had a male muscularity along with the rough and tumble attitude that was all boy, the child possessed a gentleness that the others lacked. At times, Kreswen wondered where it had come from. Such sensitivity was often thought of as weakness, and neither he nor his wife, Myrus, had ever been considered soft.

They came from hardy stock. Myrus, a petite and comely woman, was reared in the Yadren Mountains. She had developed her strong, durable disposition from tending the herds and fighting hunger in the bitterness of the bleak-times in the Fayliss range. This, though, had not changed her bubbly personality, a perfect match for her rosy face.

Kreswen had not had an easy childhood either. He had grown up in the rugged atmosphere of the Mid-Region, working in the Milch farms of his homeland. He could still remember the hungry days of the Greatfall when food was scarce and the idea of self-preservation had become painfully real. It was those difficult times that finally drove families like his and Myrus's to move to the more fertile region around Tizra, where his parents still had a small farm on its outskirts.

No, they would never be considered soft. Perhaps the fact that the child had grown up without such hardship could explain his sensitivity. To correct any imbalance in this area, Kreswen planned that when the boy grew older he would spend harvest season helping his grandparents bring in their crops. Still he was glad to see that music was an interest for his son, for it carried with it an artistic expression that he did not possess.

Myrus had a sweet voice, and she had mastered the finger harp to accompany her singing. Bracken, clearly endowed with the same gift as his mother, had already shown an unusual skill with the stam, and his father had made sure the boy had the instrument the moment his talent became evident.

Kreswen was awakened from his thoughts by the approach of a small swaim. It had crept from behind a tree and was now watching them with steadied attention. Its soft fur glistened where spots of sunlight left a patchwork on its back. Bright eyes gleamed from either side of its short black nose, and its long whiskers twitched expectantly.

The boy was delighted at the swaim's appearance. These were the friendliest creatures of the woods, and many times they appeared in front of them fearlessly, in hopes of being fed a morsel. Both father and son slowing sank into the soft grass, hoping to put the swaim at ease.

From the leather sack at his side, Kreswen broke off a bit of the leftovers from their lunch. Leaning forward, he handed it to his son. Bracken took the piece of food from his father and slowly extended it toward the animal. Immediately, it responded by creeping closer and relaxing. Soon its tiny paws reached up and gingerly removed the food from the child's grasp. It retreated a few paces and began to devour its prize.

"Why don't all the creatures of the forest become our friends, Father?" Bracken questioned.

Kreswen looked down into his son's bright blue eyes; so many questions to ask, so many to answer. He hesitated for a moment and then spoke. "Fear. Fear has captured them, Son."

"But where did fear come from, Father?"

"The animals became afraid because long ago the hearts of Ebbern's people changed. They were captured by fear themselves. A fear that the legends tell us came when they were caught in the Night Ruler's web of lies. He had snared our forbearers with it. The creatures sensed its deadly grip, and somehow they gained the wisdom to avoid us."

Kreswen recounted the modified version of Ebbern's history, known as the "Early Tales." It was a simpler way for children to deal with these questions until they were older and mature enough to hear the story uncensored.

Bracken's eyes clouded with amazement. "And why did the Night Ruler want to hurt others, Father?"

Kreswen paused for a moment before answering. Should he tell the child the frightening account the way he'd learned it as a youth, or should he leave it for another day? Of course Bracken had heard accounts from ancient writings in the Volume about the evil lord, but they'd always been put in a light that muted the full horror of the wicked prince's schemes. Perhaps it was time to pull back the veil a little. The boy's face urged for an answer. For some strange reason, he sensed that the child was mature enough now to learn a little more of the story. *Yes, perhaps this is the time,* Kreswen thought.

"Long ago," he began, neglecting the full details—in the Fourth Age, under the reign of the First Council—"when Tizra was but a small village and all Nerkush was quiet and at peace, the Night Ruler came. The Yuki herdsmen were terrified by the strange sights that appeared in the sky above them."

Kreswen had read the accounts in the historic writings, but he'd also been told the tale by his elders when he was a child. He clearly remembered those nights, years ago, clustered around a warm hearth in his home, when his ancient grandfather poured out the story of the age-old battle that had taken place in the night sky.

He drew from those childhood memories and from readings of the Volume as he continued, "Stars collided, their sparks starting fires on the plains. Some even said that war was in the heavens. From their station high in the mountains, the herdsmen could see clearly as the firmament appeared to have been set ablaze."

Kreswen remembered looking deep into his grandfather's crystal-blue eyes as the story had unfolded; he would never forget that haunted gaze. The story had been told many times in many households, but the old man added his own slant to the narrative, whispering almost under his breath.

"Many thought the fire would never subside. They feared it would burn on like the fires of the underworld until all of Ebbern would be left barren. But then, mysteriously, the fire subsided and the real horror began. Then the stars began to fall, streaking across the dark sky like fiery birds of prey, only to vanish just before they reached the ground."

Kreswen left out many details. He realized that the child was having difficulty grasping the extent of the terror that had been unleashed on their peaceful world. He didn't tell him of the wildfires that burned the pleasant plains of Umin and of the countless stories of mystery that surrounded the descent of the burning ones.

"Then came the Night Ruler, falling with the force of a renegade sun. Only his star did not burn out like the others. It became brighter as it grew closer. Everyone ran from the spot where it landed, far up on Shidow Mountain. The whole night was lit up like daytime. Finally those who were brave enough climbed up Shidow's steep slopes to seek out its resting spot. They said its radiance warmed them and left with it a peaceful feeling.

"After a while, the light grew dim, and as its brilliance faded, the Ruler appeared out of the center of the star. His countenance was dazzling, and as he came down into the plains, great crowds followed him. There was a magical presence around him, and hope seemed to spread from him like the mist spreads over the valley in the season of the last warmth."

Kreswen stopped, remembering how his elders had been angered by the treachery of those times. Yet he wondered if any of them would have had the courage that cost so many lives. "Some were afraid of him, but they were considered fools and doubters. Still others tried to stir up the people against him, claiming he was a deceiver. But those opponents all came to mysterious deaths, and before long, no one would speak against him. Finally he arrived at the City of Shurar."

"Where was that?" the boy asked.

"It was a great city where Accad is today." The boy was familiar with Accad, for his father had taken the family there for a Cele-break during the previous year. It had left a deep impression on the boy. But very little remained of ancient Shurar, only a few crumbling ruins surrounded by the walls of a museum.

"The Council leaders of Shurar asked him to lead them. His wisdom was so convincing that they believed he could guide Nerkush to a bright future. But no sooner had he taken power than the Division began. Many said it was as if light became darkness. Confusion scattered friends, families, and neighbors. Hatred ripped at the people's hearts, and they slaughtered one another without mercy. It was then, by some invisible force, that the Night Ruler vanished. But most believe that he still lurks nearby and that his influence is still with us, causing much of the evil that haunts our world."

Kreswen had studied this history years ago, along with other young people in a class on Gathering Day, when the devout families of Tizra met to study the Volume. He'd heard the story many times, but each time he had to recount the tale it left him saddened. "Some built great fortresses in which to hide. Men were sold as slaves, and great monstrous beasts roamed the land. Shadowy creatures crept from the sea and devoured men. Even in our age, there are stories that the descendants of those beasts still lurk in the Forest of Zorek waiting to prey upon those who have forgotten the stories of our elders and think of them as myths."

Bracken was spellbound as he sat beside his father at the edge of the glen. He listened to the story with an intensity that drew the ancient tale from Kreswen with new meaning.

"Most of the animals became afraid and ran from all who approached them. A few remained friendly, but even those seemed different. The land and the sea were upset and struggled with each other. No one knows the entire story, and many of the facts have been lost over the years. Of course many just laugh at these things and call them myths."

"Father," the child interrupted, "wouldn't it be wonderful if the animals had not been cursed by such things and were friendly like the swaim? He's so cute and his fur's so soft." The animal had finished eating and was watching them again, hoping for a second helping.

"Papa," he continued, "do you suppose we could take the swaim home, perhaps he would like to live with us? I'm sure he'd make a wonderful pet."

"No, Son, it's better to leave him here in the woods," Kreswen answered, "for this is his home, and we can always come here and visit him again."

Kreswen stared up into the sky, watching the white clouds as they drifted on the soft breeze. So much of what he'd told his son had become mythical to him. Even though he knew the sacred history had a purpose, it had become more of a morality tale in his opinion; something one could learn ethics from but little more. At times like this, though, he wished he could believe it all. "It has been said," he continued, more to himself than to the boy, "there is a day coming when all the animals will be our friends again. It will be the day when the Night Ruler is cast away forever. A day when the great promise will be fulfilled."

"Of course, Father, we hear it every week at the gatherings. They speak of it from the Volume. The Prince of Wonder will return, and with him the peace we all seek."

"Yes, Son, we all know the story well because your mother has made sure we hear it regularly." He continued, innocently mocking Myrus, the sincerity of her voice and tone when she told the tale. "*Then all of Ebbern will sing, and the trees will make music as they did before the coming of the Division. It will be a day of power, power that will humble the evil prince forever.*"

Bracken laughed along with his dad at the end of the sentence, a naughty little glimmer tickling the corner of his eyes. "And don't forget, Dad, how she always sings the last part." The boy's grin set the stage as he began to mimic his mother's sweet voice. "*The good Prince wants us to be agents of his wonders to prepare Ebbern for his return.*" They both giggled and playfully punched each other until an unexpected soberness came over them.

Bracken was the first to sense it, and he turned a questioning look toward his elder. "When will that be?" he asked. "Will I be alive? Will I see him come?"

"Many have said it will be soon," responded Kreswen, merely repeating what he'd heard Myrus and others report. "They believe that life as we know it now will change greatly and that the final struggle for Ebbern's world will end, and the grasp of the Night Ruler will be shattered."

He felt he had an obligation to his wife to tell his son what others said, even though he struggled to accept all of it. "It is believed that only those who have given their allegiance to the Prince of Wonder will know that the end is here. Many will have to pay for that knowledge with their lives."

Kreswen picked up a colorful stone from the ground. Turning it over, he examined its texture as he talked. He believed in things he could see, things like the stone in his hand and the knowledge that had moved their nation ahead of all the others. So much of this tale had become a traditional part of Nerkush's culture. It was just another ancient story to build holiday celebrations around and create a special season for children to enjoy. Many like him gave the custom a weak nod and went along with those who believed in it rather than stir up dissension. It was all harmless anyway, and the little ones seemed to enjoy it.

He looked across the glen toward Tizra, where he could see the dome of the Advanced Mind-Training Center. It was where Nerkush's youth learned what was real. His years spent studying Ebbern's history, its shifting cultures, and the many wars that had brutalized the population of his planet had made him secretly skeptical of these "neat little stories," but he knew it would be out of place for him to say differently. So, for now he continued the narrative.

"The truth-seers say the Night Ruler is strong and hates all knowledge of the Prince of Wonder. These sages pored over the Volume for many years and became the stewards of its teachings; they believe that he murdered the Prince to keep his plans from coming true."

"What were his plans, Father?"

"Plans to create a different world, one where all evil would be removed."

"Did the Prince succeed?"

"That's yet to be seen. But one thing the truth-seers say is that he overcame death, and that was proof enough that he will be successful someday."

Even while he was relating the simplified story, and even though he doubted most of it, the fact that it might be true troubled him. For beyond the reach of his child's comprehension were countless stories of terror and hope. It would take days to relate the threads of truth that at times seemed like myths. So many had forgotten the teachings of the Prince of Wonder.

Few gained any more than a philosophic appreciation of his life. "He taught wonderful things, and yes his death was tragic. But we have the record of his deeds, and those should be enough for us to try to follow, anything beyond that is mere speculation."

In recent years, Kreswen had come to reason this way himself. He knew how Myrus felt, and he respected her hopes. But he had yet to be sure of his own beliefs. Besides, so much had changed since the day they claimed the Prince had come back to life. There was so little evidence to prove the things written about him. Hadn't his followers soon lost the power they declared he'd endued them with? Within a centi-cycle of his supposed departure, it had become more about mere tradition. His followers allegedly used to do the wonders like he did, the ones he promised to give them. But apparently these were no longer evident.

In fact, if anyone sought to do such works now, they were considered deluded or followers of some kind of evil. It was clear to him that the growing followers of the Night Ruler had connected with energy forces that even his mind-tech training could not explain.

It was greatly debated among his colleagues whether there were powers from other dimensions and realms beyond what they could discover with their reason. If there were such powers, it was clear that the evil side had a monopoly on them.

What had happened to all the promises of the Prince? Was the story just that, a story, a beautiful but empty legend? That's why he and Myrus had argued. She believed, but he could not. His training had produced so many doubts within him. Still, part of him hoped it *was* more than a legend.

Realizing that he'd left off with his explanation, he pushed aside his own questions and told his son the story anyway. He would finish it and make sure that the child at least knew the entire account so he could decide for himself what to believe. He slipped the stone into his pouch and continued his story.

"Yes, Son, some say his coming is without a doubt. All the words of the Sayers will be fulfilled, and they promise as surely as he has died to break the spell of the Night Ruler and empower his followers to do the same, he will come to finish what he began and build a new world."

His voice trailed off toward the end, betraying his weariness with the whole issue. Attempting to change the subject, he stood abruptly and looked up the rise. His movements startled the swaim, and it scurried away. Ahead was a clearing in the forest.

"Enough of those things now. Let's go on to the orchard! I'm hungry for something sweet and fresh."

The child rose as well and ran ahead, first to reach the grove. The jippen trees were ripe at this time of year. They found one close to the entrance of the orchard, its branches heavy with fruit. They each took a jipe and munched contentedly as they walked farther into the garden.

The boy looked up, his face momentarily caught in the diffused sunlight that filtered through the branches above him. "There's something so wonderful about this place, Father. The air is so fragrant." Around them stretched row upon row of bushes and trees. Every hundred yards, another type of tree was ripening. An exceptional thing about Tizra was the variety of flora that ripened each season. Trees of all types could be planted, and fruit would grow all year round.

"Let's gather some for the rest of the family. Your mother said to bring them home for dessert." Together they picked the jippen and placed them in their side packs. After they had finished, they quickened their pace back through the woods. At the edge of the forest, they stopped and gazed down upon the quiet scene below them. Greenbrook descended beyond them until its silver-green surface slipped under the first trees at the edge of Tizra.

The city had so many trees that even mid-summer was pleasant as long as one stayed beneath them. Kreswen watched his son as he took in the grandeur of the view. He loved this child. Feelings he could not describe flooded his thoughts. *How do you tell your son how much he means to you?* There seemed no way other than to give him the best of everything possible.

"Let us go home, Bracken," Kreswen said. They set off, making their way down the rolling hills toward Tizra. He sighed as he watched the child run ahead of him. The boy had always been affectionate. But, like so many of his generation, he faced the emergence of a whole new world, and sometimes Kreswen sensed that it's pleasures were more alluring than the deep bonds of love that drew a family together.

He'd known those bonds growing up. The hardships of the Greatfall with its economic crisis and food shortages had only brought him closer to his parents and siblings. But he sensed those values were lacking in the present time. They had so much now. Families rarely went hungry, and now that Nerkush dominated much of the world's resources, they had little worry about any future like the difficult past they'd been challenged with as children. Bracken's generation would never experience this. Kreswen often wondered if this was doing them a disservice. Would the fact that they never had to fight for anything spoil them or fail to develop the character they would need to survive should another time come like the one he'd endured as a child?

He could still remember the bitterness of those times, but he also was grateful for the way it had drawn his family together. They loved each other and needed one another to survive. He'd seen how his parents had loved him. In many ways, their children were the only wealth they possessed. He had bonded with his parents, his siblings, and his friends in a way that seem to be lacking in Bracken's generation. He was troubled by this, and by something even deeper that he couldn't quite name. He found it hard to express how he felt toward his son. When a man passed through deep challenges with those close to him, the hardship created its own way of communicating intimacy deeper than words ever could. But now they all lacked the struggle that could create that bond and the beliefs those times had produced in him. Kreswen wondered if Bracken would ever understand those values. He also wondered if his son would ever grow to appreciate how much his father loved him?

CHAPTER 9

THE VALLEY OF RAKA

TAR-LYNREXS (LATE-SUMMER), 5512

S had had restored order to the compound after the earlier melee, and the remaining workers grudgingly labored again at their duties. The blistering sun had kept up its attack on Bracken's head, and in spite of the sloppy hat he had donned, his brain felt numb, his thoughts swirling within him like the dusty air stirred by the milling herds. The tedium of shoveling the grain soon allowed his mind to come into focus and his thoughts went back to earlier times.

It seemed that he had grown up all too quickly. Once he reached his fourteenth year, he had found it hard to believe all the sincere but simple ideals that his parents held. His mother had never lost her devotion to the Volume and the tales of the Prince of Wonder, but somehow they had not captured Bracken in the same way.

When he was young his mother had faithfully read him the stories from the Volume. Many had intrigued him, but soon they became all too familiar. As new discoveries from the world of sci-tec were unveiled, they truly impressed him, and the tales from the Volume seemed just that—tales, even pleasant ones but ones completely out of touch with where Ebbern was going.

The tender times with his father had grown infrequent. Kreswen had become overly occupied with his duties at the Advanced Mind-Training Center, and his mother's discontent over this soon sent ripples into his stable home. Finding himself without the peaceful security that had been part of his life for so many years, he began to seek out the haunting songs of minstrels, edge-poets, and philosophers to fill the void. By his fourteenth year, Bracken had begun questioning the choices of the Fathers.

Nerkush had been victorious in the last Great War. It had left a certain pall of hubris over his nation, and that pride clung to its leaders in spite of their claims to want to rebuild a better world. From the ranks of Advanced Mind-Training Centers across Nerkush, scholars arose to share their concerns, and this in turn stirred up a new breed of minstrel-poet that became a thorn in the flesh of the growing overconfidence that their nation seemed to display.

A subtle but relentless assault of strange ideas found their home not only in Bracken's emerging philosophy but also in the minds of many of the youth his age. These ideals beat out a different cadence than what he'd known in the past, one so alluring and mysterious that it caught his heart.

Almost as if on cue, scores of his generation began to respond to these unique philosophies and brash ideas.

New forces soon brought his land to a turning point, one that would revolutionize it, shaking its safe and stable way of life and sending it reeling into a time no one could have imagined. Weapons of mass destruction had been developed in the last dec-i-cycle that could devastate most of Ebbern if unleashed in a significant amount. They not only threatened the tentative peace won at the end of the last Great War, but they left a pall of fear hanging over Bracken's entire generation.

In many ways, it defined part of who they were. If the end of their planet could possibly come in the flash of a thousand suns, should they not live differently than any other group before them?

It was not only the distant rumblings of war and intrigue that helped to inflame these troubled times but also mysterious powers from other realms. They began to manifest themselves even in the quiet lower plains of Umin. Many claims were made concerning sightings of strange sphere-like flying craft in the skies across Western Nerkush. These accounts filled many with wonder, others with fear that somehow these signs were harbingers of fearful times ahead for all of Ebbern. Some even claimed to have communicated with beings that piloted these vessels. Bracken remembered one man in particular whose odd ideas had been part of the great changes that had come to Nerkush.

Now it seemed like the pieces of this cryptic puzzle were coming together. Somehow Bracken felt that one piece lay shrouded in the mystery of a strange man, the esteemed but peculiar astrogazer, Frim Lieter. Their last encounter had opened up whole new possibilities and a host of questions along with them. There was much about him that Bracken didn't know, much that had happened to this man while Bracken was growing up that no one knew about.

CHAPTER 10

ABOVE EBBERN

PAR-MANTRIK (FIRST CHILL), 5503

Shadow and light played across Strieme's field of vision as he shot into the sky above Nerkush. Bolts of energy tingled in the extremities of his motion cloak as he twisted away from the harsh light of the setting sun. As he did, two forces briefly clashed within him; one dark, the other light. Even at this distance, the sunlight left him uncomfortable. He pressed on anyway, drawing the edges of the flight garment tighter around his muscular body. His red eyes glowed as he scanned the horizon, sharing the data they retrieved with the read-out scrolling by on a flickering gossamer panel within his head.

Details of other adversarial entities swept through his consciousness, and he assessed their proximity against his own trajectory. There was warfare in this realm, and he needed to move with stealth. It was all part of the ancient battle waged in a high, hidden realm above Ebbern. This battle raged on while those who lived on the planet below knew nothing of it. Its outcome often affected them, but they remained unaware until the results of each battle manifested itself in the choices of its leaders and populace.

He was confident that none of his enemies would be close enough to stop him if he continued to move in his current arc. Each time he reached this height, he wanted to return to the comfort of the lower realms even though eons ago he'd been at ease within this expanse. He remembered when he could soar nearly at the speed of thought through this area. But that was before his kind had been stripped of their former powers, during their great but failed rebellion in a past epoch. The memory of that loss made him quiver with rage each time he thought of how they'd been hurled from their exalted position. Now it took great effort and the proper equipment. He shook off his anxiety and set himself to his task. He knew he must answer the summons of his master, aware that the slightest disobedience would send him to the place of chains.

His momentum ceased at the arc's apex and he glided to a halt, hovering just below the line of blue that marked the edge of space. A shimmer-gate opened next to him, and he was sucked into a quivering stream of color. Through these gates, his master could bring his presence to the higher realms. It held him tightly as the Shadow Czar's commands rushed through his mind. "Your next assignment is simple." The force behind those words gripped him with such strength that it took all his self-control not to scream out. "Our enemies have decoded our communication. The sentinels have warned me that these adversaries are seeking to disrupt our plans for Ebbern. It was here at this level that our enemy had been manifesting." The Shadow Czar had come to this high point to investigate for himself. "They will try and penetrate our shields and bring the truth to those we've deceived. You must stop them."

Strieme peered deeper into the scintillating portal from where the commands issued. Just beyond the edge of his sight he could sense something churning with a wicked strength, lashing out and then returning to a calm control. There was anger there, a bitterness writhing as if it had been churning for epochs.

He spoke when a brief window of stillness came, as if the being that had been commanding him was suddenly without breath. "But what measures should I use?"

There was a low rumble like lungs clearing of bile before the voice returned, hissing like the bellows of a furnace. "Use every weapon in your arsenal. Make dark appear as light, lies appear as truth. But you must stop them long before they penetrate your shield wall." Several shafts of phosphorous colored rods appeared in his hand followed by the next command, "Use these matter-shifters. Call the specialists together and empower them with them. I've set the plan in motion earlier, now you must carry it on. Take the wands and follow the pattern I've set in place. It will stop them. Deception has always worked; it will work with these fools as well. But blunt their plans now and don't let them penetrate our shroud. I'll send you the template. Follow my scheme exactly."

With that, the portal closed and Strieme sensed his motion cloak losing its force. He touched it lightly with one of the matter-shifters and the garment was reenergized. The device surged with such uncanny force. The rod felt as light as a breath yet it could hold things in place like an anchor embedded in a sea of stone. It had the power to shift matter into a flux that could be manipulated to form what ever the possessor commanded. It wasn't often that he'd had the honor of holding such power in his grasp, and now he held several with a fearful respect. He knew that as his master had done, he could continue to carry out their plan and continuing to create objects to deceive their enemies and hopefully keep the world they held captive firmly within their power. Now he must repeat the deception the Shadow Czar had set in motion. He hovered briefly, his eyes brightening and then dimming as the details of this process were transmitted into his mind.

Yes, that will work, he told himself as a smile curled the edge of his mouth.

He looked down toward the planet below. Placing his hand on a row of silver threads near the edge of his motion cloak, he activated the descent mode. Instantly he fell, slowing momentarily near the Pillars of Rimlex to vanish into one of its caves.

CHAPTER 11

PILLARS OF RIMLEX

PAR-MANTRIK (FIRST CHILL), 5503

The night was cold, but not too cold for a true believer like Frim Lieter. An inner fire burned in this gaunt but handsome man, and its flames kept him warm even as his breath frosted in the biting air. His neatly trimmed beard accented his fine features and graying hair, and his countenance in the moonlight appeared as smooth as the feathers of a silverhawk.

A frequent cough betrayed his one weakness as he periodically struggled against the chill. But he was determined to stay with his vigil, lifting a white handkerchief to his mouth to shield his lungs against the night's numbing presence. He had often exposed himself to the harsh elements under a dark sky because of his faith in a force beyond his planet, a force he felt sure was drawing nearer every moment.

He was crouched on a high outcropping of rock, staring into the blackness above. Other peaks rose around him in the darkness, stabbing at the stars like black and brittle shards of glass. Together, these crags formed the mountain range known as the Pillars of Rimlex. Below him, at the base of the rock, sat his trans-rig, its power-cover making sporadic popping sounds as it cooled in the chilled air.

As he watched the darkened heavens, the stars seemed to squint and emit flashes of red and green. The triple moons of his planet climbed slowly into the night sky, the last one still hugging the distant horizon. The frigid air jabbed at his neck when the collar of his coat accidentally fell across his back. He quickly pulled it tight again and continued to look into the sky.

As an astrogazer, Lieter was a member of a select group assigned to the great eyepieces and sound-sensing space probes at the Tizra Advanced Mind-Training Center. He was acquainted with other professors like Kreswen, who he'd often seen with his three sons at the Gathering Day meetings. He secretly envied Kreswen, seeing the way he doted on his oldest child, a boy named Bracken.

He'd not been blessed with children. He'd been married briefly years before, but his strange ideas had driven away his mate. To her, the thought of bringing a child into a home where the father was so lost in his study of the heavens was as chilling as the cold atmosphere in which he often spent his time. She had married him because of the stars she'd seen in his eyes, but she'd soon discovered the mind behind them was as distant and mysterious as the lights looking down on Ebbern each night.

Like many at the Advanced Mind-Training Center, he lived in a world of what he considered reason and knowledge. This had created an elite mentality among his colleagues. Over the years they'd learned to use their brilliance as a weapon; and he, more than most of the others, threw down the gauntlet of his theories, challenging his peers to prove him wrong.

In his early years as an astrogazer, Lieter was aloof toward most of his students, and when he destroyed their immature speculations with lock-tight logic, he would often toy with them. He was confident that he knew more than all of them, that no one could best him. Many resented him as a result and mocked him behind his back. He treated his fellow professors with equal conceit, so gradually even they drew away. As he recalled these things, he was glad he was different now. It was that difference in part that brought him to such lonely spots on many nights.

When had it all changed? he wondered. His eyes absently searched the skies as his mind scanned the past for some catalyst. There it was—that one evening after class, as he'd sat at his desk correcting a student's equations. His soul suddenly felt as brittle as the sharp lead tool he was writing with. In frustration, he pressed its point into the page and it snapped. At that moment, something had snapped inside him as well. Mere theories and academics could not satisfy his longing for something transcendent, he'd realized.

Then as now, staring into the night sky, he'd seen the darkness in his own soul. Within it were distant lights but no sun, no warmth. It wasn't long before his outward quest was matched by an inward one. He realized he needed to connect emotionally, to find some kind of meaningful relationship. Why was he here on Ebbern? What strange fate had placed his kind on this perfect orb? Questions like this often left him wondering but also feeling lonely.

So, in hopes of finding some warmth in his frigid world, he began to warm to others around him. He saw his students in a different light and became a father to many of them. He would guide with more than logic and knowledge, he would lead them toward truth. But not the kind Kreswen taught his children.

Long ago, he'd departed from what he considered the childish and irrational ideas of those who met on weekly Gathering Days to hear the teaching of the ancient ones. He attend them now only out of tradition. Their lessons sounded to him like simple tales fashioned to keep his race passive and trusting. Hadn't the great astrogazer Hamimep proven that Ebbern was not the center of the universe? And breakthroughs in modern medical technology had rendered the superstitious requests for healing from otherworldly entities obsolete. The sci-tec leaders not only probed the skies, they had also searched the micro-world and unmasked the secrets of the elements and how they functioned.

This new knowledge had created all the wonders that his nation enjoyed, except for one dark blot. These great tools of knowledge had also produced something that could wipe out his world: The Destroyer Weapon. It was this one disappointment that had sent him searching for something other than mere reason—the mind itself was capable of both great good and great evil. There had been so many wars on Ebbern and now armed with this new means of destruction another conflict could easily be his planet's last. Faced with this conumdrum he wondered if there wasn't some *other* guiding force in the universe that could lead his planet to a peaceful future.

Now he longed to experience whatever it might be, that something deeper, something that would take him beyond the realm of mere speculation and theories. Drawing his cloak tighter around his shoulders, he drank in the stark beauty of the vast array of celestial lights above him. It was as if someone had scattered diamonds on a black velvet cloth. How could there not be other life forms out there? He'd always believed that life existed on other planetary systems. Perhaps somehow that life had seeded and nurtured the life that had developed on Ebbern. It was this theory that had made him determined to become a Touch-Point.

The chilling air seemed to accentuate his loneliness. He longed to connect with others of his own community. But often they were put off by his eccentric ways. So the idea of becoming a link between his planet and alien beings seeking contact with his race created an opportunity for this desire to be met in another way. Over the years, he'd read the writings of earlier Touch-Points. Much of what they claimed was ridiculed by his fellow astrogazers, but something deep inside told him they were all wrong.

In a moment of spontaneity, he lifted his arms and reached out toward the stars as if he could gather and count them in his hands. He knew so many of them by name. In his mind, he called out their names. Somewhere amongst them must be another race reaching back to him. This was what had drawn him to the ideas of Brace Estim, a brilliant but eccentric astrogazer believed to be the original Touch-Point. Frim remembered Estim's theory of the multiple-phase program. Aliens, he claimed, were establishing a system called "accelerated evolution" to advance the growth of the race as well as save Nerkush from the certainty of war. They also claimed that through their advanced technology, they could alter the DNA of Ebbern's inhabitants creating a new race possessed of great intellect and immune to disease. This new line of super-beings would be like gods. So these visitors from other worlds had set up a system of Touch-Points to be the contacts for this process, trained for future leadership.

Perhaps this night would be the start of his training, and it would be worth all the waiting. So he drew his cloak around him and watched the skies with the confidence of a true believer.

After a time, movement near the horizon jarred Frim from his thoughts. A dot of light darted toward him, growing in size as it approached. A faint hum became audible to his attentive ear. Transfixed, he whispered under his breath, "They've come!" As the light moved closer, it took on the form of a bright polished disk, knifing its way toward his perch.

None of Nerkush's, or any other nations', sky flyers were shaped like this, and none could leave the atmosphere. The few permanent stations and communication satellites orbiting Ebbern had been propelled there by burning gaseous fuel. But this one moved by some hidden energy and had clearly come from another world.

The humming grew louder, and Frim trembled with anticipation, overwhelmed by the knowledge that this would be an actual Contact. At last, he would have a tangible encounter with this advanced race of beings.

Impressions wove their way into his mind. Then an internal voice spoke to him. "We are glad that you have waited so patiently, Frim Lieter." The words buzzed in his head, warm and pulsating. "Your faithfulness will be rewarded. You have known of our existence for a long time. Like the others who have known, you have had the insight to recognize the importance of our appearance. Congratulations! You will become another link in our system of Touch-Points."

Overwhelmed with excitement, Frim felt the night's chill vanish in a wave of adrenaline. He watched expectantly as the massive disk came to rest in a large quarry about a hundred yards from him. The humming sound slowly abated and again the voice whirred in his mind. "Come quickly, we have much prepared for you."

From the underside of the disk, a stairway gradually descended. Frim scrambled down from the rocks and ran to the ramp. He paused for a moment to catch his breath and then climbed up the stairs, his heart filled with excitement.

At the top, several creatures met him, each dressed in a shimmering garment that covered their humanoid bodies from the neck down. Their heads appeared like his except for an odd angularity.

Even though his hosts looked different, they radiated warmth and confidence. Staring into their dark but brilliant eyes, he felt as if he'd known them all his life, as if they'd been his dearest friends. They presented him with a silver container filled with a warm and tasty liquid. They invited him to take a seat among a circle of chairs that faced a large, three-dimensional image floating at its center.

The internal voice spoke again. "You must have many questions. There will be plenty of time for all of them. But first let us give you a little tour."

A large celestial map appeared at the core of the projection. It contained a familiar cluster of stars. Then that group grew smaller and smaller as the image expanded to include heavenly bodies he'd only been able to view at a distance. Periodically throughout the display, dots of light blinked and glowed.

Again, the voice hummed in Frim's mind. "Each of these spots of light represents another one of our Touch-Points, on planets housing our representatives. Gradually they are helping our stellar systems unite, coming together in harmony, with the goal of putting an end to violence and war throughout the known universe."

The guided tour through the stars continued with additional highlights. Frim felt he'd finally found his true purpose in life. He was eager to become another of these dots of light for his planet, eager to bring peace to a world on the verge of destroying itself.

What seemed like hours passed as his instruction continued. But so much of it only confirmed what he already believed. No wonder they'd chosen him. His unique brilliance and forward-looking philosophy had prepared him for the huge task he was being assigned.

The instructions finished with an invitation to become a Touch-Point. "Should you choose to become one of our agents, please acknowledge this by touching the light on the panel beside you."

Frim immediately placed his hand on the glowing dot. The inner voice whispered to him again, "Very good, we will begin the treatment at once."

He was unafraid as they led him to the Transition Room where the mind-expanding operation would take place.

He had read of the treatment in Brace Estim's writings, describing a mild experience but one with life-changing benefits. Through a simple operation, his mind and senses would be altered, enabling him to have telepathic two-way contact with the Disk Command Center. He would become an agent commissioned to carry the message of galactic assistance and evolutionary restructuring to others.

The beings led him to a soft leather-like couch in the transition compartment, motioning for him to lay back. "The operation is short and quite pleasant," the voice assured him. For one brief moment, Frim felt afraid, but as the probes above his head lowered into operation, he was overcome with a deep sense of well-being.

Color and sound seemed to knit in his mind as he yielded to the waves of energy that surged through his brain. His senses echoed with excitement. The operation continued for about ten minutes. Then, as quickly as the sensation had begun, it was over.

Words hummed in his thoughts again. "The operation is complete. You will find it quite easy to contact us at any time. Just remember, Frim, that all circumstances must be arranged before we will manifest ourselves. We don't want any unwelcome guests at a Touch-Point gathering."

The friendly alien motioned him toward another doorway. "This way for a tour of our spacecraft." He fell in place behind his guides as they led him along corridors and through rooms filled with various instruments. He guessed these to be navigational devices and power generators. The voice explained the equipment, but Frim understood little of what he heard and saw. Though he was a highly educated man, this technology was far beyond his ability to comprehend.

Finally, they reached what appeared to be the control room, a larger area where other creatures appeared to be busy with various tasks, apparently operating the different mechanisms for the maintenance of the space vessel. In the center of the room, another three-dimensional image similar to the one he'd seen earlier dominated the chamber. Emanating from it was a sector of stars containing the Trion constellations. Frim recognized it from the maps he had been studying in his research at the Institute.

"A familiar sight, Frim Lieter?" the voice nudged him from his wonder.

"Yes, I've done much research on this sector of space. It has always fascinated me. I had hoped to discover more about its unusual structure."

"Well then, we can help you in your investigation. Watch closely and remember." The screen instantly magnified the Trion Star System so that Frim could examine it at a closer range than he'd done before. He took rapid mental notes. What he was seeing now would increase Nerkush's knowledge of the universe by many years. The image dissolved, and he was left staring at empty air. "This is just the first of many sessions we plan to give you in the future, but it's time for you to leave now." The disk creatures pointed him toward another door.

They led Frim back through the vessel to the room where he'd entered the craft. He was invited to take a seat, and as he did he sensed the craft descending and finally coming to rest. Once they had landed, his host led him through the hallway to the main hatch. It opened on its own, and he walked through it and made his way to the bottom entrance ramp.

It was near dawn, and the chill air made him shiver. The creatures gave him a departing salute. "Bring others to your level of understanding. Time is running out for Nerkush, but our plan will save them." The thoughts filled his mind, not so much as sentences but as seed concepts that would later grow into speeches and articles.

The alien voice spoke one last word of farewell and then warned him to move back from the disk. As Frim watched, the hatch closed and then the craft began to hum and spin, rising rapidly into the gray morning light. It grew smaller as it moved away until it appeared as just another star. He watched in fascination until it winked out.

Frim strolled back to his trans-rig. Climbing into his seat, he was struck with an overwhelming sense of purpose. He had been chosen! He was special! He would be a leader in the new order! Nerkush could now have hope. The future of his planet could be secure, and the reckless use of destructive weapons could now be curtailed by a new super-race of beings that he and others like him would lead.

He switched on the power unit and steered his rig through the rough terrain, finally arriving at the highway. As he sped along the road toward his home, the sun rose above the horizon ahead of him. His senses drank in the splendor of the moment. It was a new day.

Yes, he thought, *a new day indeed.* A new day was dawning for him and all of Nerkush. The coming of that day might be years in the making, but he was sure it had begun with him on this night.

Chapter 12

Raka

Tar-Lynrexs (Late-summer), 5512

Bracken took his wrinkled handkerchief from the pocket of his faded work garment and wiped his brow. He leaned on his feeding scoop and stared out at the barren peaks in the distance, still musing despite the bellowing of the vinweok herds. Perhaps it was the bleakness of his surroundings or the need for emotional warmth, but he found himself on an inward journey into his past.

He remembered the early years with his family and how they had seemed to pass so slowly. Tizra changed, but only gradually. Its tree-lined streets stayed the same, though, keeping him cool in the hot months and sheltering him from the strong winds of the bleak time. This season with its icy days usually found him nestled cozily by a fire in the evenings with his parents and two brothers. Years had passed since he had walked in the garden with his father. Their times together had become a rarity. Life was too full of other things.

He could still remember times of closeness with his father, though, and some with his whole family. Those times were far away now and from a different season. A season that was cold to the flesh but warm to the spirit. He wished he could go back to that place and time. Perhaps he would have dealt with it differently.

He'd thought at first that Ley and the Community were more like family to him than his own people had ever been. But their recent troubles and exile had begun to cool the warm affections he'd first felt toward them. Maybe he'd been wrong. Perhaps in the years of his youth, the bonds of his true family had been forged forever, bonds stronger and more real than any of these recent relationships. What if this longing he felt was for true family, a family that the Community would never be able to replace?

The bleak wasteland where he found himself now had made him second-guess his choices many times. Had the strife among his fellow workers brought out their true character. And what about his willingness to strike back at them in anger? The barrenness of this region was laying bare his own soul. It had left him with a loneliness as desolate as Raka. Maybe the Community was not all it had been made out to be. Maybe their dreams of a new society were only that, dreams. He second-guessed even his second-guesses and knew at this point, guessing and remembering were all he could do.

CHAPTER 13

TIZRA

MANTRIK (BLEAK TIME), 5506

Flames crackled on the hexagonal hearth. "Please bring me a cup of brek, Kreswen," called Myrus from her warm spot by the fire.

"Comin' right up." Kreswen's tone was warm and loving, his face gentle and mature. "Cold evenings were made for brek." The whole family enjoyed its smooth, comforting taste, even the boys. All three were waiting anxiously for their father to join them in the wood-paneled gathering room. Laughing, they pushed one another in playful clashes. The high oak ceiling echoed their squeals.

"Papa, come here," shouted Kempec. His brother Ditten stood up, hoping to goad their father into a wrestling match. "We'll beat you this time for sure. Big giants like you are easy."

Bracken was too old to join his brothers now, but he loved seeing them egg their father on.

He was taller. His blond hair had darkened to a deep brown, and his face had lost its roundness. His blue eyes had grown more crystalline and perceptive. He joined the fun with a taunt, "Yes, Father, they've beaten a few like you this week already."

"You boys could no more pin me down than you could pin a fistra," smirked Kreswen in playful defiance.

They laughed back at him. "A fistra's ten times as big as you."

Joining the family in the gathering room, Kreswen set a steaming cup of brek on the table beside Myrus and then grabbed the youngest boy, playfully lifted him into the air. "You boys are so weak you find it hard to lift your heads up in the morning." He loved his children. This was fun, he thought. He needed to spend more time like this. He needed to be with his family regularly and not distracted by his scholarly duties. He needed their love and they needed his. "I'll beat both of you with just one hand," he shouted in mock anger, as he dove gently into the midst of the two and rolled with them on the thick floor covering.

Myrus watched and laughed along with them for a while. Taking a sip from the cup Kreswen had brought her, she returned to her reading. The Volume lay in her lap, its worn pages open to a favorite passage. Evenings like this were not only made for brek, but for the wonderful reflections she found in her book. She looked down at the sacred writing, her face peaceful. But then a wisp of stressful memory furrowed her brow. She and Bracken had been walking home from Gathering Day and he'd come up alongside her.

"Mother, last week at the Mind-Training Center, one of our teachers said that the Volume was just a collection of ideas that our ancient sages dreamed up to control their followers. Is that true?"

She gently placed her hand on the boy's shoulder. It was wider than his brothers' and she sensed the manly strength that had formed in his growing physique. She could also feel the stress that issues like this were stirring in him. She hesitated to reply, lifting her hand from his shoulder. In fact, she wasn't sure how to reply. She'd heard some of the leaders of Gathering Day give their answers to such challenges to her beliefs, but she found it hard to articulate them to others. Still, she was determined to give it her best try.

"The Volume's reputation has often been questioned. Your teacher's remarks are not the first ones to challenge its authority. Many of our scholars hold that history supports its claims." She couldn't recall any of those sources at the moment but still spoke with as much confidence as she could convey. "Besides, I consider its teaching valid not merely because of their confidence in its origins but because my own experience with the Prince of Wonder has confirmed its claims."

"When was that, Mother?"

"It was years ago, Bracken. I experienced his presence in an overwhelming way. In fact, it continues with me to this day and there are seasons when it returns as fresh as the moment it first happened."

"But that was exactly one of the points that my teacher made. That those who follow the teachings in the Volume are merely following their emotions and not rational thinking."

"Son, what I've experienced goes far beyond my emotions. Doesn't watching a sunset bring out an emotion? But that experience is based on something that is really there, something that's really occurring. Well, there are things like those sunsets that take place in other realms and they're just as real but can only be seen with eyes of faith."

"That may be true for you, Mother, but it's never occurred for me, and when I look around at so many of those who join us each week at the gathering, it appears that they've never had such an encounter. It's like they join us there merely to appease some guilt or simply enjoy the fellowship we have there."

"That may be true, Bracken, and it's my greatest wish that someday you'll know what I've experienced as well. I'm confident it will happen. The Volume gives me just such a promise."

"That's the other issue I'm struggling with. It seems that there are so many promises written there that haven't come true. Like the promise of a power from beyond this realm, I've yet to see it. All I see is ritual and tradition. The ancient ones knew it, but I see little of it at our weekly meetings."

At this point, Myrus had to admit that what Bracken claimed had a ring of truth to it. She knew her encounter had been real, but questions like this often left her wondering as well. But so much of her life now was crowded with raising her children and being a wife. So she had chosen not to overly concern herself with such issues. She would merely live out what she believed and leave such questions to wiser people. Besides, she had an inner peace that her love for her family and her example would in time be the best reply she could give to such questions. "I've had those sorts of questions too, Bracken, and even if I don't have an answer now, I'm sure in time one will come."

She put a gentle hand on his shoulder again. She hoped to give him some comfort with her touch, but his words betrayed that he still needed more.

"Well, that way of looking at things may work for you, Mother, but I need something more. I'm going looking for it even if it means you and Father don't approve."

At that point, Myrus had wanted to reply with another argument but had chosen to trust the promises that her son doubted. Instead, she had drawn him closer to her as they continued to walk home.

The noise of the family tussle brought her back from her thoughts, and the dark shadow of the memory faded as she watched the play nearby. She was older now, but still beautiful. Youth seemed to have found in her a special place of grace. She looked up at the boys again. She loved them deeply, the way only mothers know how to love. They had been a pain and a joy to bear, a struggle and a blessing to raise, a tear and a smile to live with day by day.

"Papa, you're growing weaker all the time. We'll soon have you worn out," came a cry from the pile of arms, legs, and torsos twisting on the floor.

Not weaker, but busier, thought Myrus. She thought of the hours he spent away from them. Hours at his work, hours she wished he could spend with them. At least they had special times like this. She felt thankful. She had her husband, her children, and her home. Others had not been as fortunate.

Other husbands had never come back from the long war. The bloody battle that the children knew little of had ended the year before Bracken was born. *Thankfully it's over*, she told herself. It was only a fading memory now. She remembered those years with bitterness. Kreswen had left. Her heart was broken. She was lonely. Days of wondering what the future held, and now that future held her. The war ended, Kreswen returned, and the children entered their lives. Nerkush was prospering now, and they enjoyed a good life.

But she still remembered her fears of the past, the rise of the Gray Power. Such a small country, and yet it stood and shook its fist at the whole world. Nation after nation fell before its advancing armies. Whole races were imprisoned by their army and then systematically exterminated. People feared that even Nerkush might fall to the advancing forces of this nation. This gave rise to speculations that the Gray Power's leader was the Night Ruler himself, cloaked in the form of a man. But such theories faded in the face of the final outcome. The Night Ruler would never have let himself be overcome so easily. It had taken the combined strength of several nations like Nerkush to finally overcome the Gray Power and its leader. Kreswen's generation had taken the brunt of the conflict, and many had never returned from the field of battle. Those who did come home were heralded as heroes. But now many wondered if their nation could field such a generation again. Some questioned whether the stock of youth that were growing up with the prosperity and safety they presently enjoyed wouldn't be up to the challenge of another war. Her thoughts were suddenly interrupted by the tussle going on nearby.

"Papa, no fair! You're using your other hand!" Kreswen had both boys neatly pinned. He rolled off and they joyfully clambered on top of him again.

Myrus joined the laughter even as her thoughts were pulled back again to those years when the world had transitioned and Nerkush had risen to the dominant place among the nations of Ebbern. With the help of the High Council, there would never be another war, Myrus reassured herself; the World Destroyer or Destroyer Weapon as some called it would make sure of that. Its awesome power had killed thousands in an instant. Other nations trembled now and stood in awe. But there was also the possibility of another nation discovering the secret of its power. If that occurred and conflict came again, no one would be safe. All of Ebbern would become a battlefield. Myrus gave this possibility only a moment's thought.

I will leave such matters up to the Council. I have my family to raise.

Kreswen and the boys lay back on the floor, tired from their struggles. The boys breathed deeply, but only for a moment. "Can we watch the vid-tel?" asked Ditten, running to the mantle where it rested. "*Accad Outlaws* should be starting soon." Ditten switched on the power control. After a few hums and pops, the vid-tel buzzed to life. The device was old and gave out a warbled sound and a slightly faded image at times. Many of their neighbors had the latest devices with enhanced sound and image, but because Kreswen was raising his family on a teacher's salary, they had to be content for the time being with this older model.

The announcer's voice crackled through the set. "Now for another evening of adventure with Trob Rex as he once again pursues the Accad Outlaws." The boys' eyes lit up. Energy rays exploded in the background as the theme music built to a crescendo. Trans-rigs roared. Trob Rex tel-talked with his comrades over their two-way communi-coms. Down alleyways and over rooftops, they relentlessly hunted the fierce outlaw leader, Kij Mista.

Bracken pulled the velvet cushions from the storage cabinet and passed them around for everyone to sit on. Captivated, they watched as the plot slowly built to its inevitable end. Myrus gave Kreswen a knowing smile as they watched the intrigue on the younger children's faces. But glancing toward Bracken, she noticed he was disengaged. He was only half-watching the program. He seemed more interested in the book laying open in his lap. It was one containing the writings of the edge-poets. He'd brought it home from the Mind-Training Center, and even though she disapproved of poets' writings, she was glad he had an interest in reading and not merely being entertained by the vid-tel's nightly fare.

The clamor from the action on the vid-tel brought her back to the present. Trob closed in for the capture of Kij. But wait … at the last moment, a quirk of fate! Kij escaped to plot his evil again! The announcer's voice came on over the thundering theme song, inviting everyone to watch again next time.

Myrus stood and stretched, turning off the receiver. "Let's roast some crumpts," she said as she walked across the room and into the food module. "We've still got several bags left over from grandpa's last crop. As Myrus searched among the shelves, she recalled the special time that the whole family spent at the end of Tar-Lynrexs season with Kreswen's parents bringing in the harvest. Back in the gathering area, the others looked into the fire as they talked and laughed about the announcer's funny voice.

Pouring the golden-colored cornels into a small pan, she wondered how the previous day had been for the others. She wondered if it would be worth bring it up … it seemed they talked so little anymore. *I'll just have to ask them*, she encouraged herself. *This moment is as good as any to work on the problem of family communication.* Carrying the round canister, she returned with the nut-like kernels rattling around inside. Pouring the crumpts in a black roast pan, she set them over the flames and placed the near-empty container next to Kreswen. She turned and smiled to her oldest son. "What did you do today, Bracken?"

Before he could answer, Ditten interrupted, telling everyone about the wogs he caught with several of his friends at the Stylar pond. Its surface had been frozen since the beginning of bleak time, but they broke the ice and dropped their lines into the chilled water. He was nearly hopping with excitement, "They were so big! I caught six, Papa! Momma stuck them all in storage and we're going to eat them tomorrow night." Ditten's face gave off a rosy glow.

"They weren't that big," teased Bracken. "There's only enough for half a serving."

Ditten pounced and tried to wrestle Bracken from his cushion. They laughed and squirmed until Bracken lifted Ditten up and dropped him back on his own pillow.

"I caught twice as many when I was your age. You'll never make a wog-fisher," chided Bracken. Ditten, just past his seventh year, was about to protest again when he too was interrupted.

Six-year-old Kempec began an exciting tale about the Great Green Beast he had slain that day in the dark recesses of his clothing bin. "Oh Papa, it had great big black eyes and teeth this long!" He stretched his arms out wide. His deep brown eyes filled with the wonder of his own imagination. His blond bangs fell like a curtain resting just above his eyebrows. "But I stopped him dead with one shot from my power-thruster."

The boy squinted, sighting down his finger and pulling an imaginary trigger. "He had three brothers. I killed all of them too!" he boasted.

"Where do you get all these wild stories?" asked Bracken. "You sound like you'll be a writer for the vid-tel someday."

"I'd like to do that," Kempec's voice took on a note of youthful pondering. "I could write stories about the monsters of Accad. That would be fun. But … really," he said, knitting his brows, "I did kill the Great

Green Beast and his brothers today. But they always disappear after they die."

The others smiled at each other and laughed. Kreswen took Kempec in his lap and hugged him. Ditten was about to go on again, but Kreswen stopped him. "Wait a minute. Now you boys be quiet for a while. After all, Momma asked to hear from Bracken first!"

Bracken leaned back against his pillow and answered his mother somewhat reluctantly. "Well, as I was going to say, I had a good time with Silas today. I spent most of the afternoon at his house."

Silas Yitha and Bracken had been friends for years. Even though their families were of a different race and culture, it had not been an obstacle between them or their parents. Growing up together, they had shared many warm experiences, not all of which their parents approved of. "We played some free music for a while." Bracken grimaced remembering Silas's struggles with his instrument. "Silas is still learning, but I'm confident he'll soon be playing his stam as well as me. After a while, though, we came up with some interesting sounds."

Bracken thought about his own blond-colored instrument that he'd learned to play so well. He loved to run his finger across the glistening silver strings and listen as the driving melody came forth from its sound box. He loved its versatility, for he could plug it into an amplifier or play it acoustically. He frowned again abruptly, remembering Silas's mother's reaction to their practice time. "I don't think his mother was too happy with what she heard," he said flatly.

Myrus nervously shook the roasting pan over the fire. She was irritated with her oldest son. "I feel the same way!" she said. "Silas's mother and I agreed when she called me today that you boys should stop playing that kind of music. Aren't there better things you could be doing?"

"You always say that," said Bracken. "It sounds so beautiful. I just can't understand why you don't like it."

"It seems to bring out an attitude that I feel is separating you from the rest of us, Son."

"Isn't that what your parents said about the music you enjoyed in your youth?"

Myrus held back a laugh. "That may be true, Bracken, but there's something different about the source of this music. It has such strong roots in the philosophy of the edge-poets." She paused, momentarily considering what to say next.

Myrus didn't want to push Bracken away, knowing his recent obsession with the writings of the edge-poets. But she couldn't ignore the fact that this new music embodied their ideals and mixed it with the new sounds emerging with Bracken's generation.

"I know you respect much of their writings, and I understand that. But their philosophies often challenge the very roots of our faith and accuse the Fathers of hypocrisy." Myrus felt a twinge of guilt, knowing that in regard to the Fathers, the edge-poets were sometimes right, though she wasn't ready to admit it to her son.

"In the end, what troubles me most is the way this music seems to be influenced by a strange force. I'm confident it's energized by more than just youthful rebellion. There's something almost ... sinister ... lurking there."

Bracken did not like what he was hearing, and he was sure his mother could see it in his face.

"Listen, Bracken, sometimes you have to trust the wisdom of your parents even if you don't understand why we disagree with you."

"Well, as I grow older I'm finding that harder to do."

"But you'll keep growing older until you die, Son, and once you've grown to our age you'll understand."

"I guess time will tell." He found it more and more difficult to understand his parents' narrow opinions about life. Dejected, he set his book aside and stared into the fire.

Kreswen, who had been listening quietly, stirred in his seat. Picking up an uncooked nut from the canister beside him, he popped it in his mouth and stared at his son. "I agree with your mother, Son. It may be fun, but it's a distraction from more important things. And just because something is fun, doesn't mean it's right."

Kreswen's temples had grayed with the years, but his face was still handsome. He had grown older, yet he still possessed a somewhat youthful attitude along with his gentle wisdom. Right now, though, it seemed unfair to his son. "At your age, you need to think about more than fun. You need to be more responsible. You're a young man. It's time for you to set some goals."

"Sure, Father, and be overly stressed the way my classmates are?" Bracken rebutted. "They're more interested in a top ranking when they don't fully comprehend what they've learned. There's so much pressure on them they're simply overloaded. Besides I don't think our instructors really care. They're busy making up their reports to the school governors and seldom have time for anyone with real questions."

"I know some of those teachers, Bracken," replied Kreswen. "They put in a lot of time preparing their lessons and devising ways to make their subjects interesting."

"Well, those aren't the ones teaching my classes. Most of them are under so much pressure to reach their quotas that they have little time for those who are struggling. Students like Silas, whose father left years ago, have the hardest time. There are more and more like him each year that are growing up without both their parents, and few of those in authority seem to care."

"Well, that should make you grateful that you have both your mother and me here for you."

"That's just it, you're not here that much anymore, and when you are, you seem to focus most of your energies pushing Ditten and Kempec to compete in the games. I know how much you enjoyed that in your youth, but you can't expect them to be as successful as you were."

"I'm not expecting them to, Bracken, but I do want them to do their best."

"Father, you're wrong. I've heard Ditten crying at night and complaining to Kempec that it's simply too hard. I wonder if it's more about you and your standing here in Tizra that's driving you."

Kreswen's face flashed red, and he responded in kind. "That's just about enough from you, Bracken. You've had so much handed to you, and you still seem to be lost in your reading and music. Well, you can't live on that. You've got to think about the future if you ever want to succeed in life."

"Sure, Father, and will we really have a future? Like you, I've heard the threats from Nerkush's enemies. Our leaders say there's the possibility that another war, one where we'll use the World Destroyer Weapon. Such a war could leave our planet barren and lifeless."

"I know, I know, Son. But we had our fears when we were your age, and we got through it. Somehow things will work out for your generation. So that's why I say you've got to plan." Kreswen's anger cooled as he realized his son's concerns were fueled by fear. "Don't worry, Son, I'm sure the High Council will find a way."

"It's just those leaders that I'm concerned about. They never seem to find a new approach to the problem, one that will bring us peace."

"Please listen to me, Bracken, you're too young to worry about all this now. Your training is the most important thing at this time, and having some goals will help you focus on it."

Sensing his father's change of mood, Bracken softened as well and nodded submissively. It was those goals that made him anxious. He realized he didn't want to be like his father, even though he loved him. His father's care was genuine, as genuine as the simplest sweet song he so often played on his mouth flute at night to the boys before they drifted off to sleep.

Yes, the love was there, but so was Bracken's determination to find his own life, to be his own man, to live and be the way he pleased. Even if it meant playing the free music his parents despised, he knew he must search for his own meaning in life. His soul had found liberation in its strange musical tones. They would never understand. When his family was gone, he would play the odd tunes on his stam in secret. Someday he knew he would be released from this bondage, to play what he chose, when and where he wanted.

"Yes, Father, I know you're right," murmured Bracken dutifully, "I'll think about what you've said."

"The nuts are done," said Myrus cheerfully, trying to change the mood. She lifted the pan from the fire and shook the nuts in a wooden bowl and passed it around the circle.

Kempec came over to where Bracken was sitting. He turned his trusting face up to his older brother. "Are you still going to take me fishing like you promised?"

"Of course," responded Bracken, reaching down and scooping up his little brother in his arms. "We'll have a great time, and I'm sure you'll catch more wogs than Ditten caught today!"

Bracken loved his family, and sometimes he almost forgot his determination to be different. Looking at their smiling faces around the fire, his rebellion would melt like ice on a mid-summer's day.

CHAPTER 14

RAKA

TAR-LYNREXS (LATE-SUMMER), 5512

As evening approached, the heat of the day had begun to dissipate. Still it was oppressive to all but the beasts that were now making their way back to the pens. Bracken longed for a drink of something pure and sweet like the waters of Greenbrook near Tizra. He coughed up phlegm from his throat and spit it out in the dirt. He took his soiled handkerchief out again and wiped his mouth. It was brittle with use and felt hard against his chapped lips.

More memories came pouring into his mind, almost like a cool and refreshing drink of krem. The thought made him grieve for Silas all over again, remembering so many of their wonderful nights camping under the stars, passing the drink between them. The thoughts of his past were so real he could almost taste them. In the coming hours, they would all pass before him like a set of forgotten friends, each with a story, a reflection, and a recollection. Some would bring with them sweet moments that he savored, but others forced a haunting mental wind into his consciousness that left his soul as dry as the swirling dust in the pens.

CHAPTER 15

TIZRA

LYNREXS (MID-SUMMER), 5507

Bracken and Silas sat around a low-burning fire in the forest near Tizra, their rough-sewn tunics nearly identical in the dark. For the first time in weeks, Bracken felt he could breathe freely. It seemed more and more that only here, out in the foothills could he get away from the stifling expectations of his parents and teachers. He didn't know how much longer he could put up with their expectations and demands without completely reacting; he felt the time for him to make his own way in the world was not far off.

Bracken closed his eyes and tried to let go of his scattered thoughts, tried to just focus on the music. He and Silas loved to play their stams and sing songs when they came out here; it was part of what he loved about their trips away from the city. Silas didn't have a gift for music, but he'd become an adequate player. Still Bracken was always happy when they played together.

One thing over the years that had endeared Silas to Bracken was his complete lack of guile. He knew he could trust his friend with any secret, any struggle, any dream; they'd shared many together. He almost laughed aloud remembering the time he'd made up an encounter with Lisha, just to see if his friend would buy it. It was during another of their trips to the foothills after they'd finished off several bottles of krem, and Bracken was feeling especially mischievous.

"So, Silas. That girl, Lisha. Did I tell you what happened with the two of us?"

"Whaaat? You're kidding."

"No, not at all. I ran into her on Gathering Day a few weeks ago."

"You can't be serious. I had no idea she went there." Silas had never been to Gathering Day. When he was still young and before his parents had split up, they had discouraged him from attending. To them, the teachings of the Volume were considered myths. But Bracken could see from his reaction that now he was suddenly considering the possibility of attending one.

"Well, she did. And I had a chance to talk with her. In fact, I walked her home from the meeting."

"Sure, Bracken. You're making this up."

"Honest, I'm not. I found out that she's watched us compete in comp-games. Says she was really impressed with how well we performed."

It was true that both had developed in their physical prowess and had done well in the comp-games, winning handily against their upper classmen in one of the final surge games, but Bracken knew that Lisha preferred the older guys. She was constantly seen with them walking her to and from classes.

"She mentioned me too?"

"Yes, you too, Silas," said Bracken with a twinkle in his eye. "But she said something I never expected from a girl like her."

"Yes, and what was that?"

"She said she's been listening to the edge-poets, and she's deeply concerned about the direction the Fathers are taking Nerkush."

"Now I know you're making this up." Silas and Bracken had both become aware of the growing movement in Accad and the edge-poets that had emerged there with their chants calling for a new direction for Nerkush. But surely a girl like Lisha, so caught up with her popularity and male following, could hardly even think about such matters.

"No, I'm serious, Silas. You know what else?"

"What else?"

"She says she's interested in coming with us sometime on our explorations up here in the hills."

"That would be amazing."

"In fact, she has a girl friend that's interested in you. She said she'd bring her along as well."

Silas stared down into the embers of their campfire and pondered this possibility. He poked at the coals with a stick and stirred them to life. At that moment, Bracken knew that Silas was convinced. The realization struck him accompanied with a pang of guilt, and he knew he had to come clean.

When Silas looked up, he saw the huge smile that crowded Bracken eyes into tiny slits. "Ah, you are making this whole thing up!" shouted Silas howling in disappointment.

Bracken's smile grew until he couldn't hold the humor in any longer. They both laughed and fell back against their sleep gear.

How Bracken loved his friend. That wasn't the first time he'd fooled Silas. But each time he'd admitted his made-up stories, there'd been that white-toothed smile on Silas's face, the brown eyes winking back at him under a shock of dark hair, and the deep belly laugh as he knew he'd been tricked again. It was at that moment that Bracken knew they'd be friends for life.

Now once again they were sharing those moments of friendship and laughter. Bracken looked down at his bare feet. He and Silas had shed their leather cleks nearby to cool their feet against polished stones they'd pulled from the chattering waters of a nearby stream after their long hike.

As the night wore on, they reminisced over bottles of krem. They laughed about some of their more interesting excursions to the surrounding hills, when they had tried testing out the theories they had gotten in their creature study classes with tiny wiggling things they found in streams. And there was that time they experimented with the homemade explosives they'd put together from the instruction their earth-tech teacher had given them. It had resulted in some huge explosions that they were sure would get them in trouble, but the detonations must have gone unheard for no one in authority came to investigate. But the highlight of each outing was what passed between them unspoken. They both relished the fresh scent of trees and the gurgling sound of clear waters embracing them, inviting them to explore the poetic edge of their thinking.

A gentle, almost melodious breeze stirred the tops of the evergreens in the forest around them. Something else seemed to stir in the air too. It was as if they could hear some distant song echoing quietly from behind the sky. And with the haunting melody, the presence of strangers drew closer on the wind of another world.

Bracken emptied his last bottle of krem, adding it to the pile next to the burning coals of the small fire they'd built to warm themselves against the growing chill of the evening air. Even though the valley stayed hot during mid-summer, the higher elevations around Tizra grew cold after sunset. Hour after hour, they'd talked, sung, and played their stams, their voices echoing up the narrow canyons carved from the ancient lava beds. Centuries before, molten magma had spilled down the hillside to form deep crevices where sparkling water now ran. At times, the music had taken them in flights of raging power. And then it soothed them as they played mellow riffs against the background of stream and breeze. Finally satiated with melody, they placed their instruments aside and lay back against their sleeping gear, staring up into the night sky.

Bracken enjoyed so many things about his friendship with Silas. It was unusual in some ways that two people from different races had become so bonded. But Bracken and Silas both had been raised without the slightest trace of prejudice against those of different races. Myrus had made sure he understood the clear teaching of the Volume that all the inhabitants of Ebbern came from one blood and should be respected. So even though some in Tizra looked on this friendship with an attitude of judgment, neither one of them ever let it hinder their friendship.

At the thought, Bracken studied Silas more closely, taking in his friend's unique features. He was sturdily built, like the trunk of a shiferen tree. His face was a long oval and his eyes were brown. The black locks of his hair parted on either side of his wide forehead and spilled onto his shoulders. His skin was a warm shade of ebony. His lips had the fullness that many of his race carried, and his brows narrowed slightly where they met above his nose. Silas's other distinct characteristic, one of Bracken's favorites, was the way his ears lay flat against his head and came to a sharp point where they intercepted his jawline.

Bracken cared deeply for his friend. He was one of those people he could trust. He was smart but also quiet, thoughtful, and loyal, solid with deep roots like the Shiferen.

Bracken knew he'd earned his friend's respect too, that Silas admired him for always pushing the discussion, always probing beyond the shallow ideas of his other classmates.

Bracken looked over at Silas, who was lifting his hands in an inquiring gesture, "So, Bracken, what do you think of this recent controversy between the Council and some of the professors at Accad's Advanced Mind-Training Center? Do you think the Council will ban them from teaching their new theories? One of my friends' older brothers who's attending school there told him about the controversy."

Bracken shrugged. He'd heard the rumors as well. This sort of news had a way of filtering down to the students in lower schools and even as far south as Tizra. Whenever something as intriguing as this came up, it spread through the learning centers because so many of the students had siblings in the higher institute and looked up to them for direction. "Ah, Silas, its typical of the Council. They've been doing this sort of thing for generations. Every time some new idea emerges that threatens their traditions or their power, they react. It's just the same old pattern repeating itself."

Bracken plucked a blade of grass and chewed on it. "Remember when the explorer Fitzebran unearthed the ruins of Hidenglex and proposed that there had been another race on the planet before us? They spent every effort to disprove his theories and then buried all the evidence he'd unearthed in their hidden Vault of Records. Sure, they say they've kept them there for future generations to study, but everyone knows it's fiction. They're only waiting for people to forget and then they'll be locked away for the ages."

"Well, they could be right, Bracken, maybe the whole project was a hoax like some in the Council claimed. I mean, not every discovery Fitzebran has made has proven correct. Remember the whole issue that arose over the Night Ruler debate? He said it was true. That ancient sources seemed to support his theory only to have several of the Hi-Thought Corp proving it was only a myth. Their sources seemed well researched and his, questionable."

Bracken pulled another blade from the soft soil and gently twisted it between his fingers. "Well, Silas, I think that question is still up for debate. But that's another controversy that will go on for a long time. Every time a case is brought before the Council like this, they reject it. They will never give up their power, and as long as Nerkush remains peaceful, they will stay firmly in place. So we're left with believing them or rejecting their arguments and finding others who will join us. Eventually a new generation will push out all the Fathers' old, fearful ideas and carve out a new path for our world."

Silas nodded but looked doubtful.

Bracken smiled at his friend and continued with confidence. "I guess you've heard that there's a stirring in Accad. In the heart of the city, a new community is forming. The Council opposes them, but their influence is growing. I hope we can join them in the future once we've left Tizra. In fact, groups like them are emerging all over Nerkush, small ones here and there, but there's momentum with them."

Bracken's tone and confidence seemed to assuage Silas's doubts. He thought, not for the first time, how glad he was to have a friend like Silas to navigate his emerging adulthood with. How lucky he was that they saw the world through the same set of lenses, forged from the roots of their quiet community and polished by their quest for life.

Silas must have been satisfied for the moment, as he switched to another of their well-worn topics, "It's like the way our parents hate the sort of music you write. It has an edge to it. Not only does it say what they don't want their friends to hear, but they also hate the way it sounds. I know it's just a new take on the old chants of the Ogresen. My family's race are some of their descendants. The songs they brought from their homeland seem to have a fascination for our generation. I just didn't get much of their talent."

"Well, that hasn't been the case with most of your race. I admire so many of the minstrels that have carried on the Ogresen's music. Besides,

Silas, you certainly have an abundance of their brains and physical agility. I guess none of us can have it all."

"I love what you've done with their style, Bracken. You seem to have taken it in a unique direction. I know you're not alone, there's a whole new movement of singers that are driving this sound. But why now, why in our time?"

Bracken dropped the grass he'd been playing with and stared off into the night sky for several minutes before he answered. "Perhaps there's another force at work in our world, Silas, some sort of mysterious clock that resets itself every few hundred years. Maybe it's like a hidden code that's switched off and on by some sort of cosmic timekeeper. Maybe this timepiece has a chime and we've found it. It's melodious but it's also an alarm, a sort of wakeup call to all of us. I'm not really sure, but whatever the case, we seem to be at that place where the gears of the clock are shifting and we must move with them."

Silas turned to his friend with a completely different question this time, and the rocky clearing echoed with the excitement in his masculine voice. "I guess you've heard the rumors about the last sci-tec expedition?"

Bracken pulled another bottle of krem from his pack. After taking a deep drink, he passed the beverage to Silas. "Yeah, someone said they found a mineral that has unusual powers. It's supposed to look like a gem."

"It may look like a jewel, but from what I've heard, it will steal your mind," Silas warned. "When my Dad came to visit, he told me if anyone touched it they'd end up losing their touch with reality."

Bracken sat up and grabbed a branch. He turned it over in his hands as if judging if it was fit for the fire, then he tossed it onto the coals. The flames grew brighter for a moment and then dimmed as the night closed in like a black fog. "Why would anyone go crazy just by swallowing a small stone?" The whole sci-tec story sounded like a lie to him. "I know that's what the officials say, but I doubt it. It's not the first time they've lied to hide the truth."

Silas passed the krem back to Bracken and leaned back again, cupping his hands behind his head. "You may be right, Bracken," he said, furrowing his brow. "A student at the Advanced Mind-Training Center said it's an important discovery. He says the mineral's effect alters your mind patterns. The gem's supposed to increase people's mental power." He looked and sounded unconvinced, though, "The whole thing seems kind of odd to me."

After drinking deeply from the krem, Bracken set the bottle down and picked up his stam. His fingers ran smoothly over the strings, playing a soothing background melody as he talked. The night air had changed. Another wind seemed to be moving in the trees.

Bracken could sense it, but he ignored its presence. "We'll probably never know what the stones do," he said disappointedly. "The sci-tec crews won't even say where they found them. My dad told me the High Council wants the whole matter closed. The crew's leader—Cib Mingus—he won't even mention it anymore."

"I've heard they've been digging somewhere up on Mt. Shidow," yawned Silas. There was a rumor to that effect running through the learning center just before break. It was said that a former student had been found with a gem in Accad and that the Pirax had killed him in a raid on his home. What would make someone give up his life for something apparently as stupid as a stone that would make you insane?

Bracken set his instrument down and poked at the coals with a stick. The fire burned brightly and sparks swarmed up into the night air. It was a mystery to him why no one seemed to know the real truth about things like the Mingus Gem. "No doubt there'll always be strange stories told about the Shidow area," he said.

The southern mountain had always fascinated him. It seemed as if it had some secret locked in its interior. "They say one thing's for sure, no one's going to find the sci-tec mine without a map. I know the Shidow area is a wilderness, but even a wilderness can be charted. I'm sure we could find the mine if we had time to explore the area. Look at all the things we've found here near Tizra."

As Bracken allowed the idea to drift through his thoughts, it seemed to grow. He felt a strange but powerful confidence that someday he would go there and find the mine. Almost without thinking, he went on,

"Knowing the way the Council feels about this matter, they've probably destroyed any evidence … still, if you had some explosives and a good eye …"

Silas rolled over and rested his chin on his clenched hand. The flames reflected a flickering dance in his dark eyes. A slight chill filled the air, and he looked hesitant when he spoke, "Maybe I could find out more about this whole thing from one of my friends in Demur. He's heard about a group of people up there who say the gem has magical—"

Bracken suddenly interrupted him. "Look! There's something moving up there." He pointed toward a spot just above the high trees. "Look at that, Silas! It's too erratic to be a sky flyer. Just look at the way it's moving!"

Bracken had seen many things in the night sky, but this was something new. The oval disk danced in an almost rhythmic pattern. Then it stopped. As the two of them watched, an overwhelming force seemed to pull at them. The night grew even more still until they could hear a gentle hum coming from the craft. As they listened, it sounded almost melodious, like a deep, lonely cry, like an ancient song from before the world was made.

The two friends watched intently, feeling an inner radiance. With every passing moment, their thoughts seemed to expand, lifting them into the starry sky, and just for a moment they felt one with the universe. Then the spell was broken and the glowing object began to move again. Momentarily, it performed an aerial ballet and then, without warning, it dashed away over the horizon as quickly as it had come.

For several moments, neither Bracken nor Silas spoke. Then Silas broke the silence, "What do you think it was?"

"I don't really know," said Bracken cautiously. He had suddenly become aware that there were a lot of things he didn't know. One thing, though, was becoming more certain every minute; he had to start finding some answers. "It couldn't have come from this world," he said. "There's no flyer on this planet that can move like that."

"You're right there," mumbled Silas.

Bracken was troubled. Not troubled in a bad way, but troubled nonetheless. He realized again that something inside him wasn't going to be satisfied with the High Council's lies and the sci-tec stories. Things were falling into place, and he had to find out what it all meant.

Silas sat back down and rubbed his eyes. "Oh, well, it's probably just another one of those mysteries we'll never understand." Yawning again, he pulled back his night cover and crawled into his sleeping gear. "All I really know right now is that I'm very, very tired. All that krem's made me kinda groggy. Why don't we talk more about it in the morning?"

"Sure, Silas," said Bracken, still looking into the sky and feeling tired as well. Perhaps all the challenging thinking had wearied him. He pulled his gear around him as the chilled night air settled over them.

But Bracken lay awake thinking. He had heard of others who had seen these odd glowing lights in the night sky. Their appearances had become more common. But something seemed even stranger. It was this that kept him awake most of the night. He had a question that seemed to be haunting him, one he couldn't get rid of. All of these things seemed to be coming to the forefront at the same time. The questions his generation had, the appearance of so many mysteries as he was coming of age. Somehow, he wondered if there wasn't some connection between the finding of the gem and the coming of the space disks as well. Could it be possible that one was the omen of the other? Finally, as the first light of another day appeared, he slipped into a short and troubled sleep.

CHAPTER 16

THE SHADOW PLACE

THRONE ROOM

Mantrik (Bleak time), 5509

The Shadow Czar glided above a frosted membrane forming the surface of an elaborate map. With a simple motion at the edge of his wing, he turned his massive body and hovered down toward the crystallized film, stopping inches from its surface. Reaching out with one of his talons, he set it firmly on a name etched into the face of the panel. At his touch, the entire membrane vibrated and its edges curled, emitting sparks as it strained at its moorings.

Around the name appeared a rectangular border, outlining the territory of Nerkush. To the right, a topaz liquid that lapped at the perimeter of the design represented the Sea of Auren. Other countries were defined as well, their names inscribed in a charcoal script against the map's brilliant white sheen. Countries like Addanis, Eliysim, Sapreism, and Birmez, all who had come through the Great War and still held some of their power. Other countries, defeated during the last conflict, had been swallowed by the more powerful countries, losing their right to a name. Still others, even more insignificant had been relegated to the sidelines, fading even as their names had begun to disappear from the surface of the graph.

Bouncing the tip of one of his talons on the map's surface, Shadow Czar drew in a deep breath, preparing to issue a command. When he spoke, it left most who heard him for the first time somewhat surprised, for his voice had a slight timbre, reminding them of the sound of some plaintive bell, calling out from beyond distant hills. They knew, of course, that if he chose, their leader's voice could roar with such authority that it would shake them to their core.

But now it spoke softly but with a firmness that drew his lackeys up in fearful attention. "Right here," he said, scraping the longest appendage of his hand over the surface of the map, outlining the words as he spoke them, "Yes, Nerkush," the last few letters drawn out in a long hiss through his brilliant teeth, their brightness lighting up the elegant angles of his handsome face. "This is where we must step up our next campaign. We must get them to bring out their Destroyer Weapon again and also to build more engines of destruction, massive ones. They must make improvements on the instruments of death they've formed from elements hidden in their planet's soil. Others too, more like the ones they've crafted from the tiny particles that invade their air, food, and water, so cruelly turning their natural world to poison."

He stopped momentarily, delighting in his next thought even before it formed on his lips. "Yes, the tiny, undetectable creatures that are carried on their air, the ones that spread diseases without a cure. We must inspire their sci-wizards to increase the production of such devices."

Nearby, a row of three minions stood at the rim of the map, their eyes following their master's every move, faithfully recording each of his commands. The tallest of the three spoke up. "What about the other nations? What should we do about them?" He stuttered on, "I ... I ... mean, should they increase the sophistication of their weapons as well?"

"Of course, but have them steal the secrets from Nerkush. Use their spies to procure them. This will create distrust. It will produce the kind of hate that will bring them to another war, perhaps their final war."

The tall one ventured another question. "Who will create these new weapons?"

"It will be easy. Use the same brilliant ones who pioneered the earlier versions, the ones who came from the conquered countries. Their sci-tecs who helped improve the Destroyer Weapon and its delivery systems. Now they can put their minds to work on even more diabolical tools."

"Yes, but those were the ones who murdered the millions. Nerkushians will not want them. They're appalled at those men's crimes."

Shadow Czar drew in a deep breath and held it. Then, expelling it in a sigh, he spoke, "Yes, but Nerkushians are fearful, and so are their leaders. Once they know that other nations have found a fast and efficient way to deliver these devices, there will be no protection from them, they'll want to be the first to control them. They'll do anything to get these secrets. Convince them to look the other way. Persuade them that it's in their best interest to forget the crimes of the past and allow these geniuses to continue their work."

"Yes," snickered the row of minions in unison. "Yes, help them forget the past crimes. We have ways of doing that."

"Then get to work," rumbled Shadow Czar.

"Yes, Master, to work," echoed all the servants as they touched the silver studs on their cloaks and departed to their duties on an astral wind.

CHAPTER 17

RAKA

TAR-LYNREXS (LATE-SUMMER), 5512

Bracken stirred the pot of stew on the small grill in front of his hut. Finally the day had ended. The vinweoks were back in their pens and most of the dust had settled, leaving a slight mist in the air. The rays of the distant setting sun distilled through the remaining haze, leaving a warm glow as evening approached.

Far off, above the eastern moutains range where the sun's rays lit the horizon, a huge cloud spread out, its lower portion hugging its peaks. From its center an angry red hue of sunlight burned through the white outer surface like a permanent flash of lightning. It's shape and color reminded him of a report he'd seen on the vid-tel about the cloud that formed when the Destroyer Weapon had been tested. Apparently this implement of war was still a threat to his planet's peace. Rumors had been circulating that now that other nations had similar destructive devices another war could be a threat to the very existence of his world. Such reports left him and many of his generation wondering about their future. If the rulers of his country could no longer assure its populace of their safety what right had they to lead. That's why so many of his generation felt it was time for change. It must come soon or there was a strong possibility that there would be little left of their world to change.

The glow in the cloud faded as the sun dropped behind the horizon and with it his worries were temporarily dispelled. But the heat of the day still lingered in the air, and its oppression seared his thoughts. Only one thing seemed to squelch them, memories of Lisha.

Memories of her were like a refreshing mist in his heated mind. Her grace and beauty lingered just at the edge of his thoughts. He wanted to reach out and touch her, but she was gone. He remembered how she'd been unfaithful to him. As much as he wanted to blame her, to ease the ache, he had to admit that she'd been seduced by someone with great charisma. Ley had drawn her in with his charm and power. Bracken had tried to forgive him for that, and his experience of Atorma—that blissful detachment from his pain—had allowed him some relief from his heartache. He believed he was now free from any possessiveness. He sought to let go of his anger toward both of those who betrayed him. But in moments of honesty like he was experiencing now he'd had to admit that it still hurt, and he still found it difficult to even consider forgiving her or Ley. The image of Lisha's clear bright eyes, her brilliant smile, and graceful figure surged into his thoughts for just a brief moment and then was snatched away by his sickening surroundings. In disgust, he struggled against the pervasive oppression of his present condition and forced himself to focus once more on the better times he had with her.

CHAPTER 18

TIZRA

PAR-SIMTESH (NEW SEASON), 5509

The last months of Bracken's term at the Mind-Training Center began as if nothing would ever change. He'd excelled in his history and tech classes. He also found daily physical training sessions invigorating, but he especially liked the workshops where they worked on trans-rigs and other vehicles. He seemed to have a natural gift in this realm. It wasn't very long until his teachers recognized his talent with mechanical things and urged him to develop his skills. Soon he was the leader amongst his peers in this field. As a result, he often found some of the upper classmen coming to him for help with repairs to their vehicles. He also enjoyed classes on farming where he learned everything from raising livestock to blasting tree stumps. This was especially helpful because he could put it to use assisting his grandparents with chores on their farm.

It had been two years since the strange encounter with the space disk, and life in Tizra only seemed to remain at the same quiet pace it always had. But Bracken's life had not. He'd changed in many ways. It was his outward development that was most obvious to those around him. His hair and complexion had darkened. His eyes had taken on an even deeper blue hue, reflecting a new sense of destiny. His face, having lost its youthful fat, was lean and chiseled. And he now often wore the long coat he'd ordered over the sphere-nexus from one of the shops in Accad.

It had arrived by trans-delivery along with a broad belt with a large buckle. He'd matched it with some other belts he'd discovered in a storage shed on his grandparents' farm. It was not the typical dress of his classmates, who contentedly followed the fashion of their provincial region—the traditional tunics, pants, and multicolored pullovers.

Silas wore a unique teal coat with bronze shoulder pads; he'd found it in his parents' attic along with matching pants. They were studded with ancient brass cleats that he had one of his girlfriends sew into them. Both of them stood out among their classmates as they walked across the campus heading to a meeting with Lisha and her friend Klime. "Did you see how the class leader was mocking us, Bracken?" said Silas. "I'm sure he's shocked that we don't fit in with their dress rules."

"It's to be expected. He's a leader but actually he's like the crew who follow him, laughing at what they fear. But we can't let that dissuade us. For too long that's been how things are lived out in Tizra and, for that matter, in most of Nerkush."

"So it's time for change. Like one of the edge-poets sang, *new ideas sometimes evoke new fashion.* We're making a statement that change must come."

"Indeed it must. It's my hope that this expression makes others wonder why we would do it. Maybe they'll discover that it's all part of a much bigger issue. Even small things add up and will make others start to wonder.

"Yes, our culture's got to find a new direction. If not, we're all headed for a collision that will end life on Ebbern. At least what we're doing is a start. We've got to show those around us that there's an alternative to foolishly repeating the Fathers' errors. I think it was significant that the night we saw the disk seem to be one more confirmation. It was a sign for us."

The appearance of the strange object in the night sky had stirred something deep inside them, and from that day on things began to change even more. At times they doubted, wondering if it had been an illusion born of too much krem, but they were confident now that they'd both seen it. Perhaps it had been a harbinger confirming what Bracken already felt shifting within them and the world outside Tizra. The fact that there was the possibility of life beyond Ebbern spurred them to consider the same for the world outside of their own hometown.

Bracken had especially embraced the writings of the edge-poets, the unique vocal artists who lived in a small but growing community in Demur where they chanted or sang their writings to the accompaniment of stams and drums. Another group like them was growing in one of the older communities of Accad, and from what Bracken had heard, poets like them and their followers were emerging in other large cities throughout Nerkush. But there was strong resistance to their message by those who supported the Fathers' belief. They announced their opposition through the vid-tel and other public forums, declaring that the dream of an idyllic society where all shared and all cared was more imaginary than possible.

But even in the face of this hostility, the edge-poets and their followers spoke, lived, and dressed in a different style. It clearly set them apart, but it was simply their way of making a statement that it was time for a change. It was this attire and lifestyle that had inspired Bracken and Silas to change their garments and identify with those communities. Places where people felt they could express who they truly were and lay aside the conforming exteriors that so many of his parents' age found themselves trapped in.

As Bracken had begun to voice these ideals, he'd found himself clashing with his teachers, fellow students, and even his parents who had so diligently tried to form the values of Tizra's tradition within him.

"Well, we don't have to worry about their scoffing much longer. Our final training season at the institute is nearly over," said Bracken. "It's time to chart our own course. Like you, Silas, I'm wondering what the future holds. What possible life could there be for any of us? What dreams could ever come true in a world that seems to have the same limited future it's had for generations?"

"You're right," said Silas, "add to that the way the world is changing outside of Tizra. The distant conflicts in other lands might eventually come here. It seems like there are new threats of war from across the Sea of Auren all the time."

"No doubt you've heard the latest, that the High Council has brought the World Destroyer Weapons out of hiding again," added Bracken. "They tested one of them on the barren western desert. Although few in Ebbern saw its explosive flash against the Ribbon Crags, its poisonous aftereffects are spreading slowly through the atmosphere. And now, not only Nerkush has the weapons, but other nations as well. The future of peace looks bleaker every day."

"If war comes again to Ebbern," mused Silas, "it's the last thing our planet will ever know. It will be the last of anything any of us will ever know … but death."

Just then Lisha Fleam and her friend Klime walked up to them and their whole demeanor shifted, their conversation put on hold. In Bracken's last year at the Center, things had mysteriously changed in his relationship with Lisha. Where she'd been distant before, now she was drawn to him and had actually reached out and introduced herself. After a few awkward conversations, they'd fallen into a warm relationship. It seemed that Bracken's rogue ideas and lifestyle had a sudden appeal to her. His edginess drew her to him even though her former male friends were shocked. All this added another layer of conflict to Bracken's status at the Center.

Bracken smiled at the lovely face that had now wiped away his haunting thoughts. "How's your last week of guidance going?" he asked as they all sat down together on the great lawn in the middle of the Mind-Training Center. Silas and Klime settled on the grass nearby chatting away.

"It's painful. I'm still struggling with my second class. The professor's a bore."

"I've got a few like that too," said Bracken, drinking in the glow on Lisha's face. She had a natural beauty that needed very little help from makeup. Her honey blond hair and delicate features were enhanced by a slender but well-developed figure. Her eyes were a soft brown with a hint of gold at the core of her irises. Long black lashes matched her full but neatly trimmed eyebrows. The gold at the center of each eye turned a dark amber when she was irritated, which was happening now with talk of school issues. Bracken didn't mind. He enjoyed watching her even when she was angry.

Lisha jabbed her stylus into the ground and looked frustrated. "I mean it, Guidance is so boring, as usual. I can hardly wait for the last day." Her long soft eyelashes blinked unconsciously as she concentrated on the black case in her hand. Her long and delicate fingers held her study module with a firm grip, but she was at the point of tossing it to the ground.

Behind her, other learners walked back and forth between their instruction stations, housed in circular pods ringing the domed-shaped central building. Tubular corridors, like spokes of a wheel connected the rooms to the central hub. A variety of courses ranging from studies in early Nerkushian tribal structure to lengthy investigations of the sci-tec discoveries were programmed into the learning consoles that filled the rooms.

Bracken plucked a blade of grass and slipped it between his lips, something he found himself doing whenever he reclined on its green surface. It made him feel somehow connected to the tranquil sense that ebbed from the natural world. "I'm glad this last week's free for us in the upper classes. I'm going to spend some time exploring the far canyons."

Lisha looked up from her note-recorder, its readout panel blinking red, a clear indication that it was malfunctioning. "Haven't you been out there before?" she said, sounding slightly irritated that she still had classes and he didn't.

Bracken slipped the green blade from between his teeth. Yes, he'd just been up in the canyons, but he was eager to go again. The air up there was better and the hillside was quiet and peaceful. "I've been up a few of them, but there are several I'd still like to see." He was hoping Lisha would go with him. But she only frowned and continued talking about her struggles with sub-body analysis. Ten feet away, Silas and Klime looked happily engaged as they lay side by side on the grassy carpet, talking quietly.

Lisha nodded toward them. "Klime does so well. She hardly concentrates and then always makes the highest marks. I'll have to work hard this whole week to keep up with her to end the session with a good standing."

"You shouldn't try to compete with her," said Bracken. "Yes, do your best, but don't be so frustrated."

"You don't understand. It's my parents and her parents. They're constantly on us to perform at our highest level. I mean, I want to do well, but they're driving us too hard. After our athletic comps and mind-team challenge, I hardly have time to breathe."

"So why do you do it?"

"Like I said, it's my parents. I'm not about to let them down. I know they want the best for me, but sometimes I think it's our whole culture. We're so driven to succeed that we hardly have time to live."

Bracken watched Lisha with a subdued sense of awe. Even when she was troubled, her natural beauty still came through match by her radiant hair sparkling in the sun.

Lisha knitted her brows, still frustrated with the slow response from her portable learning module. "Do you think if I used the Tc-4 mode it would resolve easier?"

Bracken reached out and took the recorder from her slender hand. "I know you're smart, Lisha, but it can be a bit of mystery. I had trouble with it till a guy in my sci class helped me with it. Here, let me try." In a way, he found it hard to believe this girl was truly interested in him. He had watched her for years, secretly hoping for her affection, yet never really believing it would come to pass. Now that she had begun to show an interest, he found it surprising. At first she seemed to be intrigued by his different ways. So many of his classmates had embraced the traditions of their parents and teachers. They had been content to mimic the instructions brought down from the High Council and they accepted the path set out for them by their leaders.

But Bracken hadn't. Ever since the night he and Silas had encountered the strange craft in the night sky, his questions had only increased. He expressed it in so many ways, in his reports to his teachers, in the way he dressed, the songs he wrote and played for his classmates, and even his attitude toward his parents. But instead of causing Lisha to dislike him as some of the others girls did, it seemed to attract her to him. She had an edge to her that was just beginning to emerge, and Bracken wondered if she saw in him a partner in adventure.

Bracken made a few modifications on Lisha's device and handed it back to her. "It should work now."

"Thanks, Bracken," said Lisha, smiling down at the now-functioning screen.

"You just needed to switch to the sub-key mode and adjust the flow rate. It took me a few weeks to learn this. You're a bright girl, you'll probably catch on quicker than I did."

Lisha switched off the recorder and dropped it into her pouch. "Sure I will," she said with a teasing smirk. "Bracken, these things come so easily for you. Why aren't you more interested in them?"

Bracken pulled another blade from the lawn. "Like I've told you before, I guess I'm just beginning to find out there are other things even more important, things that may change the future of our planet." He had begun to open his heart to her, but he still hadn't told her about the strange encounter he'd had with the space disk. But now that she seemed to have drawn closer to him, he was ready to share even this with her.

Lisha looked at him with a quizzical glance. "So are you ready to let me know something new? There seem to be so many interesting things about you that you never share with me. I hope this is a sign that you're opening up."

Lisha wanted that closeness with the young man beside her. She'd heard Bracken talk about his family, and she'd hinted to him that her parents did not care for her in the same way Bracken's cared for him. But she hadn't told him everything. She found it difficult to let him see how deeply she was hurt by others and even by her own father.

She was much smarter than her classmates gave her credit for. They pegged her as just another pretty face, and it made her mad. Of course she was aware of how attractive she was, but that only made it all the more offensive. Did her natural beauty mean that she couldn't possibly be intelligent?

And then there were the issues with her father. He couldn't see past her brother to recognize her own potential. Sure, her sibling was brilliant, but he had a way of garnering most of their father's limited attention. It hadn't always been like that. He used to have more time for all of them. She missed those times. Most of his week now was spent traveling across Nerkush selling his new invention—the Cylac rotor, a device he'd invented to help farmers harvest their crops. All of this left her with a slow, burning resentment toward him, and beneath that, a longing that couldn't be fulfilled.

Though she wasn't fully conscious of it, she looked to Bracken to fill the emotional void her parents had left, and he wasn't doing as good a job at it as she'd hoped. She wondered if he had the wisdom to match his boldness. Still, his adventurous spirit fascinated her, and his good looks only added to his whole allure. Of course she wasn't about to give away how she secretly felt about him, but that would probably change if the warmth between them continued to grow.

Bracken hesitated and then smiled back his answer. "Well, it would take some time to explain. Tell you what, if you'll come hiking with me tomorrow, I'll share it with you."

Lisha thought for a moment. "Well I may have to skip a few things, but I guess I can find the time."

A melodic chime sounded in the distance. "There's the bell, we'd better go," announced Bracken as he stood to his feet and offered Lisha his hand. "I'll walk with you."

The four of them got up and headed toward their next class, Silas and Klime following a few paces behind.

CHAPTER 19

TIZRA

PAR-SIMTESH (NEW SEASON), 5509

As Bracken and his friends strode across the broad grassy area leading to Lisha's class, a tall man approached them from a distance. But even before his frame came into focus, his melodic voice reached them. He was singing a simple but haunting melody that arrested their steps; they stopped, standing entranced as the strange figure moved closer.

Bracken soon recognized the mysterious person as he closed the distance between them. The man, Elcari Amaura, had been a teacher at the center years ago but had been removed for his odd beliefs. Bracken vaguely remembered the rumors surrounding the man's ouster. He had become an edge-poet, claiming to see visions of a new future for Nerkush. His songs had been deemed unacceptable to the High Council, and they had demanded his removal.

Bracken had just begun his training here a year before the man had left. Though that had been some time ago, he could not have forgotten him. In fact, no one who saw him forgot him. It was not just his height and striking features but the fact that he was blind. Despite his visual limitations, he moved toward them apparently unaided. His long angular body was complemented by a handsome face marred only by two dark and fleshy scars where his eyes had been.

No one knew how he'd become blind. Some said that it had been from a war on the distant lands beyond the Sea of Auren. Others said that he was born that way, but most believed it was from a ritual his parents participated in near the Pillars of Rimlex. Believing that he was an unusually gifted child, they had removed his eyes, trusting that his gift of second-sight would only be enhanced once he could no longer see the present world.

Whatever the case, he had proved his giftedness and brilliance by first rising to the top of his class at Tizra's Mind-Training Center in spite of his handicap and then, after graduation from the Advanced Mind-Training Center he'd returned to his old school to become one of its leading scholars and teachers. But then something occurred that changed everything; it started after he'd returned from a sojourn in the Desert of Morek.

He began to put his ideas into song, and it was not long until those songs became a curse to him. They had had an unusual power over some of those who heard them, especially the young. Soon he had a growing following among the students in Tizra as well as the other youth of Western Nerkush, and that's what had settled it for the Council. His reputation soon reached even Accad, where students there had taken up his ideas.

They played his songs on their stams, singing along with them in small groups gathering in the herb shops and krem rooms across the great city. The Council acted mercilessly and removed him without the slightest warning. His expulsion had happened so quickly and he had vanished so completely that soon his influence faded as some new phenomena swept through the land, leaving only a faint echo in the hearts of those who once sung his songs.

But Bracken had not forgotten them. In fact, as he stared at the man before him and listened to his entrancing voice, a rush of memories came pouring back into his mind. Even though he'd been young, he had secretly memorized some of the blind man's songs and could still recall some of their words. But those thoughts were quickly swept away by what he heard from the blind man's mouth now. He was no longer singing, but still the effect of those past melodies seemed to hang in the air around them. He continued to step closer, somehow always facing the young man he'd come to meet.

"Hello, Bracken," called the singer in a low, sweet voice as he closed the final distance between them. "I know you're there, even though I can't see you the way others do." The blind man's dramatic entrance onto the

Center's grounds drew the attention of the students, and a group began to form on the lawn nearby.

Bracken was shocked. How could this singer know who he was or where he was? And how was he walking unaided by a guide stick or another person? "What's going on?" the youth stuttered at the poet. He turned and looked at Lisha, who had the same questioning expression. He looked back at the singer, who was smiling. Though the man had no eyes to see, a strange emanation came from the place they had once been. He seemed to squint slightly, and then he began to sing again. It was in a modal scale, rising and falling in a range of over two octaves but supported by a deep vibrato that resonated so powerfully that Bracken could sense the tones vibrating in his own chest.

His first words were a prelude, "I see great things for you … Bracken!" the last syllable slowly ebbed away and then he began again in rhyme.

I see small things that twinkle and shine.
The sound of chirping at the end of the line.
I hear the spellbinding music of a simmering band
And adventures in a far and strange new land.
I see leaves bathed in a moist crystal rain
And moments of bliss filling your brain

I see the sight of your breath in the high mountain air
And a woman of mystery whose love you will share.
You'll see worlds beyond this one all made of light
But to reach them you must walk in the night
Oh, lonely traveler should you ever return
Keep truth in your heart so that others can learn
Soon they will follow your bright shining path

So you must lead them, avoiding all wrath
Some will struggle and fall in the way
But you must go on, do not linger or stay.

It is time, oh wanderer, take your first tender strides
Walk into a realm where the answer often hides
A palace of truth waits in the clear mountain snow
So step out on your journey its time now to go

The last note of the singer's voice slowly faded into the warm afternoon air. Bracken and Lisha, along with the crowd, stood around, unsure how to respond, so they just stared and whispered among themselves until the strange poet turned and slowly walked away, his departure as haunting as his appearance.

Bracken felt strange and somewhat embarrassed. Some in the small crowd of students that had gathered to hear the blind poet were giggling at the bazaar incident they'd just witnessed but others were silent, still enraptured by the soft and pleasant tenure of the voice they'd just heard. A few gawked at Bracken, no doubt wondering at the weird, future-tale the poet had told.

Bracken wondered too as he and Lisha stared at each other in disbelief. "Is that who I think it was?" she asked tentatively, the force of the preceding moments still impacting her. "Is that the professor they removed from school years ago? I'd heard the rumors surrounding him, but I had no idea that he was still around or that he could sing like that." Bracken could see, in spite of the oddity of his message and demeanor, the sheer beauty of his voice had intrigued her.

"Yes, it was. I was younger then but he left a lasting impression."

"What does it all mean, Bracken? And what was that about some 'woman of mystery'?" asked Lisha, sounding irritated.

Bracken was mystified as well but out of concern for Lisha's worries about the "mystery woman' he tried to minimize the incident. "You know as much as I do, sweet one. You're the only woman in my life, and I hope it will be that way forever … all I can say is that was really strange, but I'm just going to set it all aside and get on to class. Are we still on for tomorrow?"

"Yes," said Lisha, still a little shaken by the part of the message concerning the mysterious woman in the poet's song.

"Great. Let's meet here then and take my trans as far as the upper trail."

Klime came up beside Lisha and motioned her to move on. "We'd better be going, Lisha, the second pod's always crowded after break."

Lisha nodded, and as she turned to go, her hand gently brushed Bracken's. "I'm looking forward to a good time tomorrow."

"So am I," said Bracken slowly. Inspite of his attempt to cover his concerns his thoughts were still captured by what had just happened, and his last words just barely trickled out. "See ya …"

Lisha frowned, revealing her lingering anxiety, but still she turned and said a sweet good-bye before walking quickly away.

Bracken and Silas watched as the girls paced back toward the center. Then they turned and walked toward their next class. Silas looked confused and urged an answer from his friend. "What did all that mean? I vaguely remember that man. He was like an edge-poet but with a real edge."

"Yes, someone who doesn't have sight, but sees things no one else sees."

"Right, but really odd things. I don't think anyone understood him. I certainly didn't."

"I know. But something seemed to resonate inside me. There was a connection there. I think he was sent to me, to us. You know how we've been questioning our purpose, the direction of our nation and all of Ebbern."

"You mean it's some sort of sign?"

"Yes, that's it, Silas. A sign. A harbinger to me that it's time I act."

"So you're going to just take off to 'worlds made of light'?"

"Well maybe not something like that, but who knows what's ahead? I just know I can't stay in Tizra forever, and maybe this is what I needed to get me thinking in that direction."

"Well, whatever you do, don't leave me behind."

"Don't worry, Silas. We'll go there together."

CHAPTER 20

WESTERN HILLS NEAR TIZRA

PAR-SIMTESH (NEW SEASON), 5509

The next day had begun with a promise of warmth under another sunlit sky and, true to its promise, the golden rays heated the air to a perfect temperature. Bracken and Lisha took his trans as far as they could into the hills, leaving it behind to slowly wind their way up one of the narrow trails that led into the wilderness. A light breeze brushed Lisha's hair across her shoulders. Bracken watched with delight as the sun glistened from its highlights. The two of them had been climbing for about a half hour, the air's earthy aroma almost intoxicating.

She heard Bracken stop behind her to take a deep breath. "The cresh smells good, doesn't it?"

"Yes, it's so colorful," answered Lisha as she stopped as well, enjoying the beauty of the yellow-green plants that dotted the slope.

Starting out again, they soon came to a small brook that splashed its way down the gentle rise. Bracken helped Lisha across it. They removed their leather cleks and sank their bare feet into the tingling water. Bracken took her hand. Lisha saw his cheeks flush as he gripped her slim, soft fingers. "Be careful, there's a large rock here," he warned as they approached the other side of the stream. Reaching the opposite bank, they both sat down with their feet soaking in the creek. The water whirled and bubbled past them, its clear texture gleaming in the sunlight.

Bracken tossed a small pebble into the brook. "When I look at a stream like this, I feel refreshed. I could stay here forever, watching it, listening to its gurgling conversation. I guess that's the way I wish people were … pure … alive … transparent. Always fresh and always clear."

Lisha gazed down at the rocks on the bottom of the streambed. Their multicolored surfaces, polished smooth by the rushing water, shone back at her. "It's not often you meet someone like that." She thought about Bracken and the way he'd begun to open his heart to her. The more she got to know him, the more he seemed just like that. "I've always hoped to, but it seems like everyone is caught up in their own desires."

Bracken curled his toes in the gritty soil near the creek bank and then dipped them back in the stream. "I agree. People don't seem to have time for the things that I feel are truly important."

Lisha pulled several small thistles from her skirt "My father's a good example of that. He's more interested in selling Cylac rotors to farmers than being with me and my mother."

Lisha stopped rather abruptly. Why was she so quick to share with Bracken? Again she found herself telling him things she would seldom tell anyone else. Too often she would hide her real feelings inside. Everything was so bottled up; her growing bitterness toward her father was hard to hold onto. Now everything was coming out to Bracken. She watched him as he threw another pebble into the brook. She'd always known there was something more than his striking features that appealed to her. He seemed to have an intriguing but warm glow in his eyes, as if a fire burned in his soul, and his pupils mirrored its flickering. It made her trust him with her deepest thoughts.

There was another thing that moved her. She knew it from the way he looked at her when she spoke. He was truly listening to her in a manner others didn't. In a way her father failed to. He was with her in the moment and not distracted like her father often was with his other worries and priorities.

They sat quietly for a while and then Bracken broke the silence. "As we've shared before, you're not the first person to look at things this way. I've felt like that for a long time, and it's the narrow mindset of our little village. It's time to move on. Leaving Tizra will be a pleasure. There's nothing really here that I want anymore, except our friendship."

Lisha looked intently at Bracken. "Why's that? This is your home. Your family's here. You've grown up here."

"I guess that's part of the problem. I've lived with these things long enough."

"What things?"

"Oh, the town's too small, the thinking too narrow and selfish. Nerkush is larger than just this little valley. The universe is bigger than Ebbern."

"That's obvious."

"I know, but it's something more than that."

"Like what?"

"Like maybe there's something outside. Something outside of Tizra and something outside of Ebbern."

"What do you mean?"

"Haven't you heard the rumors about the space disks? They're suddenly showing up everywhere. They're supposed to be from out there," he said, pointing into the blue above them. He paused for a moment, caught up in the emotion of his theme. Turning his gaze from the sky, he looked intently into Lisha's eyes.

"Then there's the appearance of the Mingus gems. They're said to open doors to another dimension." Most of the students at the Mind-Training Center had heard rumors about the strange stones, but to most of them they were only odd and funny stories to be laughed at but never really believed. "I've even listen to the songs of a few edge-poets who have hidden messages about them in their music. They sing that it clears a pathway of perception into another realm."

"Sure. I've heard those things as well. But the two events are worlds apart. What possible connection could they have? Anyway, how do you know if the disks are real?"

"Because ... I've seen one."

"You have?"

"Yes. Silas saw it too. In fact, that's what I've wanted to tell you. We had an encounter with one the year before last." He pointed back toward the sky. "It was right near here. Ever since then we've kept it to ourselves, but now it seems more important than ever. It's as if it was a sign to us that change has come to our world. Another signal that there is something significant in store for our generation."

Lisha paused for a moment before responding. She didn't know whether to believe Bracken or not. But she decided to see where their conversation would lead anyway. "Well, now that you've seen one, what do you make of the whole thing?"

"I think there's a connection."

"Between the disks and the gem?"

"Yes. If only you'd been there. When the disk appeared, Silas and I found ourselves momentarily lifted and transformed as if we had discovered our purpose. That somehow we're connected with the entire universe. What I've heard about those who experience the gem is similar. They have this awe-inspiring moment when they are lifted, expanded, and then find life's purpose. Yes, I'm guessing there's a connection, and I'm planning to find out."

"How?" Lisha giggled, humoring him. "Are you going to grow antennae to contact them and just ask for a ride on a disk?"

"No," he snarled back playfully, though she saw he looked a little hurt. "I'm going to see if there's a connection. I'm going to Shidow to try and find the hidden Mingus mine."

"Oh sure, you'll just run up there and trip right over it," she laughed. "You've got to be kidding." Lisha had heard strange rumors from many of her fellow students and teachers at the Mind-Training Center. "I was told by one of the sci-professors that it was all made up and that no one would ever find the Mingus mine. It was just like all the other old legends that have grown up around that mountain."

"Well, I think he's wrong." Bracken was visibly upset now. Sensing his irritation, she backed off.

"Maybe you can find it, Bracken," she said, smiling reassuringly at him. She liked him, and even if some of his ideas were hard for her to believe, she would overlook them. "If you do, please bring back one for me," she said, her voice warming toward him.

He softened under her grace. "I guess I'll know for sure once I've gone there. Sad to say it won't be for a while. I've promised my father's parents that I'll help them on their farm with the next two harvests by then by brother Ditten will be old enough to take over for me. Then I've got at least the first year at the Advanced Mind-Training Center to get out of the way. But once that's through, I'm on my way up there."

He looked back down the hillside toward Tizra and sighed. "One thing I know, I'll be able to see things more clearly when I'm away from Tizra. It'll be good to find more who agree with me. I'm tired of being told I'm wrong by most of the people around me. I think a lot of questions will start to be answered then."

Bracken lapsed into silence, thinking of his parents, the Fathers, and his teachers with their constant clichés and admonitions: "Be successful, be someone your parents can be proud of!" And, of course, their quoting of the Volume, and all its phrases that had seemed so worn-out to him. He couldn't believe in something he had never seen. He believed in things like the brook that was in front of him. Not in stories about any hidden evil prince who lured people off the true path. He could see evil all right. It lay in the threat of the World Destroyer Weapons.

The fear of their awesome power being unleashed by some madman in a moment of passion seemed to invade even his peaceful moments, moments like this one. Pictures of barren, charred landscapes flashed in his mind. "Something has to change, you know, Lisha. People have got to open their eyes and start to really care ... to be themselves and quit scuffling in the game of smashing others to put themselves ahead, the way nations on this planet do now."

He looked into her brown eyes for a moment and then turned away as a warm flush flooded him. He was finding it so easy to love this girl. She was beautiful not only outside, but inside. He was touched that she had shared her struggles with him. He was happy, too, to see that she had a desire to learn and to explore what he was seeking. She seemed intrigued by his different ways. When he thought about it, though, he wasn't quite sure what had drawn her to him but he was glad to see her interest growing.

"You know, Lisha," he began again, "most of those I've grown up with seem to have their greatest joys jostling their trans-rigs on the boulevards or talking about the last girl they took down." He frowned, the edges of his mouth turning down and his pupils pin-pointing for a moment. "It's always the same. Drink lots of krem or nectol when the Rest Day comes, joke, and act smart. Try to impress girls like you. I just don't want to be that way anymore, and I guess I never ..." he stopped.

Lisha was looking at him with a gaze that melted him to the core. Her eyes were alive with a warm glow. The breeze stirred her blond hair. Her lips were moist, the slightest hint of her white teeth peeking through.

"When did you start to feel this way, Bracken?" she asked.

As he stared at her, he felt a deep urge to reach out and pull her to him. He longed to press his lips against hers and to hold her in his arms. Instead, he went on with his answer. "I guess it really started when I was young. I began to wonder about things, like the stars, the sea, the snow on the mountains. Why are they so beautiful? What are they there for?"

He plucked another green blade and held it up. "Even things as small as this tiny piece of green. It seems all part of a wonderful mystery, so natural yet somehow so eternal. How can I understand what all this means? How can others just ignore all this beauty for the sake of the shallow things they value? I know I'll find answers. It's like pushing through a dark haze toward the sun. Shaking off the shadow of narrow thinking, I mean. I've found there are more important things in life than what we're being molded to believe. Don't you feel that way?"

"Yes, I can really identify with what you're saying," Lisha stared into his eyes for a long moment, and Bracken saw there that something deep was forming between them.

"Besides, there are others who feel the way I do. They've been away from this little village. They've seen the new things that are happening in Accad and Demur, and they've told me about them. I suppose that, too, is part of the reason I've changed." He remembered how he'd spent his nights secretly listening to the recordings of the edge-poets that friends who had visited Accad brought back with them to Tizra. He had listened to them so many times that their messages had come to be part of him as if their ideas were already inside of him and their poems along with their songs had merely awakened them.

Lisha wanted to hear more. "What did they say about Accad, what did they tell you?"

Bracken moved closer to her, resting his hand gently on hers. "There's something happening with a small group of people down there. They think like you and me. They write and sing about a new era, a mysterious but wonderful age, an age coming to all of us. We just have to care about one another, believe in it, and it will come."

"Is that all they believe?"

"No, there's one other important thing. They want Nerkush to dismantle the Destroyer Weapons and bring an end to the constant wars on our planet."

As Lisha looked deep into Bracken's blue eyes he sensed questions there. Perhaps his ideas sounded rebellious, almost blasphemous to her. But he thought that it might be part of the reason she liked him. He was bold enough even to believe in something others found wrong. But searching her expression he also wondered what her fears were. Did she care about the future of their planet? What if war came again? What if they used the Destroyer Weapons and it turned Ebbern to ash?

"This is what you've been hoping for too, isn't it? You've been hoping to find people who believe like you. People who believe in life and not destruction."

"Yes, and I want to be part of them, even though a lot of narrow people think they're all strange. My father's one of those narrow people. He's always griping about the group who lives in Accad's old neighborhood. He told me he saw a few of them on his last trip down there and said they were really crazy."

"It seems like those who look for something real in this world are always considered odd," said Bracken. "But I've learned the truth about them. They're honest and bold people. Their poet-minstrels have such hope for the future if they can bring about change."

"That's so true, Bracken. I'm becoming more convinced of it every day." Lisha's voice seemed to caress him. Against the striking glow of her face, the beauty of their surroundings seemed to fade. She was the most beautiful girl he'd ever seen. As they talked, Bracken yearned for her. He could sense her responding to him. Bracken began to speak again, "I guess that's why …" then his voice trailed off. Her face had completely captivated his attention. For a moment he hesitated, unsure of what to do next. But her smile soon dispelled that question.

Reaching out slowly, he touched her shoulders and pulled her close. His fingers brushed across her lips, over her delicate cheek, and then ran through her silken hair. She closed her eyes, savoring his touch. He pulled her closer and their lips met. It was a gentle embrace that soon flamed into a passionate and inextinguishable fire. In the heat of that moment, they forgot about everything but each other. Even the sound of the brook was lost on them as it continued to gurgle happily long after the sun ceased to dance on its surface.

CHAPTER 21

RAKA

TAR-LYNREXS (LATE-SUMMER), 5512

For as long as he could remember, Bracken had loved green things. Whether it was the lushness of the forest near Tizra or the verdant reflection in the pools beneath its trees, the natural world always seemed to refresh him. But here in the desert, the parched vistas seemed to suck the last bit of moisture from his soul. It was in moments like this that he sought refreshment in his memories.

He had relived that first time he and Lisha had explored the foothills above their village and the joy they'd found in each other's company. That escape had been the first of many as their love for each other grew. In those next three years as they pursued their relationship, the common ideals and dreams they had seemed to weave their souls together.

All that was gone now, those hopes were as frayed as his tattered work clothes. Was it the way she'd betrayed him or just his stubborn lack of forgiveness that kept them apart? Sometimes he wondered if he'd ever know; at other times, he wished he could forget her completely.

Bracken sniffed at the familiar aroma of his dinner slowly warming on the fire. It would be filling but almost tasteless. He raised an earthen cup to his mouth; its contents carried with it a slight taste of brine but it was wet and that helped wash the last bits of grit from his throat.

He longed for a drink of water from some cool mountain lake, like the one he'd drunk from when for the first time he'd arrived the Pool of Tibtem at the base of Mount Shidow. His thoughts reached out for those moments and all that followed after it.

CHAPTER 22

MOUNT SHIDOW

PAR-SIMTESH (NEW SEASON), 5512

Deep in the Shidow wilderness, Bracken knelt beside the cool water of Lake Tibtem and took a refreshing drink. As his cupped hands broke the pool's surface, they momentarily disturbed its glass-like appearance. When the lake grew calm again, he could see his tan reflection wobbling on the face of the blue-green water. Now that he had finished his commitment to bringing in the two harvests on his grandparents' farm, and with his first year at the Advanced Mind-Training center behind him, he was ready to begin a new chapter in his life.

The journey from Tizra had been exhilarating; each marker on the road seemed to trigger the ticking of an inner clock as he counted off the time bringing him closer to the answers he sought. Would he finally step into his destiny? What wonders would this journey hold for him? He couldn't help thinking of the blind poet's words, "oh wanderer" … it made his heart soar with anticipation.

He had opened the sky-hatch on his vehicle and the warm sun had turned his skin a shade darker than when he'd left. His trans-rig had brought him to the base of the mountain, but as versatile as it was, it couldn't manage the rocky outcroppings that ringed it. That was of little consequence, for he preferred walking the final distance, fording streams and letting the cool water wash the grit from his footgear. He'd brought his stam along as well, hoping to compose some new songs inspired by the pristine environment.

He used the tracking device on his com-patch, bringing up its small graphic display to give him the coordinates to the lake. The last part of his journey had been over some rough terrain and it had left his feet tired, but his spirit feeling free. He looked out across the surface of the lake. Its wetness appeared inviting. Shedding his clothes, he dove in and swam several yards. The water was crisp, and his skin tingled as icy fingers jabbed his senses awake. Climbing out, he stood and stared up at Mount Shidow, its massive sides, the color of dull purple rising toward its snow-covered peak. He breathed deeply of the mountain air, and its scent seemed to clear his mind the way the water had cleansed the dust from his sweaty body. His head grew light and the high altitude seemed to weave a spell around him.

Somewhere in that mountain is the sci-tec's mine, he told himself. I'll find it if I have to look for a week. A snow-cold wind echoed down the high cliffs and blew over him. Chilled to the bone but refreshed, he dressed and began to set up his base camp. After a day of rest, he would begin his search.

On the far side of the mountain, someone else had been searching as well, only his search had just ended.

Ley Os quickly tightened the ignition wires to the poles on top of his charge generator. He raised its arm, his knotted muscles flexing, and forcefully thrust it down again. Beyond him, in the side of the mountain, an explosion discharged tons of rock from the face of a hidden mine. Os's ruddy, bearded face broke into a smile. The sci-tec crew had made very sure no one would ever get into this place again—or so they thought. Its chief miner, Cib Mingus had gotten out with a massive amount of the stones before they shut it down, but now the supply had grown slim. Os needed to go to the source, so he'd come to Shidow using the few clues that Cib had given him.

With the dust still settling, he ran to the mouth of the excavation. He entered it, ducking his head slightly and then slowly moved deeper into the opening. Using a small search lamp, he examined the stability of the support beams. Assured that all the rubble had settled and the girders remained firm, he walked cautiously ahead, his footsteps echoing down the long narrow shaft.

Later, he reached the spot Cib Mingus had told him about. A metallic wall with a hatch in its center crossed the tunnel, sealing it tightly. The burnished anti-rust surface reflected the beam from his search lamp. On the wall to his left was a row of storage lockers. He opened them, finding the protective clothing and helmets necessary for entering the chamber containing the Mingus gems. The coverings looked stiff and worn, but Cib had assured him that they would give him sufficient protection against the rays of the Mingus Effect. Os set his lamp on a rock and began to change. Somewhere in the distance he could hear the drip of water as it seeped through the porous rock and splashed into a subterranean pool.

He'd been a miner for years working in mountains that ringed the Valley of Raka as well as the hills hidden in the dense Forest of Zorek, and now, just recently here on Mount Shidow. Digging around for treasure had had its disappointments—too many played-out claims and false hopes had left him desperate for a strike. But long ago he'd given up his search for mineral wealth. He had found something much better. Cib Mingus had introduced him to the real riches.

He knew that the sci-tec guys thought only they had the kind of minds and equipment that could search out the powerful stones and treasures this mountain held. Sure they had the right "formula", but now he'd found it too. That was one good thing about coming from a wealthy family. It had afforded him the best education, allowing him to master engineering at the elite schools he attended. It was thanks to that education that he was so adept at operating the sophisticated equipment that could detect new and unusual substances.

For months he'd probed in the Shidow region using the detection devices that Cib had trained him with. He'd used them to scan the rock and soil looking for the precious stones and the mine's entrance. Once he'd found it, he'd immediately created an elaborate map to help him on his next visit so he wouldn't have to use the same complex apparatus to find the mine again. None of this gear had been cheap, but he had all the resources he needed. If Cib had left him a map it would have been so much easier and less expensive to find this place. But he'd not had time before the sci-corp came for him.

His family's wealth had been a blessing and a curse—money had never been lacking with them. There was always plenty; if only he could have said the same about affection and attention. But his parents didn't have the same kind of emotional attachment to him they'd had with their wealth. Ley saw through his parents, the way they used their power, money, and influence to control others. It was their constant quest. He had to admit he saw their same sense of drive and ambition in himself, but not for money. He was searching for something that would help him connect with others and find the community that never existed in his own home. He wanted to use his resources for the common good, not just for personal gain.

It was that quest that brought him into his current career and ultimately brought him into friendship with Cib Mingus. His wise mentor had exposed him and many others in Accad to the gem and its power. Guided by Cib, Os had taken several excursions into his wondrous realm. Cib claimed this would be the one thing they'd been looking for to create the new kind of culture Nerkush so desperately needed. One adventure with the gem and Ley had been convinced as well. Of course the authorities had silenced the wise old miner, but not before he'd given Ley a supply of the gems and enough clues to know where to look for more. If only he'd made the map that he'd always promised to make. For some reason he never got around to it.

Inspite of that Ley owed much to Cib and now finally, he was fulfilling his destiny, he was becoming the catalyst of the change he dreamed of for Nerkush. The ever-growing demand for the gem was proof of that, wasn't it? The fact that he would be the one source people came to for their supply of the stones was proof of his destiny. He smiled at the thought.

Making sure the protective clothing was snugly sealed around him, he punched out the code on the lock console. A combination of lights fluttered momentarily on the readout panel and then held brightly, forming four parallel lines. The hatch opened with a hiss, and Os stepped into the chamber.

The sci-tec crew had done a good job sealing off this area. It hadn't taken them long to realize that no one could work there without protection from the Mingus rays. He'd heard stories of how the early ones had been unaware of what was happening to them until they'd been caught up in the effect. But gradually they'd discovered how to control and harness the stones and protect themselves from their power. The gems' effect was greatest when a person took them internally, but with so many of stones in the same place, the mine created a symbiosis that was overpowering. If you weren't wearing protective clothing, you might be propelled into some unknown dimension, never to return.

On the floor of the passageway and in the walls, stones of various sizes emitted a soft glow. Ley stooped to collect the ones on the floor and filled several of the containers he'd brought with him. He could always come back later and dig the others from the rich vein opened by the previous miners. Os examined each gem closely through his helmet's visor before placing them in the silver-colored boxes he had brought with him in a large shoulder pack. He knew that if they were not properly contained, he would be unnecessarily exposed to their effect.

Having collected enough to fill his knapsack, Ley left the mine. He stood safely back from the entrance and sealed it again with a small explosive charge. Assured that it was well hidden, he grabbed a handbag he'd left outside and plunged into the surrounding forest, heading back towards his rig and eventually to Accad.

Sometime later when a burly stranger broke through the brush and appeared at the lakeside, Bracken was not completely surprised. He had heard the distant explosions and half expected whoever had caused them to eventually make himself known since there was only one trail that led back to the main road and that trail started here at the pool. But what did surprise Bracken was the nature of his visitor.

Os seemed to have a faraway twinkle in his eyes as he approached and extended his hand to Bracken. "Name's Ley Os." The man's tone of voice was almost ethereal. "Been mining in this place for years." Even if it wasn't true, it made a good cover story for why he was there. "You might have heard my blasting earlier," said the miner, setting his handbag on the ground.

Bracken stood up and greeted the stranger, "Good to meet you. I'm Bracken. My home's in Tizra."

"Fine town. Usually stop by there on my way to Accad. Not a bad place for a rest in the shade on a hot day." Os ran his fingers through several days stubble and looked back up the mountain. "Beautiful sight, isn't it? It always seemed strange to me that more people don't travel down this way. Guess they still believe those old rumors about the stone of fire that fell back in the Fourth Age."

The miner knelt down beside the lake's edge, took a deep drink and then splashed some water on his sweaty face. "Fine with me. I kinda enjoyed being here by myself. Haven't seen much of anybody since the sci-tec boys left."

"You were up here when the sci-tec team came through?"

"Yeah, they tried to run me off the mountain, but I just hid from them. Didn't want me aware of what they were doing. One of those official expeditions, you know, all hush-hush and everything. But I'm not about to be intimated by them. I come prepared for any possible situation." He spread apart the edges of his handbag, allowing Bracken to see its contents. It contained several weapons. What looked like at least six energy eggs and an igniter tube with its case of pellets, lay side by side at the bottom of the bag.

"You certainly do," said Bracken, clearly recalling what some of those weapons could do. "My friend and I discharged one of those eggs when we were younger." He thought of the time he and Silas had purchased one illegally, learned how the settings worked, and then tossed it into a smiidgion shack in a ranch near Tizra. He still remembered how the powerful blast tore the small shed to bits and how mad the smiidge farmer was with them for frightening his animals. Luckily they had gotten away without being reported to the authorities, but he still remembered the shouts of the angry smiidger.

Bracken looked up from the handbag and then at the straps of the shoulder pack still on Os's back. "So if you were up here when the government guys were around …" he said hesitantly, "then you probably know what they found up here."

"Sure did …" Ley grew suddenly still. He took his pack off and lowered it gently to the ground, resting it safely against his leg. He gave

Bracken a funny, almost suspicious look for a moment, and then as if catching himself in that pose, he smiled again. "And what would you be doing up here?" he said, sitting down and loosening the laces of his dusty boots.

Bracken looked back at Os, hesitating for a moment. Os was probably ten years his senior. His face was still youthful, even with the few wrinkles near his eyes. There seemed to be a charm about him that made Bracken feel at ease. "Well, to be honest, I was hoping to locate the sci mine. I wanted to see if those magic stones I've heard rumors about really exist."

Os pulled off his boots and looked up at Bracken, squinting through one eye. "Sit down, friend. It kind of hurts the neck staring up at you like this."

Bracken obeyed, sitting down across from him.

"So you think they really exist, do you?"

"Well, from what I hear, they're being circulated by the thousands up in Accad. A lot of people claim someone's bringing them in."

Os nodded, "Yeah, I've heard that. Some of the corrupt and greedy ones on sci-crew were selling them, but most of those stones are gone now, carried off over the Sea of Auren by greedy traders."

Bracken ran his fingers through his wet hair, combing it into place. "Besides, I don't think the sci-tec crew would bother coming down here on a hunch. You saw them. You ought to know."

"Sure did. Made the biggest stink you've ever seen. Threatened me with prison if I didn't leave. Made me promise not to come back here for at least six seasons. But I just hid here near the lake until they left."

"Well, do you think they found anything?"

"They sure did. But they would never tell me. No, I got all my facts from the one who discovered the place. A guy called Cib Mingus. That's how the stones got their name. He'd been tinkering around on this mountain for years using his detection sensors and calculations to find them. He actually was looking for another type of stone and just stumbled on the gems. Even though he was part of the sci-crew he never agreed with the High Council. He wanted to openly share them with everyone." Os shoved his tired feet into the cold water and sighed.

"They say he's dead now. The whole thing's rather mysterious. No one really knows for sure." Of course Ley knew what really happened. He knew that the High Council had Cib shipped off to some island prison off the coast of Toplana. But thankfully not before he'd secretly left a huge supply of the stones behind with Ley.

"So you talked to him. Did he tell you anything about his discoveries?"

Os grew quiet. Who was this guy Bracken? He could be working for the Pirax. But he doubted it. The kid looked too innocent. Ley wondered whether he should share his secret. He looked up the mountain for a few moments and then back to Bracken. He might as well. This youth was just the kind of person who'd be open to the whole thing. Besides, he felt a personal mandate to make the gems available to all who would try them. He was on a quest to introduce a whole generation to their power.

Bracken seemed a lot like the hundreds of others he had met in Accad. All of them had been searching for answers, and he'd always been willing to share with them what he'd discovered. In fact, he felt as if he'd been born for such a time as this, as if his destiny was somehow tied up with the stones and the emerging group of youth seeking answers.

Like a lot of them, he was sick of where Ebbern was headed, and these stones might be just the key to changing the course of his generation. And if this generation could be changed, then the course of Nerkush and Ebbern might be changed as well. He was a man with a mission, and Bracken was one more candidate for a change.

Os picked up his shoulder pack and popped open the top. He removed one of the silver cases and then snapped the bag shut again.

Bracken stared at Os and then at the metallic container in his hand. He felt a strange sense of wonder and excitement. Somehow without Os telling him, he knew what was in the case. He asked anyway, blurting out his question. "What's in there?" he said, pointing at the object in Os's hand.

"In here, Bracken, is what you've been looking for. The Mingus gems."

"That explains the explosions I heard earlier today. You know where the mine is. How did you find it?" Bracken felt an awesome sense of delight. He almost reached out and grabbed the container from Os.

The miner watched him, and Bracken knew he wasn't hiding his eagerness well. But instead of opening his treasure, Os only smiled and put it back in his pack.

"Why'd you do that?" asked Bracken.

"There'll be plenty of time for the stones later," said Os warily as he glanced around him. "Something feels strange about this place all of a sudden."

Bracken noticed that there was no com-link on the miner's wrist just a white strip crossing his tan where one had been. "I see that you don't have a com-patch, Os."

"Yeah, I never wear those things when I want to remain incognito."

Os removed an omni-sensor from his pack and lit up its array. "The High Council's following so many of us now with their sphere-trackers, it's like they've got eyes everywhere. I've got to make sure they haven't followed me here."

Bracken watched as Ley probed for the presence of strangers, sliding his hands over the sensor panel and monitoring the read-outs.

Os looked up at his new acquaintance and gave a mischievous grin. "Looks like I've slipped by them again. This device scrambles their data and cloaks my movements. Still, it's weird, I somehow feel we're being watched."

Ley placed his device in his pack and slipped his boots on again. He stood abruptly. "It's time I be movin' on. You're welcome to come with me to Accad. If you're still interested then, I'll make sure you experience the power of the stone once we arrive there."

Bracken looked around, feeling a little bewildered as he tried to decide. "Okay, just give me a few minutes to pick things up." He tossed a few things into his bag and threw it over his shoulder, pointing back down the mountain to where he'd parked his vehicle. "I've got my rig with me. If you're going through Tizra on your way back, I could drop it off and ride with you into Accad. I'd just like to bring my stam along with me. I was hoping to write some new songs here. I believe Accad will be just as inspirational as this place."

"Fine," said Os, putting on his shoulder pack again and grabbing his handbag, "the highway runs right by it. Sure, bring your instrument if you'd like."

Bracken collected his things and followed Os up the rise that led back toward the north road. At the crest of the hill, the miner stopped. He stood and gazed suspiciously up the surface of a huge cinder cone to their right. Satisfied that he could see nothing unusual, he relaxed and turned, walking on.

If he had bothered to look back a brief moment later, his reaction would have been entirely different. From high up the face of the crater, he would have seen the flash of metal in the sun. The reflection came from a magni-scope held in the pudgy hand of one of three men crouched behind a high outcropping of boulders. The three watched quietly until Os and Bracken slipped from view. Then without a sound they climbed down from their perch and hiked back to their waiting trans-rig. Climbing in, they followed from a distance as Os and Bracken drove north.

CHAPTER 23

ABOVE MOUNT SHIDOW REGION

PAR-SIMTESH (NEW SEASON), 5512

Whenever Michess descended to places like Shidow, there was always a hint of similarity to the realms he usually inhabited. The mountain's environs and its pristine character retained a few traces of its former beauty. But even in its ancient glory, it had never compared to the higher spheres.

But he was not here to enjoy the scenery. He knew he must stay on task. The command had been direct. *Watch!!* But now he felt compelled to ask, "Should I not act?"

If he intervened at this time, perhaps he would protect Bracken from things that watched and lurked just beyond his field of vision. But as quickly as he entertained such a thought, the Voice spoke firmly: *Not yet. Just continue to observe for now. Harm may come, and at that moment, should I call for it, you will act.*

Michess quickly found contentment in the command he'd been given. He never doubted the wisdom of the One who had spoken to him. It would be foolish to do otherwise. But he could see that a great conflict might be ahead. So he followed the unfolding activity with a continued sense of concern mixed now with a reminder that an intelligence greater than his own was watching as well.

CHAPTER 24

ACCAD

YIANE (FIRST WARMTH), 5512

Accad was a busy metropolis. Commerce flowed in and out of its ports, making it one of the most important cities in Nerkush. A wide variety of traffic coming from the east and over the Sea of Auren intersected in this oceanside city. Common goods, as well as strange enchantments, bulged from the shelves of its marketplaces.

People of a hundred different origins met in its busy streets where pedestrians as well as huge, gleaming trans-rigs jostled one another. High buildings, where the commercial elite managed the economics of Nerkushian life, clogged the areas near the wharves. Other clumps of glittering pillars were scattered around the city, some housing the rich, others the various offices of authority.

The Hall of the Fathers, the meeting place of western Nerkush's ruling body, jutted its polished stone façade into the air near one of these clumps. Flocks of birds nested in nooks near the top of its high pillars or scrambled by the hundreds for the simple offerings of grain that visitors scattered in the open square before the building.

Ley Os's trans-rig moved along a boulevard in front of the archaic building; the sight of it seemed to make Ley and his passenger grow suddenly resentful. Their bitterness churned to the surface. Their faces looked sour as they stared at the rulers' headquarters. The high arched pillars and stone façade looked cold, hard, and unyielding. *Just like the Fathers*, thought Bracken, *such rigid, hardened, and unprogressive men.* Men that ruled Nerkush with a firm, unloving hand. Men with their own interests in mind.

Ley spat into the street as his rig pulled past the building. "The selfish ruling the ignorant," he muttered. "It won't be that way forever. They have to surrender their control someday but until they'll hold onto power anyway they can."

Bracken agreed. It seemed that the ruling authorities were invading every area of their life. He looked down at the com-patch on his wrist. Its indicators glowed a cold blue, confirming his access to anyone in his group of friends with a few strokes of his fingers. "You've probably heard that the Fathers want to tie our com-links into their network."

"Yes, the sphere-net is a great thing, but I have the suspicion that they're using these coms to track us."

"I know. It's sad. I like being able to connect with my friends and family anywhere quickly and easily."

"Well, as nice as that is, there'll come a day when we may have to abandon them. If you want my opinion, the ultimate goal of our leaders is to monitor all our communications. It's all about control."

"Yes, they want that control because they're afraid. Afraid of losing their power and position." Bracken recalled how accustomed they'd all become to instant global communication through devices like his wrist com-patch and other sphere links in their homes and offices. "I'm still amazed that this device can so easily link all of us."

"It's great, but you probably know it's all built on sand."

"Sand?" Bracken had learned that in class, but its significance hadn't hit him till now.

"Yes, it's a derivative of those same grains people run their toes through at the beach."

"Seems I remember some old saying about the danger of building your life on that stuff rather than something solid." They both remembered the proverb and had a good laugh.

"Yeah, the global link may all come apart someday, but for now the 'Rax loves the fact that they can spy on us anytime they want."

"Didn't you tell me someone in the Community was working on a way to scramble our communications so they couldn't track us?"

"Yes, someone is, but I'm not sure how reliable it will be."

"The 'Rax's schemes are just one more thing limiting our freedom."

"They're just servants of the High Council. I guess the Fathers' objective is total control and those troopers are just their henchmen. Besides that, they've got a whole covert group feeding information to the 'Rax."

"Are you sure?"

"Listen, Bracken. If you knew my background you'd understand. My family's money has bought them great influence. They've been moving behind the scenes for generations, controlling our leaders with their money."

Bracken thought of his sheltered life in Tizra. He'd never known lack, but living in a family that was supported on a teacher's salary made money something they had to watch carefully. "Well, it must be nice being raised around such wealth."

"It's not as great as it appears. When riches are in such abundance, they often take the place of what really matters. That's why the Community appeals to me. It's about family, and that's something money can never fill."

"I guess people like your parents and others with wealth are the real ones in control."

"Yes, and they'll do anything do keep that power even if it means not caring what happens to us. That's exactly why they're restricting our freedoms."

Bracken turned back from watching the building and gazed ahead up the street. "They're sure trying to, like the whole thing with the gem. If you hadn't met Cib Mingus, it would probably still be a mystery."

"Yeah, old Cib was a real help. He's given this generation more than he'll ever know. Os patted the pack on the seat between them.

Bracken looked down at the bag containing the Mingus Gems. Staring at the backpack, he felt a sudden surge of desire. He wanted to open the bag, pop open one of the cases inside, and gaze at the glowing stones. He wanted to look into their mysterious secrets. He wanted to plunge into the depths of their enchantment.

"What are you going to do with all those stones?" he asked hesitantly. "You can't possibly use them all yourself."

Os smiled back at his new acquaintance. "I don't intend to, Bracken. Most of these are gifts for people I know in the Community. I'm planning to deliver some of them today and the rest later on to others who are helping get them out."

Bracken felt a little put off by the Mingus peddler. It looked as if he would have to wait until some of the stones had been delivered before Os would share one with him. Why the wait, he wondered. Perhaps Os was merely testing him to see if he really wanted to touch the gem's power.

Bracken looked up from the pack and across at Os. "I'm really looking forward to experiencing the gem." He tried hard to suppress his eagerness as he spoke. "This is the kind of thing I've been looking forward to for some time. I've come to believe there's something more to existence than the limited things we perceive in this realm." Bracken had heard the chants of the edge-poets as they sang of other realms, timeless and limitless places entered through cleansed portals of consciousness.

"Well, you won't be disappointed, my friend," said Os. "The Mingus dimension is a world beyond anything you can imagine."

Bracken saw what looked like laughter in the man's eyes as they penetrated Bracken's façade. "Be patient, my young friend. You'll have your turn soon enough."

Bracken nodded and felt a lump in his throat as Os headed his rig on up the boulevard.

As they approached the next intersection, Os's sense-tector went off. The red light on his instrument panel blinked and an audible hum filled the car.

"What's that?" asked Bracken.

"One of the Pirax hover-eyes must be tracking us."

"I've heard about those, but what does it mean?"

"Probably that the 'Rax are going to pull us over."

Os touched a spot just below his instrument panel, and a hidden drawer appeared. He tossed the pack with the Mingus stones into it, followed by his handbag from the backseat and touched the panel again. The door closed with a *whoosh*. Bracken looked closely at the panel, but the door was undetectable.

Just then a silver-and-gray trans-rig pulled across the intersection in front of them. One of the officers inside motioned for them to pull into the side street to their right.

An odd shadow drifted across the pavement beside Bracken. He looked up and saw a gray object with a glistening lens piece at its center hovering over them near the top of one of the nearby buildings. So that's what the hover-eyes looked like. It made him shiver just to know that his movements were being monitored.

As their rig came to rest beside the curb, another 'Rax rig pulled in front of them as the other closed in behind them. The 'Rax officers in their body armor stepped from their rigs. Three walked toward them while the others stood watch. Pedestrians along the boulevard stopped and stared at the unfolding drama.

As the lead officer approached Os's side of his vehicle, he spoke out a command. "Shut off your drive unit and get out of your rig. Both of you." The agent's voice crackled through his voice modulator. It sounded almost metallic. "We need to search your vehicle."

"Do you have a search-cred?" queried Os.

"We don't need one, this is just routine."

"I'm sorry, sir, but without credentials I'm going to have to say no," insisted Ley as he and Bracken got out of the vehicle.

Os defiantly raised himself up to his full stature as the 'Rax agent approached; but still, at over six feet, he seemed small against the officer in his body armor.

The voice crackled again. "Move out of the way." The second agent pushed his way into Os's rig and began looking under the seats. The third moved to the rear and activated the storage compartment latch. It popped open, and he began to dig through it.

"You can't do this," shouted Os, clearly agitated. He made his way toward the back of his rig, but the 'Rax operative muscled him aside. He stared back at Os, his eyes like dark coals peering out of his helmet's vizi-port.

"Like we said, it's just routine," echoed the second agent as he continued his search. The two nearby 'Rax rested their hands on their holstered weapons.

"If it's routine, then why are you searching my rig?" said Os as he walked back to where the first agent stood. "We're good citizens. Just like you, sir."

"Sure you are, Os," snapped the agent.

"So you know my name?" Ley sounded surprised.

"And we know what you're doing. You're bringing illegal substances into our lovely city." The words were harsh, but the 'Rax's instincts were correct.

How do they know? wondered Bracken. The answer came in the officer's next words.

"We've been tracking you for a long time, Os, and we're confident we'll find what you're smuggling."

A crowd had gathered, clearly fascinated by the scene unfolding before them. But as the officers' hands hovered over their energy thrusters, the onlookers instinctively backed away.

Bracken could sense it too. Was this whole thing about to go from bad to worse? He hadn't expected this sort of nightmare to be part of his visit to Accad. What was Ley going to do?

In the next second, he had his answer.

"Listen, sir, we've just come from a camping trip on Shidow. We're tired from our long drive." Ley raised his hands, palms out in a sign of submission. "Sorry I was a little touchy. I apologize for being so rude. You guys put up with a lot of guff. I should have been more sensitive." Ley smiled sheepishly, matching his conciliatory words with a body language of apparent surrender. "It's been a long day and I'm worn out. Go ahead and look all you want."

The 'Rax leader grunted an acknowledgement and looked over his fellow agent's shoulder. "You find anything yet?"

The second agent backed out of Ley's rig. "Nothing."

"Same here." said the other 'Rax, finishing his search of the storage compartment. He slammed the cover with a look of exasperation.

Just then, a signal went off in one of the 'Rax's rigs. The second agent touched the com-link at the side of his helmet and muttered something. A series of voice commands, most of which were inaudible to everyone else, buzzed in his interior speaker.

"Looks like there's an emergency in the Ortrin sector. They need all of us."

The lead officer turned to Ley. "You're lucky this time, Os, but we're going to find what you're smuggling eventually. Just a matter of time."

"I'm not quite sure what you're after, Officer." said Ley, feigning ignorance. "But, again, please forgive me for my earlier rudeness."

"Yeah, you're forgiven," mocked the officer as he led his men back to their vehicles.

"Good luck with your emergency," said Os under his breath with a smirk. "Let's get out of here, Bracken." With that, they both climbed into Ley's rig and drove off in the direction they'd been heading before the stop.

A quarter of an hour later, they entered one of the most unusual and intriguing sections of Accad. They'd arrived at the Community. As they drove through the colorful street, a calmness seemed to envelope Bracken, and the earlier anxiety from their encounter with the 'Rax began to drain away.

The Community was truly a unique place. He'd watched the stories about this place on the vid-tel. He'd also heard about it from a few of his classmates that had slipped away from their parents to see it when their families had visited Accad as tourists. It was made up of a different breed of newly arrived inhabitants who now lived in this oldest section of the city. They seemed to have collected here as if drawn by some hidden force. They came from all over Nerkush, each from different regions, cultures, and backgrounds. Yet it was apparent that several things had drawn them here and drawn them together to form their community. They seemed to be seeking the same things. But perhaps the greatest thing, the most powerful force bringing them together, was a sense of the timeliness of their quest. They wanted to transform their world. The appearance of their small borough clearly reflected this.

Houses and shops, sensitively but uniquely decorated, expressed the desire for a break with the usual humdrum. Greenery sprang from the most unusual places, wooden boxes filled with flowers and shrubs hung from windowsills with the glass above them painted with bright, transparent, and colorful patterns. Other similar arrangements were placed on sidewalks and alleyways.

The ancient houses in the area had been painted in deep, earthy colors. The streets seemed to have a sense of the primitive blended with the modern. It was a gentle contrast to the rather sterile atmosphere of Accad. The most striking example of uniqueness, though, was the colorful and handcrafted clothing of the area's inhabitants, who casually walked its streets and frequented its various shops. Their attire was so unlike the dress in Tizra and the rest of Nerkush.

Bracken found it all enchanting and exciting; everything he'd hoped for through all those years of feeling so alienated in Tizra.

Ley parked his trans-rig near the Brazen Eagle herb shop, one of his favorite stops. "You'll love the proprietor, Bracken," explained Os. "He's a rather jovial man. Known for his long and scraggly multi-tinted beard. It's kind of a reflection of his place—a little messy, but it dispenses some spicy liquids and tantalizing food.

Os carefully removed one of the gem containers from his pack and placed it in a second handbag he'd taken from the secret compartment. Grabbing it, he motioned for his new companion to follow him. "Leave your stam in the rig. It will be safe."

Bracken shouldered his own bag and followed his new mentor. Glancing about suspiciously, Ley locked his vehicle and started down the street toward the Brazen Eagle.

Unnoticed by both Os and Bracken was the black trans-rig that had followed them from Shidow.

It had pulled over a half a block down the street. Two men, their eyes shielded behind glare guards, sat slumped in the front seat while a third in the back focused a powerful sight amplifier on the two friends as they strolled toward the herb shop.

CHAPTER 25

ACCAD

YIANE (FIRST WARMTH), 5512

Reaching the entrance to the Brazen Eagle, Ley pushed open its large wooden door. At its center was a massive bronze bird of prey embedded in its stained wooden surface. As they entered, Bracken was swallowed up by pleasant chatter and mellow musical strains that played a counter score in the room. The smoke-filled air above the tables lingered like a pleasant incense over the relaxing customers. Sawdust covered the floor and the walls, yellow with age displayed a few odd paintings hanging at irregular angles. Looking closer as his eyes adjusted, he could see a small crowd gathered near one end of the building.

On a low stage in front of them sat what Bracken figured was an edge-poet singing to the accompaniment of a stam. Bracken wanted to stop and listen, but Ley motioned to him. He sheepishly responded, following the miner as he sauntered to the service bar and leaned against its counter. Behind it a heavy-set man bent over a large earthen crock, pouring hot herb liquid into it.

"How's business, Bryten?" Os asked quietly.

The man looked up to reveal a bearded but jovial face and pleasantly responded, "Well, Ley, I haven't seen you in weeks! Thought maybe you decided to stay up on that mountain of yours for a while."

Os smiled back and winked at the man. "I've got some good news for you, Bryten!"

The proprietor abruptly lowered his voice and then glanced around the room. Assured that no one was watching, he gave Bracken the once-over and then spoke. "This kid okay?"

"Sure," said Ley, stroking his beard and sniffing the pleasant odor drifting in the air. "Think I'd bring him with me if he wasn't? Met him up on Shidow. Kid's hungry for a touch of the stone."

Bryten's doubts seemed to vanish at the mention of the gem. He grinned back at Ley.

"Well, how about our little deal?" The fat man said, his eyes staring greedily at the pack hanging from Ley's shoulder. "Did you bring the stones?"

"Sure did. You want them now?"

Bryten tilted his head toward the opposite end of the building.

"No, no, not here in front of everybody. Use the side door. Leave them on the table near the Zhemix vats."

Without a word, Os followed the man's instructions, returning a moment later. "I'll be expecting your payment in the usual way," said the gem peddler, as he took two sticks of dried fruit from a bowl on the counter.

"No problem," said the bearded proprietor. "It'll be there on time."

"Good."

"How do you find your way around up there on Shidow, Os? The place is mysterious."

The mingus dealer tapped the bag at his side. "Simple Bryten. Made myself a map. I carry the directions with me at all times. I'll never get lost."

"Sound's like a good plan. Well make sure you call on me after your next trip up there."

Ley jabbed the fruit into his mouth, breaking off a piece to chew. He handed the other piece to Bracken and motioned for them to leave. "Let's go, Bracken. I'll show you the sights," said Ley as he headed out the door and into the bright sunlight.

Leaving the Brazen Eagle, they stopped by Ley's rig to pick up another case of the gems and Bracken's pack and stam. From there, they strolled through the leisurely atmosphere of the Community. People lounged in doorways, soaking up the sunlight. Some played on instruments while, here and there, couples embraced openly. Many of them wore floral arrangements around their necks and in their hair. Strings of beads and tinkling bells hung from tan necks and bare ankles. Smiling faces bobbed up and down along the crowded sidewalks. Ley and Bracken returned their greetings with grins of their own. Many approached Ley with words of thanks and questions about the next delivery of Mingus stones. Bracken's excitement grew as he pondered the way Ley moved smoothly among the people in this part of Accad. The stone peddler was clearly a leader here. Bracken knew he had little to say and much to learn.

Rounding a corner, they stopped in front of a miniature castle-like stone building. "This is my place," said Ley proudly as he fumbled in his pocket for the lock activator. Across the street was a long rectangular park. People danced and relaxed on the grass beneath tall, leafy trees as they listened to a group of musicians play.

"Sounds good!" Bracken admired the skill and ease with which the band played. "Who are they?"

"Chepa Ayan's group," answered Ley, finding the activator and touching the button that unlocked the huge oaken door. "They're known as Golden Flight. I haven't met them yet. A touch of the gem would improve their sound, though. They've asked me to meet with them tomorrow. It should be interesting, to say the least." They stood listening for a few more minutes, and then Bracken followed Ley into the house. He was led down a long hall with rooms on each side and then upstairs to a large sitting room. The room was decorated in simple but versatile decor, the typical setup of a man without a companion. Throw pillows and lounges were scattered around the room, giving it a clean but disorganized appearance. Doorways led into bedrooms on either side.

"Have a seat, Bracken," said Os, putting down his bag nearby and pointing toward a comfortable-looking cushion.

Bracken set down his stam and sloughed off his pack. He sank into the pillow, exhaling a relaxed breath, hoping to keep his eagerness for the gem's touch from being completely obvious. He felt a little anxious about his first experience with the Mingus. He was eager to use it but had some questions first. "Before I use the stone, could you tell me a little more about how it works?"

"It's quite simple." Ley took a seat and poured them both drinks from a silver decanter on the table between them. "There are basically two kinds of stones. The more powerful variety is deep green. Cib Mingus said that's what started the whole problem with the sci's. The stones are so powerful they lift you completely out of this dimension. In fact, the most powerful don't have to be ingested even though I recommend you do. The minute you touch them they start to transport you. They sci-techs lost a few of their crew that way. That's when the Fathers decided to hush the whole thing up."

"What happened to them? Did they ever discover where they went?"

"Yes, eventually one showed up in a completely different place than the chamber where he took the stone."

"What did he say?"

"That he'd encountered beings with such beauty and power that it changed his whole life. He resigned his position and lives out near Raka somewhere."

"Creatures with power and beauty? Sound amazing."

"That's what scared the High Council. When they heard that there might be some power that they knew nothing about, they decided to seal the whole thing up."

"But what's with the disappearing thing? How could the stones do that?"

"I guess they open some sort of portal into another dimension, and when you get exposed to ones powerful enough, they transport not just your mind to that world but your entire body."

Bracken took a sip from his drink and set it back on the table. Doubt filled his mind. "That sounds kind of frightening to me. I mean, if I'm not sure I'll come back, I don't think this thing's for me."

Os swallowed the liquid in his own glass and flashed a knowing smile back at the youth. "Calm down, don't get too excited, Bracken. It's all a matter of technique. Just simple understanding of what's happening. Besides, I'm not about to give you a stone with that power."

Os sounded sure of himself and Bracken felt more at ease. He listened intently as Os continued explaining. "It's a matter of simply yielding to the effect and not fighting against it. Besides, you'll start out with the weaker variety. It'll be no problem."

"Go on, tell me more." Bracken pushed aside his earlier anxiety, wanting to know every detail.

Os took another drink, letting out a satisfied belch before answering. "Well, the weaker ones are light blue. They seem to work mostly on the mind, and their effect lasts about eight hours. Like I said, it won't be any problem for you."

"What about my stam? Can I play it?"

The gem dealer had no idea how good a musician the younger man was, so he'd hesitated to take any chances. He'd seen others who had little talent attempt to play under the gem's influence and it had ruined the experience. "Maybe next time, after I've heard how good you are. Besides, there are enough new things ahead of you tonight without adding another one to it.

Hoping this excuse had settled the matter about the music, Os set his glass on the table and reached for his pack. "Well, are you ready?"

Bracken felt nervous and was suddenly a little unsure. Not wanting to miss what might be his only chance at the stone, though, he pushed away his fears. "As ready as I'll ever be."

"Great! Let's begin." Ley removed one of the silver cases from his bag. "Cib designed these containers, and they work quite well. Not the slightest amount of leakage," assured Ley.

"Who goes first?"

"You. That way I can make sure you'll be all right your first time out. After that, you should be familiar enough with it not to need my help."

"What do we do now?"

"Open the box by this button," Ley pointed to a small stud on the side of the silver case. "Then simply remove one of the stones, put it in your mouth, and swallow." Ley sat back and smiled.

Hesitantly, Bracken followed the instructions. He pushed the button, the lid popped open, and there were the stones, giving off a soft glow. He gingerly removed one from the container and the snapped the lid shut. It was about half the size of his fingernail. Gripping the stone gently, he lifted it to his mouth and hesitated. Then tossing aside a quiver of anxiety, he swallowed it, washing it down with the drink in front of him.

At first, nothing appeared to be happening. Then gradually Bracken began to smile. Soon he was overwhelmed with joy and fell back, laughing uncontrollably. As the effect increased, he lost complete consciousness of Ley and his surroundings. He seemed to be tumbling down a furry, warm tunnel of peace.

Ley watched benevolently as Bracken slipped into a blissful trance. Assured that his friend was all right, Ley reached into the same container, lifted a gem to his mouth, and swallowed. He leaned back into the cushion behind him as deep, knowing smile broke across his bearded face.

A couple of hours before dawn, Bracken began to recover from the gem's pleasant effects. Gradually regaining an awareness of his surroundings, he noticed Ley seated near him, staring peacefully at a lighted candle in the center of the room.

Lifting his head from the cushion, he spoke softly. "That was greater than I had anticipated. Such beauty! Such color! Such dimension! It's beyond words!"

"I know," agreed Ley, then with a poetic flair, he added, "and it's limitless ... cosmic prairies that stretch forever filled with purple sage ... uncharted seas of bliss. It's the very thing this community has been longing for, a power that can change our world for good. It's an experience that will lift everyone to our ultimate destiny as a race. It's a new frontier to venture into, perhaps the ultimate frontier."

Bracken sat up and smiled, his face full of wonder. "Now I see why the Fathers kept it a secret. They must know that if the people get a touch of this, the foolish laws and limits they place on us will no longer hold."

Ley looked across at Bracken, his eyes reflecting the soft light of the candle. "Yes, once the sci guys told them about the stones' power, they knew they had to stop their release."

Bracken stared back at Ley momentarily and then returned his gaze to the candle. "It's all beginning to make sense."

"Those narrow fools knew all along what would happen if the people got hold of the secret. But it's too big even for them. It's beyond anyone's control. Something else has a hand in what's happening. That's the reason we've all gathered here in the Community. There's a new hope for Nerkush …"

"And you …. I mean we, hold the key!" interrupted Bracken excitedly.

"Exactly! You're catching on fast, Bracken. It's not about me. I've got my part but it's bigger than all of us." Ley's voice had taken on a tone of harmonious rapture. "It won't be long before all of Nerkush will begin to see the light."

"It's all fitting together," responded Bracken enthusiastically. "It's becoming totally clear. I'm so happy, I can't stand it." Bracken fell back again and began to weep for joy. Something deep was occurring inside him. That which he'd known was there for many years now was finally before him.

Ley smiled knowingly, a small tear rolling down his own cheek. He'd convinced one more soul, brought one more member into the growing flock of blissful believers.

It was near dawn when the two of them slipped from Ley's house into the morning twilight on their way to the Brazen Eagle for breakfast. Ley had his ever-present handbag clutched closely to his side. Bracken had grabbed his pack as well and shouldered his stam in its carrying case before heading out, thinking maybe he'd get a chance to perform on the stage at the herb shop. They walked serenely down the quiet thoroughfare as the stars blinked in the predawn darkness. The sun wouldn't be up for at least another hour. As if lost in a dream, the two of them seemed to wander aimlessly.

So complete was their wonderment that they failed to notice several figures moving through the shadows behind them. Bracken somehow sensed a presence, but not soon enough to understand its meaning. Without warning, he heard the whosh of a heat pellet as it flew near their heads and then burned, with a hiss into the wall beside him.

Fear shook them from their blissful thoughts, and instinctively he and Os bolted down the street away from the source of the deadly attack. Several darkly clad figures slipped from a nearby alley and ran after them. Bracken's heart pounded. Suddenly alert, Ley jumped into a sheltered entranceway and jerked Bracken in after him. Reaching into his bag, he pulled out his own igniter tube, its burnished surface flashing in the light of a street lamp.

A surly voice came from a secluded doorway across the street. "All right, Os, we want the map! We know you've got it! Bryten told us. He took a little convincing for him to give up your secret. Let's just say he'll heal in a few weeks."

"That fool sold me out,' cursed Ley.

"Just give it up and we'll leave you alone." The voice was icy, fearsome.

Bracken looked at Os, who seemed to be running through his options. Ley's eyes took on a darkness that he hadn't seen before. At first it looked merely like fear, but as he listened to Os's response, he could sense that fear turning to hate. "If these toughs think they're going to get it that easily, I'll have to inform them differently," he said under his breath. "How do I know you will keep your word?" he called out coyly to the attacker.

"Just toss it into the middle of street, let us pick it up, and we'll be gone. If you don't, we'll move in and burn you bad, Os!"

"Okay, man, here it is."

Bracken gave Ley a puzzled look. Slowly, Os drew out a different item from his bag, where it and several other letters had been tucked in beside the real map. The other item was also on heavy parchement and would fly far once it was thrown. He tossed it into the middle of the street. "Ok, there it is." *They must think I'm unarmed* reasoned Ley quietly, as he waited for his opposition to act.

Ley reached into his pouch again and pulled out two smooth energy eggs. "Here, Bracken, you may need these."

Bracken took them and slipped them into his backpack. He had seen the effect of their explosive power and wondered what they would do to those pursing them.

Ley suddenly drew back deeper into the doorway pulling Bracken back with him.

Gradually, a figure moved from the shadows and ran for the folded piece of paper in the street. At the same moment, Ley thrust a small fire pellet into his ignition tube and raised it to his lips. Aiming carefully, he billowed his cheeks. The pellet lit as it rushed from the cylinder. It struck the squatting figure. He moaned once and then collapsed. The next moment, two pellets struck near their heads, fizzling into the wall. Ley ducked back into the shadows, watching as two other figures moved toward him, weaving in and out of doorways down the street.

"You'd better run for it, kid," warned Os. "I'll draw their fire and then come after you."

Bracken cautiously edged out from the doorway and then ran. Flashes of light streaked by him as more heat pellets whizzed over his head. Then one hit the wall beside him, pieces of the plaster pelting his face and stinging his eyes. Momentarily blinded, Bracken stumbled to the ground. He hadn't expected this, and in the chaos of the moment he was caught completely off guard. It wasn't that he was afraid of a fight, he and Silas had had their share of running off bullies bigger than them, but he wasn't used to fighting with explosive weapons. But if he had to, he would use them.

Brushing the spattered fragments from his face and blinking his eyes, Bracken hid behind a trans-rig up the street and watched the unfolding battle between Os and their pursuers.

Alone now and frustrated, Os scrambled madly across the pavement and down the street, moving the battle away from Bracken. The miner slipped behind a parked trans-rig. He seemed suddenly territorial, Bracken thought, like some animal stalking another rival that had invaded his domain. But as Bracken watched the scene unfold, he sensed this was something deeper, that Os was fighting for something else. He was fighting for his position. He wasn't just protecting the Community but his place as one of its leaders.

Just then, another volley of heat pellets burned into the trans-rig where Bracken was hiding. To his left he saw a darkened alleyway. Sprinting toward it, he hoped he could move out of the line of fire. From there he could retrieve one of the energy eggs that were in his pack and prepare to use it. Clutching tightly to the strap of his stam case, he held it in place as he ran. How he wished he'd left it behind, but it was too late and the instrument was too valuable to just toss aside.

Once he reached the passageway, the darkness there seemed to swallow him up. Cautiously, he poked his head out from his hiding place and watched the action continued to unfold. But a moment later, another heat pellet burned into the wall beside him. *Where were his assailants?* It was clear by now there were several. He knew he had to find a better position. With that in mind, he headed down the alley hoping to discover a way around his assailants and to move up on their flank.

Back on the street, Os crept to the other end of the rig and came up with his tube to his lips, just as a black shape shot out from seclusion. He fired. The missile struck his pursuer in the arm, spinning him about. Groaning, the man slumped into the doorway.

"I don't know why you want that map so bad. You'll never get it this way!" warned Ley, shouting at the other figure. "You think you can move in on me. I've paid too much for what I've got, and no one—not you or the 'Rax—is going to take that away from me."

Quietly, the other shape backed off down the street. Convinced that his assailants had been sufficiently discouraged, Os retraced his steps looking for Bracken, but he couldn't find him.

Bracken came out of the shadows at the other end of the alley and crept tensely along, hugging the side of the buildings that lined the street. Reaching another alleyway, he turned into it, hoping it would bring him up behind his foes on the street he'd left earlier. He was on edge, and the terror of the preceding moments had drained him, but he was intent on lashing back at those who had struck at him and Ley.

His mind swirled with questions. Who was after them? Why did they attach so viciously? How had something as wonderful as the gem become a commodity to fight over? Then, without warning, a cloaked figure pulled him into a dimly lit doorway. No sooner had Bracken vanished from the corridor than a volley of heat pellets struck the wall where he had been moments before.

CHAPTER 26

RAKA

TAR-LYNREXS (LATE-SUMMER), 5512

This "valley" could hardly be called that. It was more like a pan to heat food on. Its wide, flat surface broken only by sporadic clumps of sand dunes, stretched out until it met the high mountains that rose in the distance like the walls of a prison cell.

He'd heard someone once say that when you're in confinement you have lots of time to think—about the choices you've made and the actions you'd taken. In a way, Raka had become a sort of jail and now he had lots of time to think.

His run-in that night with Ley's enemies had made him face the cruel reality that all was not peaceful in the Community. Somehow in that idyllic society there was still greed and violence. He knew someone would have to make a living selling the gems, but the fact that people were fighting to control the supply and willing to potentially murder for it was way beyond what he'd expected.

There had also been the force with which the gem dealer had responded. He obviously knew that there were others besides the Pirax that were after him, and he was prepared for them with weapons. But as Bracken reflected on what Os had shouted back at his assailants that day in the alley, it was clear that he'd go to any length to protect his investment. Could there be a bigger motive here other than just the romantic one of sharing the wonder of the Mingus stones with a world that needed a new direction? The changes he'd seen in Ley out here in the desert made him wonder.

Once in while, a breeze from the Eastern mountains would come up in the evening. It was like a cool breath that reminded him of how the blind edge-poet's words that day at his school had lifted him and helped to start him on his journey. But now the air in the valley was still and lifeless. And in a way, the words he'd heard from the sage now seemed just as inert and empty as the atmosphere around him.

Every day the relentless heat seemed to not only bake his body but his brain as well. As dazzling as his experiences in the Mingus realm had been, it was almost like his mind had been slightly seared by some of those encounters. In fact, he wondered if that wasn't what had happened to Ley as well. The gem dealer's attitude had become brittle, and his words no longer carried the refreshing tone they once did. Now, sometimes they seemed as dry and tasteless as an overcooked meal.

Ley had become increasingly paranoid. On some nights, he muttered in his shack about the thugs back in Accad and the threat of them pushing into his "territory". Why, Bracken wondered, was there a battle for these gems? Why did something that so elevated one's consciousness have to be fought over like money?

One night in a dream, Silas and Lisha both came to him. The three of them joined hands and danced to the sound of Golden Flight's music. As they spun like children dancing in a circle, dust rose up from their skipping feet and became a cloud. It was like the fog that swallowed Silas at his moment of death; Lisha spun away from him to be lost in the vapor. He clung to his friend's hand tightly, but then suddenly Silas slipped away to vanish into the cloud with only his cries echoing after him. The cries woke Bracken from the dream, and he spent the rest of the night thinking of his departed friends. How he longed for both of them. Silas would never return, but perhaps he could win Lisha back. Such hopes haunted him, but even as he thought of her, the pain of her betrayal caused him to bury such desires.

One of the few delights that remained was the brilliant display of stars that filled the night sky here in Raka. Each night they would capture his imagination before he fell asleep. He remembered how he'd seen the silver spacecraft come out the night sky near the Pillars of Rimlex. He wondered where its occupants were now. Perhaps the Disk People would bring his planet the salvation they needed. But as often as he'd looked for them in the heavens, he always fell asleep without their appearance.

So the days passed, and each one seemed to increase the barrenness of this valley and with it the aridness of his soul. Bracken had to look hard to find even the tiniest bit of hope in his heart, and with each investigation it seemed to become even more devoid of any promise.

Like the lonely wilted tree that grew beside his shack, all that had once been so verdant to him had gone out of his life. He missed the way the color green seemed to refresh him, and at that moment he missed one of the greenest places he'd ever been. He'd been told of its allure for the first time by the mysterious stranger who had rescued him from his attackers that night in Accad. The stranger who had later introduced him to the lush Forest of Zorek and the mystery that lay within it.

CHAPTER 27

ACCAD

YIANE (FIRST WARMTH), 5512

Not long after the sudden rescue, Bracken found himself sitting in the Brazen Eagle, sipping tea to calm his nerves. His stam case rested on the floor beside him, and his pack was stuffed even closer on the seat next to him, now crowded with its lethal contents. He wasn't expecting another attack here, but at this point he wanted to be ready for anything.

The man that had saved his life sat across from him clothed in a hooded cloak and smoking from a well-worn pipe. Dalfang Niekolt had introduced himself once they were both out of range of their pursuers. Then he quickly escorted Bracken down several alleys and through a back door into the safety of the herb shop. The place was full; it was one of those establishments that remained open continually because of the clientele that visited at all hours.

As Bracken looked around the room, he felt safe even though he was now suspicious of the owner who had possibility betrayed Ley. But when he went to the counter to order tea the man appeared to not recognize him. Then he reasoned that the proprietor probably saw new faces all the time. As he had taken his seat with Dalfang he scanned the large crowd and it gave him the assurance that danger would probably not follow them into its busy environment.

Bracken told his rescuer that he'd been set upon mysteriously while out for an early morning walk. He'd been vague about his involvement with Os. He wasn't about to give that information up to a stranger.

Dalfang was a rugged man, but a wise one. He was old, but his age had done little to diminish his strength. His gray beard and pale-blue eyes gave him the face of a scholar. Bracken soon learned that the wizard-like stranger lived in the Wilderness of Zorek, but from time to time made brief visits to Accad. Bracken considered himself lucky that their paths had crossed in the twilight and that the strong arms of the older man had pulled him to safety. But what he didn't know right then was that something far greater than luck was involved in their encounter.

Bracken looked across the table at his new acquaintance. *What a unique man*, he thought. The Forest of Zorek was a wilderness few people bothered to visit. All but the rugged types avoided it, yet this aged man seemed to be all the better for living in its hostile environs.

Over the next several hours, the two of them talked and drank more tea, its mood-altering affect gradually calming their nerves as daylight filtered into the room through its few windows. During that time, the stranger asked Bracken many questions about his home, family, and philosophy. It made him feel good that someone older expressed an interest in his ideals and actually seemed to agree with him on some of his major points. Bracken soon realized that much of the talk had been about him; taking another long sip from his mug, he set it down on the table and looked quizzically at his new friend. "Don't you ever get lonely living in Zorek?"

The older man smiled back, his eyes squinting warmly. He seemed to be as fascinated with his young friend as Bracken was with him. "I suppose that's a possibility, but I have a purpose for being where I am," said Dalfang, his voice resonating pleasantly over the garbled conversations in the background. Even though it was early dawn by now, the Eagle was still half filled with patrons. "Of course, there are others coming to live in Zorek. I see them from time to time. They are beginning to realize that living here in this city tightens the nerves and binds the senses from true awareness." The sage-like man sounded confident. His tan face displayed an eagle-like nose that spoke of majesty. "Some have come there and others will join them, it's merely a matter of time."

The depth of maturity Dalfang exuded fascinated Bracken, not just in the words he spoke, but in the way he spoke them, so confident and peaceful. There was a genuineness that seemed to surround him. He found himself transfixed by the soft glow in the man's eyes, hanging on his every word.

"Zorek is a pleasant place, I wouldn't live anywhere else. But I have an even greater reason for being where I am. It's one I don't often share with others." Dalfang paused and waited at this point, quietly sipping from the cup in his hand, his long fingers wrapped firmly around the earthenware mug. His hands were weathered by the wilderness life, but still appeared articulate when he used them to illustrate his conversations.

After a few minutes, Bracken broke the silence. "Well, aren't you going to tell me what it is?" He wanted to pry the answer from the man in his eagerness, but though he spoke hastily he kept his voice quiet. Somewhere in the back of his mind he wondered why this strange man whom he had just met was willing to share something so apparently secret with him. *What was going on?* First there was his meeting with Ley Os on the mountain and now this strange encounter with the man from Zorek. It made him wonder if he wasn't being moved by some greater energy than his own toward a unique destiny. He remembered the harbinger he and Silas had seen that night in the sky near Tizra. He also recalled the prophecy that the blind oracle had given to him years ago at the Mind-Training Center in Tizra. What strange forces might be at work in his life? Or perhaps it was all just some silly string of coincidences. He pushed the thought aside, eager to hear more from his new friend. Bracken sensed he should be patient and let it come in its own time.

The two of them waited there without speaking for long minutes, listening as a musician across the room played soft melodies on his stam. The air was filled with drifting clouds of smoke from the pipes of several other patrons who sat puffing contentedly around the shop. The semi-sweet scent of incense burning in small containers near the entrance mingled with the stronger odors flowing through the air, creating an intoxicating aroma.

Then Dalfang slowly began again, "You see, it was not an accident that I was nearby tonight when you were attacked. It was meant to be. In fact, I knew some time ago that it was going to happen."

Bracken stared back at his rescuer in disbelief. "What do you mean? How could you have known? You told me you just arrived here." "Did someone tell you that I'd be attacked?"

"No, it wasn't that at all. I knew about it through a vision." The older man paused for a moment as if waiting to see Bracken's response. Confident that the other was still listening inspite of his strange statement, Dalfang continued. "This may be hard for you to understand, but not everything that we perceive comes through our five senses. There's another sense, one called Fenessence."

Bracken was not unfamiliar with the name. He remembered that somewhere in the past, his father had told him that the ancient followers of the Prince of Wonder had believed in Fenessence. He'd also told him that there were two kinds. One taught in the Volume and one that came from another place, a dark place; one he should avoid at all costs. But its use had long ago fallen out of practice. In fact, most today had rejected its use, saying it was no longer needed in the modern age. But he'd also heard rumors that another group had arisen and was actively experiencing it, a group that the edge-poets had predicted.

Bracken took another sip of tea and then set his cup down. "Yes, I remember hearing something about this ability, but it's no longer needed in our time."

"A tragic mistake indeed," said Dalfang, setting his cup down beside Bracken's on the wooden table and lifting his worn hands to animate his words. "If there was ever a day when we needed something more than reason, it's now. Reason is good but limited. There are many other ways of knowing about our world than mere reason."

"Sure, but so many look at this Fenessence as just another fantasy dreamed up by those who will not acknowledge the new learning and discoveries supported by the sci-scholars."

"Yes, but opposing evidence has come to the forefront that refutes that view. Look at what some of the great minds at our sci-tec schools are revealing, declaring that there are dimensions existing side by side with ours. You must realize that those who rely on reason's limitations have led us to a way of life that values only what can be seen or touched. Even a child knows that life is more than that."

Bracken remembered his encounter in the Mingus realm. There was so much he hadn't realized, things he'd never seen before, yet they had been so close. There were other realities, but his blindness to them had kept him far away. One encounter had changed him and opened up a whole new way of perceiving things. Yes, he had to agree, and so he continued to listen even more intently to the sage-like man across from him.

"There are many other worlds to explore, my young friend. As I said before, even some of the greatest thinkers on Ebbern have found that their sci-tec research into the nature of our world reveals other realms, ones that run parallel to ours."

"I tend to believe them, but what of it?" Bracken didn't want to automatically accept everything he was hearing. His challenge was coming from his new attitude, the one he'd developed as he pushed aside the ideas his father had placed on him. Yes, this man was unique for his age, and Bracken admired him for that; but then again, he could be just like Kreswen, only a gentler, and apparently wiser, version but still someone who believed in legends and antiquated ways of looking at life.

"Have you ever heard of the world of Vonervyn?" Dalfang's frame seemed to grow beneath his leather cloak as he spoke.

Bracken hesitated before he answered. Of course he'd heard of Vonervyn. It was one of those legendary worlds that the edge-poets sang about. It represented their ultimate ideal of peace for Ebbern in the future. They proclaimed that if everyone worked together in harmony they could achieve a time of love and peace. Over time, the ideal had become more a symbol than an actual place. But still there were those philosophers who had recently come to Nerkush from beyond the western reaches of the Sea of Auren. They taught a growing group of eccentric followers that such a place existed, and they even claimed to have led them to it. One famous group of edge-poets from another country had all become followers of this belief. But most of those in Nerkush cast doubts on their claims and declared openly that such teachers had no place in their country. So like them, Bracken had come to think of Vonervyn as a dream-tale, the kind of thing that he had lumped together with myths about the Prince of Wonder and the other stories he had heard as a child. That was all they had ever been to him, just stories; sometimes nice ones, but ones that had become increasingly ridiculous and boring as he'd grown older. So he hesitated to answer the wizened man for fear of giving away his skepticism.

Finally he put his musings into words, "Yes, but I never put much thought into it. You know those things are considered myths by a lot of people."

Dalfang answered gently. "That's partly true, but what many fail to realize is that myths are often based on fact. People have been skeptical of such things, but mostly because they are too preoccupied with vain pursuits. You see, there really is a world of Vonervyn."

Bracken looked down. He felt slightly embarrassed by his new friend's sincerity but moved ahead with a query. "What exactly is Vonervyn, anyway? I've heard so many conflicting theories about it. I seem to remember my parents telling me that followers of the Night Ruler had deceived the poets who proclaimed it. They told me that these sages had invented some elaborate teachings and produced false wonders to make it appear good. Still, I must admit that there was one teacher at my mind-training center who I respected, and he believed strongly that there was such a place."

Undeterred by his young companion's skeptical reply, Dalfang continued his story. "Vonervyn is a vast realm of beauty and peace that few have ever found." The aged man went on for several minutes describing the wonders of the idyllic world he proclaimed.

Becoming a little bored with the subject, Bracken gazed out the window behind Dalfang. The street was coming to life. It was nearly mid-morning now. "Well, if it's so beautiful, why haven't more people found it?"

"Because its gates have been kept hidden from ancient times."

"Gates?"

"Yes, one is hidden in Zorek Forest. One of its Guardians, known as the 'Ancient Keepers,' showed me its entrance years ago when I was your age. He commissioned me to take his place as a keeper of its door. He told me to wait till the right time came and people were ready, people like you. He said then I should share its secret and many would come to its peaceful world."

Still unmoved by his companion's tale, Bracken motioned for the man behind the counter to bring them more tea. When he arrived, Bracken requested an herb that he hoped would revive him. The stress of his earlier trauma had left him drained. In a few minutes, the new brew arrived, and the scent of the hot liquid promised to restore him. He took a deep breath through his nostrils and, gradually letting it out, he asked, "So this strange realm—if it's real, who else has seen it? Have you shown anyone its entrance yet?"

Dalfang looked at Bracken with a knowing smile. "This is why I'm here right now. The vision I was given concerning you had an additional purpose in our meeting. You see, I wasn't sent just to pull you out of the path of those explosive pellets, I was sent to guide you. Somehow the skills you will learn in the future are linked to what you'll experience in the world of Vonervyn, and I'm here to convince you of its reality."

"So, you're serious. You were sent here through a vision activated by this Fenessence. And this Fenessence was given to you in some strange world called Vonervyn?"

"Correct, Fenessence actually is one of the side effects of visiting Vonervyn. You see, each of us has a latent ability to perceive and move in this realm, but once you've visited this new world, it's released on a whole new level. Its effect unleashes the power to do things that logic and reason have no explanation for, powers to amaze."

Bracken sensed his skepticism increasing. He looked back at Dalfang with a growing incredulity. Then, as if his odd friend knew what Bracken was thinking, he did something completely unexpected.

CHAPTER 28

ACCAD

YIANE (FIRST WARMTH), 5512

Without another word of defense for his claim, Dalfang took his cup of hot brew and moved it to the center of the table. He stared at it intently for several minutes. Then holding his fingertips to his temples, he spoke three strange words. "Evek, Riynek, Scevek." Immediately, the cup began to vibrate, and then without warning, it gradually rose from the table.

"What's happening?" gasped Bracken. "Are you causing that?"

Dalfang ignored his young friend and continued to focus on the cup as it rose higher. Then as if moved by a hidden hand, it slowly glided toward Bracken, gently descending until it came to rest on the counter directly in front of him.

Bracken was speechless as he stared at the cup and then looked back into the wizened man's glowing eyes. "What you've just witnessed is merely one of the latent skills that visitors to Vonervyn develop," said Dalfang with an air of authority. "There are many more."

Bracken, his mind still spinning under the display of Dalfang's mysterious powers, sputtered, "More, as if what I just saw wasn't enough. That alone would make any unbeliever a convert."

"Oh yes, there are a lot more. There's the power to see into the future, to know what others are thinking, and even to bring healing." The glow in the wizard's eyes had dimmed, but his enthusiasm had not. He looked deep into the face of the youth across from him with an intensity that gripped his young friend. "That's why you've been chosen to come to Vonervyn. You have a destiny, Bracken, and you'll need these powers to fulfill it. Even though you were skeptical, I had a feeling you'd change your mind once you realized this is more than a fantasy. That's why I gave you this small demonstration, to convince you of the forces in me that you're dealing with and the potential that lies in your own future."

At that moment, Bracken needed no more convincing; instead he was eager for answers. "So, okay, it's real, but how did you do that?"

"Like I told you, my young friend, Vonervyn has gifts to unveil in us far beyond your wildest imagination. They'll be released in you once you've spent time there. What I've just shown you is only one of them. So many more wait to be opened to you. All you need to do now is shake off your doubts and come there."

In the place of Bracken's previous skepticism there was a growing desire to move into this realm of power. He suddenly realized what this could mean to him and others. He would now have a way to convince them that not only should they explore the Mingus dimension but that it was only one of the many new doors that were opening to his generation.

The old man had been right, Bracken told himself. He had been skeptical, but Dalfang's warm confidence and what he'd just seen was changing all that. Another desire had now replaced his doubts. "Yes, I'm ready to go there now. When do I start?"

"If you're willing to trust me, I can lead you to its western gate. It's near my home in Zorek."

"So how can I find your place?"

"Just follow this map."

Dalfang handed Bracken a piece of parchment. He opened it and read the title at the top: The Door to the Anindi Passage of Vonervyn. Beneath the lettering was a cleverly drawn illustration showing the Forest of Zorek, and a rustic cabin with a narrow path leading away from it to a beach on the shores of the Sea of Auren. The road to Accad ended near its sandy border, sketched at the bottom of the map. Bracken folded and tucked it away. "So if I show up there, you'll give me the guided tour, so to speak?"

"I guess you could put it that way, but actually there are others who are much better guides. I'll introduce you to them."

"Fine. I'll come right away. I just need to locate the friend I lost in that near disaster you saved me from." Things were suddenly moving forward at a pace Bracken had not expected but now willingly embraced. He sensed that he must move with this strange and unanticipated turn of events, that the path he'd longed for was finally unfolding before him.

Dalfang shook the embers out of his pipe and stuffed it in his bag. "Good, then let me go on ahead and prepare for your arrival. Vonervyn's inhabitants don't take well to unannounced visitors." The bearded man took a final drink from his cup. "There are a few other matters I must take care of here in Accad before I leave, so I'd better be on my way. See you soon, my young friend."

The wizened man rose from his chair to leave, and Bracken stood with him, pulled from his seat by the force of the man's charisma. The youth extended his hand to the older man. "Thanks again for saving my life back there."

"Don't mention it. I saved it for a good reason!" Dalfang shook Bracken's hand in return, gathered his cloak around him and nodded good-bye.

"Good-bye," said Bracken. As he watched the older man walk out the door and into the morning mist, he wondered if this encounter would be a turning point in his life, if his life had just been changed forever. Whatever the case, he knew he had one other question that needed answering. He had to find Ley and discover why their last encounter had taken such a violent turn.

CHAPTER 29

DEMUR

YIANE (FIRST WARMTH), 5512

At that moment, across the Bay of Accad in the City of Demur another young man had a rendezvous with someone who would change his life as well. Demur lay at the base of a range of low rolling hills. Streams cascaded down their green surfaces and spilled into the Sea of Auren. At the mouth of one of these, a group of houseboats bobbed on the water, their weathered hulls creaking as small breakers lapped against their rotting sides.

Several boats floated beside a pier marked Wharf Twenty-Nine. In the last stall, her mooring lines dripping with water, rested the *Cedar Ark*. Chepa Ayan, leader of a band known as Golden Flight, sat on her deck in a rope chair, enjoying the salty breeze as he watched seabirds glide in smooth arcs overhead. One, circling above the water, suddenly dove beneath its surface and appeared moments later with a thrashing fish in its beak. "Quite a catch," he said, admiring the rather large ock in the bird's mouth. Chepa took a long draw on his pipe. The gray smoke drifting from its bowl curled around him.

Although he appeared outwardly peaceful, inside he was anxious. That evening, he and his group had an appointment with Ley Os. The thought excited and worried him at the same time. He wanted to experience the power of the gem, and Ley was the rumored purveyor of its magic. Therefore, he had arranged a meeting with the gem dealer. His contact had come through his friend Grey Winstad. Grey had not only embraced the gem's power but had introduced the stone's magic to his band. It had changed them and their music. Chepa knew it was time he took some risks. He needed a change. His group needed the change or they would miss their chance to go with the strange tide he sensed was rising among his generation.

As eager as some were for the music his band played, he secretly knew that it was too much like all the other groups that existed across Nerkush, too much like the music of their parents' generation. His group needed to come up with something that was uniquely their own, something that represented the changes that were coming among his friends. It was time to portray the special purpose that so many felt they were born for. But he'd heard that there was always a risk with the stone's power. It was the side effects and potential dangers that worried him most. New experiences always seemed to hold problems for doubters, he told himself, but he had to be open. Life didn't wait for stragglers. Turning these thoughts over in his mind, he chewed on the stem of his pipe and waited.

He had nearly finished his pipe-full by the time his group began to arrive. Nev Broc appeared first. He was a jovial man who wore his shaggy hair down over his broad shoulders, his face covered in a thick black beard and his clothes loosely hanging around his ample waist. His right hand gripped the handle of his keyboard case tightly as he walked up the pier. Chepa took the pipe from his mouth and waved Broc aboard. "You're early for a change."

Nev stepped from the pier onto the deck. The boat rocked slightly as he sat down in the chair next to Chepa. "I know. I had some things I wanted to talk over before everyone else got here."

Chepa filled his pipe again. "What's up, Nev? You got a new song you want the group to do?"

Nev took out his own pipe. Lighting it, he stared intently into Chepa's eyes. "No, nothing like that."

"What is it, then?"

"Well, first of all, I was wondering about this guy, Ley Os. I know some of the others are excited about this gem thing. But do you think it's safe?"

Chepa took a deep drag from his own pipe and then expelled the smoke in a steady steam in the direction of the distant sea bird before answering. "I've heard the same rumors you have. But I think we need to explore some new avenues or we're going to remain in the same musical rut we've been in for some time."

"I agree Chepa that a lot of people in the Community have experienced its power and it's opened up some amazing things for them. They say it's great. But others, well, just haven't come back, I mean in their minds. But it could be more than that. I've heard rumors that some vanish completely. You know, they've gone to another dimension and never return. Doesn't that scare you just a little?"

Nev looked out over the still waters of the bay and then back at Chepa. The air was calm, almost as if to reassure him that he was making the right choice. But in spite of the placid surroundings, Nev's brow furrowed with a hint of anxiety. "Then there's this other issue with the authorities. You know what the High Council has said. They've ordered the Pirax to come down on those they suspect of using the stone."

"I know, I know," Chepa replied, echoing his friend's concerns but with a slight edge of skepticism in his voice. "You can't put your trust in rumors, Nev. If we did that, we wouldn't try anything new. Sure there've been some scary things reported with the gem, but most of what I've heard is positive. As far as the authorities, well the High Council is always going to be that way. They'll suppress any unknown factor, even if it's good. But they have to find us, and who are we amongst so many? It won't be long until all our generation will be using the gem."

Chepa stopped for a moment and put his feet up on the boat's railing. Yes, there were problems with the stone. But he had convinced himself that the potential good outweighed the negative aspects. He needed what the gem promised. He needed something like the Mingus Effect to lift him out of the dead and boring mold his music had fallen into. "I think it'll be all right Nev," he said with a sigh. "We don't have much to lose by trying it just one time."

"Perhaps you're right," responded Nev. He looked down at the com-patch on his wrist, its tiny indicator blinking green, "But now that so many of us are tied in with the sphere-grid, it scares me. It's great being able to communicate so quickly with each other, but it makes it easier for the authorities to track us. I'm sure it won't be long until they're listening in on our conversations. With the stance that the High Council has taken toward our community and message, what will they do if they discover we've experienced the gem?

"No doubt there are risks with something like this, but I believe its effect on us will be worth the chances we're taking." Chepa sounded quite assured, but inside he still felt the same uncertainty that he could see in Nev's face.

"What was the other item you wanted to discuss, Nev?" ask Chepa.

"It was about the hololight projectors. Are we going to introduce them tonight?" Nev was anxious as ever about the apparatus that would create three-dimensional images of the band and then project them to appear anywhere in the audience.

"Well, I think we should give Madrik the opportunity to try them out. He's been working on them for weeks now, and I believe he's worked out the problems he was dealing with earlier."

"Okay, but they may really shock some of the gathering."

"Well, that's part of their attraction. I think it will only enhance our popularity. Besides, that's exactly what I want our followers to expect from us—the unexpected."

Content with Chepa's apparent wisdom, Nev took another long pull on his pipe and added with a smoke-filled breath, "Well, it will be quite a night."

Later, one by one, the group came down the pier carrying their instruments. Several of them needed help carrying the heavy power units, which magnified the sound. Three of the band's avid followers helped them with their equipment. Together, they lugged the heavy cases into the main room of the houseboat.

The boat was perfect for their music. It was the last one on the pier. Isolated from most of the other boats, it sat far enough out on the water that the sound of their amplified music didn't disturb anyone. The main room was large with bare-wood beams stretching across its high ceiling.

Despite its size, Chepa had gotten it for a song because of the boat's age. Glass windows enclosed one side and gave the band a beautiful view of the inlet as the sun moved higher in the sky. Across the bay they could see the outline of the taller buildings in Accad some of them appeared lit with tiny fires as the sun glinted off their windows.

The group spent the rest of the day rehearsing and mixing with the young women who came each day to listen to them play. Groups of these attractive girls often brought other female friends with them, and late in the afternoon two of them came up the pier accompanied by three slightly older ones.

The new women had raven-colored hair spilling down in long luminous strands over their garments. Their blouses and skirts were cleverly woven with strands of silver and gold and looked like intricate tapestries. All three had piercing green eyes that seemed to vibrate as they spoke. Glistening jewelry hung from their slightly pointed ears, enhancing their fine facial bones. It didn't take Chepa and his bandmates long to be completely captivated. They invited their guests to take a seat on one of the many worn but comfortable couches scattered around the practice hall. The band members set aside their instruments and listened with fascination as the women introduced themselves. The tallest, who called herself Tristixsen Pythian, was the obvious leader. With a commanding presence, she introduced her companions, Simish and Yssmey.

As Tristixsen spoke, her teeth flashed white like the light of Ebbern's moons, enhancing her flawless skin and fine facial bones. "We've heard great things about your band, Chepa." She pointed to the younger girls, "Your friends here invited us to find out for ourselves. But we're not here to listen to your music. We have another purpose. We've come to bring you a special message."

"A special message?" queried Chepa, giving his mates a bemused smile. He turned back toward Tristixsen with an almost defiant look, a little taken aback by her boldness. "So what possible 'message' do you have for us?"

"One that I hope you're prepared for because it's coming whether you're ready for it or not."

And with that, Tristixsen went to draw the curtains over the windows as her friends took candles from their bags, lit them, and then placed them in a circle on the floor in front of their leader.

CHAPTER 30

DEMUR

YIANE (FIRST WARMTH), 5512

The warm glow of the candles softened Tristixsen's striking features. As she stared into their flickering light, her green eyes seemed to capture the essence of the flames, reflecting their fiery dance. After a while, she lifted her gaze and looked directly at Chepa.

"Have you heard of the Creeds of Adriyen?"

"Of course, our teacher at the Academy spoke of them years ago in one of our lessons." Because Chepa's parents had been wealthy, they'd had him educated in one of the private mind-training centers known as the Academy where this bit of history had been debunked as a mere legend. "Edge-talkers supposedly proclaimed them after the Greatfall. But all that was myth. Most believe their prophecies were dreamed up, and as far as I know they never came to pass."

Tristixsen was not the least bit phased by Chepa's attitude. "Well, in spite of your cynicism, I believe they are true. In fact, I've translated one of them into our modern vernacular. It's not word for word, but I think I've gotten the basic message. I've even updated it with some rhyme. I'd like to sing one to you. Would you humor me?"

Chepa's skepticism was not about to give way to this woman's persistence, but her beauty captivated him. If it meant he might get to know her and her friends better, he would allow her to go on. He nodded his approval.

Tristixsen took a wrinkled scroll out of her colorful shoulder bag and slowly unrolled it. As she did, the other two women began to chant. Their voices were melodic and ethereal. As their chant turned to a soft humming, their leader opened her mouth and out flowed the poem as a song.

On Ebbern's globe at a crucial time
Poets of song with words that rhyme
Are sent forth to gather the youths so fine.
When the time comes—this will be the sign:

Red will be Ebbern's three sister moons
Minstrels will travel from the desert of dunes
They will sing with power their wonderful tunes
Till all in their generation finally attunes.

It's for just such a day the movement longs
Everywhere they gather like hungry throngs
Listening to the magic of the wonderful songs
Lifting up their voices they will right all wrongs

Guiding with wisdom the group they have spawned
They will lift their stams like a magical wand
Announcing the saviors from the world beyond
Declaring with power a new day has dawned.

So listen now, all who can truly hear
The time of their coming is finally here.
The days turn to night and the night into days
But wise will be the council from their glistening haze.

So listen, all you children, now is your day
Your song to the stars prepares their way
Now is the moment to have your say
Ebbern is dying and will surely decay.

So no longer sit idle accepting your fate
Be not bowed low with this fearful weight
You are the ones—your hand's on the gate
So open it now for your joy will be great

Tristixsen's final words hung in the air like a sweet haunting fragrance. No one spoke, refusing to break the spell the poem had invoked. Finally the raven-haired leader looked deep into Chepa's eyes, holding him with her gaze. "So we believe you are these minstrels. We're absolutely sure," she said, nodding to her companions. "The three of us saw it when we read your star-graphs. The young girls gave us your birth dates, and they all match. So you see, we've come to guide you in this calling."

Temporarily captivated by the mood that the poem's beauty had created, the bandleader had almost been swayed. But now Chepa's incredulity returned in the face of Tristixsen's bold prediction. He felt manipulated. Looking over at the group of younger women, he said, "So they gave you our birth dates, did they? I'm not sure if I want them around us if they're going to give away our personal information."

One of the younger girls began to protest, but Tristixsen stopped her. "It's not the girls' fault. We tricked them. We told them that we wanted the dates so we could bring you a nice gift when your special days arrived." She stood abruptly to her feet and walked forcefully toward the bandleader. Stopping just inches from him, she reached out and placed a slender hand on each of his arms.

Chepa felt a charge of energy surge through his whole body. He tried to pull away, but the soft fingers held him. The power of Tristixsen's grip was clearly not coming from her feminine strength. It was something otherworldly that held him. Then her gaze focused on him, and he melted under its allure and warmth. "Be careful, Chepa. You are truly called. But if you allow your arrogance and fears to close your mind, you'll miss the one opportunity that the stars have given you. What your generation needs is a leader with a force beyond the limitation of this natural realm. Ebbern must have someone who will guide it away from its current path toward destruction. We sense that that person is coming. But they're not coming from this planet but from a higher place. This is why we've come to you today. You have a part in all this. We have seen the signs and omens. They all tell us that your group is about to come to a place of prominence and it's for a reason. You see, your band has been chosen to prepare others for the coming of such a being."

Chepa felt his resolve draining again. It was as if he'd been gripped at his core by unseen, sensual hands that massaged away his resistance. He stared back into the green eyes that had captivated him, and suddenly a vision appeared before him. He saw Golden Flight performing in a broad open space against the backdrop of jagged mountains lit by a crimson sunset. Someone else was with his band. Another member he'd never seen before playing a stam beside him. But this new musician moved with them in perfect harmony as if he'd played with them often. A large crowd was gathered before them. He could hear their music, but it was different. It sounded quite unlike he'd ever heard it before. It had an energy and rhythm that was hypnotic.

He watched as thousands swayed before him as if held in a trance. As he listened and watched the aura before his eyes, he heard their song rise to a climax. A loud vibration shook the whole stage where his group was standing and then it echoed high into the sky above him. In the next instant, a veiled face shimmered before him and spoke with a power that both stunned and fascinated him. "You are the chosen ones, Chepa, you and one you'll soon meet. Together you will announce our coming and bring peace to all of Ebbern, and then from there on to all of Nerkush. You have come to this place for this hour. But you must answer this call. If not, you will soon be forgotten and someone else will take your place. You are the ones, Chepa ... this is Golden Flight's hour ..." As he listened, time seemed to stop, and he drifted in a cloud of peace. All seemed at rest until the scene faded and he was once again looking into Tristixsen's enchanting gaze.

She released her grip. He felt suddenly weak, as if he would collapse, but she reached out and placed her fingers on his forehead. Instantly his strength returned. "I know what you saw and heard Chepa. I saw it as well," she said, holding him now only with her alluring gaze. "Do you see how important it is that you respond? Surely you are called for this hour."

Chepa was overwhelmed with affection for the woman before him, and he reached out to draw her into his embrace. She didn't resist. In fact, she returned his hug, their bodies molding together with pleasure. Caught off guard by her willingness, he released her. As he drew back, her look continued to invite him and acknowledge that she was eager for more. But then she caught herself as if remembering something she'd left undone. "One final part to the message." She turned now and faced all the band members. "You are about to meet with a man who will bring one more part to your assignment. He will introduce you to an element that will change your music. Listen well to him, you have much to learn."

Still caught up in the moment, Chepa looked around the room at his startled friends. They were as surprised as he was. "Wow, that was overwhelming. It's hard to describe what I've just seen, but I believe that these women have been sent to us."

Tristixsen smiled at them all, "And now that you've heard what we were sent to say, we must go." She gathered her friends behind her like a lioness leading her cubs, and as mysteriously as they had appeared they all padded softly out of the room into the gathering twilight.

CHAPTER 31

DEMUR

YIANE (FIRST WARMTH), 5512

It was late in the evening by the time Os arrived. By then, all of them had grown a bit nervous wondering if the oracular message they'd been given was real. They had sent the remaining women and the band's helpers away to keep their meeting a secret.

There was a soft rap on the door, and when Chepa answered, Ley slipped into the room with the poise of a diplomat. He greeted each of them with a firm handshake and a knowing smile. "Good evening, friends. I've been looking forward to our time together."

Chepa spoke for the rest of the group, a slight quaver in his voice giving away his excitement. "So have we. Especially after what happened earlier." The bandleader described to Os the encounter their group had with Tristixsen and her companions.

He listened with a faint smile curling at the edge of his lips. "Ah, yes, the Pythian sisters. They visited me as well. But it was in a dream. In fact, it's been a recurring dream. I met them years ago. They swept into my life, spoke a word over me, and then just as mysteriously slipped away. Other than in the dreams, I haven't seen them since. But they made it very clear in the visions that I was to meet with you at some point." He let out a nervous little laugh, and the others joined in, hoping to dispel the tension in the air.

"It's funny how something as silly as a dream can change the course of your life. Those ladies are strange, strange but beautiful." His words trailed off momentarily as he pictured their striking features. Then he caught himself and looked up at the group. "Anyway, sorry I'm late. I had a slight interruption yesterday. I've been running behind ever since."

Os was still a little on edge from his encounter the previous night. After the clash with his enemies, he'd returned home hoping that Bracken had gone there. But when he'd discovered the youth was not there, he'd returned to the streets looking for him. His search had been fruitless, so he finally stopped by the Brazen Eagle in the afternoon and the owner had told him how Bracken had shown up there but had left after talking with a hooded stranger. It had taken the rest of the day to deliver batches of stones throughout his network of purveyors and then rest briefly from the effects of the previous night's ordeal. All of this had left him wondering and a little worried, but he hid any anxiety under his smooth and practiced demeanor.

Chepa motioned for Ley to take a seat near the window. "That's all right. We're glad you made it."

Os sat down, slipping his pack off his shoulder. "Might as well start right now, since I'm late. I guess you've all heard what this is like. That's usually how I get customers, you know, word of mouth. If you weren't eager for this, you wouldn't be here. Well, let me tell you, all of you are in for a fascinating encounter, one that will not only change you in an amazing way but one that will change your music in a manner that you can't even imagine." Os paused for a moment, a note of caution rising in his voice. "But you need to start this journey right, so listen closely."

Gathering around him, the others watched as Os brought out a silver container and opened it. A group of the blue gems glistened against the black lining in the case. Even before the light in the room caught their crystalline shapes, they seemed to sparkle. "These are the stones," he said, almost gloatingly. "Swallow one, and it's a new mind, a new life, a new person." He slowly moved the case, letting each of the group stare at its contents.

"Beautiful," whispered Chepa, as he gazed at the glowing jewel-like stones that rested in the silver box. "How do they work?"

Os carefully explained how to release their full effect. "Right now, all of us are being touched by them. They radiate a powerful energy once they're exposed to the air. In fact, if you had enough of them around you, it wouldn't be necessary to swallow them. But taken individually, they must be ingested to have the full effect. Their power will increase after you swallow one. The surface of the stone is sharp, but once it's in your mouth, its edges dissolve and you'll be able to swallow it. As its effect grows, it will fully melt and be absorbed into your system. Don't be afraid. These are the weaker varieties. They will be quite safe for your first voyage."

Ley held out the box and offered one of the blue gems to Chepa first. As Os looked around at the wonder and desire on the faces surrounding him, his heart swelled with pride. This was what he was here to do. He felt like some cosmic shepherd guiding his little flock to high mountain pastures of delight. He would lead them and protect them.

Hesitantly, Chepa lifted the stone from its silver container. Ley knew well the slight tingle he must feel in the tips of his fingers.

"I can feel its power already," Chepa said, as if reading Ley's thoughts. He slipped the stone into his mouth as Ley had instructed. Leaning back in his seat, he watched as the others took their turn with the gems. Nev was the first to react. He began laughing almost uncontrollably. Soon all of them joined him, giggling, falling out of their chairs in delight, and rolling around on the floor. Gradually this stage passed.

Chepa was astonished by the initial sensations from the gem. But as the Mingus Effect increased, an impression of hopelessness momentarily overcame him. He realized he couldn't stop what was about to happen to him. The effect grew in its intensity, pushing aside every other feeling. But just as the sensation crested, his anxiety quickly vanished as a new and wonderful world enveloped him.

The colors in the room became more vivid. His vision became suddenly keener. He lifted his hand and gazed into his palm. It was as if he could see his pores and skin breathing. His body fluctuated between chills and warm flashes. He watched the others around him. All of them appeared to be experiencing the same thing. "This is crazy, isn't it, Nev?" His words seemed to echo off the walls as he spoke.

"Yesssss …" responded Nev, "I can't quite take it all in. My whole body feels like it's gone to sleep. Your face, Chepa, it's bending." Nev began to laugh and then abruptly stopped. "I feel like I'm falling through space and drifting out of my body." He hesitated for a moment and then relaxed again. "I've stopped now."

The whole room began to pulsate as though it was alive. Color and sound seemed to harmonize in a sensual symphony. Undulating waves of warmth flooded through Chepa's mind and emotions. He felt himself sinking into the soft cushion of his seat almost as if he was becoming one with it.

Ley advised them from time to time as they moved deeper into the experience. "Keep relaxing; everything is going just fine."

Chepa found his body vacillating between extremes of peace and nervous anxiety. "It's like flowing down a river," offered Ley. "Release your fears and leave them behind … drift." Ley's words had a penetrating comfort to them. "It's as though we are all floating on a gentle sea. The breeze has caught our sails and we're outward bound. Relax and release. Soon the flow will begin, and then you'll understand." Ley's voice seemed like a firm but gentle hand lifting them higher and higher above any fear they might have had.

Gradually, they began to talk again. "How long will this last?" questioned one of the others. "It seems like we've been here for hours."

"This is but a brief transition phase," answered Ley. "In a few moments, we'll be moving deeper. Your mind's beginning to absorb the Mingus impulses. Our voyage has just begun."

Chepa felt at ease again. He looked around. Things were different. The atmosphere seemed to glow. "There's a cloud of light filling the room. Can you see it?" His gaze fell on Os and stopped. "What is it, Ley? What's going on? Look! Your face is glowing."

Looking away, Chepa glanced around the room. Everyone's face was radiant. But, as he turned back to Ley, it was evident that his face was brighter than all the rest. In fact, his whole body projected a hazy, soft platinum hue. Suddenly, Chepa wondered how he ever could have doubted Ley's sincerity. He was filled with respect for this unusual man who had guided them to this moment of bliss.

"Continue to relax," Ley repeated again. "We are entering the maximum stage."

Chepa and the others found themselves unable to sit up. Every molecule in their bodies seemed to have dissolved and flowed into the stream of love that surrounded them. Above them, Chepa noticed an increased intensity in the light that pervaded the room. Like a rainbow waterfall spilling down over them, a river of multi-colored light flowed into the room. As each cascading color washed over his body, Chepa felt himself becoming less and less aware of the room and the others until he lost all consciousness of them.

Hours passed. Vast webs of pastel lights collided with bright green, red, and yellow stars. It was impossible to find words to express his feelings. What was the use of vocabulary when words had lost their meaning? Thoughts would bubble to the surface of his mind and then burst with a seeming fragrance of herbs. His senses wove a lavish garment of pleasure that clung snugly to his body.

Then from the center of the streams of light, a figure appeared. The being's face had a warmth and peace that captivated the young musician. Then the apparition spoke. "I know you're troubled about the future of your planet and those of your generation. But one is coming who will bring peace to your world. Rest in the assurance that once he appears all will be well." Then slowly the vision faded, but the words still filled Chepa's mind like the lingering fragrance of the sweetest flowers. Was this what Tristixsen had predicted? Then with a fresh rush of pleasure, he understood it all. It was their time. Now not only could they play a new type of music, but they also had a new message to sing with it.

"We are about to enter the highest phase," Ley's words rippled across the room. "The stones are a gift. They magnify that which is endless. They lengthen that which has no end. They make time deeper, and draw out profusion. With bright, radiant pleasure they fill the soul beyond its capacity. This is now the time we have been waiting for. You'll be able to play music, music like you've never heard before ... the song of dreams ... like a cresting wave, it's coming."

Chepa's heart felt like it would burst as Ley's words echoed his own thoughts. His ears tingled as a faint melody brushed across them, and his mind began to create song after song. Riffs of poetic melody entwined with each new creation. He looked down at his body. He moved his hands and then his feet, as he pulled himself up. The others were soon standing also. They moved slowly over to their instruments. Chepa picked up his stam and began to strum it. The waves of sound almost knocked him to the floor. He had never heard sound so pure, so alive. "Did you hear that?" he asked. "It's beautiful. Beautiful, overwhelming, impossible." Chepa began to play again and the others joined in.

Nev touched the keys of his instrument and a sound like the tinkling of shards of crystal, a ringing of tiny bells and the thunder of a waterfall all in perfect harmony blended together as if in a whirlwind of whispers. There were sounds there he'd never heard before and new rhythms to be explored. Then in the next moment, a whole new set of melodic vibrations emerged and with them a fresh approach to using them in the symphony that grew as the band played together.

Soon the room was filled with sound, each musician moving smoothly together, each one discovering a dimension on his instrument he'd never known before. They played song after song; old ones they had known for years, new ones they composed as they played. Each chord in the new progression accented the preceding one, harmony and rhythm built to a crescendo. As they sang a new song, their voices blended with the ease of accomplished vocalists.

Let us take all our fears
Cast them deep in the sea
Let us leave all the past
Let us take up the key
Open the shining door
Run free, run free
Now is the hour to let it be
Let it be

Ebbern's liberation has finally come
We announce it with our stams
We announce it with our drum

Gather tribes of children to glowing light
Gather all you children and shake off the night
Now is the time for the one who's so bright
Now is the time when our world he'll unite

"We've never played like this," shouted Nev above the throb of instruments as his fingers danced across his keyboard. "Every one of us is in perfect unity. I've never been able to move my fingers so quickly and smoothly." Nev was smiling, Chepa and the others were smiling, but Ley Os was smiling most of all. It seemed that the night around them smiled as well. It seemed that their boat floated on a cosmic tide that surged out into the universe even as the natural tide surged out of the bay and into the Sea of Auren.

Os took a small musical pipe from his bag and placed it to his lips. He played a haunting tune to their song. As he played, he danced around the room, his boots pounding out a rhythm beneath him. With each strike of his heel, a fresh sense of power surged in the musicians. A cloud of silver dust rose from the floor and filled the air. But it was unlike any dust they'd ever seen. It was like bits of tinsel, and it sparkled and glittered as it wafted about them in an unseen wind. As his feet continued to pound on the deck, they sounded eerie and ancient like the thunder of cloven hoofs on the soil of another world.

A few days later, and after more journeys into the realm of the gem, the band played again. Crowds pressed toward them as they stood on stage in the Sea Sphere, the floating hall that was moored on the shore of Accad Bay. People from all over had come to hear them. It wasn't just the usual crowd. Others had come from as far as Tizra as a result of rumors that had been circulating about the stone's impact on their music. But it was not only Golden Flight that performed that night, other groups like them, groups that had stepped into the Mingus realm in the preceding days and months, joined them. Groups that Ley Os had introduced to his mysterious stones. Chepa looked out over the mass of people who had jammed the auditorium, eager people, he told himself, *looking for what we have*. He smiled inwardly, assured that he would give them even more than what they had come for. This was the beginning of a new Nerkush, a new Ebbern. It was a wave of enlightenment for all those who would listen.

Madrik activated his hololight projectors, and images of the group appeared among the throng. Surprised at first, the crowd reacted with suspicion as they stared at the likeness of the various band members projected throughout the crowd. Some reached out toward the forms and quickly realized that they were mere projections but seemed fascinated by the quality and life-likeness of the images.

Recognizing the crowd's uncertainty, Chepa sought to reassure them. "There's nothing to worry about. What you're experiencing is the invention of our friend Madrik. He's just one of a growing group of artists that are combining Nerkush's latest technology with their creative ideas. He's using his craft to bring us as close to you as possible. Our group recognizes that our concerts are so much more than one-dimensional productions. It's truly about all of us creating something together. We've wanted a way for each of you to feel as if you are a part of this creative moment. Together all of us can produce a synergy that will enhance the music and carry each of us to a new level of experience."

With that, the band began to play again, their projected images perfectly reflecting each of their movements. Uncertain at first but gradually adapting to the new level of intimacy that the images created, onlookers soon began to interact with the projections, dancing, imitating and interacting with the created forms.

Throughout the evening, the music climaxed time and time again. There were songs about passionate love, broken hearts, and of course the celebration of life. But now the group began to add its new songs as well. It wasn't long before everyone in the room entered into the same ecstasy that the group felt. As a united body, people swayed and rocked with the pulses of music. It was as if inwardly they all agreed with what the group announced through their songs. Many of them had been initiated into the Mingus realm through the network of purveyors that Ley had established, and they clearly understood the message of the songs on more than one level. Even the songs that were old standards took on a new meaning, subtly coming through in the new arrangements. The time had passed for them to listen to the Fathers. They had their own lives to live. One of Golden Flight's songs echoed this sentiment and the hidden underlying communication that it carried with it.

I've been forced in a mold like an ingot that's been cast
I've kept the empty rituals and worn them like a mask
It's become such an empty foolish task
Let us leave them
Not believe them, we're free, free at last

Stones of power, stones of light
Stones that drive away the night
Cib had told us they were right
Gems that give another sight

Let us take them
Let us share them
As our souls take flight

Undulating bodies echoed his words. They wanted freedom, liberation. Sexuality and liberty blended in their movements. They would make it their anthem, their declaration. It would be theirs now without restraint. Chepa looked around the room as he performed, taking in the expressions on the listeners' faces. He saw lonely children, searching for more than mother's shallow affection and father's strict discipline. They pleaded for life. The Law of the Fathers had restrained them long enough, and now was the time to make their own world. Chepa's group and groups like his would help them. So would Ley Os.

The room began to glow with a radiance that bathed everyone in a gentle light. A shower of ethereal stars, unseen by most, fell from high in the ceiling onto the holo-images and hid within them. The dancers' pleasure increased. Their focus and interaction with the forms intensified. Chepa watched with an aloof sense of knowing. Very few of them understood what was happening to them. But Chepa could see it. He could see the brilliant stars of energy within the holo-images interacting with the throng. Unsure what it all meant, he assumed it was the power of the Mingus stones, and he was content to accept it as one more of their amazing side effects.

But then some of the stars morphed as Chepa watched. Dark, evil forms appeared within them. Bewildered, he watched as they changed again to light. Was there some unseen conflict at the heart of this radiance? Perhaps there was a sort of rivalry even in this realm of delight. Maybe he would have to focus part of his energy to drive away something that was taking advantage of their newfound experience. Was it possible that there were wicked entities seeking to invade this space with their own agenda? What would happen, he wondered, to those who couldn't see what he saw? It left him perplexed.

But what he couldn't know, what none of those in the crowd knew, was what awaited them after these moments of bliss. Most would be strong enough to shake off the grappling claws of devilry, but some would be held firmly in the clutches of evil hiding inside the light. Then slowly, day-by-day, they'd be dragged away to an inner emptiness.

But all this would be revealed in the future, and Chepa, Bracken, and their companions would have to struggle with the reality these unseen beings brought to so many who had unknowingly invited them into their world. Edge-poets and philosophers would soon provide their insights as they addressed the dilemma, claiming that this was what always happened when new ground was taken. There would always be risks and victims. But at this hour, most in the sphere remained unaware; dancing till the sun began to rise over the quiet waters of the bay.

CHAPTER 32

RAKA

TAR-LYNREXS (LATE-SUMMER), 5512

Even when twilight settled over Raka and the dust from the herds had dissipated; the air was still unreasonably hot. The sweat of the day's labor, crusted with the powdery mix from the stables, clung to Bracken like a stale veneer. Washing it off brought little relief because the odor of the beasts still clung to him but he bathed anyway using a cloth and pan of water.

Once the sun had settled beyond the horizon, he would often trek to the one high spot near their compound and watch the shades of magenta and gold change to gray as the final bits of light faded into night. From his perch, he could see the distant entrance to the valley as a tiny gate with ridges on either side; it appeared deceivingly small, but he knew how high those rocky citadels were from having passed through them on his way to this desert.

Raka was vast, and one could easily be lost in its wasteland. Yet in all this great area, only one spring of water had been found. Only here on Shad's land had the farmer managed to coax from the nearby hills a steady stream of moisture. The same held true for vegetation. Only the hardiest of scraggly desert plants were able to survive. Here and there a lonely shriveled tree subsisted but bore no fruit and few leaves.

It seemed to mirror the desolation that was creeping into his mind. All his great hopes and the promises of the Community appeared to be withering. Had he made the right choice in setting out on his quest? Had the words of the blind prophet simply been a mirage like the phantasms that arose amid the heat of the day in this bleak valley? Was he still on the right path or merely wandering aimlessly? He needed answers, but he simply didn't have the strength or desire to pursue them.

He lifted his drinking can to his lips and emptied its final contents into his parched throat. He recalled another place where moisture filled the air and trees grew in abundance. A deep aching at his core longed for the inner drink his soul had taken from that place, even as his body longed to drink from the sparkling brooks in the forest of Zorek.

CHAPTER 33

FOREST OF ZOREK

YIANE (FIRST WARMTH), 5512

From his secluded spot high on the ridge, Dalfang watched Bracken struggling up the ravine. Behind him, almost hidden in the trees, sat his home. Its storm windows, framed between rough cedar siding, were open, allowing the ocean breeze from the Sea of Auren to blow through his parlor. In the distance, he could hear breakers as they crashed against the rocky shoreline.

Bracken stopped his climb beside a chattering brook and knelt down to drink deeply from its chilled waters, filling his canteen with the cool liquid when he'd finished. He was carrying his stam in a shoulder case beside his backpack. The weight of the two bags was adding to the stress of his climb, and he had begun to sweat under the extra load. He needed the refreshment the stream offered, and he needed the beauty of his surroundings to refresh his agitated thoughts. After his encounter with Dalfang, he had spent three days looking for Ley but had been unable to find him.

The proprietor at the Brazen Eagle had told him about the group called Golden Flight that lived across the bay and was scheduled for a concert at the Sea Sphere. He said he'd heard rumors that Ley was with the group in Demur. He was reluctant to believe the ower after his betrayal of Os. But he had few options. Then Bracken remembered how Os had told him he was scheduled to meet with the band.

He spent a frustrating day and night trying to catch rides to Demur, and by the time he got there, the concert was over and no one seemed to have any idea where Os was. So he tossed aside his hopes of finding the gem dealer in Demur.

Returning to the Community in Accad, he was told that Ley had gone to the Shidow region but had left a quantity of stones with his network of suppliers, who were actively introducing seekers to the Mingus realm. Bracken quickly found new friendships with that group, and for the several days he lived with them in the Community, taking more and more treks into the Mingus realm. He'd started to play his stam under the influence of the stone's power as well and had come up with several new songs. It wasn't long before he had a following. They seemed to love his playing and were moved by the message in his lyrics. But in spite of his growing popularity, he was not content.

Gradually his fascination with the pleasure of the stone was replaced by a hunger to go farther into its higher realms. Twice he had taken the more powerful stones that had physically carried him into another dimension. But each time he returned, as delightful as each quest had been, he still had many unanswered questions. It was then that he recalled his encounter with Dalfang, and something told him he might find answers by visiting the wizened sage. So he had finally come to the Forest of Zorek, seeking direction from the man who had saved his life. He remembered how Dalfang had used Fenessence to lift the cup into the air in the Brazen Eagle. He wanted that same power, power to impress his friends, power to effect change amongst his generation, power that could potentially alter the course of his nation toward peace.

Dalfang waited patiently as he watched Bracken fill his canteen and start out again, his eyes warming with a calm glow. He was happy to see that the youth had come to Zorek. This had been his hope since their encounter back in Accad. He had great expectations for this young seeker. He felt it was part of his mission in life to guide and shape this generation toward a better future, and he knew that the realm of the gem could only take them the first step toward their destiny. He reached out to the youth with his mind, *"You're almost here, a few more steps."*

Refreshed, Bracken walked on. He had been hiking perhaps a half hour. His footgear left waffle prints in the dark-brown soil wherever it appeared between the crusty rock surface on the hillside. Soon he would be at the top.

Dalfang met Bracken at the crest of the hill. "So you've come." He greeted the young man, gripping each of his shoulders in his strong and weathered hands. Looking squarely into his eyes, he welcomed the young hiker with a broad smile. The firm embrace of the older man along with his warm welcome seemed to bring a peace to Bracken.

"Yes," gasped the young climber, speaking between breaths. "That last hundred yards was rather steep." He turned to look back down the ravine, his chest heaving. "I thought I was in shape. Guess I needed a little of this."

Together they gazed at the blue water of the Sea of Auren below them. The distant horizon collected a bank of white, puffy clouds that moved slowly toward them on the crisp breeze. "Looks like we're in for a change of weather," offered Bracken.

"You never know how it will turn out here," replied Dalfang. "Those clouds hold little rain, but the fog should be in by morning. It's always wet." Dalfang glanced into the woods and then back at Bracken. "You'd probably like some refreshment after your climb. Follow me, there's a meal waiting at my home."

Bracken walked behind the older man, along a ridge for a while, and then they turned abruptly into the woods. The tall trees pointed firm fingers of evergreen at the clear sky above them. As they entered the forest, its lush undergrowth exuded a fragrant aroma. A variety of herbs grew wild along the trail. Looking ahead, Bracken could see a quaint mountain cottage wedged neatly between several giant trees. Its wooden porch squeaked as they crossed it and entered the parlor. The breeze blew at the burlap curtains that hung inside the open windows. "Find a seat at the table," Dalfang offered, gesturing toward a rough-hewn wooden chair. "I'll join you in a moment."

Bracken sat down. Glancing around the room, he took in its soft earthy atmosphere. Chairs of wood and leather were clustered near the fireplace, evidence that others besides Dalfang had been there warming themselves from its glow. Ashen logs were all that remained now. On the mantle above and resting on tables around the room were unique vessels holding a variety of plants. The interior of the cabin was nearly as lush as the surrounding forest. The table was made from beautifully carved wood. Intricately sculptured legs supported its polished top. Bracken liked the homey atmosphere of Dalfang's world. The woods and mountains seemed to extend their peacefulness into the cabin. The bustling pressure of Accad seemed miles and years away.

Dalfang returned to the room with a pitcher of liquid in one hand and a bowl of fruit in the other. He offered them to Bracken and took a seat beside him. "Do you find your surroundings pleasant?"

"Quite restful." Bracken leaned back in his chair, thinking about the peace he felt, savoring the moment. "This is jipe juice!" announced Bracken as he took a drink. "Where did you get it?" Bracken hadn't had any since he left Tizra. The familiar taste of the sweet liquid caused his thoughts to momentarily drift back to his home.

How were his father and mother? Ditten? Kempec? Where was Lisha? He missed her the most ... the times they had shared their thoughts, visions, and dreams. If only she were here to enjoy this experience. He promised himself he would bring her here someday.

Dalfang woke him from his thoughts, "I have several trees in my orchard in the meadow beyond the spring. That drink came from some late season Jipe. They seem to ripen later here in Zorek." He pointed out the window to a clearing in the woods.

Bracken nodded as he took another drink. "I can see why you've made your home here. The forest is alive and yet completely unthreatening. I'm going to enjoy my stay." He plucked some of the fruit and ate thankfully, drinking in his surroundings. "This forest is so green and inviting, I can't imagine anything more pleasant. Yet you tell me Vonervyn is even more beautiful. I find that hard to believe."

Dalfang folded his arms across his chest and began to address Bracken as a father does a son. "Believing is something you'll have to learn more about later. As for Vonervyn, your reaction is not unusual. But understand this, young friend, merely because you fail to grasp what I'm telling you now in no way changes its existence."

Dalfang was momentarily upset by Bracken's unbelief and wondered if he should scold the youth. But he paused and then changed tack, taking on a tone of encouragement, "Try to understand that what I'm telling you is evident all around you."

Bracken squirmed a bit, feeling like a child. "What do you mean by that? I can see it's beautiful, but I'm not going to try and read some fairy tale into it."

"Of course not. Simply observe." Dalfang pointed to a tiny insect that slowly crawled across the windowsill. "Do you think our little friend here has any knowledge of our plane of existence?"

Bracken looked at the creature with amusement. "I doubt it. He lives in his own world."

Dalfang looked satisfied. He was starting to get somewhere. "Exactly! Yet we exist, don't we? Now just think for a moment, if suddenly he were given the capacity to understand as we do. It would be overwhelmingly beautiful for him and a bit disturbing to say the least. The realm of the insect is limited."

"And so is ours." Bracken nodded, acknowledging his growing sense of awareness.

"You're catching on quickly, my boy."

"So, what you're saying is that there's a higher realm for us as well. That's become obvious to me lately." He'd known this since his journeys into the Mingus dimension, but Dalfang went to places beyond this world without the gem's power.

The sage pointed out the window to where a tiny winged creature did an aerial ballet, "The worm metamorphoses and comes forth as a citizen of the sky. And you and I must move on as well. We can go anywhere we wish if we know how. We can become beings of a higher realm if we only learn the keys to that world."

"What kind of world are you talking about?"

"One that's infinite … a world in which we evolve ever upward until we become like the one who made this world. And then … and then we can create our own worlds and fill them with what we choose." Dalfang's eyes squinted as he unfolded these truths.

Bracken was ready to see the evidence. "It sounds great. Now all I need is to experience it."

"Fine, that's what I brought you here to see." Dalfang glanced out the window toward the treetops. A soft golden light touched their branches.

The old man stood to his feet, taking a staff that rested against the wall near him. "We should go, the sun is moving toward the sea, and we need to reach the gate before dusk."

"Can I bring my stam and pack with me?" He wasn't about to leave either one behind, so he was relieved to hear Dalfang's reply.

"Sure, they love music in Vonervyn."

Bracken followed as his guide led him from the cabin door and deep into the forest. Branches of great trees formed a green sanctuary around them as they moved along the twisting path. After a half-hour's walk, they came to a clearing. Granite cliffs pushed themselves together, forming a narrow canyon at the bottom. Bracken watched with amazement as Dalfang gingerly climbed and jumped between the rubble of rocks strewn in their path. The older man broke the previous silence of their climb with an utterance that sounded as if he had been reading Bracken's thoughts. "I've walked this trail often, young one. My feet are familiar with each step. Follow on, we're nearly there."

The first chill of evening was settling as they reached the head of the path. It dead-ended into a solid wall of granite. Although Bracken wasn't sure of what to expect, he began to feel he had followed a foolish old man on a crazy chase. Once again, it seemed that his elder had read his thoughts.

"Don't be fooled by appearance, lad. Secrets must be well hidden. Mysteries like Vonervyn do not open their doors to stumbling fools and skeptics. "Have a seat and listen," ordered Dalfang quietly but firmly. Bracken found a seat on a large rock behind him. "This is no time for doubts," the elder continued. "You haven't come this far to throw away your faith … trust me and you will soon see."

Dalfang's form seemed to take on an awesome majesty in the twilight. His eyes glowed even more brightly as he pulled the hood of his cloak over his head to warm himself against the evening chill. "Here lies the Anindi Passage to Vonervyn." He pointed to the wall of stone in front of them.

Bracken's eyes slowly followed the granite wall to its crest. Above them the sky was pink, as the fading sunlight splashed itself on the previously distant clouds. An almost overwhelming stillness hung in the air around them. Bracken began to feel foolish again and had a sudden urge to run away from this madman. He pushed the thought away.

"The key to this door lies in your tongue," continued the sage. "A few short syllables will turn its lock. The code is simple. But, remember, it must be kept secret."

Reaching into the leather bag at his side, Dalfang withdrew a polished rectangular piece of metal and handed it to Bracken. On its surface were scribed these words:

IVEX · HITH · MINAE · TRAE TRAE · VO · REM

"All you must do is speak those words and it sets the plaque vibrating. The metal is unique. It pulsates at a certain rate, nothing else works. It can't be duplicated. Those vibrations activate the device that triggers the door. Once the vibrations reach a certain pitch the gate will open. But be sure to focus all your energy on each phrase until nothing remains but the pure resonance of each word. When I first sought to unlock this gate I struggled, but gradually I learned to bring every thought into complete concentration on the words. Sometimes it will happen on your first attempt, other times you may be required to speak them more than once. But it will always open if you are faithful and persistent."

What is this idiot telling me? Bracken argued within himself. This mindless ancient thinks granite will move by talking to it. *Bracken, you have really made a mistake this time, you'd better head back before it's too late. You'll probably have to spend the night here.*

"Quiet your thoughts, Bracken." Dalfang's soft but authoritative voice interrupted his doubts. "How long will it be before you understand Vonervyn is a parallel universe? It's not in this dimension. Here at this rock is where the two worlds meet. Simply repeat the words with me and push away your unbelief. You must try."

Bracken hesitated for a moment and then spoke reluctantly. They began almost in a whisper. Behind him, Dalfang quietly mouthed the words as well.

"Ivex Hith," the younger repeated each word. "Minae Trae Trae ..." he paused, feeling foolish. What was he doing? The words sounded awkward in his mouth, and he was reluctant to repeat one more syllable. But he'd come this far, he'd spoken the first part of the phrase. Why not finish it and prove the old man wrong? So he completed the code. "Vo Rem." All was still for a few moments, and Bracken was tempted to toss the placard on the ground. But then before his next breath, the plaque began to vibrate. It trembled in his hand until he could hardly hold it. Then a faint hum began. A few heartbeats later, it had grown to a loud ringing. Then suddenly, the granite face dissolved; Bracken stared in wonder. A minute before, all he could see was solid stone. Now there was a glowing passageway dawning before them.

"Amazing," sputtered Bracken. "That was faster than I expected."

"Well, let just say you had a little help."

"You mean ..."

The slightest smile curled at the edges of Dalfang's lips. "Most people need some assistance the first few times. But you'll catch on eventually." The mentor pointed into the glowing passage. "But enough of this tarrying, there's much to see through there. Let us go."

Humbled by the sight, Bracken obediently followed him into the light-filled tunnel almost stumbling from the overwhelming sense of awe that increased as he walked forward. No sooner had they stepped into the corridor than the granite wall reappeared behind them, its smooth, gray surface bathed in the final rays of the sunset near its crest.

CHAPTER 34

TIZRA

YIANE (FIRST WARMTH), 5512

While Dalfang was introducing Bracken to a new world, Frim Lieter was hoping to do the same for his students. It had been several years since his first encounter with the disk and its intriguing occupants. At first he had eagerly shared the encounter with his colleagues, but most of them had been incredulous, leaving him even more alienated. So, over the years he was careful who he told of the strange rendezvous. As a result, he'd only found a few who would listen and none who would take him up on his offer to have an appointment with the strange race from outside Ebbern's planetary system. But things had changed in recent years, and even some from the highest ranks of Ebbern's society had spoken openly of their own experience with strange objects in the night sky. Yet, almost all of them remained perplexed by the experience because most of their observations had occurred with the spacecraft at a distance, and were therefore unexplainable. Still, there was a growing interest in this new phenomenon, and it seemed like it was the right time to open the subject again. This time he would share it with those who he hoped would be more open to his message: his students.

It was late afternoon as Frim stood in front of his astrostudies class at Tizra's Advanced Mind-Training Center. Normally, the study room had a rather sterile atmosphere, but at the moment it had taken on a warmer feeling. Rather than lecturing, Professor Lieter was sharing from his heart in response to queries from his audience. The intensity in his voice made it clear that, as controversial as his subject was, he was a believer. The unusually alert students listened with rapt attention. Frim was responding to some of the offbeat questions his pupils had asked. Although they weren't exactly in line with the normal studies on heavenly bodies, it was an interesting sidelight—a sidelight with which the noted teacher had had much experience. The direction the topic had taken provided the perfect opening for what he'd waited years to share. He smiled and made careful eye contact as he warmed to his subject. "You see, the entire celestial network is far too vast for us to presume that we are alone. There may not be any visible signs of life in our own planetary system, but considering the vast array of stellar bodies, the possibilities are unlimited."

A tall, thin student held up his hand. "If that's so, what would be the nature of this other life? I mean, would it be intelligent?"

Frim's lower lip curled down in speculation. "Why not? Can we be so shortsighted and proud as to imagine ourselves to be the only intelligent creatures inhabiting this vast universe? Undoubtedly," he continued, his eyebrows slightly raised as he addressed the whole class, "many of you have heard the theories of Brace Estim concerning contact with life from outside our planetary complex. He concludes that not only is there evidence of intelligent life, but there's evidence that life is seeking to make contact with us." A wave of whispers and murmured comments rippled across the classroom.

A youthful-looking boy held up his hand, a slight expression of unbelief on his face. "You mean this space disk stuff that he's been reporting?" Brace Estim, the controversial astrogazer, had been removed from the faculty years earlier for espousing his theories about extra-Ebbernian life. But before he'd left the academy, his theories had made a deep impression on Frim; and after his encounter with Semie, he had an even greater motivation to promote what he knew were no longer theories. He just had to find a way to share them without creating the sort of controversy his former mentor had.

"Yes," continued Lieter, a bit defensively, his gaze sharpening. "And why not, when you realize how foolish it is to suggest that we are alone. What have we done to explore such possibilities? A few dozen space probes, some sphere-link satellites put into orbit, and of course that brief but truncated space program to one of our moons. It's all been nothing more than a little cautious tinkering at the edge of infinity."

Frim's tone became an almost gentle pleading as he sat down on the front of his desk. His voice was quiet, but the intensity in his eyes increased. "Nerkush needs to expand its efforts in this area. When you consider the fact that presently we are capable, should war occur, of annihilating this planet, it becomes obvious that we have few alternatives. The inhabitants of Ebbern must make a step of moral and intellectual evolution, or we will undoubtedly destroy our race. If we aren't capable of doing that by ourselves, then it's not beyond the realm of possibility that a more intelligent force would desire to intervene and help us make such a step. I liken it to a parent helping a child learn to walk."

At this point, a somewhat skeptical pupil interrupted Lieter with another question. "That sounds possible, but what proof do you have? I've heard the theories and even been to Estim's lectures in Accad." Since his expulsion at the training center, Estim had moved to Accad and now gave lectures in rented halls where a more progressive populous was open to his theories. Still, only a few people really believed and followed him. "The former professor's theories seem to have caught on there somewhat. I must admit that I have some friends who even claim sightings of such objects. But the whole thing leaves me with a vague feeling of disappointment. Something like this that offers such hope for our world appears quite evasive. Apparently we can't quite tie it down." The slightly bookish student ended his question with a hopeful query. "What I really want to see is concrete evidence that it's true."

"All right," Lieter said simply, with the air of a man who was confident he could back up his claims. "I'm willing to give you proof, but only to those who will show a sincere desire for such evidence." His bold statement left his hearers stunned. He looked slowly around the room, enjoying the impact of his statement. Then once he was confident he had his listeners' complete attention, he spoke again. "How many then?" he inquired, motioning for a show of hands. About a dozen slowly responded. "Very well." Frim continued more seriously, his studious face reflecting a growing sense of confidence.

"Those who've raised your hands, stay behind after class. I'll talk with you more. The rest of you are free to leave. Be sure to complete your reading assignment by the end of the week. See you at our next class!"

CHAPTER 35

VONERVYN

YIANE (FIRST WARMTH), 5512

Having passed through the gate of Vonervyn, Dalfang and Bracken now stood on a green hillside dotted with trees, their narrow trunks topped by multi-colored leaves. Two huge standing stones rose up like sentinels, guarding the entrance.

Above them, the sun of another world shone brightly in the cobalt-blue sky. Its color reminded Bracken of the Sea of Auren at midday. He circled to take in the view. Rolling hills with crimson and amber shrubs scattered between the trees filled the landscape. In the distance, a lake glittered in the daylight like a piece of jade lying on a bed of lime. Beyond it, snowcapped peaks stood like a row of stoic pillars guarding a single distant moon, its faint light bleeding through a green mist that hugged the mountaintops.

"I can't believe it," shouted Bracken as he fell back in awe. "It's really real! You weren't crazy, I was. You aren't the fool, I am. Wait till Silas hears about this." Bracken sloughed off his bags and fell back, rolling in the grass, laughing, bubbles of pleasure surging within him, the fragrance of this place increasing his intoxication. Just like his transference into the Mingus realm, he had come into another dimension. Only this one came without the aid of a stone of power. Now all he needed was a simple phrase and the perseverance to hold his focus on its resonating energy. Dalfang stood still and smiled, drinking in his surroundings but with the familiarity of a frequent guest.

Gradually, Bracken composed himself. Still somewhat overwhelmed, he listened quietly as Dalfang instructed him. "You're welcome to remain in Vonervyn as long as you wish. There's much to learn and enjoy. When I first arrived years ago, I was so entranced I lost track of time for weeks.

"No doubt you did," chuckled Bracken. "What a weird and wonderful place. I mean, when you told me it was beautiful I never imagined this. Is everything else here just as amazing?"

Dalfang raised an arm and slowly turned, pointing out things of interest here and there around them. "Oh yes, and so much more. It will take you months to explore all that's here just in the lower regions. Then in the upper regions there are more portals to other worlds. It's endless."

"And what I'm feeling now, will that continue as well?"

"I am sure you will always find things quite pleasant here." Dalfang pointed to granite stones rising from the earth not far from them. "But should you wish to return to Ebbern, simply come to these markers and repeat the code. It's much easier to return than enter here. I've never failed to get back even on my earliest attempts." The older man smiled with a somewhat fatherly look at his young friend.

"I'm sorry to say I have to leave you for now, as I have other pressing matters to attend to. But I know you'll find your way into the joys of this place. Besides, I've arranged a guide for you. He'll be showing up shortly. We'll speak again soon."

He turned and began to walk toward the obelisks, speaking as he went. "Take your time and stop at my cabin before you leave."

Bracken looked up from his place on the grass, somewhat aghast that his guide would want to leave such a lovely place, having just arrived. "You're leaving already? We just arrived. Why go now?"

"I'd like to stay and introduce you to more of this realm's beauty, but I have urgent matters to attend to back in Zorek. Besides, you're safe here. There are others who will make you welcome and show you around," said Dalfang continuing to walk towards the standing stones. Reaching the entrance he stopped, turning back with a smile and a wave of his hand. Then he spoke the secret phrase, and the golden passage appeared again. Stepping into it, he vanished and it disappeared.

For a long time, Bracken sat quietly in the grass, looking into the sky and savoring the clean air. With Dalfang gone, at first he'd felt a little insecure; but as the warm sun and gentle breeze embraced him, he sensed the tightness in his stomach gradually melt away.

Why wouldn't anyone feel welcome and secure in such a place, he wondered. He thought of his own world, the stresses and worries that so many of the edge-poets chanted about. This was why they had created their Community with the hope of a better world. But in spite of their dreams and efforts, terror, oppression, and uncertainty crouched like an evil creature ready to pounce upon that hope and tear it to shreds. The Fathers had their agenda and the power to carry it out. The Pirax were the arm that enforced their will and these agents seemed to delight in the suffering such an assignment brought to their victims. The members of the Community were struggling against this onslaught. Maybe a sojourn in a place like Vonervyn would renew them.

So, perhaps this was the place for so many of his kind; escape to this land of enchantment and forget about the Fathers, the Pirax, and the threat of the World Destroyer Weapon. As he soaked in his surroundings, a growing sense of mission increased in his heart. This was all part of his destiny … along with the strange harbingers he'd encountered from other worlds and his experience with the gem. It was all falling into place. He was to lead others, to help them find a way out, to find meaning beyond the shallow message of an empty life in their present existence.

Perhaps this place would be a refuge where he could renew his strength and solidify his dreams, returning to Nerkush with a fresh sense of purpose. He would bring others here, and together they would form a movement that could change the destiny of his old world. He continued to luxuriate in the soft grass until a faint harmonic whisper awakened him from his dreaming.

Looking up for its source, he heard a melodic sound coming from a small, forested rise to his right. Then, as if on cue, a figure emerged from the strand of trees and slowly approached him. Bracken stood up, watching expectantly. The creature was about seven feet tall and walked with a graceful gait. Two large ash-colored eyes with specks of cinder where there should have been irises dominated its angular head. At the center of its cornea, tiny particles shimmered as if lit by an inner fire. Bushy hair grew back over its skull from a high forehead. Its graceful ears came gradually to a point. Its balletic walk betrayed a muscular form beneath its green, leaf-like garment.

The figure smiled, its comeliness enhanced by a row of brilliantly white teeth. Its large eyes seemed to expand even more as the creature spoke in a sing-song tone, "I see you are enjoying yourself." His head bobbed as he talked, and his voice's slightly melodious tone seemed to tickle Bracken's eardrums. "It's hard not to be happy here in Vonervyn." The being looked toward the nearby obelisks and then back at the new visitor. "I see you've just arrived … Dalfang brought you, I assume. He informed me you'd be here."

Bracken stared in amazement bordering on humor, as he watched this funny creature articulate. An inner warmth clutched him and stilled his voice, so he just grinned.

"Dalfang's a good fellow," his new friend continued. "He's brought a few like you here before. They all seem to have the same strange look when they first arrive." The creature's large eyes didn't blink once, which only seemed to increase its uniqueness. Besides its peaceful manner, as if to confirm its otherworldliness, its body seemed to emanate a soft glow. Turning to its right, the creature motioned Bracken to follow. "Come with me. It's my delightful duty to show you around. Oh, and yes, I know what you're about to ask. My name. Well, I'm known as Dimishta, son of Curaa." The elf-like being winked pleasantly finally moving its long eyelashes. "Come along now, there's much to see," said his host, setting off at a brisk pace.

Bracken collected his bags and hurried after his host. He pumped Dimishta with questions as they walked toward a large cluster of trees on the horizon. "What race are you?"

"We're the family of Filanleys. We came to inhabit Vonervyn after losing our former home." The Filanley seemed almost homesick for a moment, his eyes losing their brightness as the inner fire dimmed slightly. The being quickly covered his dejection with a smile. "We were driven from it by a strong lord and his army who made war against our leader. We were powerful, but they outnumbered us two to one. It wasn't very pleasant for a while. I mean, we weren't accustomed to this kind of life, but we've adjusted gradually."

"Why would you find it hard to adjust to such a pleasant place?"

"Oh, if you only knew. Our present environment is a huge step down. But I'm afraid you wouldn't understand."

Bracken evidently had touched a tender spot with his host, so he moved on with another question. "Who is your leader?"

"His name is Wiscim." The Filanley pointed toward the snowcapped peaks. "He lives high in the Knasir Mountains. Perhaps you'll meet him someday."

"Dimishta, how long have your people lived here?"

"Ages." The creature's voice sounded strangely distant for a moment, like an echo in a long tunnel. "I am quite old myself. At least six thousand of your years."

"Hmm, you look well preserved."

"Our kind don't age in the normal sense."

"I can tell." Not completely satisfied with the answers, but impatient to discover their destination, Bracken changed his line of questioning. "Where are we going now?"

"To a party. My good friend lives in those trees ahead. Since Dalfang informed us of your visit, I've been preparing and have invited many friends." The cluster of trees was closer now, and Bracken could make out movement under their shade. Dimishta pointed toward them as he spoke. "When Dalfang told us a visitor was coming, word spread rapidly. We all love a party, and each new visit means another celebration. There should be a good size group to welcome you." Bracken could hear the sounds of plaintive music drifting in the air. Strange forms appeared to be moving about beneath the trees. "You'll be glad to know that one of your kind should be there as well."

Bracken felt a sense of pleasant surprise at this latest announcement. "Good, I'll be interested in seeing who else Dalfang has brought here."

"Oh, she didn't come here through the western gate, but through the Kutim Passage under the northern mountains," replied Dimishta.

As they approached the party, people emerged from beneath the wooded canopy to greet them. Dimishta introduced Bracken to a number of the Filanleys, few of whose names he remembered past the introduction. They all seemed happy, eating and offering him various types of fruit and an amber liquid in silver goblets. Music came from a group of creatures sitting near one of the tree trunks, playing upon strange-looking instruments.

The area beneath the trees looked as if it had been fashioned by some organic magic into various rooms and levels. Nowhere was there any evidence of a nail, saw, or hammer. It was almost like each living space had been formed by some strange nature-based magic. His guide took him on a tour of the dwelling, explaining some of its comforts, like the marvelous soundproofing each offered, providing its residents with guaranteed nights of peaceful rest.

Bracken quickly found himself in several animated conversations with his new friends. Like Dimishta, though, they seemed to be doing most of the talking. Eventually he found a seat at one of the tables. Looking up from his food, he saw a young woman approaching him through the crowd. He stood to greet her. She was tall and shapely. Her red hair cascaded over her shoulders and her lightly tanned skin accented her green eyes.

Before Bracken could speak, she smiled and then spoke. "Hello. It's so good to see one of my own kind here." She placed her hand gently on his arm as she sat down beside him. Her long crimson robe, topped with a thin gossamer half cape, accented her thin waist and ample breasts. Bracken felt a tingle shoot through his body as her hand continued to rest lightly against him. "My name's Brish, Brish Tremiley." Her voice was soft and breathy but sincere.

"I'm Bra ... Bracken," he stuttered a little, overwhelmed by how striking his new acquaintance was. He fumbled around for his next sentence but could only come up with, "It's good to meet you as well." He had so much to ask. Not sure where to start, he began with the typical approach.

"How long have you been in Vonervyn, Brish? It must be for some time. I mean, you seem quite at ease here, like it's home."

"Yes, its grace does grow on you the longer you stay. So I make frequent visits here, and each time I try to stay longer. Soon you'll start to feel close to the others here. For instance, your guide, Dalfang, and I are old friends by now." Brish glanced around. As she talked, her eyes sparkled like fish flashing about under a mountain stream, taking in the activity of the party going on around them. But gradually they seemed to light on him more and more until finally she gave him her undivided attention. She seemed to enjoy Bracken's presence. "Yes, Dalfang and I have been acquainted for some time. But he wasn't the one who originally brought me here. I came through the Kutim Passage beneath the northern mountains. My guide was Eshtar Cosh. Did Dalfang mention him?" Brish's teeth dazzled gleaming white as she talked, her eyes punctuating her sentences with captivating animation.

"No." Bracken thought for a few moments. It seemed odd that Dalfang hadn't told him there was another way into Vonervyn. He smiled back at Brish with another question, still awkwardly trying to make conversation. "How long have you been here this time?"

"About three months. But the beauty of the place soon slows time down, it's almost like you start to forget about it. Each day brings something new and unusual. I've never been happier in my life." Brish continued to share stories of delight between sips of the slightly intoxicating liquid that the Filanley kept topping off as they made their frequent rounds, checking to see that their guests were comfortable.

Bracken enjoyed listening to Brish talk so much that he was caught by surprise when the conversation suddenly took an unexpected turn. "As delightful as Vonervyn is, something has begun to trouble me recently."

"What could possibly bother you in a place like this?"

"It only began with my most recent visit here. I'd never sensed it before. But now, each night the most horrible feeling seems to overwhelm me just after sunset. It seems to come in with the evening air. It's been increasing each night. I was shocked at first. I never expected that Vonervyn held anything but peace and tranquility."

Brish seemed to tense up, but Bracken could tell she was trying to cloak her anxiety, not wanting to trouble Vonervyn's newest visitor. She spoke softly now, as if to calm her unease. "I wasn't frightened at first. I didn't think there could be anything evil in this beautiful world. But now that it is growing more intense, I've found myself becoming extremely anxious. I'm almost afraid to go home this afternoon."

Bracken wondered why Brish was so quick to share her worries with him. After all, he was new to the place and probably unable to offer any practical advice. But he found his heart reaching out to her anyway, hoping to dispell her fears. Perhaps a few songs on his stam would calm her and bring some peace to her troubled thoughts.

Not sure how to respond he asked, "Haven't you told Dimishta? He must know what it is."

"Yes. I've asked the others here about it, but they don't seem to understand what it could be. They seem to be pleasantly ignorant of the whole thing." Brish looked hopefully into Bracken's eyes. "Perhaps you can come back to my place after we're through? Maybe you'll be able to find out what it is."

Bracken found it strange that Brish would confide in him even to the point of inviting him, a stranger, to her home. But perhaps it was the fact that he was from Nerkush as well and offered a perspective that none of the other residents of this idyllic land could.

He looked reassuringly into her eyes. "I'd be glad to."

The party around them continued unabated as they talked to one another, sharing their backgrounds and the strange destiny that brought them together in this unlikely place. Although their conversation continued pleasantly, his chest felt tense as he thought about what Brish had told him. His best attempts at chasing away the foreboding only gradually reduced the pressure rising in his blood. He felt it pushing aside the joy he'd sensed earlier. Like an ugly worm gnawing at the surface of a pleasant fruit, with its goal to reach the core, he could feel something there gradually eating away at his peace as if it had taken aim at his heart. But then Brish looked deep into his eyes, and the sensation he'd felt when she first appeared came back with such intensity that it momentarily pushed away his worries.

Did this delightful girl have some hidden power that had lessened his fears? The more she gazed at him, the more he was sure this was the case. And if she had such power, what other skills did she possess? Why had that skill not helped her with her own worries? What was the source of her craft, and would it always be so benevolent? She was alluring but so was a roaring fire on a cold night, only you didn't want to get too close to it. But for now he was delighted by her energy and longed for more.

He looked back at her, hoping to match the warmth she'd just shown him. He wondered what a girl like Brish would be doing in Vonervyn. Why would she be here alone, and what had prompted her to leave Nerkush? Was she a forerunner like him? Did she have a destiny similar to his? He felt a surprisingly deep kinship with her even after such a short time together. It seemed they were fellow pilgrims in this new world.

"How did you ever end up here?" he asked.

"I was in an advanced mind-training school in Toplana. It was a complete bore." Bracken was familiar with Toplana, a city in northern Nerkush. "I bumped into Eshtar there. Actually he found me and told me about Vonervyn. He said he'd been sent to me through a vision or something like that."

Bracken nodded, "That's how it happened with Dalfang and me."

"I was skeptical at first. I'd heard what most people hear ... Vonervyn's just a dream world, the only reality is life in Nerkush. But Eshtar took me to a secret chamber inside his house and, just like you, the next thing I knew I was here. It was even greater than I dreamed, and continued to be ... at least until these strange events began."

"I know. When I first stepped out of the passage, I was overwhelmed. I can see why Dalfang was so eager to bring me here. I know many people who would love this place."

A knowing and eager look came over Brish's face, "I've learned much here. I'm sure that Dalfang has shown you some of the amazing things that start to activate in you once you've spent time here." Brish's emerald eyes seemed to pierce right to Bracken's heart as she spoke with increasing animation. "I've started to use some of these amazing gifts already."

"Yes he did. In fact, he showed me one when I first met him. It was what convinced me to even consider this place."

"Good. As I said, I've started to use some of them already."

"Like what?" asked Bracken, eager to learn more.

"Well, I've started to read others' thoughts."

"Sure you have," said Bracken with obvious incredulity. But he didn't want to offend this very attractive girl who had taken such an interest in him, so he quickly repressed his skeptical look. "So, how do you know you can do this?"

"Ok, let's do a little test."

"All right."

"Just relax, let all distracting thoughts go, and imagine something you'd really enjoy."

Bracken smiled as the first thought entered his mind. An image of Brish, her mouth open in a slight smile, her full lips glistening and her bright eyes gazing warmly at him. "Okay, I've got one."

Brish's face flushed slightly. "Not that one."

Bracken opened his eyes and caught the slight embarrassment on his new companion's face. He wondered if she actually did see what he was thinking. He gave a slight chuckle and pictured his friend Silas.

Brish closed her eyes again. She was quiet for a long moment and then said, "I see a name. It starts with an 'S'. He's really close to you. I see you sitting by a fire sharing krem. More's coming to me now."

Bracken stared back at Brish in amazement, watching as she squinted her eyes and wrinkled her forehead. There was a long pause and then suddenly she spoke. "Yes, his name's Silas."

"How did you do that?" Bracken sputtered.

"Well, I just let go in my mind and these words and images just start to fill my imagination. Of course I use the words Eshtar taught me."

"What words are those?"

"Oh, I forgot to tell you. When I received the entrance phrases that he gave me to get through Vonervyn's gate, he also told me that once I'm here a while and want to start activating the new skills I would acquire, he would give me the phrases that would trigger them. He wrote them on a special cloth that I keep rolled up at home. I've memorized them now, so I just repeat them in my mind each time, and just like that it works."

"How long were you here before these things started to occur?"

"Oh, I would say around the second month."

Bracken reflected for a few moments, still marveling at how accurate Brish had been. "Well, I certainly have some surprises to look forward to. I hope you can teach me all you've learned."

Bracken felt almost childlike for a moment, as if he was suddenly the juvenile, and this alluring girl, who was clearly younger than him, was in fact so much wiser. He stared back into her eyes, tender now by his obvious hunger for more wisdom, and she responded graciously, almost temptingly.

"Sure, Bracken, in fact I've much to teach you, even though I've just begun learning myself. There are things I've seen here that leave me astounded, and I can't wait to share them with you. It will come to you, just wait. I can see how truly hungry you are for them."

As Brish spoke, Bracken felt himself pulled closer. There was something about her that hadn't been there when they first began to talk. Her viridescent eyes looked as if they were endless pools of green light and her words were soothing as a pleasant breeze on a scorching day. He wanted to know all she knew and more. He wanted the power to know others' thoughts, to move things with the power of his mind.

It was becoming clear why he'd been led to this extraordinary place. He was a pioneer, a trailblazer and now he would go back to bring many of his peers to this new level. He reached out and took Brish's hand. "Yes, I believe I will. Indeed, not only do I want to move deeper into these gifts but a lot of people I know could greatly benefit by this and all the experiences we have here."

"I agree. It's exactly the kind of place my friends need," offered Brish, squeezing his hand and then releasing it. "Most of them are filled with strife. It would help them find peace. Plus, once these gifts start to activate in them they'll find better things to give their minds to than the krem-drinking parties and other shallow things that fascinate them now. I've been thinking about going back and bringing them with me. But first I wanted to really explore Vonervyn and know my way around before I introduced anyone else. I think they would think I was just crazy. But like Dalfang convinced you, I'm sure I can convince them. I just wanted to make sure it was safe, and I was sure it was … until now," Brish turned to Bracken and took his hand again, squeezing it tightly.

Just then, Dimishta interrupted their conversation. "You'll have lots of time for talking later. Right now we'd like to present Bracken with our welcome leaf." A crowd quickly gathered around them, as Dimishta raised his voice. "We'd like to let our new friend know how glad we are that he's come to join us here. Bracken, you are welcome to stay as long as you like. Build a home here as Brish has done. Bring others here if you wish." His voice took on sincere warmth. "We know the problems of Nerkush and trust that Vonervyn's soothing atmosphere will settle many troubled lives. Wiscim, our leader, has given us a new charge. We're no longer to keep this world to ourselves, we're to export our tranquility and peace. We're to open our gates to others like you. Too many years have gone by, and we've kept this hidden. That will be the case no longer." The Filanleys gathered around Bracken, smiling brightly as Dimishta finished his speech. "Now receive this welcome leaf as a token of our friendship."

The Filanley held up a ring-shaped piece of green material. Its texture was similar to the garment he was wearing. Motioning Bracken to hold out his arm, he slid the bracelet of green around his wrist. It felt snugly comfortable. Bracken smiled a thank you, and all applauded. "Also, Striray, one of our leaders, wants you to know that you can stay in his home until we prepare a better dwelling for you tomorrow."

"Oh, but he's going to stay with me tonight," injected Brish.

"Okay then, just as long as he's well taken care of," smiled Dimishta. A chuckle went through the crowd. The elf-like creature turned to his guest. "We'll see you on the morrow. I have some business to take care of in the south." Dimishta waved a good-bye and departed, a few others leaving with him.

"Let's go now too," whispered Brish. "I want to get home before sunset."

Bracken thanked his new friends for their hospitality, grabbed his gear, and then left with Brish.

CHAPTER 36

FOREST OF ZOREK

YIANE (FIRST WARMTH), 5512

The cluster of evergreens stood in tight rows, forming a wall against any possible intruders. Several had been twisted together by some supernormal force, sealing any possible opening. Sap oozed where the trunks and branches had cracked under the stress of this rearrangement. Such a fortress was necessary whenever the Shadow Czar called for a meeting with one of his higher minions on Ebbern's surface. From a distance came the faint sound of waves breaking against rocks. A slight sea fog hugged the tops of the trees that had not been molested. Nearby a path led up a canyon to where it dead-ended against a sheer granite wall.

Normally, a grove like this would be alive with wooded creatures. The bigger ones were gone now. The small ones that remained crouched in stunned silence, peering up from holes and from beneath rocky clefts where they had gone to hide.

The forest was still now, except for the deep breathing of two dark forms. In place of the fragrant sea breeze, a sulfurous stench hung in the air.

The smaller of the two forms, a flux-morph specialist, bowed deeply as it drew near the other, "You called for me, Master."

"Of course," said the giant figure, the last syllable hissing from its mouth. "You would have been foolish not to come immediately, Lyslaink."

"Your summons is always my priority," responded the smaller creature. He wondered why he'd not been summoned to some lower chamber. Maybe his master wanted to spend some time on this level in spite of his danger of exposure. He quickly pushed aside such speculation, knowing that if we wasn't quick with an answer he'd be disciplined. "What is your pleasure?"

"You must bring a disturbance to Vonervyn. It's time to torment some of the new ones at ease there."

A slight shadow moved over Lyslaink's countenance. "Won't that lead to speculation on their part?"

"Of course, but we can deal with them. Every garden has its poison creatures; even paradise has its serpent. But we must let them think we want their best. It's easy. Pleasant lies quickly soothe those we trap."

"What sort of disturbance? How much terror must I use?"

"The effect must be complete."

"Why?"

"We must keep them fearful. We don't want them to ever find a place of true peace. That's why we seek to expand our terror to every realm. I've already had one of my agents at work sowing fear. You will help increase it."

"That will be a pleasure indeed, my lord."

"You must keep them wondering, always wondering."

Lyslaink looked up at the dark lord. He was the one wondering now. "Why, though? Don't we want them to forget about their destiny and drift until it's too late?"

"They will anyway. That's what makes our efforts so enjoyable. Even while they fear, they persist in their pursuit of pleasure. And so the noose simply grows tighter, the chains heavier."

The Shadow Czar's eyes narrowed, and a slight vapor filled the air as he slowly expelled his breath. Almost imperceptibly, Lyslaink could see the dark lord's gray tongue lick his lips and then dart back between his perfectly formed teeth. He was so elegant and stately, but his appearance bore a harshness as if it had been lacquered with aging veneer. "Pleasure indeed."

"As you've requested, I've been tracking the young one who came into Vonervyn today. What of him?"

"Let him alone for now, unless he gets in your way."

"Is that a possibility?"

"His movements have been predictable till now. But one never knows. Don't worry, though, I have plans for him. I'm personally going to enjoy the suffering I bring to him at the proper time."

"So what resources do you want me to use in Vonervyn?"

"One of the Octi-orges should be adequate. You seem a master at creating these devices, each new one more deadly than the last. Plus, I like the fact that they can always be recycled if damaged. Remember, only bring them close enough to the victim to create fear, then draw back."

Lyslaink had an arsenal of machine-like creatures he could bring to life for his heinous purposes. But none was more effective than the Ti-Or, a nickname he'd given it. "A wise choice, Exalted One."

"Send me a report immediately."

"Absolutely."

The Shadow Czar pulled his cloak firmly around his massive figure, signaling an end to the meeting. He touched the brass ring on his wrist, vanishing the next instant from the wooded enclosure. Lyslaink followed his leader's movements, activating the device on his wrist and disappearing as well. Now only a faint cloud of vapor drifted in the clearing. Much later the forest creatures crept out to inspect the damage done to their wooded homes.

CHAPTER 37

VONERVYN

YIANE (FIRST WARMTH), 5512

The sun was setting behind them as they walked toward Brish's dwelling. Like servants bowing to their master, here and there shadows from tall evergreens fell across the rolling hills. At first, she seemed happy to be out walking, but as they drew near to her home, she became noticeably anxious.

"What you're afraid of isn't real." Bracken tried to reassure her, taking her hand as they walked along. "It's only a fading memory of something from your life back in Toplana."

Brish cheered up a little and smiled. "You're probably right." As they came to the top of a small hill, she pointed out her home. "There's my place ahead."

Brish's house looked like a typical Vonervyn dwelling. Wood-like material artfully woven formed its roof with a leafy waterproof fabric gracefully stretched over it as a covering. Small window-like openings covered in a transparent gauzy substance punctuated its walls. To the side of her home was a field enclosed with a rail fence. Inside, a small herd of blue-furred creatures milled about. They ran to the fence and watched the couple as they approached the dwelling. They seemed to eye them with a lonely, hopeful look as if wanting to be fed.

"Brish, what are those interesting creatures?"

"Oh, those are my giismis. Aren't they cute? They used to be vigorous and fierce, but I've learned how to tame them. It was one of the gifts I've learned to use here. They're as gentle as lambs now."

Bracken stared at them as he and Brish walked on. For just a moment, there was a flash of recognition in their eyes, as if something else was looking out at him but then it was replaced just as quickly by their hungry stares.

As they approached the entrance, a huge door greeted them and then mysteriously opened of its own accord. *That must be another one of her powers*, Bracken told himself. *One I'd like to have as well.* He imagined impressing Silas with it. Truthfully, he had begun to imagine a lot of things he could do with the powers promised him here.

When they stepped inside, Brish led him through her dwelling, and he recognized a few Nerkushian touches: pieces of familiar furniture invitingly placed here and there, handcrafts and artwork adorning the walls, paintings, and even a few sculptures pleasantly arranged to catch the eye.

"Your place is lovely. I assume that's some of your work on the walls? They're beautiful."

"Thank you, Bracken."

"And what about this statue?" he inquired as he approached a twisted crimson figure standing on a black pedestal. It appeared as if it had been a beautiful bird wreathed in fire and contorted by the flames."

"Oh, just the expression of a dream I had once. It has a certain dynamic to it. Like two forces colliding … hope and terror. Sometimes I have strange dreams."

Strange indeed, thought Bracken.

Brish continued to show him around the house. The sitting room looked out on a small garden. Nearby were two quaint but adequate guest cottages. She explained that she often had visitors, so the Filanly's had built the cottages for her to house them. The kitchen and other rooms were paneled in dark wood and covered with more of Brish's woven tapestries. She showed him the small guest room where he would spend the night.

"I usually invite my guests to stay in the cottages by the garden, but I'd feel safer if you'd stay a little closer tonight," she said, leading him back to the main room. "Please make yourself at home."

Bracken found a seat on the couch. Brish joined him a few minutes later, carrying a tray filled with luscious-looking fruit. She set the food on the table in front of them, lit a candle at its center, and then settled in snugly beside him. As she did, the strange tingling he had felt earlier returned. The energy he sensed was more than just the allure of her beauty; it was something much deeper, a force that seemed to come from within her. It attracted and fascinated him but also left him a little perplexed. In the midst of his contemplation, she turned to him and smiled with a warmth that melted away his questions.

"I'm glad you're here Bracken. It's reassuring that you'll be close by tonight."

"I am pleased you want me here. You're a lovely woman, and I'm happy that my presence is a comfort to you."

Dusk was quietly moving from the east as they talked. Brish went about her dwelling lighting several candles and then joined him again. Everything appeared peaceful, but Bracken could sense a growing uneasiness in Brish. He tried to comfort her, hiding his own anxiety. "Like I said, there's really nothing to be afraid of. I'm here now. If anything does come, I should be able to take care of it." Bracken reached down on the floor where he had deposited his stam with his pack resting beside it. He patted his bag to make sure the energy eggs that Ley had given him were still there. In the past, he would never have thought to keep such weapons. But the street battle with Os's enemies in Accad had changed his mind. He had kept them secret from Dalfang as well, not knowing what the wizened sage would make of such destructive things. Now that Brish had shared her fears, he sensed a protective confidence that emboldened him. Whatever was out there, he knew he could handle it.

He looked at Brish's face. All her earlier confidence and forceful allure seemed to have vanished. He wanted to comfort her. In fact, he wanted to do more than just comfort her. He wanted to hold her, to protect her, to squeeze all her fears away in his arms. Her look seemed to invite his affection.

The moment seemed filled with possibility. Here was this beautiful creature alone with him, apparently eager for his protection and attention. It would be so easy just to move closer and embrace her.

Then he remembered Lisha. He would never betray her. Not even for a few moments of pleasure. Somehow, as he thought about her, all temptation drifted away. He reached out and held Brish's hand reassuringly for a moment and then let go. "You'll be all right. Cheer up."

The words had barely left his lips when a dreadful presence invaded the room. Frightened, Brish moved closer to him and began to tremble. "See what I mean, it's here. I'm not making this up. Why is it here? Where could it be coming from?"

Bracken felt chilled to his marrow. Brish was definitely not imagining things. He stood up and looked around. Where was the source of this terrible presence? Brish stood up beside him, staring out the window. Suddenly, she screamed and pointed in horror through the front window into the blackness outside.

Bracken reached down and grabbed his side pack. In the next moment, his adrenaline moved him to the door. He opened it, squinting into the darkness, trying to see what had frightened her. Something moved in the distance. Then it stopped. Silence. All he could hear was the thudding of his own heartbeat and Brish's breathing behind him. "If you can, blow out the light behind you."

Brish crouched down and moved along the floor till she reached the candle on the table. She blew and the flame flickered. Exasperated, she blew again. Still the light persisted. Then once more and the room went dark. She threaded her way back to Bracken and clung to him. All was silent except for their nervous breathing. The moments seemed to creep by. The air was heavy; it enveloped them, almost suffocating them. Then once more, something moved. A hulking shape in the dark crawled toward them.

"There, do you see that?" cried Brish. She swayed a little, as if she might faint. She gripped Bracken's shoulders, holding herself up. Then Bracken saw it. Out of the night a metallic glimmer, shrouded in a cloud of darkness, floated toward them. Unexpectedly, a dreadful whirring sound began to shake the ground beneath them. Flaming eyes appeared in the midst of the miasma.

Bracken felt something gripping, tugging at his core, drawing him toward the murky apparition. He held onto the doorframe. Threatening tentacles appeared from the cloud and moved along the ground toward the house. Bracken's mind had suddenly gone blank ... the only thought he could manage was *How is this all happening in such a peaceful place?*

Brish fled to the rear of the house, screaming hysterically.

"Bracken, snap out of it," he told himself. Quickly, he reached for the energy eggs in his pack. Holding the small oval weapon in his hand, he set it to discharge on impact. He resisted whatever force had so mesmerized him and stepped through the doorway.

He stopped a few feet out and hurled the weapon at the advancing specter. Then he turned and ran into the house, retreating after Brish.

A powerful explosion rocked them off their feet as they reached the back of the room. A hideous scream rose to a crescendo and then died away, leaving the night air still again.

Brish relit the candle. She and Bracken waited for several anxious moments before slipping back toward the front door. The energy egg had done its work. A direct hit to the creature's mid-section had brought it down. Shards of metallic and fleshy substances were scattered about on the ground.

Brish still held onto Bracken but sighed with relief. Bracken gradually became aware of something dripping down his fingers. He lifted his hand to discover that he'd been wounded. No doubt a shard from the explosion.

"You're bleeding, Bracken," gasped Brish. "Let me get something to tend to your wound." She ran into her bedroom and returned with a medi-kit. She led Bracken into the food prep room and ran water over his wound. After gingerly applying some salve to it, she bound it with cloth she'd torn from an old bedcover.

"There. That should do for now. Tomorrow we can visit Dimishta. He claims to have special healing powers. This will be a time for him to prove it to me."

Once the bandaging was completed, their attention returned to the earlier conflict. They made their way to the front of Brish's home and looked out toward the site of the explosion. For a long time, they stood staring at the dismembered creature. Then Bracken blinked several times.

"My eyes must be deceiving me … It can't be happening … This is insane." Just as strangely as it had appeared, the creature started to disappear—the scattered remains disintegrated into thin air before their eyes.

"Bracken, hold me," said Brish. "I feel so weak. I can't take it." They huddled together, watching till there was nothing left of the creature. Now there was only a tormenting memory and a few ashen marks on the ground.

"It's all right now. We both just need to calm down."

Brish loosened her grip on Bracken's arms, but she was still trembling. She took a long, deep breath. "You'll never know how glad I am that you're here. Thank you, Bracken." Gradually, Brish seemed to compose herself and the earlier chill was replaced by the stillness of the warm night air.

Then an intriguing, majestic sight began to fill the sky. Brish smiled, "This happens every night in Vonervyn, Bracken. It's the fire-dragonflies' dance of bliss."

Together, they watched as the sky erupted in a dazzling display. Tiny luminous winged creatures spun a ballet of light in the darkened sky.

The sparkling glow had a soothing effect on both of them. Their anxieties slowly melted away. They watched, entranced, until the creatures vanished, leaving behind a faint glimmer.

Bracken's initial joyful feelings about Vonervyn began to return.

Brish sighed deeply. "I'm exhausted. I think I'll go on to bed." She got up and moved toward the door. "Good-night. Again, thanks for all you did."

"Glad I could. I'm going to stay out here for a while," responded Bracken. "I've got some thinking to do." He remained near the door in the ebbing light the fireflies had left behind.

He looked out at the distant hills, dimly lit by the stars. The giismis softly bellowed from their pen, a plaintive tune. He stared at them for a moment; that sound was almost human. Perhaps Brish had taught it to them. A lot of the beings in this world seemed to do odd things. Maybe he could teach creatures to sing like that someday.

The terrifying experience was only a fading memory now, almost as if it had somehow been swept from his mind by a gentle breeze. He felt secure, warm, comforted. All was quiet around him. He reflected on the joys of his first day in Vonervyn. They pushed away all his worries. Nothing remained of the earlier dread. This place was too wonderful to be kept hidden. He promised himself he would leave in the morning and return with his friends. He had to bring them here. He couldn't wait another day. Lisha especially would love it.

He stretched, and yawned. He was tired. Taking one last gaze out into the night, once more he told himself he must bring his friends here right away. With that firmly resolved in his mind he turned and headed to bed. Behind him, the last essence of the dragonfly's radiance faded away.

CHAPTER 38

TIZRA

LYNREXS (MID-SUMMER), 5512

Bracken had been home from Vonervyn for several weeks. The wound he'd gotten from the explosion had healed, but in an odd way. Dimishta had used his nurturing powers, chanting some strange words and applying a special salve. The result was a pure white scar left on his hand in the shape of a small diamond. Periodically he rubbed it, his fingers following its outline. As strange as it was, it reminded him that his experiences in Vonervyn had been real. So had all of the strange encounters he'd enjoyed since he'd left Tizra, and he shared them with great enthusiasm.

Lisha and Silas were not as excited about his adventures as he'd hoped they'd be. He'd spent days explaining to both of them about his experiences in the realm of the Mingus gem and how it had change him. He was so eager for both of them to experience the flights of inspiration and pleasure. He couldn't say enough about Ley Os and the Community. Of course he'd tried to capture the wonder he'd experienced in Vonervyn, but it just seemed like a dream to them. He knew that's why they had to experience it firsthand.

After much debate, he had finally convinced them to at least go with him as far as Accad. From there, he was sure they would see things differently. The Community would have a positive effect on them. Everything would be fine once they all got out of Tizra. Getting out, though, wasn't that easy. His parents were seeing to that.

"You're what?" Kreswen snapped angrily at his insistent son. They stood together in the central room of their comfortable dwelling. Myrus sat in the corner, pretending to read. Outside, the sun had passed midday and was slowly moving toward the eastern hills.

Bracken stood firmly in place, his face a mask of defiance. "That's right, Father, I'm not going to go to the Gathering Day meetings anymore." Tomorrow would be the weekly assembly.

In recent years, he'd grown bored with the mindless singing and worn-out teachings of these gatherings. And since his return, they'd become unbearable. He could not longer hold in his views. "Please hear my hear my heart. The Volume promises a power from a world beyond, but the meetings seemed to contain so little of that power." Now that he'd experienced the realm of the gem and the power that was there, he found those promises even emptier.

Kreswen's voice rang with displeasure at his son's attitude. "Don't tell me that, young man! It's enough that you've been gone for days without letting us know where you were, and then the way you embarrassed us last time by leaving the Gathering. I don't want to hear that kind of talk this evening."

Bracken had surprised his parents at the last meeting by getting up in the middle of the care-speaker's message and leaving. As good as the leader's intentions seemed, the whole message was no longer connecting.

"Please, Bracken," injected Myrus, her brow wrinkling slightly. "Your father's right, it was embarrassing. Now please don't make matters worse by being this way." Myrus rose and walked over to her son, resting a motherly hand upon his arm.

Bracken's tone softened slightly under his mother's touch. "I'm sorry, Mother! But I've made up my mind. There's just nothing here for me anymore. I see things differently now."

Bracken's patience was running out. He felt like his mother's affection was suffocating him. He looked at the worn Volume lying in the chair where she had left it. "For instance, that silly book you read all the time. Don't you see there's more to life than those dead, old sayings you treasure so much?" Bracken broke off suddenly, thinking before he made his next statement.

Kreswen seemed to calm down a bit, his tone more confused and hurt than angry, "I just can't understand why you're acting this way, Son. I could possibly understand your point if going there wasn't so important for your future. But like your mother always says, the writings of the Volume have more than temporary value."

The note of gentle concern in Kreswen's voice made it all the harder for Bracken to respond. "I know all those things, Father. I simply don't believe them anymore. Sometimes, I'm not too sure you do yourself," he added harshly.

"You know better than to talk to your father like that," interrupted Myrus, taking her hand from his arm. "Now I want you to apologize for your attitude." The atmosphere was growing tense again.

Bracken's rebellion solidified. "I can't, Mother. That's the way I honestly feel, and I'm not going to change. In fact, there's something more I've got to tell you." He hesitated, looking at these two people he both loved and resented; Kreswen, with his unyielding but fatherly way, and Myrus, who cared too much sometimes. Stress had drawn a grim picture on their normally pleasant faces. "I'm leaving Tizra tonight," announced Bracken abruptly.

The room grew completely still, his parents reeling from the surprise. "Where are you going, Bracken?" Kreswen finally managed.

"To Accad, Father. Silas and Lisha are going with me. We'll find a new life there and new friends as well." He was sure his two friends must be having similar confrontations with their parents right about now. "There's another type of gathering there. It's called the Community, and they're like a family to one another. They've come from all over Nerkush. It's as if we realize it's time now for our generation. We wish to build a new world together, one that's not in the image of the old with the dictates of the Fathers ..."

Bracken pointed toward the sacred book. His jaw clenched in anger for a moment, and he said firmly, "and the worn-out ideals that come from the Volume."

Kreswen's eyes seemed to flash with anger, but then his features took on a resigned look and he said gently, "You're of age now, and we can't stop you. You'll have to leave your trans-rig here with us, though, until you've paid off your part of it."

Bracken felt helpless at these words, but his frustration quickly turned to resentment when he realized his father was playing the last card he held to keep his son from leaving. Angrily, he pushed by his parents and ran to his room, collecting his stam and the things he had packed earlier.

Ditten and Kempec stood in the doorway of their bedchambers, somewhat stunned by what they had overheard but aware that it was the inevitable result of what they had seen growing in their brother for some time.

Bracken stopped and hugged each of them but then quickly headed for the front door. His rage reached the boiling point as he grabbed the entry latch. "All I can say," growled Bracken, as he pulled the door open, "is that it doesn't matter to me if I ever see either of you again." With that, he stomped out.

Kreswen and Myrus slowly came to the threshold and watched as their eldest son moved quickly out of sight down the tree-lined street. Above, the sun had spattered high clouds with bits of red and purple, almost as if they'd been bruised by the angry scene Bracken had left behind.

But Bracken felt only a sense of exhilaration as he walked away. He was on his own at last. He could walk the road he chose now, a road that was soon to turn in a direction he'd never been before, a path leading into the unknown and to another world.

CHAPTER 39

HIGH REALM

LYNREXS (MID-SUMMER), 5512

A circular array of brilliant white wings, like a white flower closing for the night, came together at the foot of the One whose voice walked among them. Above them, a remote canopy of stars formed a vivid cathedral of light. These ancient beacons stood as a witness to the words now spoken. "I've heard your thoughts, and you misunderstand. Yes, echoes of the past hostility have found access through this young one. Sadly some of his statements are true. But even as the foe moves to splinter the harmony of his loved ones, there are other agents who move in that world. I will guide them. They will know what to say. Of course you remember that nothing surprises me, even when members of your own ranks rose up, it eventually fulfilled my purpose. I knew it was coming because I stand above and beyond it."

A murmur of understanding from the folded pinions fluttered like a breeze across petals of lace. But such was the strength of these beings that on Ebbern this murmur would be considered a mighty wind.

"The power that I've endued you with is only a hint of what awaits those below who come near to me. There will be a day when this wanderer and many like him will discover again what has been lost for generations."

These words inspired a melody of praise from beneath the feathered cluster. The throng of voices built slowly to a crescendo until it seemed to rattle the distant stars.

"With this discovery will come a melodic sound that has been waiting for an epoch to arise. It will join yours and break the chains of those in darkness."

The strain of voices continued, assurance evident now in each inflection.

"So, continue in the confidence I have given you. Many others who have never seen your kind believe in the one who commands you. They are the *old ones* who remember the ancient promises hidden in my words. They can bring to the forefront the memories of a past generation that knew my power. They may be old, but in their words are seeds that will grow until they accomplish the purpose that is embedded in each passage. These *old ones* are my emissaries too and they will succeed."

The murmur moved once again, and now the flutter was a symphony that none below could even imagine. If they had heard it, their souls would have been lifted as if by a force of nature beyond their world.

CHAPTER 40

TIZRA

LYNREXS (MID-SUMMER), 5512

Bracken made his way toward a small farm that lay near the outskirts of Tizra. Even though he was still angry with his parents, his initial rage had quieted, and a mellower attitude had come over him as he'd walked through the placid lanes of his humble town. Their peacefulness stilled his displeasure, and in those moments of grace he remembered his grandparents. So he'd resolved not to leave without seeing them.

Immediately after he'd left his home, Bracken had contacted Silas, and Lisha through their com-patches. He'd told them that he no longer had his trans-rig and that they'd all have to catch a ride to Accad. They'd agreed to meet at the big shiferen tree near the outskirts of Tizra later that day.

Bracken loved to visit his grandparents' home because it was so tranquil, and he needed to calm himself. They had tilled the soil of their fertile land for most of their lives. He had many fond memories of summers spent there working the fields and tending the livestock with his grandfather, Srenken. He recalled how at the end of each day, his grandmother, Ysinta, had brought them cooled mugs of keptim milk from the chilled vats she kept in her cellar. He and Srenken would sit watching the colors change against the eastern hills as Ebbern's sun moved slowly toward the horizon.

Srenken always had a story or history lesson that captivated Bracken and was quick with a solution to queries that his grandson would bring up. Once again, Bracken trusted that his grandfather would also have answers to some of the questions he was dealing with now. He was confident that his elders' wisdom would still the fears, anger, and conflicts that stirred in him.

He followed the tree-lined streets of Tizra until they dissolved into unpaved lanes shrouded by fields of grain. His grandparents' house sat squarely in the midst of one of these, nestled beneath tishwood trees with several fenced barns and outbuildings scattered nearby. He walked up the steps to the aged house, the creaking slats on its porch announcing his arrival. He didn't need to knock. Instead he called out the names of his loved ones as he opened the huge oaken door at the front of the house.

As his words echoed through the ancient dwelling, he considered again why he'd come. The previous confrontation had left him rattled. He needed a wiser, more mature person to speak to his issues. He knew he would find it here.

Why couldn't his parents give him room to explore what he had discovered? Why were they so rigid in their views? Then there were the encounters with otherworldly forces that had left him so mystified. It all seemed exciting and stimulating to his adventurous side, but it also left him troubled. He was sure Srenken would have some jewel of wisdom to set him at ease.

"We're back here," called Ysinta, her sweet voice comforting and familiar. "We've just started to eat."

"I know," called Bracken toward the source of the earlier call, "I smelled your sumptuous cooking the moment I opened the front door." Leaving his stam and the things he'd packed for his trip by the front door, he made his way through the hallway. As he did, he passed by rooms on both sides, each filled with well-kept antique furniture crowned with a thin layer of dust.

Both grandparents rose from their places at the table and greeted him as he entered the eating room. "Oh, Bracken, it's lovely to see you," said Ysinta as she drew him close.

He felt her tiny but sturdy frame beneath her simple clothing, its strength a testimony to her years of labor and self-discipline. Her sun-worn face spoke of the decades spent toiling beside her husband, but it also held a radiance that testified of an inner light.

Srenken's face matched his wife's in years, but his huge body and ample arms overwhelmed Bracken as he smothered him in a firm embrace. "So, the wanderer has returned," said Srenken. "Myrus told us you've been to Accad recently and even as far south as Shidow. Sounds like you've had some interesting adventures. Sit down and tell us all about them." He motioned to an empty chair and spoke to Ysinta. "Bring our traveler something to eat, and I'm sure he'd love some cool keptim milk as well."

"I'd love some," said Bracken. "It's been too long since I've had the joy of its tingling chill soothing my parched throat."

"How's the family?" ask Srenken. "I haven't seen Kreswen since the last harvest. He must be busy with his teaching and writing."

Bracken understood the hidden message in his grandfather's words. Other priorities had come into all of their lives and the schedules of those priorities put demands on all of them. He asked himself why he hadn't made this journey sooner. "They're all well, Grandpa, just busy. My brothers are busy with their schooling and athletics. Of course, Mother wants to be at all of their activities. I guess she's staying in touch with you, though. I don't know exactly what Father is working on now, but he's hoping this year's research will get him the advanced degree he's been laboring on for years. He deserves it. I just wish things were more like when I was younger. You know, when he and I had time to explore Deep Forest together. Mother has prodded him to take the whole family on a trip there for years, but we just don't seem to get around to it."

Ysinta set a steaming plate of food in front of Bracken, matched with a full mug of chilled keptim. He took a long drink of the cool liquid before starting in on his food. "Well, since you haven't seen me in a while either, I'm sure you're wondering what's brought me all the way out here."

Srenken turned to his mate with a smile that invited her response. "Yes, it's been a while, and last year we only saw you once. We understand you have other interests now, but we'll miss your help when the harvest comes this season."

"I know, Grandma, and you know how I've always helped you in the past. As hard as it is every year, I've enjoyed it, especially the evenings when I had time to hear Grandpa's wisdom. I'm sure Ditten will be as great a help as I've been in the past. But I've got a lot going on now. New friends, new ideas. There's so much happening across Nerkush these days, so many changes taking place."

"We've heard about some of those changes, Bracken," said Srenken, "but as strange as they may seem, they're really nothing all that new. Each generation has had to face its challenges and upheavals. The sad thing is, when these issues arise, people are quick to cast aside the wisdom of their elders. It's almost as if they can't learn anything from both the right choices and the mistakes of their forefathers."

"But this time it's different, Grandfather," said Bracken. "You see, I've had some encounters recently that have made me doubt most of what I learned years ago from Mother and Father. I know they meant well, but their ideas just seem like fantasies now. The same with some of the 'truths' the mind-training instructors and High Council leaders cling to. They link their arms against any change. But it's not working anymore. That's why a whole generation now seems on the brink of a new age."

"Like I said, Bracken, none of this is really new. I remember when Kreswen went through a similar search to the one you're taking now. Myrus told us about a lot of the conflict in your family. But again, it's nothing new. It's simply a journey of discovery. We've all made it at one time or another. My elders didn't like some of the things I proposed in my day either. It's not that we don't learn new things as time goes by, but I need to add a warning here. It's just that with each new set of ideals there are also dangers. One of the greatest of these is the subtle pride that comes with the idea that no one's ever seen it the way we do now."

"I can understand, Grandpa, but what do you think of the reports that the High Council is deploying the World Destroyer Weapon again? Our enemies across the Sea of Auren now have the capacity with similar armaments to bring destruction on whole cities. We can no longer count on the great waters that separate us to keep us safe."

"Yes, I understand it's a different world. Our sci-tec discoveries have made things more dangerous. But it's always been dangerous when we give in to greed and violence. You know the history of Ebbern. We had wars within our own borders that resulted in a whole generation nearly being wiped out."

Bracken listened intently to his grandfather, taking eager bites of the delicious food. He loved and admired his grandparents. Everything about them from their peaceful farm to the food that now warmed his stomach was a testament to the quality of their lives. He could never deny that, even if he thought their sheltered existence in this idyllic place left them out of touch.

Bracken took another long drink on his beverage. Then he looked intently at his grandfather and almost whispered, "You know, Grandpa, that I've always respected you and Grandma. You've always been there for my family and me. You have great wisdom, and up till now I would never have doubted it. But things have changed radically on Ebbern in these last few years. I feel like we're on the verge of something potentially devastating and that our world is coming to a point of no return. If something radical isn't done soon, there won't be another generation to enjoy our lovely planet. You know as well as anyone what the destroyer weapon can do. If enough of them are ignited, it could easily sear our entire planet. We'd be just one great big heap of charred ash drifting in space forever. I know your generation had its wars, but it never had the power to destroy the entire globe. That's why I think all these strange things I've encountered have started to occur now."

Srenken leaned toward his grandson, a new intensity in his voice. "Strange things? What sort of strange things?"

Bracken hesitated momentarily before replying. He'd not shared any of these things with his family, even the encounter with the strange disk in the night sky years ago. It had been a secret that he and Silas had been afraid to reveal. He'd kept it all in but now he didn't care. He wasn't sure if his grandfather would believe him, but then he remembered that he had always been able to share with him even when he told him odd things. Like the stories about the chi-wogs he and Silas found deep in the caves near Rimlex, where they had explored in one of their early adventures. Even though the chi-wogs had escaped on the way home and in spite of the fact that most people believed the little creatures had become extinct years ago, his grandfather had believed his tales.

With that memory fresh in his mind, Bracken responded. "Silas and I were out on one of our wanderings. It happened one night several years ago when we were camping in the hills above town. A glowing disk appeared in the night sky and seemed to sing to us. Then it flew away at a speed that none of our flying craft could even come close to. I know it probably sounds crazy, but it was real. Then there are other things ..."

Bracken stopped for a moment, not sure if he should go on. But Srenken encouraged him, "Go ahead, son, we're listening," he said, turning toward Ysinta with a look of concern.

"Then I've had encounters with the Mingus stone. It took me to places I could never have imagined. It changed me, opened me to a whole new way of looking at life and the beauty of our planet." Bracken spoke faster as he warmed to his subject. "Then I visited a place called Vonervyn. It's a world I find hard to describe. I traveled there through an inter-dimensional portal that opened with a spoken command. Its entrance is hidden in the Forest of Zorek. But, again it's another encounter that made me realize that things are not what they appear. There are other realms and other worlds that have made me see our own in a completely different way." Bracken was suddenly aware that he'd poured out a huge amount of information, a lot of it strange, to his grandparents in a short time. He was concerned now that he'd overdone it and even brought up things that they'd probably never heard of. So he was suprized by his grandfather's reponse.

Srenken also took a deep drink of keptim and after setting it down returned Bracken's gaze. "You may think we're isolated, Bracken, but we get the news even out here at the peaceful edge of Tizra. We've heard of some of these things. I've read about them in articles in our local print. The vid-tel commentators have also explained this Mingus Effect. But we've heard it's dangerous, Bracken."

"No, no, no, Grandpa. It's not that. Of course I want to discuss that issue with you as well. But I wasn't under the influence of the gem when I encountered the disk, and it didn't take a magic stone to open Vonervyn to me."

"Okay, son, I'll take your word for it for now." Srenken folded his hands and rested them on the table. He looked over at Bracken's grandmother intently and then slowly turned his loving but serious gaze back to his grandson. "You may not have known this, Bracken, but I've always believed that there are many forces hidden from us, and yes, there are other dimensions like the ones I've heard about with this gem's influence. Ones that we can see and others we can't except by some unique revelation. But there are pitfalls on these pathways, and you need another kind of 'road map' when you journey there. Not everything that feels right is right. Some of the roads lead to death."

Somewhat surprised by his grandfather's sudden candor, Bracken stared back at Srenken with a puzzled look. "No, you never spoke of these things before, Grandpa. Why not?"

"Well, simply speaking, I didn't think you were ready for them. But it's apparent that's all changed now."

"So what are these 'road maps' you're talking about?"

Srenken got up from his place at the table and went into the other room, returning with an old but well-kept copy of the Volume in his hands. Bracken had seen his grandfather reading from it many times over the years. He'd read Bracken the stories from its pages when he was young, and as a child he'd been fascinated by them. But now, as he had told his parents so many times, they were just clever but empty stories like many of the legends that had come down through time from Ebbern's many philosophers and keepers of history.

Bracken was sure that he was about to get a lecture like the ones that Kreswen had given him recently. He almost got up from the table to leave, but something seemed to hold him there. Maybe it was his thirst for another draft of his grandmother's beverage, or maybe it was the sincere look on the faces of his grandparents that brought a sudden peace to the moment.

Srenken set the ancient Volume down and placed his hand gently on top of it. "You see, Bracken, your father's generation could have experienced the sort of things you speak of, things from other dimensions. The words of this book teach us about special gifts."

"What kinds of gifts, Grandpa?"

"Gifts that give us unique abilities. Abilities to understand hidden things through visions and dreams. The capacity to know the future along with insights into the secrets of people's hearts. The skill to perform miracles and signs that will amaze, and even a talent to bring the healing of disease. These may not be exactly the ones you're encountering now and maybe not the same way you're experiencing them, but they chose to ignore similar things."

"Why did they ignore them?

"They chose to pursued the comforts of this life first. Perhaps it was the hard times of the Greatfall when food was scarce and we had so few things in this world to enjoy. I can understand why they made such choices. Hunger and fear can make the most committed of us change our ways even while we hold onto the shadow of our former beliefs. But those beliefs were founded on real things, Bracken. They knew that there were whole realms for them to explore if they took the promises of the Volume to heart.

"New realms. That's what I'm trying to tell you. That's what I've been discovering, and now you're telling me that the Volume talks about such things?"

Srenken lightly tapped the cover of the sacred book with his hand. "Exactly. Where do you think the truth-seers discovered the words they shared with us in these writings? Some of them encountered beings from other realms. Some experienced visions. Maybe different than the ones you've described to us today. But they were powerful encounters that changed them and gave us this book. Some were even lifted into the sky by a force beyond our realm and saw things of such beauty that words were not fit to explain."

"But that was all so long ago. It sounds to me like little more than myths and empty tales. Besides, don't some of the teachers at our Gathering Day say that all those things ceased in times past?"

"Yes, but your grandmother and I know that's not true. We saw these sorts of things when we were young. There were teachers then that plumbed the depths of this book and found reasons to believe that those abilities had not died out, they had merely been neglected and forgotten."

"Then why didn't you search them out and bring them forth to others in our time?"

"Sadly other things pushed all that aside. I watched it happen to so many of us who had once hoped in these wonders the Volume promised."

"What sorts of things would make you neglect such gifts?"

"You see, Nerkush became prosperous again and dominated Ebbern with its military, we felt secure. Our nations had the destroyer weapon, and the rest of Ebbern was afraid of us. Soon simple pleasures were replaced with more expensive ones, and before long no one wanted to live without them. We were soon content to seek comforts and pleasures in the things we could see and touch. And our sci-tec philosophers told us that the sort of promises the Volume held were just myths like so many other legends from our past. But of course that's all changing now. With the possible threat of Ebbern's annihilation, your generation is looking for answers. My only concern is that you're seeking them in the wrong places."

Bracken was stunned. In all his years with his grandparents, he'd never heard them talk to him like this. "I can't believe you're telling me all this now. Why didn't you before?" Did you really think I wasn't ready to hear these sorts of things, Grandpa?"

"Bracken, I guess I had lost faith in the promises of this book as well. It's been so long since I've heard anyone really believe that there's any real power here."

"I can understand that. All it's ever been to me is exciting stories and good sayings. You see, I've experienced things in the realm of the gem you can't imagine. It's true, and I've encountered a reality there that I believe could give Nerkush and Ebbern the answers that we desperately need right now."

"I can understand how you feel, son. But be careful—not all the 'truth' you experience is real. I don't fully understand these realms you speak of, but one thing I want you to remember—the Dark One can put on light like a mask. In all your adventures be aware of this, and remember, as powerless as the promises of the Volume seem to you now, the Prince of

Wonder is real. This I know for certain, even if many of us did not see that power in our day."

Bracken emptied the remains of his beverage. Perhaps Srenken was right. Maybe there was some sort of power in the promises of the ancient book that rested under Grandfather's hand, but he'd never seen it and he wasn't about to believe it now. He looked back at his grandparents with a sincere longing, grateful for their love and concern but still doubtful. He realized that if he were to explore the claims they'd made about the Volume, it would take time, time he didn't have, time that none of his generation had. They must act now on what they knew was real and change the course of things before it was too late, before the disaster he saw coming arrived.

"What you've said sounds interesting, Grandpa, but it all seems too familiar and rather mundane. Thanks for sharing, but I must follow my heart."

Looking out the window, Bracken realized the light outside signaled that sunset was not far off. He must be moving on. It was clear that he'd have to hurry if they hoped to catch a ride on the highway before dusk.

Bracken rose from his place at the table, his chair scraping across the floor. "I'll remember what you've said, Grandpa, but I need to be going now. I know one thing for sure—I must follow the path I'm on for now. Thanks for listening to me, but I need to leave. I'll be back, and I'll let you know what I find in the strange new worlds I'm exploring."

Bracken realized he'd been abrupt, but he sensed an urgency in his mind and knew he must move on. He knew his grandparents would understand his eagerness to head out on this great adventure. They'd always been willing to support his quests, and this time would be no different.

Srenken and Ysinta walked Bracken to the door, where he collected his things and said good-bye.

They stood for a long time, watching him make his way through the fields glowing golden in the late afternoon sun. Then they turned and quietly walked back into their home, shutting the giant door behind them.

CHAPTER 41

PLAINS OF UMIN

LYNREXS (MID-SUMMER), 5512

The road to Accad passed near the Pillars of Rimlex. This odd configuration of granite hills rose like rows of broken teeth from the rolling plains of Umin. Great fields of grain made a patchwork that, seen from the air during the day, spread like a quilt over the fertile prairie. At its center, a broad winding river meandered like a lazy snake crawling toward the sea.

Bracken sat musing at the side of the road, still slightly angry over the plight of having to leave his trans-rig behind. He was also feeling some remorse for his harsh tone with his parents. They had been so good to him over the years, and he cared for them deeply; but as great as all their love was, it couldn't help him now. He had to follow what he felt was the path opening before him and others his age. No doubt he'd come back to Tizra and visit his parents. There'd be time for reconciliation then.

Even though it had been late in the day, Bracken, Lisha, and Silas had caught a ride from a friendly farmer just as they were hiking out of Tizra. After a long drive he had dropped them off at an intersection near the Pillars and then headed west toward his ranch.

It was dark now, and the starry heaven gave off the only light, as the tail lamps of the farmer's vehicle grew smaller in the distance. All three of Ebbern's moons were on the far side of the planet. Nightfall seemed to close in like a murky blanket and with it a sense of foreboding settled over the three of them. The stars that had at first looked warm now appeared cold and eerie. Something strange seemed to be making its way toward them.

Not far from the perimeter of the Pillars rose a small knoll garnished by a few lonely trees. Hoping it would provide more shelter and privacy for the night's rest, Bracken and his friends headed off across the fields being careful not to disturb the ripening grain.

No sooner had they settled beneath the sprawling oaks than guide-beams from a group of trans-rigs appeared in the distance. Coming from the direction of Tizra, they slowed as they approached the intersection. Instead of turning to the west as the previous vehicle had, they took a small dirt road to the east that passed near their clump of trees. Unsure of the nature of the caravan, Bracken's group remained secluded as the line of what now appeared to be four trans-rigs rumbled by them on the rough road. The vehicles came to a stop just beneath the base of the Pillars.

Silas squinted into the night trying to make out the scene more clearly. "Seems strange that anybody would be out here this late. Who do you think they are?"

Bracken crouched beside his friend, not answering until the vehicles had moved on. "I don't know. It could just be a party group looking for a secluded spot for a good time." Bracken led his friends out from beneath the trees and stared off toward the rough peaks. Faint echoes came from the group as they left their rigs and began to hike up the small ravine. Passing between two of the larger pillars, they vanished down the other side.

Quietly, Lisha came up behind Bracken. "I don't see any festivities. It seems rather odd. I'd like to know what's going on."

"I agree with Lisha," Silas said. "One of those rigs looks a lot like one I've seen around the Advanced Mind-Training Center. It's white tail section stands out even in this light. Maybe they're a part of the strange group I've heard rumors about. You know, the one Professor Lieter started." Silas's voice took on a mocking tone. "Several have said they meet out here to connect with the 'space' beings." Maybe if we get a little closer we can find out what they're up to?"

Bracken shrugged. "Okay, we'll check it out. But I don't want to be discovered butting in where I'm not wanted." Bracken took Lisha's hand and squeezed it tightly. "Come on then! Follow me, but let's be careful not to make a lot of noise." Quietly, the trio headed off toward the pillars.

Cautiously, they moved up the path that the others had taken, following the trail between the high rock outcroppings. The ragged pillars, lit only by the distant stars, seemed to stare down at them like stoic sentinels who at any movement could come to life and forbid them from passing. As they neared the top, Bracken whispered, "Remember, let's keep quiet and make sure you don't dislodge any loose rocks."

Creeping to the tip of the ridge between the two pillars, they carefully peered over. The sight that greeted them seemed to confirm Silas's suspicions. A stone's throw away, the mysterious group sat on a large flat rock talking amongst themselves, their voices only slightly audible to Bracken's group. One of the students, a square-shouldered youth, was addressing the professor. "Dr. Lieter, how long do we have to wait? I don't mean to sound impatient, but we've been here several times now and not seen what you've promised." The young man's concern had a hint of pride in it. He obviously wasn't the type who liked to be embarrassed, and after all their previous trips here others back at the school had started to question the group's hopes.

"As I told you before, it may be several hours or merely a few minutes." Frim's high voice was gentle and encouraging, like that of a true believer.

Lieter had brought them here several times without results and the group had grown more skeptical with each trip. When they'd first arrived here weeks before, they'd been full of faith. But from what he felt tonight, this could possibly be the last time they'd be willing to take such an outing. Frim could sense their doubt as he listened to them chat quietly amongst themselves. Some, though, seemed to believe in spite of previous disappointments, for they were focused on the night sky, scanning the horizon from one end to the other. These were the ones Frim had great hope for. They would become contacts like him, true believers in the message of the Disk People. Gradually, though, as all of them lingered, a calm came over the group almost as if the starlight had cast a magic powder on them. It increased until an overwhelming feeling began to fill the night air, slowly encouraging them to lay aside their doubts.

"Be patient, Yono, this will be a good chance for you to do some firsthand study of the heavens. Note the large constellation immediately to the south of the Starry Pitcher." The teacher extended his thin index finger toward another bright configuration that formed a triangular shape with a dusty spray of stars at it center. "Can anyone tell me about the nature of this system—its name, number of stars, relative individual size, distance from our planet, number of solar systems?"

A murmur went through the group of students as they hurriedly refreshed one another's memories. "All right, who will be the first to answer?" questioned Lieter, his thin frame silhouetted against the bejeweled night sky.

A rather stocky but intelligent-looking girl responded first. She pushed her sight assisters up on the bridge of her nose as she began. "That is the Trion Star System, sir." The girl had an oddly deep voice. "Most astrogazers estimate that it contains at least seven hundred stellar bodies, although they haven't been able to arrive at an exact figure because of an unusual tendency that leaves whole sections in a cosmic cloud. I believe Professor Glinit has developed a theory concerning this particular effect. Am I right, Professor?" The girl looked at Lieter, confident that she was correct, her round face shining like a small moon in the dim light.

Frim was obviously pleased by his pupil's eager knowledge. "That's right, Catine. Because of that cloud, many theories have emerged about what's at its center. Go on." Catine continued reciting her well-learned facts.

Back on the ridge, Bracken turned a cynical look toward his companions. "See, Silas, there's nothing strange going on here. Look at their teacher pointing out constellations to them. It's just a group of students from the Training Center on a field outing probably waiting for some meteor shower the professor has promised them."

"I know. I can see for myself," said Silas, looking dejected. "I guess we'd better go back and get some rest. Sorry, Bracken ..."

"It's okay, Silas. You know I'm always up for investigating strange things, but this just doesn't look like one."

As the three companions began to creep slowly away from the ledge, they were startled as one of the students shouted. His cry was loud enough that Bracken and his friends could clearly hear his words. "Look! Professor Lieter!" The students and their teacher jumped up and turned toward the eastern horizon. A shining disk of light was rapidly approaching, skimming over the distant fields. The whole group seemed frozen with wonder by the sight. Only Lieter had the composure to speak. "You see, Yono, it's just as I told you; they have come, we just had to be patient. They promised me they'd appear, now that I've been made a contact." The professor sounded satisfied. He was basking in the glory of the approaching revelation. "They've homed in on my mind waves. Soon they'll be speaking to you through me."

"Why's that, Professor? Why can't they speak to us directly?"

"They don't generally communicate through vocal language like we do. Until mental contact is established, I'll be their mouthpiece."

Now convinced of the unusual nature of the situation, Bracken and his group cautiously climbed back to their observation post and watched in amazement as the glowing disk neared the group below them. A loud hum pushed away the previous stillness. The space vehicle filled the whole sky as it came to hover a short ten yards from where the students stood. Without warning, a beam of light shot from its surface, focusing on Frim Lieter's entranced face. His whole frame appeared like a suddenly metamorphic butterfly, glowing in the light of a new day. He began to speak, his voice amplified and its suddenly strong tones clear, carrying easily as far as Bracken's group. Captivated by the professor's transformation, the group's attention shifted from the space disk to their teacher. An ominous voice issued from his vocal chords, so unlike their usually squeaky dissonance. "Be restful, friends!" the deep voice comforted. "We are among you for your own good."

The soothing modulations played a peaceful tune on the tense strings of the watchers' anxieties. Gradually, they began to relax.

"As Professor Lieter told you earlier, this is a contact gathering. Some of you did not believe him. That is understandable."

Bracken crept closer, awed by the sight. Frim stood firm, a gleaming sentinel of another dimension, illuminating the darkened landscape around him. The voice went on. "You are not the first to hold such questions, but now it is time to let such destructive thoughts vanish."

Catine looked at the disk nervously and then back to the professor. "Who are you?"

"As your instructor told you earlier, we are the inhabitants of the Trion Stellar System. Some of your race have labeled us Trionites. We have come to bring you to a higher level and stop the path of destruction your planet's leaders are on."

Yono stepped out of the group and advanced hesitantly toward the glowing orb. "Then you've really come to help us, just like he said?"

"Certainly, and let this be a lesson to you. Such men as Professor Lieter are of great importance to your world. You should have trusted him more completely. We don't mean to scold, though, merely to encourage."

Once again, Catine stared up at the glistening object, her round face reflecting its light. "Will we be able to be like Professor Lieter?" she asked eagerly. "I mean, able to contact you and make others aware of your purpose?"

"Yes," the graceful voice instructed. "All of you may become contacts if you so desire. Something I hope you all will do. There appears little time for your race if such a response does not come from more of your people." Several clicks and whirls sounded inside the disk. "We will take you aboard now. And after a briefing on our goals, we will perform a simple procedure that will allow you to become contacts like professor Lieter. So, let us proceed with the matters at hand. In a moment you …" the voice stopped abruptly.

Slowly, almost as if he were mounted on a swivel, Frim turned and faced the ridge behind which Bracken and his friends were crouched. "Our sensors perceive the presence of others beyond that rise."

Another beam of light leaped from the surface of the disk, illuminating Bracken's trio. The voice intoned again, and increased a note of firmness in its still gentle flow. "Come out! You won't be harmed. We intend only peace."

CHAPTER 42

PILLARS OF RIMLEX

LYNREXS (MID-SUMMER), 5512

At first, Bracken and his friends felt compelled to run, but realizing the bright light of the craft exposed them, the three obediently but warily scrambled over the rocky rise into the view of the entire group. "We didn't realize what was going on," declared Silas as they drew closer to the group, a look of stunned embarrassment on his normally placid face. "We'll be happy to leave and never mention a thing we've seen."

"That won't be necessary," the oracle replied calmly. "We can easily erase your memory of this incident if we so desire." The voice stopped for a moment and then went on, the ominous syllables somewhat warmer. "But maybe there is another alternative. Our scanners tell us that you've heard our offer to the others through Professor Lieter. Perhaps you desire to join those who are becoming contacts."

Lisha and Silas, completely unsettled by the chilling encounter, drew back at the offer, but surprisingly, Bracken stepped forward. "I'd like to know more about this. If you can stop Nerkush from its senseless drive toward destruction, I'm interested. It's good to discover a force that's seeking to increase awareness among the men on this planet—even an alien force."

Bracken could hardly believe he was speaking with such boldness, but since he'd had a touch of the gem and stepped into the world of Vonervyn, strange things like this didn't frighten him, in fact they stimulated him. And since he'd cut his ties with his family, he was ready for any new adventure.

Almost as if the Trionite sensed Bracken's eagerness, it responded pleasantly through the professor. "Very well, then, you may come. What about your friends?

Both Silas and Lisha shook their heads no. "It appears they've decided not to. Then your friends can remain behind. We have no desire to force our way on your people. The process will only take a few hours. You'll be back with them soon."

Anxiety covered Lisha's face as she stared at Bracken. "What do you think you're doing?" she moaned. Her limits were already stretched by the stress of leaving Tizra, and now this encounter was pushing her toward a crisis.

"She's right, Bracken," Silas said, staring up at the bright, hovering oval. "You don't know what will happen to you if you enter that thing." Silas was up for the initial adventure that had prompted them to leave Tizra, but ever since their encounter years before with the glowing object in the night sky, he'd been haunted by a deep fear. He'd never revealed it to Bracken, but it was always there, just faintly perceptible beneath the surface. Now, with the hovering object's appearance at such close proximity, his worry emerged full-blown.

Bracken turned to his friends with confidence. "If they wanted to harm us, I'm sure from what we've already seen they would have little trouble doing so. If you don't want to go, fine, but please let me. You two are starting to sound like my parents." Bracken's voice took on an unusually crisp authority. "It's time people stopped worrying about themselves and started doing something to change the foolish destiny of this planet."

Both Silas and Lisha looked taken aback by Bracken's newfound authority. But instead of driving them away, it seemed to draw them toward Bracken. "Okay, if you—"

The alien voice came to life again, interrupting their conversation. "I'm glad to see you're coming. Your friends have no need to worry. You'll be returned safely in a while. This is the first phase of the process and only takes a brief time." Lieter had begun to move toward the glowing craft, speaking as he walked. "Please follow the professor."

Inside the space disk, the series of clicking and whirring sounds continued as servo-drive motors came to life. Gradually its smooth surface was broken, as the outline of a rectangular opening appeared. A gleaming metallic stairway extended itself slowly to the ground. A faint green light illuminated a corridor, stretching back from the craft's entrance. An almost human creature, his body layered with a glistening garment, stood by it, extending a welcoming arm toward them.

Frim stepped up the stairway, confident from his earlier experiences with the Trionite. The others followed, somewhat shakily, but eagerly interested. At the top of the stairway, their alien host introduced himself to each of the group as Talay and then asked for each of their names in return. Bracken was the last to vanish through the door of the floating spaceship as Lisha and Silas watched anxiously below. The stairway retracted and the hatch closed, sealing with a hiss.

"I hope he'll be all right," whispered Lisha.

Silas muttered half-heartedly, "Well, all we can do now is trust that these aliens will keep their word."

Lisha looked dejectedly at the disk. Now that Bracken was gone, and his confident attitude was no longer there to assuage her, Lisha wondered where all of this was leading. As benevolent as these beings appeared, that alone was not enough to calm her doubts. She wondered what their ultimate intentions were. And why was Bracken so trusting? Maybe it was all the experiences he'd had in the strange new realms he'd been exploring. But what about her feelings? What about her opinion? She wasn't used to her point of view being so quickly ignored. Then on top of that he'd left her alone. She felt momentarily abandoned.

That thought brought a bitter memory. *Just like my Father*, she couldn't help thinking. Yes, that was exactly how she'd felt when her father abandoned the family for his business. Now Bracken was abandoning her for this latest thrill. She loved his taste for adventure, but this was a little too much. She could forgive him, sure, but seeds of doubt began to grow in her heart. Even if she wouldn't admit it to herself, she needed security along with adventure.

Silas's words interrupted her thoughts. "Bracken acts a little crazy at times, but I guess he's got to be his own man."

"I know, but I was hoping he'd consider me now that ..." The sudden increased hum of the saucer's power source drowned out her last words. Bracken's two companions watched as the disk climbed back into the sky and vanished over the horizon, their hearts full of wonder but also apprehension.

Inside the speeding ship Bracken felt his body pressed heavily into the comfortable seat his Trionite host had offered him. The others in the group were seated beside him, their chairs forming a circle facing the being who had welcomed them aboard. Their host's body only seemed slightly affected by the g-forces that pushed down on them like a massive hand. They watched in awe as the expansive landscape beneath them appeared on a large three dimensional view-projection suspended above their host.

As inspiring as the sight on the viewer was, Bracken found his new surroundings of equal interest. The interior of the craft was a world of its own. Uniquely designed alloy-like panels with opaque rectangles of green light dotting them, ran from ceiling to floor. Their pale illumination cast an ethereal atmosphere over the chamber. Elsewhere, readouts blinked on instrument panels before the watchful eyes of the several aliens seated in front of them. Undoubtedly, they monitored the speed and navigation of the spacecraft. Near the doorway stood a lone alien. His hands operated a hexagonal panel studded with various markings mounted beside squares of colored light. The spacious room reflected the aura of a technology that had reached its apex. Some of the things appeared similar to the technology that was currently in Nerkush but other systems around him were unlike anything he could imagine.

Periodically, through their flight, the Trionite host who stood facing the group communicated with his guests. He was no longer using the professor, though, but implanted his words directly into his listeners' minds. "As I mentioned when you entered, my name is Talay." His thoughts were pleasant, but Bracken felt a sense of apprehension. Something wasn't quite right. Even though he was in awe of the being and the technology all around him, still deep inside he felt a bit uneasy. It must just be the newness of his surroundings, Bracken told himself. Besides, he'd been unsure in Dalfang's presence while he waited for the gate to open. Now he had to overcome some unbelief again.

The alien smiled placidly. His eyes were narrow ovals coming to a peak at the top, almost like teardrops. "Your planet appears to be a lovely place from this vantage point. It's sad that such is not the case in reality." The alien's mental conversation seemed to rise like sparkling bubbles in Bracken's thoughts. "Yours is not a unique problem. In the known universe, we have discovered several other planets that have similar crises occurring upon them. Each of them has come to the brink of destroying themselves."

Talay's smile dimmed a little at this point. His thin, bony hands were clasped gently together across his waist. "They'd developed a technology they were neither willing nor capable of controlling. But we've been successful in changing their destructive course. Members of their race became contacts, and soon they turned the tide. We sent them out as heralds of peace and empowered them with an authority that convinced even the most skeptical in their world."

Yono leaned forward in his cushioned chair. "Are you going to use similar tactics in dealing with the problems there?"

"As we have explained to Professor Lieter," said the alien, his answer filling each of the group's minds simultaneously, "we are but one unit of an interstellar assistance force sent to aid races such as yours, and yes we're hoping that such an approach will turn things around here."

Bracken gazed intently at the Trionite standing across from him. "Can you give us more details concerning your program for us?" he asked.

The guide momentarily ignored Bracken's question. Somewhere deep in the heart of the craft, the lumbering of its energy force changed noticeably. "Forgive my interruption but we've reached observation level. If you'll notice the view above my head, you should be able to get a clear picture of your planet below. I didn't want your questions to delay the spectacle of seeing your home from 500 miles out in space, a luxury afforded few of your people." The Trionite joined the others as they gazed intently at the splendor of the blue-green glow reflecting off the surface of Ebbern. "Going back to your question, Bracken," their alien friend went on, returning his glance to the group, "we hope to raise the overall consciousness of your sphere."

Catine shifted her weight, still staring at the scene above. "How long will that take, Talay?"

"Perhaps a generation, Catine. But gradually as the contacts increase and our presence becomes accepted, we will be able to make an open display of our purpose."

"Then we're to be the first phase of that plan?"

"Exactly," acknowledged Talay, in what appeared to be a smile curving on his face. "Soon others will join you, and there's time for—"

Yono interrupted, a slight note of tension in his masculine voice, "That's what I don't understand, Talay. It seems to me that we're at the crisis point now. How can we wait another generation?"

Professor Lieter turned to face the others from his spot at the end of the seats. He appeared to have come out of his trance. "Don't you realize that this single ship has the power to hold in check all the armaments and arsenals of our entire planet? It will be a simple thing for our Trionite friends to hold back the release of these destructive weapons until we have reached a state of maturity. Then we will be capable of dismantling them and putting our technology to a more fruitful use."

Two flashing hexagons appeared in the center of the 3D image, accompanied by a buzzing. "Nothing to be alarmed about!" the Trionite assured them. "That is merely the signal that our leader is now ready to address you." At this point, even Frim Lieter looked surprised. "Yes, this is a special occasion that even you, Professor Lieter, have yet to experience."

The blue-green sphere of Bracken's globe vanished from the projected image, leaving the area momentarily blank. Then it came to life again. A shudder of amazement went through the group as the veiled form of the Trionite leader appeared. Talay explained that the energy veil that shrouded the leader's entire body, revealing only a faint outline of his appearance, was necessary for his protection. The leader's life was of the highest importance and had to be shielded while the expedition was in this primitive section of the universe.

"My name is Semie," announced the shrouded image. "Please receive my warmest greeting. I have but a few moments to speak with you, as my duties are many." Even though the leader's form was veiled, a strong sense of authority emanated from him. His guests stared back in awe. "Let me say that I am glad that you have been chosen to assist us in the multiphase program. I hope all of you will take the treatment we'll be offering and become contacts as Professor Lieter has done."

Semie's voice filled the observation room. The audio monitors strained under its deep resonance. His message thrilled them, enthralled them, and even seemed to command them. It felt so easy to obey, to help because they were chosen. "Dedicated people like yourselves are a great asset to your race. If you are agreeable, the triumph of our cause will be completed more easily. Our forces will be in contact with you in the future, as the program evolves. I seriously encourage you to take the treatment and join the ranks of the professor. You are the vanguard of your race and the ultimate hope for the future of your planet. Good-bye and good luck." With that, the image vanished, replaced once more by the emerald-blue planet.

For a few moments, all of them sat quietly. Then Catine spoke softly in almost a whisper. "He certainly is powerful. I hope we'll be able to talk with him again." It had been powerful, but still there was the slightest hint of doubt in Bracken's mind. Somehow everything was too perfect, too right, and too sterile. Bracken felt mentally seduced. But why? Everything Semie said made sense. His plan would no doubt save Ebbern, and this had become a growing mission for Bracken ever since he'd tasted the power of the gem. He was truly a man on a mission.

"A certain possibility," said Talay, "if you become a contact." He stood and moved toward the entrance through which they had arrived. "If all of you will follow me, we can proceed with the treatment." Now that they were hovering above the planet, the strong g-force they had been experiencing earlier was gone. But still they were not weightless in the zero-g atmosphere; some sort of gentle gravity held their feet lightly against the deck of the ship as they rose from their seats.

The group followed Talay quietly down the hall. As they reached an intersecting corridor, they turned to the right and entered a softly lit chamber. They all were encouraged to take a chair. Suspended above each was a metallic probe with two padded circles on a Y-shaped extension. Talay walked behind every member of the group, adjusting their chairs and the device.

"Now, if some of you feel hesitant about this and would like to wait until later, that would be fine. We do not desire to force anyone into this programming." No one but Bracken seemed to feel any apprehension. Slightly ashamed, he hid his fears and smiled back at Talay as the alien adjusted his seat. Talay looked down at him with ancient, empty eyes. "Sit back then, and relax. We'll begin in a moment."

The Trionite took a seat in front of the group beside Frim, who had no need of the treatment again. The apparatus slid gently into place over each person's head. A soft hum was all that acknowledged the beginning of the cycle. Once the sensation began, each person relaxed completely—all except Bracken, who suddenly stared in disbelief. Before his eyes, the surrounding walls of the ship began to lose their sophistication. The winking lights and complex readouts slowly vanished. In their place appeared curving walls of stone. The Trionite himself changed in appearance, looking fearfully hideous. Bracken quickly reached above his head and pushed away the probes.

Talay stood and moved toward Bracken, his appearance once again benign and friendly. "Is something the matter?"

Bracken shook his head slightly, not wanting to admit what he'd seen. "I don't know. Everything started to look different when the process began." Bracken shook himself again, hoping it would clear his senses. Gradually the polished walls and winking lights returned. Once again, he felt he was on a genuine spacecraft. "I'm okay now. I guess I was just a little dizzy. Maybe it was the effect of space travel."

"Shall we continue with the treatment then?" Talay inquired softly.

Bracken felt a sudden hesitation, even though he was completely supportive of his host's mission. He'd definitely seen something unusual a moment before and couldn't shake it from his mind. He sensed he needed to hold off. "No, I think I'll wait, for now."

"Very well," Talay said. "Just wait quietly until the others are finished. Our ship is presently returning to the contact location. Once on the ground, your equilibrium should return quickly."

Bracken watched as the others around him enjoyed the pleasantness of the treatment. He was about to admonish himself for stopping the procedure when the probes lifted from the other passengers. Each one had an elated smile and began to share the beauty of their experience.

Talay's voice rose above the chatter, instructing them. "We have landed now. You can return to our contact point."

Quietly, the group followed him to the disk entrance and received a farewell as they descended from the craft. "You will be contacted for further assignments in the future. Until then professor Lieter will instruct you. Good-bye."

As Bracken reached the bottom of the stairway, Lisha and Silas ran to meet him. "What happened?" they both said in unison.

"It's a little confusing. Maybe in the morning my head will be a little clearer and I can explain it then."

Lisha hugged him, and he returned her squeeze. "I was afraid you wouldn't come back." Bracken caught something strange and frantic in her eyes. What did she mean he wouldn't come back? He wanted to ask her, but Lieter came up behind him at that moment and pressed a hand to his elbow.

"I don't know what happened to you in there, but I hope it won't keep you from following through and having the treatment. We need more like yourself who see the urgency of the hour."

"That's something I'll have to think about after my head clears a little." Behind them, the stairway retreated. The humming of the spacecraft increased as its door sealed. Bracken and the others turned and watched the disk spin away into the night.

After it had vanished from sight, the professor turned to Bracken held out his hand. "Here's my contact information, please get in touch with me when you've made a decision."

Bracken took the card and smiled shakily back at Lieter. "I'll do that. Right now, though, I'm really tired." Looking up into the night sky, he felt the anxiety he'd sensed earlier in the craft returning. His surroundings seemed eerie and strange. For some reason, he wanted to get away from the area of his recent encounter. "Do you suppose you could give us a ride back toward the highway? There's a clump of trees there we'd like to spend the night camping under. If we're going to catch a ride in the morning, it will help to be a little closer to the road than where we've originally planned."

"Certainly."

After a short and bumpy ride, the professor dropped them near the trees where they planned to camp. "Don't forget to contact me." Bracken yawned a thank you, agreeing he would.

The starry night gradually brightened as the planet's three moons rose high in the sky. But that had little effect on the trio as they collapsed into their sleeping gear beneath the trees and fell into a deep sleep.

CHAPTER 43

PILLARS OF RIMLEX

LYNREXS (MID-SUMMER), 5512

Bracken stirred from his slumber. The late morning heat was making his sleeping gear uncomfortable. A shaft of sunlight beat down on his face through an opening in the tree branches.

Thoughts of the previous night's encounter came spilling back into his mind. But as forceful as they were, the confrontation with his parents also occupied his attention. He felt remorseful, but fighting against that emotion were the memories of their beliefs and requirements. Last night's encounter was proof that they had no idea what the real issues were and what he was truly dealing with. He loved them but hated their narrow views. The conflict soon dominated his thoughts. After a while, the inner battle became unbearable, so he pushed it away and tried to sleep a little longer.

Squirming, he moved away from the irritating sunlight. The small stones that had seemed insignificant when he had fallen into weary sleep now pressed annoyingly into his back. He rolled over, only to find his ribs nudged by another row of sharp pebbles. In disgust, he sat up to the new day.

Beside him, Lisha's soft face was peaceful, her long lashes gently closed against her high cheeks. "You're a beautiful girl," he whispered to her under his breath. She stirred slightly. He felt so deeply about her. They had so much to discover together.

In the distance, a morning-call warbled across the fields, its cry carried on a breeze that stirred the ripening heads of grain. Bracken looked over at Silas. His sleeping face was also at peace.

Bracken felt a deep bond with his friend. It was good to be on this adventure with him. All those years dreaming, learning, discovering new ideas together and now they were finding things they had never imagined.

Stirred by the heat as well, Silas rolled over and sat up. "Good morning, Bracken," he mumbled, rubbing his eyes with both hands. He squinted at his friend until his pupils adjusted to the morning light. "Last night seems like a dream. Did all that really happen? I mean, you soaring off into the sky. I know it happened but right now it all seems so unreal. Any chance we were just imagining it."

Bracken stretched his long arms toward the leafy ceiling. He knew it was more than a dream. He knew he'd experienced something transcendent out there. Something of mystery. Something that had opened a door to a whole group of possibilities. But he wanted to turn it over in his own mind before revealing its full impact to his friends. "I know how you feel Silas, but it wasn't a dream. I'd like to pretend that it was for now."

"That's fine with me," said Lisha, awake now and resting her chin on a cupped palm. Her hair was disheveled from the night's rest but still radiant, struck by flickers of sunlight. Her eyes blinked away the night's slumber as she gave Bracken a cuddling embrace. "I'm glad you're here with me and not orbiting out there somewhere," she said, pointing toward the turquoise sky. Bracken nodded in agreement, kissing her lightly on the lips.

"Yes, that was a little more than what I was expecting for our first night away from home."

"It was for me too," said Silas as he climbed out of his sleeping gear and stared off toward the Pillars. There was no evidence of the encounter of the previous night. He yawned and picked up his things from the ground. After stuffing them into his pack, he slipped it over his shoulder. "I wonder how long we'll have to hike before we find a place to eat."

Bracken shook out his gear and rolled it up, "Probably a couple of hours at least unless we catch a ride."

Drawn by the distant sound of music, Lisha pointed toward the west. "Look over there by the highway, maybe that's our ride. I wonder who that is?" A large trans-max was pulled off to the side of the road with its power cover propped open. Two people labored under its shade, while several others sat around on the ground listening to others playing music on their stams.

"It looks like they're having rig trouble," said Bracken as he helped Lisha roll up her gear. "Maybe we can help them. I've worked on a few trans-maxes before."

Packing their remaining things, they hefted their packs along with their stams and started toward the road. Field birds and gold-wings flew ahead of them, disturbed from their places by the three friends as they walked through the tall grass.

As they approached the stalled vehicle, three of the people sitting outside acknowledge them with smiles. Bracken responded with a smile and introduced himself and his companions. "Hi, my name's Bracken, this is Lisha and Silas. We're from Tizra. We're heading toward Accad." Some of the new group looked familiar to Bracken, especially the two who had been playing their stams. Then he remembered. They were part of Golden Flight, the group he'd seen playing in the park on his recent visit to Accad and the Community. He also remembered what Ley had told him about his visit with them. *This is good news, we'll be right at home,* he told himself. So the warmth of their greeting did not surprise him. Two of the group laid aside their instruments and rose to say hello.

"Morning, friends," one of them acknowledged, his light frame clothed in a colorful garment topped off by a multi-hued scarf around his forehead. "My name's Chepa." he said, "And these are some of the members of my music group—Nev Broc and Naavin Shor."

The two nodded hello, an air of self-assurance on their faces. "We're called 'Golden Flight.' Perhaps you've heard of us?"

"Yes," nodded Bracken, "in fact, I heard you playing in Accad recently."

"In the Community?"

"Yes. You were playing in a park across from a friend's place. His name's Os, Ley Os. Have you met him?" Bracken smiled, hinting at the possibility of a shared secret. "He told me he was planning to pay you a special visit."

Chepa looked at his friends and smiled knowingly. "He sure did."

Bracken was inwardly smiling now as well, realizing that something significant was taking place on this lonely spot on the road to Accad. It looked as if one more piece of a fascinating puzzle was fitting into place. Perhaps it was part of a plan that was all coming together. It gave him a sense of destiny, almost like a calling. Bracken could tell it was increasing with each step he took away from Tizra and the narrow world of his past.

He felt instantly at home with this group. "If you've met Ley, that's great, then we're among friends."

Chepa turned and nodded toward the trans-max. "We're on our way to an engagement up north. We're having a little trouble with our power-drive. We've got a couple of people working on it."

"Maybe I can help," offered Bracken, moving around toward the end of the rig. "I've worked on a few like this in Tizra."

The trans-max was a unique form of transportation. Its large but sleek metal body was lined with tinted convex windows. Glancing through them, Bracken could see that the interior had been sectioned into sleeping quarters and a traveling lounge. It sat on a set of ten circular air cushions with massive hubs. At the front, the pilot cab was spaciously decorated, the guidance controls brightly polished. Several attractive girls were watching through a colored pane at the rear of the trans just above the power-drive.

Chepa introduced Bracken to the two men laboring over the energy generator. They were hesitant at first but gladly moved aside when Chepa explained Bracken was familiar with the mechanism. After conferring with the two frustrated workers and a few moments of tinkering, Bracken announced that he had found the trouble. "It looks like a gap in your MU, the Motion Unit." Bracken remembered how this problem came up often in his repair classes back at the Mind-Training Center; his teacher had taken special care to train his entire class in how to repair these troubled units. "They malfunction all the time. Looks like the issue with MU was caused by the flow register being out of line. It shouldn't take long to repair, though. Do you have any expandable form-links? I'll need them to calibrate it."

"I'll check the storage locker," said Chepa, pacing toward the entry port and vanishing inside.

Bracken brushed aside a bothersome lock of hair from his eyes as he grappled with a faulty device. The tools he had to work with were not the best, but he was soon making progress.

Back by the side of the road, two of the group picked up their stams again. Silas and Lisha sat down with the others, listening as Naavin and another member countered one another on their instruments. Lisha was fascinated by the rhythm. Her body swayed freely with the sounds. The driving but pleasant melodies encouraged Bracken as he worked.

After much noisy rummaging around, Chepa returned with a set of form-links. "These are old. I hope they'll work."

Bracken took the worn-looking package from Chepa. "The packaging looks a little tattered, but what's inside should be okay," he ventured. "I'll need them later to calibrate things when I reseal the flow register." Setting them aside, he squeezed back into the power compartment.

"Like I said, we're headed for Accad," Bracken continued, momentarily pulling his head out of the power compartment and pointing off toward the Pillars of Rimlex. "We were camping last night near those Pillars. You probably won't believe me, but we had the strangest encounter with a group there."

A slight hint of a smile formed on Chepa's lips. "Some strange things have happened to me lately, so I'm not as skeptical as a lot of people. Tell me about it."

Having just met Chepa, Bracken was a little reluctant to open up about the matter. But the experience was still so real to him that he felt compelled to share it. "You're probably going to think I'm crazy."

"I've been accused of that many times. So don't worry, I'm really fascinated now."

"Well, we ran into a professor and a group of his students from the Advanced Mind-Training Center. We thought maybe they were just on an astrogazing outing. But we'd heard rumors about strange appearances of space disks in these parts, so we followed them."

"I've heard those stories as well. In fact, some of my friends claim to have had sightings like that. It's never happened to me, but it would be great to see that sort of thing sometime. Our universe is so big, there's got to be others out there."

Bracken nodded, encouraged. "So we followed the professor's group and listened in on their meeting. The next thing you know, this disk comes spinning out of the sky. The beings who piloted it spoke through the professor, and I got an invitation to come on board."

Chepa rolled back his head and let out a hearty laugh. "You're making this up, aren't you?"

"I know it sounds wacky, but I'm telling you the truth."

In spite of his initial jesting, Chepa appeared to be sincerely listening. "So what did you see? And what did they say?"

"They said they were bringing a message of hope to our planet. That our leaders have brought us to the brink of destruction and that they've come now to move us on a new path. Some sort of rapid evolution that would change our culture."

"Sounds like just what Ebbern needs." Chepa turned and stared off at the distant pillars. "I've heard lots of rumors about that place. Our group had an unusual encounter with three sisters. Their leader gave me a prophecy that might have some connection to what you've brought up. Maybe I'll meet up with those Disk People someday."

"Well, the way things are happening these days I wouldn't be surprised." A little worried that maybe he'd shared too much, Bracken buried his head in the power compartment again and changed the subject. "Where's your band headed?" Bracken's voice echoed in the oily chamber.

"We're on our way back to Demur," said Chepa, leaning over Bracken's shoulder, trying to understand the dynamics of the broken apparatus. "We've been on a rest trip near Mount Shidow. It's a beautiful spot, and we needed to unwind. We have a cabin near the old cinder cone, beside Srific Brook."

The interior of the craft's power compartment was growing warmer. Bracken wiped a bead of perspiration from his forehead. It sounded like too much of a coincidence to him. Maybe they'd had another purpose for visiting Shidow. Perhaps they'd been on an errand for the gem dealer. "So you met Ley," Bracken repeated, hesitating a moment, but then he brushed caution aside. It was best just to get things out in the open. "I guess he let you in on the Mingus gem?"

"Yeah …" Chepa stretched out the word, a little unsure as to how much he should say to this new acquaintance.

Bracken looked over at him, trying to gauge his mood. The man was hesitant, but that was normal. With all that the 'Rax were doing to suppress the Mingus movement, as far as this group was concerned he could be one of their agents. This bandleader had to decided if he could trust Bracken. His expression seemed open and he went on, "Yeah … what an experience. It's changed our whole approach to playing."

Bracken smiled, "It changes a lot of things. It did for me."

"So you've had some journeys in the Mingus realm? I guess that's what you were doing with Ley."

"Yes, and it wasn't long till that led to experiences playing my stam under its influence."

With the mention of music, Bracken sensed Chepa's hesitation beginning to disappear. "That's the way it was for us," said the bandleader. "It all really started then. Since that first session with the gem, our music's come alive. In fact it's moved us into a new dimension."

Bracken struggled to center the flow register, his grip slipping. "Interesting," he grunted, grasping the device firmly again and forcing it into place. "I've only played with a few others. You're a whole band. That must be an amazing thing performing together under the gem's effect. I'd like to try sometime."

"We should be able to take care of that once we get moving. After your help, it's the least we could offer." Chepa looked at Bracken's gear lying on the ground. "Looks like you're hiking. We'll be glad to give you a ride."

"Great! You're going to Demur, huh?"

"Yeah."

That wasn't exactly the answer Bracken had hoped for. He wanted to go to Accad. But Demur had its own charm. Perhaps he'd enjoy its bayside atmosphere, especially if it were enhanced by a touch of the gem's power. "Sounds fine. Anywhere but here will be great."

Besides, Demur was just across the bay from Accad. He was sure he and his friends could catch a ride to the city once they'd arrived at Chepa's place.

The musician squeezed closer to Bracken, peering over his shoulder into the chamber. "You seem to know what you're doing in there. Appreciate the help."

"It's nothing. Glad I could be of some assistance." Bracken pointed toward the device in Chepa's hand. "Pass me the form-links, please. I need them for the final adjustment."

Chepa looked relieved, "Glad you came along. I was afraid we weren't going to make our performance at the Sea Sphere."

"The Sea Sphere? Tonight?" Bracken paused and looked at Chepa. "I've heard about the performances there. It sounds like an exciting place." Bracken turned back to the engine, measuring the position of the flow register and then calibrating it with the links as he sealed it into place. "I've always wanted to go there. Do you play there often?"

"I guess you could say it's where we got our start." Chepa stood back and rubbed a kink in his neck. "It's become our home base. All of us live nearby. By the way, Ley Os plans to meet with us tonight. I think he'll be surprised to see you with us."

Bracken thought about the gem peddler. Things were working out better than he'd hoped. Now Lisha and Silas would have a chance to experience the gem. "I'll be glad to see him. I wanted to share his little secret with my friends."

Chepa smiled. "I'm sure he'll be happy to oblige. In fact, we'd be happy to as well."

"You mean you have some of the stones with you?"

"Well, you know Ley's somewhat of a salesman. We've got plenty now."

"Great. And my friends, can they?"

"Sure, it would be our pleasure. Especially after what you've done for us here," said Chepa, pointing to the power compartment.

Bracken finished and wiped some of the dark lubricating compound from his face and hands with a rag Chepa offered him. The two stood back and examined the work at a distance. Their forms threw black shadows on the roadside. "We'd better give the unit a try, though. None of us will be going anywhere if the register doesn't stay in place."

"You're right," Chepa called for their driver to start the power unit. The propulsion device came to life with a loud roar. Bracken listened closely for a moment and then shouted to Chepa above the noise. "Sounds like it's holding!"

"Good! Let's get back on the road. We need to make Demur by evening."

Bracken explained both of Chepa's invitations to Lisha and Silas as they loaded their gear into the storage unit on the side of the rig. They looked relieved but also a little anxious as they climbed aboard the transmax. Following them aboard, Bracken took his stam with him instead of leaving it in the storage compartment.

The interior of the giant rig was decorated with an earthy plushness, its comfortable seats making the riders feel immediately welcome. The vehicle soon pulled back onto the roadway. One of the band's girls offered everyone a mildly intoxicating drink and something to munch on. Bracken leaned back beside Lisha, enjoying the comfort of their new surroundings.

Chepa reached for his stam case. Snapping open its locks, he rested the instrument on his lap. "So, you play. Why don't you let us hear some?" He handed Bracken the expensive instrument, which Bracken could tell was well cared for. The stam was like Bracken's, it could be played acoustically or hooked to an amplifier to carry its sound to a crowd.

Admiring the exquisite stam, Bracken carefully placed it in his lap and plucked the metal strings. Intriguing tones vibrated through the air. A different but inviting warmth filled his body. It was a common occurance now since his encounter with the Mingus stone. Thrilled by the quality of the sound, he began to play several of his better-practiced compositions. The intriguing melody soon had his listeners entranced.

After a while, Chepa signaled Bracken to stop and then opened the small amber container he'd pulled from a cabinet overhead. The interior of the trans-max took on a greenish-blue glow as the gems' light flooded the compartment. Ley had given the canister to him as a present and said that it would keep the stones in their pristine state and would be adequate in stopping any leakage of the powerful rays.

Even though Bracken had explained to Lisha and Silas about the Mingus stones before, he once again reassured them of the delights ahead. Chepa encouraged them as well with promises of pleasure and insights awaiting them once they imbibed.

Most of the group was eager to experience the stones' power again. All agreed that Eire, their driver, should abstain. They were quite sure that it wouldn't be wise for him to try and navigate the trans-max under the influence of the Mingus effect. The only other reluctant one was Nev Broc. As the case passed into his hands, he refused to touch the stones.

"What's wrong?" asked Bracken, a little surprised that Nev wouldn't join in. "You're not driving. This stuff's amazing. Why pass it up?"

"It's the Fear," offered Chepa. "His last 'voyage' was a bit too much."

"The Fear, what's that?" ask Bracken.

"It's some odd thing that happens under the stone's influence sometimes," explained Chepa. "Ley sold us a bunch of the stones, and we've been experimenting ever since, sometimes every day for days in a row. But then some of us started to have this overwhelming anxiety attack us. It was like someone was watching us, as if we were pawns in some cosmic game. We felt mocked."

"I've never experienced that," said Bracken.

"Glad to hear it. Perhaps you never will. But after you experience The Fear, we've found it's better to hold off for a while before you go back under the stones' power."

"What could it be?"

"It may just be the body's way of dealing with the changes we're experiencing. You know we've all heard stories about sea divers that went too deep or sky flyer pilots who went too high, too early in their careers. Maybe it's just something like that. But the good thing is, it wears off after a while. I'm sure Nev will be back joining us again soon."

Bracken looked over at Lisha and Silas who had been listening in on the conversation. He could tell they were a little uncertain now. He smiled at them both, and with all the persuasion he could muster he joyfully egged them on. "Don't worry. It's no big thing. I've never had what they're talking about and I've tried it several times. Besides, I'll be here right alongside you. It's going to be one of the greatest things you've ever experienced."

Lisha and Silas both gave sheepish smiles in response. And following Bracken's lead, they reached into the case as it passed by, each choosing and then slowly swallowing a gleaming gem.

Bracken watched happily as both of his friends were soon deeply under the stone's influence. He could see they were delighted as well, and they reclined peacefully into their comfortable seats between fits of laughter and joyful contemplation. They smiled at their enhanced view of the realm where they lived before and exulted in the pleasure of the new one they were discovering as they went deeper under the stones' power.

Inspired by the joy he saw on their faces, Bracken handed Chepa's stam back and took out his own instrument from its case and began to play with a fresh inspiration.

"Not bad," noted Naavin, taking his own instrument to join in. The rhythmic throb of harmony soon filled the lounge as Chepa and the rest of the group began to play along.

"Bracken should sit in with us on a few numbers at the Sphere tonight," said Chepa over the driving melodies. "I think the people will love him."

"A great idea," added Naavin, a gleeful smile forming on his lips. "Let's rehearse a couple of his songs."

"Yes, I think people will really like him," agreed Chepa between spells of laughter. "His playing is a great addition to our group."

Bracken smiled as well, happy in the joy of new friends, pleased that Lisha and Silas we're doing so well under the stone's influence. The trans-max lumbered down the road, a hive of melodic sound and pounding rhythm as it hummed its way toward Demur.

CHAPTER 44

BAY OF ACCAD

LYNREXS (MID-SUMMER), 5512

The Sea Sphere floated on the sheltered Bay of Accad near Demur. Giant mooring lines, like threads of a silver web clutching a round egg, held the globe firmly beside a wide pier. Golden Flight's transmax pulled up near the rear entrance. A few of their helpers unloaded the band's equipment. The large baggage rattled the wharf, as it was being unloaded and hauled into the Sphere.

Chepa led Bracken, Lisha, and Silas on a tour of the performing hall while the band's helpers unloaded the rest of the instruments and set them up on the stage. The music center was one of the most unusual Bracken had ever seen. He felt privileged to have Chepa give them a guided tour. A large transparent floor, the entire diameter of the globe, stretched out in front of the platform, revealing the lower part of the Sphere falling away beneath it. Above his head, the concave walls of the ball rose toward their apex. A unique array of fixtures hung from the ceiling. Once activated, this would turn the Sphere into a glittering ballroom. A transparent gauze-like material was stretched in contour with the walls and about a foot in front of them over the entire surface of the Sphere. Chepa pointed out the walls, as the three of them stood in the center of the vast complex. "Behind that covering are some of the special atmosphere producers. Tonight, when they're turned on, you'll see what a fascinating world this place can become."

Just then someone called from the entryway. "Hey, Chepa," waved the figure as he moved toward them across the crystalline deck.

Chepa turned and waved back. "Ley, good to see you!" As Ley Os approached, Chepa nodded toward Bracken. "Recognize my new friend?"

Os looked happily surprised to see Bracken. "I certainly do," he said, a sense of relief obvious in his voice. He greeted Bracken with a smile. "Right after that little encounter we had with those bandits, I thought you were done for, either in a med-unit somewhere or that you'd run back to Tizra, scared away by those thugs." Turning his attention back to Chepa, he said, "I never expected to see you two together, though."

With sincere spontaneity, Os hugged Bracken, throwing both arms around him in a genuine embrace. Bracken hugged Ley back, feeling a surge of appreciation for the role Ley was playing in all their lives.

Bracken pulled slowly back from the embrace and smiled at Ley and Chepa with real warmth, "It's kind of a surprise for both of us. We ran into Chepa and his group near Rimlex. They had a little trouble with their trans, and I helped get it running again. They offered us a ride, and here we are."

Bracken was glad to see the gem dealer again. Their Mingus experience and the predawn battle had knit Bracken's heart with the older man. Bracken was also relieved to see that Ley had survived the attempts on his life. "Where did you disappear to after that trouble in Accad? I went back to your place later, but no one answered my knock."

"There are plenty of places to disappear to in that city. I wasn't about to go home right away after what happened," answered Os. "I was worried about you as well. I went back to my place later, but we must have missed each other. I spent several hours searching the streets for you, but the next day the proprietor of the Brazen Eagle told me he'd seen you safe and calming your nerves with cups of his tea."

"Well, at least we're both safe." Bracken was about to mention how Dalfang had saved him when Ley interrupted.

"Who are your friends, Bracken?" Os glanced briefly at Silas and then turned and gazed into Lisha's eyes with a charming stare. "This one is particularly lovely."

Lisha felt a little embarrassed by Ley Os's enchanting manner. She had never met anyone who could capture her attention so quickly. Strangely, she found the gem dealer completely fascinating within just a few moments.

She wasn't sure whether she should respond to his suggestive look or merely remain aloof. Finally, she smiled shyly back and then looked to Bracken, hoping to escape Ley's haunting gaze. Perhaps it was his frequent encounters with the gem that had given him the magnetic power she felt flowing from him. She looked to Bracken for rescue, but at the same time she secretly enjoyed Ley's attentions.

Bracken seemed unaware of the subtle exchange between Lisha and Os. "This is Lisha and Silas. They're two of my best friends from Tizra."

Ley had not taken his eyes off of Lisha. She could feel his stare. The mysterious attraction she felt toward him a moment before continued to grow. Finally, Ley turned his gaze back to Bracken. "You have good taste in friends, Bracken, very good taste. By the way, have you shared our little secret with them yet?"

"Yes, I've told them all about the gem. That's part of the reason they came along with me, and thanks to Chepa they've already experienced it.

Silas cleared his throat and eagerly addressed Ley. "It was amazing. Wouldn't you agree, Lisha?"

"Yes it was," said Lisha, still flushed with the afterglow of the gem's influence. "In fact it still is," she said, laughing and smiling gratefully at Os now that she knew he was the one responsible for all the joy she was sensing.

"Well, you've just had your first journey, lady," said Ley with a wink. "There's many more ahead if you want them. If you do, you just let me know and I'll be happy to oblige."

Os gave her another wink and then turned his attention back to Chepa, placing an affirming hand on his shoulder. "It's what has helped make this man's group one of the most unique musical sounds in Nerkush. His blue-green eyes danced with a secret joy. "They're on a mission now. They're bringing a message that there's more to life than meets the senses and much more yet to understand." Ley smiled at Chepa and then turned to Silas, acknowledging him in a more personal manner for the first time by placing his hand firmly on the young man's shoulder. "So you're Bracken's other friend. I'm glad to see there are those close to him from other races. This speaks a lot to his character, and it obviously happened before he ever came under the influence of the Mingus Effect."

Silas smiled back at Os and then nodded toward Bracken. "Yes, we've been friends for years. Grew up together in Tizra."

"Sounds like true brotherhood." Looking squarely in Bracken's eyes, the gem peddler continued his talk. "You found it naturally. Not everyone does. But that's what the Mingus will do to all who embrace it. It will create a brotherhood between all cultures and races. It's just a matter of time. The shadows of our world hide the lurking ghosts of prejudice. Obscurity is the guardian of hate, but the gem will expose those lies, and with the power of its influence, bring a real unity among us all."

Os's words had a poetic rhythm to them. His way with words had no doubt been enhanced by his many excursions into the world of the Mingus.

Chepa patted Silas on the back, vouching for Ley words. "He's absolutely right. That's the power of the gem." With a knowing look, he glanced down at the pouch at Os's side. "And it appears he's brought some with him."

Ley put his hand on the leather bag hanging from his shoulder. "Yes, there's plenty for all of you."

Chepa motioned to the rest of his group. They had finished unloading the equipment and were lounging on the stage. "Good. I was hoping the group would have a session with the stones before we went on tonight."

"That's why I'm here," smiled Ley. Chepa pointed toward the door to the musicians' lounge. "Let's go. There's no better time than the moment."

The group walked unhurried across the Sphere's glass-like deck. Their footsteps echoed in the empty room.

Chepa was walking between Bracken and Ley. "You know, Ley, Bracken's quite a musician."

Ley looked pleasantly surprised. "I knew he had a stam, but I never got to hear him play."

Bracken grinned back at Os. "We'll, you're going to."

"You going to play with the group tonight?"

Chepa interrupted him as they reached the door. "He sure is. I think you'll like his playing, Ley. He's great. He's sitting in with us on a couple of his own compositions. I can't imagine what it will be like once he's had another touch of the gem."

"I'm looking forward to finding out," said Ley as the group disappeared from the hall and walked down the corridor leading to the musicians' lounge.

Bracken spent the next hour going over his two compositions with the band. Confident that they had the songs down, Chepa and his group left Bracken to continue his rehearsing. He went over and over his verses, making sure he would be able to play them even under the influence of the gem. Ley had given the band the Mingus stones earlier, and they'd eagerly slipped them into their mouths in a unified motion, laughing together like children setting off on a new adventure.

Entering the music hall later that evening, halfway through Golden Flight's second set, Bracken was confronted by an overpowering sight. He had expected the room to be wondrous once its atmosphere producers were activated, but what he saw before him as he mounted the stage exceeded the limits of his imagination. The hololight projectors were active all around the room and Bracken saw his image flicker in the glistening spheres scattered around the hall.

A sea of curious faces stared into the spheres and then up at him from the audience. People dressed in a rainbow of colorful clothing clogged the massive floor. He strapped his stam in place and gazed at the dome overhead. Hues of amber, magenta, vermilion, and ruby mixed on the laced white outer surface of the curving walls. Dancing pigmentations seemed to spill over the onlookers as a kaleidoscope of light beamed down from above. Each tint of light shimmered with life. Every motion of the people around him released energy within him. It was as if their collective joy animated every cell in his body. The effect of the gem was at its maximum just at that moment.

Overwhelmed by the beauty around him, Bracken's soul bloomed in awe and adulation. Turning to the others in the group, Chepa gave the signal to begin. As if ignited by the blaze of a fiery dawn, Bracken's heart erupted with joy. His fingers sprinted on the strings of his instrument, detonating an explosion of arousing sound. Leaning forward, he sang into the microphone. His voice, an unleashed prisoner of silence, exalted in song like the chorus of an anthem:

Wanderer, find your home
Depart your vacant tomb
Let the stars inspire your flight
Shake away the webs of fright
And soar …

Wanderer, set your course
Break the binding force
There are treasures to be found
Listen closely to the sound
And roar …

You are new, you are now, you are the breath of life
You are free, you are here, you are the death of strife
Hate will melt beneath our gaze
In the loving nights and the endless days
No more the fist of hate, gone forever suffering's gate

The crowd came to life at his words. Hundreds of bodies swayed, coupling, spinning, caressing. A rippling ocean of desire linked everyone in the Sphere in a bond of fellowship. Voices echoed back to Bracken from the audience and elsewhere, beckoning for more, whispering for further blessings. The members of Golden Flight smiled at each other, and Bracken laughed with them. In melodic union they played on, each verse building another layer of sensation until Bracken's second song brought the concert to a climax.

At the end of his session, a resounding ovation from the listeners echoed through the Sphere as Bracken descended from the stage and allowed Chepa's group to continue their concert. As he pressed his way through the crowd of admirers to the musicians' lounge, Silas and Lisha, who had been watching from beside the platform, greeted Bracken with almost reverent astonishment. "That was overwhelming," shouted Silas above the din of the crowd. "I've heard you play great before, but never like that. The gem has changed you."

Bracken smiled in agreement, drawing Lisha close to him, her softness warming him with the heat of love.

"I'm so glad you brought me along, Bracken," she said invitingly, running her fingers gently along his arm. "I'm sorry I didn't trust you more at the Pillars."

Ley met them in the lounge with an intriguing prospect. "This is Naavin's brother, Roon." He introduced them to a tall, but ample-looking man. "He's invited us to his estate in the hills near Oak Forest. It's a great place. We can unwind there after Golden Flight's session without being bothered by strangers. You and your friends can ride in his rig out to his home."

"Sounds good," replied Bracken, acknowledging Ley's new companion. "I'll look forward to it."

CHAPTER 45

WATCHING SHAFT

LYNREXS (MID-SUMMER), 5512

They had many words for it. It had always been there with them. It contained melody, harmony, rhythm, pitch, tempo, timbre, dynamics, and a host of others things that only eternity would reveal. It was part of their language, and they'd never been in a world without it.

They listened as the planets gave off their sound and the stars sang in a harmony so complex that they had been studying it as long as they could remember and still were unable to fully grasp its depth.

Michess was grateful to inhabit a place where this element was prominent. He had only known a brief period without the sounds of joy. He recalled years before when there had been a short time of stillness, the days when he and the others looked on with horror as the Prince of Wonder had apparently been murdered. But then, to their delight he'd returned, triumphant as he ascended from the lower regions. Now he was enthroned again, and all of them looked forward to those moments when they could return from their assignment to be in his presence again.

He remembered with wonder the memory of the great Prince's time on Ebbern centuries before. Of his struggle and the final victory as he emerged from the oblivion that most had thought was final. This exploit had become one of their great themes, and all around the Prince the sounds of triumph played without end. Michess was looking forward to returning to that place and joining its continual celebration.

But now he hovered, looking down through a watching shaft at the one he'd been assigned to. As he listened to him and others at the Sea Sphere perform, he wondered at the plaintive melodies and limitation of their instruments. Their playing had a few elements that he enjoyed but countless others were missing. Some of it sounded harsh, almost grating at times even though it contained melody, harmony, and a few other aspects.

He hoped there would be a day when those who danced in the Sphere below him would somehow hear what he heard within the world high above them.

Much of his assignment had been spent merely watching. There had been messages from his brethren that an assault was possible against the group he'd been assigned to. What was he to do? Was he to intervene? Only time would tell. No order had come from the one who'd called him to watch. So he continued his vigil, patiently enduring the meager sounds that arose through the shaft.

CHAPTER 46

OAK FOREST

LYNREXS (MID-SUMMER), 5512

Strieme found himself on assignment in a pleasant place. He had the distinct sense that this would probably not happen again for some time. So he chose to enjoy it as long as he could.

The orders had arrived earlier along with a company of effects functionaries who had been putting things in place. These specialists could do amazing things with basic matter. They had recently been on assignment near Rimlex but were now temporarily authorized to help him. He would need all of them to create the encounter he imagined. They stood, waiting, their motion cloaks hiding their presence from the woodland creatures around them.

He listened with pleasure to the sounds of tiny creatures chirping in the wooded setting. He breathed in deeply. The scent of grass moving though the clear air made him dread the fact that he would soon return to the acrid realm he normally moved in.

His reverie was interrupted as the sensor array in his mind clicked on. The message came through quickly, and as he read it he understood why he'd been sent here. The voice of the Shadow Czar was clear. "I'm ready for a harvest now. It's time to take one of their ripened souls. He's well fattened, so I'm looking forward to this. The feasting should be glorious. Their suffering is such delight, especially at that moment of "truth". A haunting laugh followed the last word, then a choking sound as the speaker sought to regain his voice. After a few moments of clearing his throat, he continued, "Is it all arranged?"

"Yes, everything's in place here. The resources have arrived, their displays are in place and should work perfectly. They've been assembled within the home and around the crest."

"Have one of your agents notify me when the moment comes. And I'll move into place."

"Without question, Great One. We'll be standing by."

Once the voice had vanished, the sweet sounds of the forest returned. Strieme drank in the peacefulness of his surroundings again and enjoyed his wait.

CHAPTER 47

OAK FOREST

LYNREXS (MID-SUMMER), 5512

Roon's land was spread over a mesa with his home perched at the top of a winding canyon road. A giant oak forest covered the surrounding hills, its twisted wooden forms mysteriously shadowing the ground beneath. A cobblestone trail, lit by burning torches, led the way to the huge oaken door of their host's sprawling dwelling. Like the surrounding woodland, the earthy but palatial manor had come to be called Oak Forest as well in honor of its inviting environment. Bracken enjoyed the sense of his new surroundings. The woods' green scent gave off a deep, welcoming feeling, and the house had its own natural beauty that blended with everything around it.

Roon led them into the spacious great room that dominated the floor plan of the house. At one end, a massive bay window looked out onto a broad deck and the canyon below. In the distance, the still waters of the bay spread out to meet a lone moon rising above Accad's silhouetted buildings on the harbor's far side.

Roon's attractive mate, who he introduced as Duvalla, greeted them with a cordial smile and a tray full of food. She wore a long caftan tied at the waist with a silver cord. She and Roon seemed to be a matched pair; he with his dark curly hair, neatly trimmed black beard, and dark complexion and she with her thick hair that fell in tight curls ending at her waist. Her pointed nose gave her an air of elegance matched by her deep brown eyes.

Munching on the tasty snack, Bracken and his friends followed her as she showed them their rooms for the night. Afterward, she led them out onto a sprawling deck that overlooked the canyon.

They watched as Estals, the delicate birds native to the area, floated at the edge of the precipice. Gliding from side to side, they hovered effortlessly in the moonlight until drawn by some hint of food. Then they dove toward the canyon floor, screeching with delight as they snatched tiny winged creatures from the air.

When Bracken and his friends returned to the gathering area, the front door burst open. Chepa's group, along with their girlfriends and helpers, came streaming in asking for food, drink, and comfort. Soon they were all sitting in a circle near the huge fireplace.

Ley produced several of the glowing stones, enough for the whole group. He passed them out with a wink, explaining that these were a milder variety of the gem whose effect would be more gradual and mellow. They were soon gone, consumed by those who eagerly plucked them from Ley's silver container.

As the group mingled, eating and embracing their intimate companions, the atmosphere came alive. Bracken felt at home. He could tell that his new friends admired him. It would be a good evening. Soon the stams came out of their cases, and music enveloped the room as Chepa, Bracken, and several others joined in. Swaying with the tempo, the friends rode the increasing cadence to its peak.

As the effect of the gem increased, Bracken felt a force beginning to flow through his body uniquely connected with his playing. It added a gracious ease as his fingers danced over the strings, but it also seemed to gradually overpower him, beckoning him to give into it. Like tingling tentacles of pleasure, the mysterious force surged through him, enhancing his playing and transporting him deeper into the gem's power.

Back and forth went a test of wills: the warm influence tugging, inviting him to give in, and his own desire resisting, even fighting, determined not to surrender. His will hovered between the two choices, uncertain which direction to go.

He was just about to yield when Roon rose to his feet and began dancing around the room. Animated by some hidden force, his tall body swayed and jerked, casting multiple shadows on the walls from the flickering firelight. His dark and chiseled features, accentuated by his movements, gave him a sensuous magnetism. As the intensity of his dance increased, his eyes stayed keenly fixed on the fire.

In his hand he held a narrow shaft of wood. He shook the pole above his head and then in triumph slammed its end into the floor. Holding it tightly, he used it to center his body as he danced in a circle. Then from a nearby chest he removed what appeared to be a skull. Lifting it to the top of the shaft, he slid the head in place. It made a snapping sound as if it had been made to fit.

A deep wailing chant came from his mouth as he rocked back and forth, shifting from foot to foot. He was obviously deep within the spell of the Mingus Effect. In fact, the more intense his movements became, the more the stone's power seemed to surge through everyone in the room. He began to laugh. A deep, eerie laugh that sent a chill into the air. Slowly his face began to transform until it was frozen in a ghastly gaze.

At that moment, Bracken felt a rising sense of confusion. It was so strong that he had to stop playing. Hidden fingers of energy stroked him, tempting him to play again, to play and never stop, to lose himself.

He resisted and shook away the feeling. Glancing across at Silas, he saw terror in his friend's eyes. What was going on? What sinister presence had bent the gathering toward this dreadful tone?

But many of their companions appeared not to see anything grotesque. Looking at the faces around him, Bracken saw that most of the group had been entranced by Roon's dance, and the other musicians continuing to play with joyous intensity, blissful smiles covering their faces.

Abruptly, Silas stood up and ran from the room, out the door and onto the broad deck. Worried about his friend, Bracken laid aside his stam, jumped up, and followed Silas out onto the expansive deck. Something very strange and overpowering had enveloped both of them back in Roon's gathering room. But what it was, Bracken was still unsure.

The night chilled Bracken as he stepped outside. In the distance, he could see Silas standing alone, staring at the darkened sky. One of Ebbern's moons stood like a lone sentinel in the shadowy night. He moved cautiously toward his friend. The stars glistened and mockingly winked down at them. The universe seemed to be bending and twisting around them. When he reached Silas, he was standing at the end of the deck that jutted out over the canyon.

Drawing up beside Silas, he found his friend still troubled but also looking a bit sheepish. "I don't know what it was, Bracken, but I just saw something sinister, almost evil in Roon's eyes. It was pulling at me, smothering me."

Silas stared down over the edge into the canyon. The drop to the bottom was long. Spike-like rocks poked up at them from the below. As he looked down, Bracken felt something pulling him toward the crags. Instinctively, he drew back and gently took Silas by the shoulder to turn him around toward the house.

"It was strange. I sensed it too," agreed Bracken. He tried to move further away, but Silas seemed rooted where he was.

"I'm sorry, Bracken, I just had to get out of there. Do you understand?" Silas was trembling, but from more than the chill of the night air.

"It's all right," Bracken reassured his companion. In spite of the fact that the deck was skirted with a waist-high railing, he wished Silas would back away from the edge; he was so close, and things felt so strange. "It was probably something out of your past memory, you know some sleep-terror that bubbled up from inside. Give it time, I'm sure it will go away."

"Yes, I'm sure it will," acknowledged Silas, comforted by his friend's words.

Behind them the melodious sounds continued, oblivious to their quick departure. Whirling tones and hypnotic rhythms stirred themselves together. Bubbling, bouncing, rumbling sounds churned in their ears. Then, enticed to look back toward the great room, they watched as a stream of ethereal fog began to drift from the house. Bracken wondered if Silas saw it as well. One look at his friend told him the strange substance wafting toward them also captivated Silas.

Pushed by the rhythm, it billowed out around them and then cascaded over the edge of the canyon, forming a large pool of glistening light that filled the ravine. Around the rim of the canyon a tide of similar mist joined the flow increasing its size. Silas along with Bracken followed the mysterious stream with their eyes as it spilled over the edge of the deck and like a shimmering white carpet spread before them. Bracken wondered if it was real. It couldn't be, he told himself.

Then he thought of Lisha. Was she still inside? Why hadn't she come with him to comfort Silas? He should have invited her to join him. Was she taken in as well?

He turned, looking back toward the house to see if she had followed them out. He could see dancing shadows playing across the windows of the house. One of the dancing silhouettes looked like Lisha's. They flickered above the glistening fog like the wings of some bird of prey, black and haunting. He looked closer at her outline but then its shape shifted. He walked closer to the house to make it out better. Another form shifted apart from hers, unnatural and unfamiliar. He turned away from it in confusion.

When he looked back out into the night, he saw Silas stripping off his clothes. "What are you doing?" shouted Bracken, staring at his companion in disbelief.

Silas was clearly in the midst of some sort of epiphany as he returned his friend's shout. "Don't you see him, Bracken? Look, he's calling me to join him."

A glowing face appeared, calling out of the swirling fog below them. *What?* Bracken thought. *Who is it?* He wanted to question, to find out who this was. Yet other voices told him to rest, to be at peace, to trust. He felt almost magnetically drawn to look at the face as well. It was so beautiful … fascinating.

He could hear it speaking inside his mind, and somehow he knew that Silas could also hear it. "I am comfort, I am home. Come, I'll help you. You have no need to fear."

Bracken felt the draw toward the face increasing. He sensed its warmth and love. His whole being wanted to surrender to its power. It pulled at him, drawing him closer to its peace, closer to its rest, closer to the edge of the cliff.

"The pool of light," said Silas, "it's beautiful, don't you see it, Bracken? So sparkling ... I've got to dive in."

Bracken shook himself, trying to break free of the strange spell. *What is Silas doing?* he thought, shuddering inside.

His friend had climbed on top of the decks railing. *I've got to stop him before its too late!* Bracken cried out inside, yet he found himself frozen, weak, and suddenly unable to move.

Struggling, he finally broke the trance and reached out toward his friend. But Silas had stepped forward. Stretching out toward the glowing face, he dove forward into nothingness, leaving the edge of the cliff behind him. For a brief second, he hung in the air, suspended like the birds they'd seen earlier that evening.

But it was too late for Bracken. In a perfect swan dive, Silas plunged into the pool of light.

For a moment, all was quiet as Bracken stared in disbelief. Then the fantasized bubble of beauty popped, and the swirling, mesmerizing cloud was no longer opaque. In that moment, the dream was over. He heard Silas scream just before his body crashed into the rocks below. Then all was still again as wafts of fog swirled up from the canyon floor and returned to the house, drawn by the music within.

CHAPTER 48

OAK FOREST

LYNREXS (MID-SUMMER), 5512

It was nearly midday, two days later, as a somber Bracken sat staring off toward the Bay of Accad. He was sitting with Lisha and Ley on Roon's sun deck. The platform's giant beams anchored firmly to the side of the canyon held it safely suspended over the twisting gorge that led back toward Demur.

Behind them, the spacious house was quiet, some of the guests had left early that morning, and the others were still hiding in a cloud of sleep from the memory of the previous crisis.

Bracken felt barren inside. His friend was gone. Dead. And even with Lisha here, he still felt alone. A loneliness only the shadows knew.

"I'm sorry we had to handle things the way we did," apologized Ley, lifting his legs and plopping them over a cushion at his feet. His face was gaunt from lack of sleep. He took a sip from the glass of tart liquid in his hand. "But I hope you understand we couldn't let the Pirax have any idea that Silas had been using the gem."

"Couldn't we have told them he picked one up from someone at the Sphere?" mused Bracken, his voice slightly distant, a mask of mellowed shock still lingering on his face. "Then at least his parents would know he didn't go berserk of his own accord."

Bracken shuddered at the memory of the heartbreaking call he'd made to notify Silas's mother of her son's death. His body, now in Accad, was soon to be shipped back to Tizra for burial. Bracken knew he would be expected at Silas's memorial service. But he was torn. How could he return with so many conflicts there? Would he be blamed for his friend's death? Would his parents come at him again? He had finally decided it would be better to get answers about why Silas had died rather than go back to Tizra at this time. Besides, was Silas really living in Accad on a stone slab or had his soul transcended this realm for a higher one? That was something he had to find out, and the answers certainly weren't waiting for him in the stifling atmosphere of Tizra.

"We don't want to bring up the gem at all," replied Os. "You saw how they searched everything in Roon's house. It was good that he had the hidden room beneath his floor to hide our *supplies*."

Bracken agreed. Once he'd run back into the house with the news of Silas's death, they had immediately sent word to the medical authorities but just as hurriedly they'd hidden Ley's supply of stones in the chamber beneath the floor in Roon's study. And just in time too. The Pirax sky flyer had arrived a short time later and the commander prodded his team to search the entire property.

"I was afraid to even bring up the subject of the stone. The 'Rax have been suspicious of me for some time, and I'm sure they'd use an occasion like this to pin me."

"I remember what they said when they pulled us over the first time I was with you in Accad. It was apparent to me that you where under suspicion then." Bracken stood and walked to the edge of the platform. He stared down at the rocks beneath him. The spot where Silas had landed was empty. All that remained were bloodstains where his head had struck. He turned away, trembling, the horror still fresh in his mind. "After bringing so many of us into the Mingus realm, you've gotten quite a reputation. Surely someone's betrayed you to them."

"Hearing rumors is one thing," said Ley, "tying me to a case like this is another. They'd lock me away if they could get any halfway-decent evidence. They want to suppress everything that defies their limited sense of reality."

Ley looked at Lisha while he talked, her delicate profile silhouetted against the blue sky. Even though he was seeking to reassure Bracken, another agenda was emerging in his mind. What was this beautiful girl doing with Bracken? She was much too pretty to belong just to Bracken. Why couldn't he share her with him?

It was not uncommon for some of the girls who followed Chepa's group to be handed off to Ley for a night of pleasure. They had a sense of obligation toward him. After all, wasn't he the one who had brought them such delights through the stones of power? *Why should this luscious one be withheld from him?*

The first time Chepa had offered Ley one of the band's female followers, he was grateful and thoroughly enjoyed indulging in her delights. But now he felt he deserved it, felt it was part of the spoils of his exploits for risking his life to bring the treasure of the gem to the waiting throngs of The Community. What about Lisha? Shouldn't Bracken be willing to share her with him? If it weren't for him, Bracken would never have met Golden Flight or discovered the delights of the gem. And hadn't the kid seen the exchange between him and Lisha? All his young friend had to do was just give the girl the right signal.

But something else was on Ley's mind and it was troubling him. Bracken was growing in his confidence. He was not merely a compliant follower any longer. After watching the youth perform at the Sea Sphere, Os saw that he was a rising star. He noticed the way Chepa and the others in the group were drawn to Bracken. His talent and enthusiasm appealed to them, and it was becoming a possible threat to Os's leadership.

He continued staring at Lisha while he talked, drinking in the allure of her form. "If they trap me, it will severely cut back on the supply of the gems. No matter how much we care for him, is Silas's death worth risking that? Thanks to the Mingus, most of the Community in Accad is already discovering a positive alternative to the shallow Nerkushian way of life. Another few years, and half this country will feel the same way."

"I know, I know," muttered Bracken despairingly. "It's just hard to accept that Silas isn't here." Tears welled up in Bracken's eyes. "We were so close ... like brothers. I'll get over it, but there's just one thing I still don't understand."

Bracken hesitated for a moment, staring down toward the terrain below, "If the gem's helping so many people find happiness, why did Silas die?"

"Some people can't quite handle it, I guess," offered Ley. "Pioneering, to the best of my recollections, has never been free of mishap. It's a sad thing about Silas, but you've got to look at the positive side of the stone's influence."

"Ley's right," agreed Lisha, her brow wrinkled in concern. She missed Silas too, of course she did. But she felt reassured. She tried to share her comfort with Bracken. "You've certainly found a new plateau of expression through the gem. Look at the way the people enjoyed your playing the other night."

She stood and went over to stand beside him. She rested a reassuring hand on his arm, "Maybe that face he saw was really calling him to a higher world." She paused for a moment, reflecting on their friend's death. "Haven't you been telling me that there are dimensions and worlds we know nothing about? Spheres of life all around us, and we're completely unaware of them."

Bracken nodded and looked up at her, but her words were of little affect. How could words, even her heartfelt words, fill the void he was facing now?

Lisha looked into Bracken's eyes, her own filling with tears. "You know how much I cared for Silas too."

How can she say that? thought Bracken. Did she really understand his loss? She hadn't spent the weeks, days, and hours with Silas like he had. She hadn't known him from childhood. She'd never explored, hunted, and gotten into mischief with him like Bracken had. He saw the tears, but the words just seemed empty. Maybe all her empathy was coming from the emotional power of the lingering Mingus Effect. He wanted her to stop talking and just be there for him, but she continued.

"Somehow, I feel that even though his body is dead, somewhere he still exists, maybe even happier than we are."

"Perhaps," muttered Bracken, still unconvinced as to Lisha's sincerity. But then he corrected himself. Maybe he was judging her too harshly. She was just doing her best to comfort him. He reached out and squeezed her hand and she squeezed back reassuringly. "Yes, you may be right, Lisha," came the words from Bracken, but he sensed that she could tell his heart wasn't in them. In fact, he sensed that this whole issue instead of drawing them together was actually driving them apart.

Ley took a final drink from his glass and then amplified Lisha's commentary. "I've seen enough phenomena in the Mingus realm to know that there are powerful forces working out there. They may seem strange to us. Nevertheless, I am convinced that they are working for our good."

"You're probably right," Bracken said, finally relenting. He stopped for a moment to taste the drink he held in his hand. It had gone untouched until now. "I really hope to learn more about the gem's effect. What I've experienced so far has been tremendous."

Lisha felt an increasing indebtedness toward Ley. Her admiration for him was growing as well. Her experiences with the Mingus stone had changed her and opened her to things she could only have imagined a month ago. His words seemed so wise. He was like a father to their group. "I agree with Ley. Even in the face of Silas's death, I still feel so completely free and at peace." She smiled at Ley, hoping to encourage his benevolence. "I hope we'll be able to try the gem again soon."

"Me, too," added Bracken, taking a deep breath and slowly expelling it. "Another touch will probably help me understand better what happened to Silas."

"No doubt it will," agreed Ley. "And I already have such an excursion in mind. I guess the others failed to tell you, but Golden Flight is one of the main attractions at a little get-together over in Accad this afternoon. We'll take the gems there."

Bracken seemed pleasantly surprised by the thought of another performance along with a journey to the Mingus realm. "They certainly did. What sort of get-together?"

"Oh, nothing much," laughed Os, a joking expression on his face. "Just a few thousand people from the Community getting together for a little celebration. Judging from the way the crowd responded at the Sphere, I'm sure they'd be quite pleased to hear a few sounds from you as well."

"When do we go?" urged Lisha, increasingly surprised by the growing fascination she sensed for the Mingus peddler.

"As soon as the others are ready," answered Ley promisingly. "It shouldn't be long, though, I've heard some stirring from the house." Ley looked back toward the dwelling. Lisha watched him for a moment, admiring him. When Ley turned back, he found her eyes on him. "Accad's beautiful this time of year. You'll love it," he said.

"Good, I'll go change then, and get ready." She let her eyes linger just a little longer on Ley's before heading for the house. It was temptingly pleasant for a moment. But then she asked herself. *What am I doing?*

Why was she so taken with Os? Perhaps it was his power and the power of the stone. She loved Bracken, but Os seemed so alluring, the look in his eyes so confident and commanding. She felt like a child, a child who needed his wisdom … a child who wanted to please him. She toyed with the idea of giving in to his subtle invitations. It would be fun, she told herself, even if it meant upsetting Bracken.

"We'll use the gem when we get to Accad," Os announced as he recovered from Lisha's unexpected beckoning glance. She had turned her face back toward him one final time as she walked gracefully to her room.

Bracken hadn't seemed to notice the exchange, though. He was staring off toward the shimmering blue surface of the distant bay.

Ley thought for a moment and then spoke to the musing Bracken. "Could you do me a favor?"

"Sure. Anything, Ley."

"Roon has to stay behind in case the Pirax come back. He wants to make sure they don't discover anything we might have overlooked. He was planning to help take some of the group's heavy equipment in his other rig. But now we'll need someone to take his place. Chepa is driving over. Do you think you could ride along with him?"

"I'd be glad to help," offered Bracken, still slightly pensive.

"Fine, then. There's just one problem. His lift only has room for two people. That means Lisha would have to ride in the max with us."

"That's okay, it would probably be more comfortable for her."

"Great!" grinned Os, rising and looking back toward Roon's dwelling. I think I see Chepa now. He's heading up toward the rig stall. Come on, we can help him load the equipment."

Putting a friendly arm around Bracken, Ley walked with him from the deck. "You'll feel better about Silas after another touch of the Mingus. Until then, just try not to think about it."

"You're right, Ley," admitted Bracken, cheering himself up with thoughts of anticipation. "I'm looking forward to visiting the Community of Accad again."

Arriving at where Chepa was loading the equipment, the two helped him lift the larger pieces into the spacious bed of the assist rig. After a tedious period of struggling with the ponderous amplifiers, the three completed the loading.

A weary Chepa climbed into the hauling vehicle's cab and touched the ignition button. Carefully watching as the propulsion readouts came up to level, he set the rig in its warm-up function. "We should be ready to go in a few moments," he announced, turning around to examine the stability of the cargo they had just loaded.

Bracken brushed dust from his hands. "I'll go and explain to Lisha what's happened. I'll be right back."

Bracken and Ley walked back into the house where Lisha was chatting with several of the girls. He quietly walked up behind and slipped his arms around her. "I have to go ahead with Chepa. He needs help with the equipment."

Lisha turned around, looking surprised. "Can't I go along?" she glanced out toward the idling rig.

"No, there's only room for Chepa and myself. Ley says you can ride with the rest of the group in the max."

Lisha shrugged and turned to Ley with a look of favor. "I guess that will be okay."

Ley's eyebrows rose slightly, accenting the twinkle in his eye. "We've got plenty of room."

"We'll meet at the park, then," said Bracken as he kissed Lisha good-bye.

CHAPTER 49

A SHADOW HIDE NEAR OAK FOREST

LYNREXS (MID-SUMMER), 5512

For as long as he could remember, Hyslevix, a low-ranking but powerful minion of the Shadow Czar, had felt an inward dismemberment. His soul was splintered like a shattered mirror. Each piece reflected back a part of him that once was perfect and content. But the knowledge of how to reassemble it was beyond his understanding. The dark lord had promised him that it could have been done easily, but now ages later it still remained disjointed. He had to live with it just as he did with his leader's other broken promises.

At least he could find some pleasure in his work—his latest orders brought him a sense of excitement. His master's harsh words were pleasant to him because they meant suffering to those he despised. "The time has come to break their unity. We will find greater success as we scatter them. This recent death will be a catalyst. It's a natural point at which to drive a wedge."

Hyslevix breathed in the commands as if they were a fragrant breeze. His soul may be divided, but at least he would find some relief and delight in seeing others divided too.

"Use the suspicion scheme. I've trained you to slacken their hope with lies until they doubt each other's intentions. It will only be a matter of time before they are at each other's necks. But we must act soon. No doubt those who oppose us have seen our actions and will move to counter us."

Hyslevix knew the routine. He had watched those higher in the chain of command move into the minds of their victims through the thought channels, planting their lies and leaving their victims twisting in mental anguish. Strieme had been one of his first teachers in this technique and taught him first by a very personal method. He'd made Hyslevix a victim of the dreaded torture. Then after Strieme had tired of toying with his underling's mind, he'd released him and finished training him in the art of Theema. So one could say Hyslevix knew it from the inside out. That's what made it so effective. Once you'd been a victim, you knew exactly what approach would bring the most misery.

First, plant seeds of betrayal in their thoughts. Sow doubts and suspicion with it, mixing in just the right amount of angst. Once the pain was applied, then all that was needed was to slip in the half-truths, accusations, and innuendoes holding out the promise of relief if one would believe the lies. He'd seen this procedure succeed many times, especially on himself.

He knew it must be done soon. Assuredly other forces were arraying against them. The Shadow Czar would not be wrong. If he was assuming they would move against his plots, then it was a certainty. So with the command came a sense of urgency.

"Report to me once their unity has been broken, and I will engage my next plan. We will certainly succeed, and with it you'll find great delight."

The words of the dark lord collected within Hyslevix's mind and dripped like a gentle rain on the floor of his inner core. It was a bitter drizzle, but one that seemed to bring relief simply because—like so many of his race—he had learned to find pleasure in the suffering of others. The cerebral moisture slowly turned to a mist that fogged the broken mirrors of his soul, temporarily softening the emptiness that reflected back into his mind.

He encouraged himself, "Duty calls and evil pleasure awaits." With that, he was on his way.

CHAPTER 50

ACCAD

LYNREXS (MID-SUMMER), 5512

On their drive to Accad, Bracken opened up to Chepa about Silas's death and the questions it raised concerning the dangers in the Mingus realm. He'd also told him that he was considering exploring the option that Vonervyn offered him. In fact, he encouraged Chepa to go there with him on his next visit. The musician sounded interested, but for the time being he seemed content to explore more of the wonders that the Mingus realm offered.

By the time Chepa pulled his rig up near the stage area, the park was already overflowing with people, many of them obviously under the effect of the Mingus gem. Those who weren't had plainly been intoxicated by some other means. Many things were available in the illegal markets on the back streets of Accad. The sound of musical pipes along with tinkling percussion instruments rang and jingled among the gathering.

As the support crew came to unload the equipment, Bracken jumped out of the service rig and followed Chepa toward the trans-max parked by the stage looking for Lisha.

He was not prepared for what confronted him. Lisha stepped out of the vehicle and greeted Bracken with a smile, but she was clearly distracted. Her eyes reflected an excited inner fire—but it wasn't because she'd seen him, it was distant and elusive. She brushed by him with a light embrace and then walked a short distance away, turning back to watch as the others descended from the rig.

The musicians and Ley greeted him warmly and headed for the stage. Ley spoke to the confused Bracken as he passed. "Lisha's already used the gem. We decided to go ahead on our way over. The ride along the waterfront was so beautiful, she wanted to see how it looked through new eyes. She really seems to have found something exciting under the effect this time."

"Is she going to be all right? She's acting kind of strange," asked Bracken apprehensively. He watched as Lisha stared in apparent captivation up into the sky.

"She's fine," assured Ley, casting an approving eye toward Lisha. "She's a beautiful woman, and I believe she's beginning to discover part of herself she never knew existed. Don't worry, though. I've been watching out for her. I've helped a lot of people through these things. We haven't forgotten you, Bracken," assured Os, handing him the Mingus case. "I've left one special stone in here for you. After a while come and join us. Just be sure to wait until you've passed the initial phase before you leave the trans. By the way Chepa's decided to hold off for now, he wants to look out for everyone."

Bracken noticed Ley's eyes narrowing for a moment, and he wondered what the man was thinking.

But all he said was, "Lisha will be with us, so you don't have to worry."

Feeling uncertain but eager for a touch of the stone again, Bracken followed Ley's instructions and disappeared into the trans-max, closing the port behind him.

This time when he swallowed the stone, he felt a dreadful shudder go through him. This must be a more powerful one, he told himself as he slipped under its spell. The next hours were lost in a whirl of sensual luxury.

Pulsating music was the first clear sensation he felt as the effect began to level off. No doubt the sound of Chepa's group preforming nearby was the source. Physically unsteady, but confident in his euphoria, he climbed from the trans-max and walked toward the platform where Golden Flight was playing. Something was missing. He felt good, but he realized suddenly he wanted Lisha beside him. Where was she?

Mesmerized by the driving sound waves and the swaying crowd, he felt suddenly disoriented. To calm himself, Bracken sat down on the grass. He felt his body tingling delightfully beneath the barrage of musical pulses coming from Golden Flight's instruments. The separate parts of his environment began to melt into one. Captivated by his joyous surroundings, he wasn't immediately aware of his growing derangement. Before he knew it, he was hopelessly overwhelmed. Where was Lisha? What if something bad had happened to her? He had to find her now.

Standing to his feet, Bracken struggled against the flow of people around him. Many danced together, others alone as if caught up in their own world of bliss, oblivious of anyone else. Several stood almost frozen in delight, staring up at Golden Flight, entranced by the modulating sounds coming from the stage. He bumped into others clumsily, apologizing, taken back by vacant stares and sometimes hostile glances.

He stopped and shook his head to clear his thoughts. It was then that he saw Lisha. She was spinning around in apparent ecstasy, holding tightly to someone else. Uncertain at first who it could be, Bracken walked closer only to see that it was Ley Os.

At first it didn't make any sense. Why would she be clinging to Ley, but it was clear from the look on her face she was deep into the moment, radiating a sensuous glow he'd only seen in her during their most romantic moments together.

A stab of pain plunged into his soul, and suddenly he wanted to run. He felt alone, crushed as hurt twisted a knot tightly around his heart. But instead of running, he slowly turned and walked back toward the max, tears welling in his eyes. Why would she betray him like this? And how could Os do this to him? What did all the good speeches about unity, brotherhood, and love mean in the face of something like this? Had Os so easily deceived him?

A feeling of savage hatred burst from his heart like a fiery arrow. A sudden bitterness squeezed his soul in a tormenting grip. Struggling with the pain of betrayal, his mind in a flurry of bewilderment, he climbed the steps into the trans-max and then collapsed into a lounge chair near the back. He strained to regain his rationality, squirming in the painful mental trap.

Surely Lisha cared for him. Or did she? Maybe he was crazy. Maybe she had never cared. Maybe she'd just used him to get out of Tizra. It was irrational, but he imagined it anyway. Tormenting thoughts he'd never had before streamed into his consciousness. His altered mind was wide open as strange new voices told him lie after lie. Yes, that was it. Perhaps she never really cared, and never would again.

Nearly at the point of breaking, he looked for relief. Perhaps somewhere in the swirl of the stone's influence he could find peace. He probed his thoughts. Seeking … hoping … waiting … Then direction came, as if something or someone had heard him. From the core of his mind something whispered, "Give in to my comfort, let go of your suffering." He allowed the sensation of the Mingus to overpower him. He sensed it cradling him, inviting him to give in to its effect.

Then he felt his agony replaced by an odd sensation. Every painful emotion suddenly vanished. It was as if a cage had been swung wide open, and the ferocious beast that had been tearing his soul apart had fled. Something deep within him seemed to resolve, as if all his torment was drowned in a rising tide of pleasure. He found himself letting go of everything he had ever cared about: Lisha, Silas, his family. It was all swallowed by a massive wave of pleasure, and he was free. Free from Lisha, free from himself. In relief, he slipped into a dream. He slept for hours.

The trans-max was quiet, and it was dark outside when he awoke. A misty fog was beginning to settle over the street. At first, it appeared as though the vehicle was parked near the scene of his previous struggle. Instead, he discovered as he glanced out the window that it was sitting on a quiet residential street lit by night lamps. Something behind him rattled, and he turned to see Chepa coming from the front of the vehicle. "It's good to see you awake," said Chepa, a note of concern in his voice. "We weren't sure you would come around before tomorrow."

"Where are we? I can't seem to make it out." Bracken's head swirled.

"This is Ley's house," replied Chepa, pointing toward Ley's castle-like home.

Bracken squinted out the window. "Oh yeah, now I remember." Bracken followed Chepa out of the trans and helped him seal the door.

"We're all staying as Ley's guests tonight."

Momentarily, Bracken thought of one guest who probably was being made quite welcome at the moment. He closed off such thoughts from his mind with a fresh feeling of resolve. He was different now, he told himself. He cared, but he didn't care. Lisha was free to be who she wanted.

"I guess you know Lisha's with Ley."

"I know," smiled Bracken, unmoved by Chepa's statement.

A security buzzer released the latch and allowed them in after Chepa acknowledged who they were through the guard-tel. They walked down a darkly lit corridor, stopping at the second door they came to.

Chepa pointed toward a cozily decorated room containing two beds. "We'll be staying down here tonight." The house was quiet except for the occasional sound of laughter coming from above. "Most everybody's retired for the night," announced Chepa, settling down in his bed. Bracken was surprised that Chepa was without female companionship. It seemed there was always some delightful beauty hanging on his arm whenever he laid aside his stam. Bracken guessed maybe Os had assigned Chepa to keep an eye on him.

Chepa nodded in the direction of the corridor, "If you want something to eat, there's food prepared in the room at the end of the hall."

"Good, I'm hungry. Get a good night's rest," said Bracken as he made his way down the hall.

Opening a door to a dining room, he saw its main table was filled with food. Bracken noticed Nev sitting quietly with his girlfriend, eating a late-night snack. "May I join you?" he asked, taking a seat at the table. The room was filled with plants, and a few candles flickered here and there.

"Of course, there's still plenty left." The three of them ate without much conversation. Nev and his companion slipped off to their room with a "good-night" shortly after Bracken arrived. Finishing the meal, he washed up and returned to his room. In spite of his earlier rest, he fell asleep easily on the soft cushioned bed.

Later that night, he woke to the sound of sobbing. After a moment, he recognized Lisha's voice whimpering painfully in the darkness. Bracken arose from the bed, threw back the covers, and walked down the hall. The soft light from a candle lit the passageway. At the bottom of the stairway, he found Lisha, her head between her knees; she was shaking.

Startled by the sound of footsteps, Lisha looked up.

"Bracken," she gasped, standing up and embracing him. "I'm so glad to see you. I thought you had gone." Her face was wet with tears, her hair disheveled. She looked up at him, her voice broken and pleading. "I went looking for you in the max, and it was empty."

"I'm staying down the hall in a room with Chepa," responded Bracken, his voice slightly aloof. "I hope you've been having a good time tonight … with Ley."

"Oh, Bracken, don't talk like that. I'm so sorry," she whimpered. "I just don't know what came over me. You must understand." Why had she done it? She felt full of shame. She'd been used.

"I think I understand. You chose Ley over me." His words were harsh as he spit them out. They smashed into her already fragile emotions. "I thought we meant something special to each other? But obviously you don't care." Bracken's face was twisted now into a bitter mask. "I wonder if you ever cared. I'm beginning to think that you just used me to get out of Tizra."

Lisha recoiled under this assault but then forced herself to reach out, extending her hands and arms toward him. "You must know I love you. I realize I made a mistake. Can you forgive me?"

"I'm not sure I can." Tears came hot from his eyes and spilled onto his cheeks. He quickly brushed them away. "Why would you hurt me like this?"

"Everything was just so new, a whirlwind of pleasure. Something told me it was time to be free, to experiment, and Ley was the perfect guide. And you seem distant sometimes. It's like you prefer your adventures to being with me."

Bracken folded his arms. "But you've known that's part of who I am. I've got this calling."

Lisha's arms collapsed into her lap. "That's the problem. Too often it's about you. And you just weren't there. But he was. Ley was there directing me, giving me all his attention. He was like a rock, solid, confident and most of all wise. That when things turned dark and I needed someone to hold onto."

"Why didn't you come and find me?"

"Ley said you'd gone back to Roon's place to hang out with some of Chepa's girlfriends."

Bracken pointed down the hall toward the street, anger rising in his voice. "What do you mean? I was in the trans-max the whole time."

"We never went back there. He suggested we walk here to his house. He said he wanted to show me some of the colorful houses and shops in the Community."

"Okay, but why did you embrace him? I saw the way you were dancing with him."

Lisha looked down, folding her hands as if to calm herself and collect her thoughts. "He said it's a way of life here in the Community. We share love on every level."

"Are you serious?" said Bracken, his voice lower now but still angry, each word like a punch striking her in the heart.

Lisha drew in again but then in a moment of defense lifted her head and looked at him slightly defiant. "And so I thought that's what you were doing. So I went with it."

"Just went with it? Where did you learn that phrase? From Ley?"

She recoiled again from Bracken's assault, dropping her head and cradling it in her hands. "Yes, I just went with it. But then all the beauty and color just went away and everything became dark. I was scared, really scared. And I needed someone wiser and experienced. He was there. His words pulled me up out the blackness. So I clung to him and then things just moved on from there."

"Things moved on from there, huh. Well I hope you had fun."

Lisha looked up at Bracken again her mouth turned down in a bitter curve. "No, I just felt used. Once he'd had his fun he turned cold."

"Well that's how I feel now. Cold." Bracken recalled the moment of peace he'd had earlier when he'd let go and the pain had gone away. So he sought it out again, and when he sensed it returning he hid there hoping for relief.

Once more, in a final effort of reconciliation, Lisha stetched out her hands toward Bracken. "You've got to understand. It all happened so quickly. I was so confused. Bracken, I'm asking you to hear my heart. I'm truly sorry. Can't you forgive?" All she wanted now was for him to hold her, to comfort her. But now he was different—distant and cold.

"I do understand. You're your own person now. You have to find your own way. Ley's part of that way."

Bracken didn't believe the words, but he knew they hurt her. Bitter voices filled his mind and promised relief through one means. *Give her the pain she'd given him.* It felt good to hurt her. She had hurt him. Now, it was her turn to hurt. The voices increased, surging inside him.

But even as he took delight in revenge, another part of him wanted to embrace and forgive this girl he'd loved so much. But it was true, he was different. A stoic-like air of confidence rose up in him, taking over. "I'm glad you could enjoy each other." There was a mocking tone in his voice.

The girl's tears began to flow again. Lisha's beautiful face looked contorted and tortured. "Ley is horrible," she moaned. "It was all so beautiful and seductive, but when it was over it was so different." A look of increasing dejection clouded her face. "He doesn't care for me, he just deceived me so he could have me."

"You're wrong, Lisha," responded Bracken quietly. "Ley cares. I care. But you have to learn to let go." It was true, he told himself. This was what some of the edge-poets had chanted, and now he understood it. They had been taught it from the tower-dwellers, the men who lived in seclusion, and by the force of their will and years of self-denial had finally reached Atorma, a state of true bliss that left one free from caring. Their songs taught a faith in the power of the mind to transcend feelings. Yes, he'd buried his pain and found bliss instead. But it hadn't taken years for them to reach Atorma. He'd found it in an instant under the sway of the gem.

Bracken reached out and gently took hold of Lisha's hand. "Quit holding on to your emotions. You have to stop feeling before you can learn to really care."

Lisha suddenly drew back from Bracken, clearly shocked by his words. He could hear how his own voice sounded, distant, possessed, and compassionless.

"What are you saying, Bracken?" she pleaded, moving further away from him. Moments before it was clear that he'd been hurting. His words had made that plain. But then he'd turned aloof, spouting some strange ideas that meant nothing to her. He seemed distant now and beyond any hope of reconciliation. "I told you I was sorry. What do you want? Please help me. I'm so confused, and you're acting so cold."

"Lisha," Bracken whispered firmly, his face drawn and anxious, "I am trying to help you. But you must let go! Go back to Ley. I'm sure he can make you happy again."

"Oh no," she moaned loudly, turning and backing for the front door. "What's happened to you, Bracken? I've got to get out of here."

"Please, Lisha. Let me tell you what happened to me earlier. I'm free now to care for you and not cling to you."

"No, no! I don't want to hear it." With that, Lisha turned and ran for the front door. She pulled it open and ran out, crying into the fog filled night.

CHAPTER 51

WATCHING SHAFT—HIGH REALM

LYNREXS (MID-SUMMER), 5512

Michess had seen many things in his time. Of course the use of the word *time* had its limitation because even though he remembered the moment of his emergence eons ago, in many ways time seemed irrelevant.

He'd seen things in the realm below that left him puzzled and grieved. He'd watched in horror as the youth had plunged to his death in the canyon. Why had he not been allowed to intervene? He never questioned the wisdom of the One who directed his life. But the incident left him bewildered. He had to remind himself that he was in a school of sorts, a place of learning that constantly brought new experiences before him, some wonderful, others appalling and painful. From his exalted place, he saw things he'd never imagined. As protected as he was from what lower beings experienced, he still had a certain empathy. And that empathy was on high alert right now.

How could this sort of activity go on and no one intervene? It was a rhetorical question. Because he knew that once major intervention took place full accountability would come with it. So it was mercy to hold back. But a mercy that was painful for all, including those who watched.

He had seen pain like this many times, but each time it shocked him. As he observed the victims being caught and some even dying in the midst of their torment, he wondered how they could go on this way. He was horrified to see the recent rejection and accompanying emotions that had played out below him. In their world of excess and pleasure, these creatures seldom found room for what he knew to be one of the greatest virtues. Forgiveness. How had he known such an ideal? It was because he'd learned it from the One who had assigned him to this watch.

It was a universal theme; the way of love and forgiveness. His cohorts talked of it all the time. They wondered how it was possible. Where had they seen it? It had been shown to them when they saw the Great Prince release all those who had wounded him from results of their hurtful choices. How had he done it? Once again it had been part of the very nature of the One who ruled them. This gracious release of forgiveness was a wonder to him, for even though he had never needed it, just watching its effect on others left him in a state of reverence.

And so, what had just happened below him left him mystified. Where would these fragile creatures ever find the power to release one another from the hurts they inflicted on each other, and would such a time ever come to them?

He hoped some of them would learn from their suffering. That the hardships they were facing would bring them to a place of compassion. But would they learn in time? Danger was clearly encroaching. It was evident in the recent death. He had an increasing sense of urgency that the one he'd been assigned to would soon need his active protection. He was conforted by the fact that he could call on his brothers at that time. Of course any action would have to be ordered by the One who commanded them. Until then, it was clear that he must watch and wait for that order.

Timing was so important. Until then he turned his attention to things below and stared down the shaft again, watching, fascinated, hoping to see the day when the one he watched now would understand what truly was occurring around him.

CHAPTER 52

ACCAD

LYNREXS (MID-SUMMER), 5512

Bracken slowly walked toward the open door. A few swirls of early morning fog brushed by him as he reached the entrance. He could just hear the padding of Lisha's footsteps retreating through the dense mist. Bracken's face took on a slightly pathetic expression as two conflicting affections clashed in his heart.

Momentarily, he thought of pursuing her, but as he hesitated, the feeling began to dissipate. Resolved to remain in the safety of non-commitment, he tarried in the doorway.

Temporarily distracted, he didn't notice the sound of other feet clattering toward him. Suddenly, four armed figures materialized from the haze. Before he was able to react, they had raced up to the door and overpowered him.

In a roar of pounding confusion, he fell against the hardwood floor, his head aching from several unexpected blows. Stunned, he lay quietly as he heard his assailants clamor through Os's house, rousing the sleepers and forcibly assembling them upstairs in the spacious gathering room.

A short time later, a pair of strong arms belonging to a grizzly looking man, yanked Bracken to his feet and pushed him to where Ley and the others had been collected. Coming into the room, he realized that Ley and their assailants were already deep into a dangerous confrontation that wasn't going to end well. But for some strange reason, Chepa gripped Bracken's arm and pulled him closer to the group. He looked at Bracken with just a hint of a smile. What was going on? Did Ley have some plan for escape? Was Chepa trying to prepare him?

"We're not going to take your word this time, Os," growled a short, squat man, his fingers clutched tightly to an energy thruster. Its blunt snout was pointed directly at Ley's head. Obviously deadly, the weapon's explosive potential seemed to match its owner's lethal temperament. He frowned, his face frozen in hate as if it had been permanently tattooed in place. "We want the map, and we'll get it if we have to break apart this building, along with you and your friends." Three other tough-looking men stood beside their leader grimacing their agreement and waving their weapons slowly back and forth at Ley's group.

"That won't be necessary," answered Ley smoothly, his voice casual. He smiled warmly at the fat man. "I'll give you the map, if that's what you want. But first, please answer one question."

"What's that?"

"Oh, I was just wondering what you intended to do with the gems once you've found them? Undoubtedly, you know the effect they have on people."

"I'm aware of it."

"Then you must realize that once you're exposed to the Mingus, you'll be looking at reality a little differently. In fact, you'll probably stop this foolish bad-man business and learn how to love others."

The portly figure smirked a tart response, sucking in his protruding stomach. "A definite possibility if I was planning to use the gems myself, but I have no such intention."

"Then what possible interest could you have in them?"

"It's business, Ley, strictly business."

"Oh, so I see what you have in mind and you're looking for the map. Let's see …" Ley shifted his glance above the fat man's head and concentrated on a painting hanging on the wall on the far side of the room.

The assailants shifted, nervous and impatient and gripping their weapons a bit too tightly, but as their leader turned to look where Ley had been staring his companions turned their heads to see too.

At that moment, Ley motioned to those in his group to move back closer to the wall.

Not seeing anything of significance, the man with the weapon turned back toward Os, completely oblivious to what had just occurred. "My interest is money, Os, the same ultimate motive you have yourself."

Ley took a few slow steps back and joined Bracken and the musicians near the wall. "Oh, but you're wrong, my friend. If financial gain was my motive, you certainly wouldn't find me distributing the stones so freely."

"Those are free samples," sneered Ley's obese opponent, not taken in by Ley's smooth response, "they're only a come-on. Once someone tries the product, they come back for more. That's when the price is attached."

"Such lack of trust in others," replied Ley, his body now parallel with his friends. Ley remained confident in the face of this dilemma, but no one else seemed to share it. He winked at Bracken even while the others stared warily at the vicious weapons pointed their way.

The chubby man's impatience seemed to boil over, his red face snapping his reply. "The map, Os, and no more questions!" The barrel of his thruster panned across the captives.

"All right," sighed Os, his face now scowling in apparent despair. "It's here behind this …"

Suddenly a loud explosion shook the house as an energy egg vaporized the front door of Os's home. The fat man and his cohorts turned in surprise as the first members of a Pirax Assault Squadron stormed down the hall. Before anyone had time to respond, they were up the stairway and bursting into the large gathering room.

Others quickly filed in behind them, their boots clacking on the floor and their weapons held ready. For a moment, the two armed groups eyed each other. Then without warning, a volley of fire erupted between them.

Explosive charges burst, penetrating human flesh. Men fell moaning. Ricocheting projectiles bounced from the 'Rax's shining shields, detonating harmlessly in a flash of sizzling light.

In the midst of the commotion, Ley moved quickly to the wall and touched a small stud beneath a picture frame. To Bracken's and the others' amazement, a steel partition slammed down from the ceiling, instantly separating them from the battle on the other side.

"What's going on?" shouted Nev, in shock, mystified by their instant escape.

"Quite simple," explained Ley, as he turned and activated a switch on the opposite wall, inducing a mechanical humming sound beneath their feet. "I had this escape mechanism installed when I bought the house. I never thought I'd use it to avoid the likes of the fat man. It was mainly for an unexpected run-in with the Pirax. It looks like we've had both."

Muffled explosions resounded through the wall. "They should take care of each other nicely." The whine of the motors beneath their feet suddenly ceased. Os reached down to the floor and pulled aside a thick carpet.

Beneath it an outline of a hatch appeared in the floor. Ley gripped a handle on its surface and pulled it up in one fluid movement to reveal a stairway descending into a dimly lit passage. "This corridor leads to a hidden exit in the park. We can easily escape."

Os's countenance became more intent as the noise of the battle increased in the background. "All of you, listen closely!" he shouted over the noise of the explosives. "Split up into small groups. We'll be less obvious that way. After you leave the tunnel, hide. We'll have to avoid contact with each other for a while. A week or two at least. So find someone that will hide you until then."

"Where will we meet after that?" asked Chepa.

"At Roon's house," Ley responded, as he started down the stairway. "Stay undercover until then. Let's go quickly now … it won't take the 'Rax long to break through that wall if they start using their energy eggs against it."

Chepa and Bracken found themselves paired together. Bracken pushed Chepa ahead, hurrying him down the stairway. "Listen, Chepa, I know a perfect place to hide. If you want, you can come with me to Vonervyn, we'll be safe there.

"Vonervyn? Oh yes, I remember now. That place near Zorek?"

"Yes, once we're there and through the portal, the 'Rax will never find us. Dalfang will make sure of that."

"Sounds great," nodded Chepa, running ahead of his companion as they rushed after Ley down the shadowy passage.

CHAPTER 53

NEAR THE FOREST OF ZOREK

LYNREXS (MID-SUMMER), 5512

Bracken took another sip of the warm brew in his mug as steam rose from its surface, meeting the chill of the morning twilight. He stood watching a large wave break on the shore a short distance away. The sea was as dark as wine, and a brisk wind blew over it turning the crest of each wave into a frothy white. He took another sip and watched dawn spread out its petals of light and open like a rose.

He and Chepa had managed to catch a ride with several people from the Community. As they headed out of Accad they stopped by the home of another bandleader and managed to convince him to loan them a couple of stams and some camping gear. No matter what was happening with Os and the Pirax, they were committed to their music and wanted to make sure they could continue to practice.

The two couples that picked them up in their ancient trans were headed off for a break. It turned out they loved the area around Zorek and planned to spend several days by the Sea of Auren. When they'd seen the two musicians with their stams standing on the highway seeking a ride, they'd been delighted to give them a lift in exchange for some music. So the two minstrels had been happy to oblige, filling the vehicle with melody as they headed up the highway toward Zorek. On the way there, during breaks in their movable concert, Bracken explained more to Chepa about Dalfang and Vonervyn along with his experiences in its fascinating realm.

When Bracken and Chepa finally arrived on the beach below the Forest of Zorek, they'd been a day into their journey from Accad. Rather than climb up the canyon to Dalfang's in the dark, they had chosen to spend the night at the beach. Arriving near sunset, they had camped in the sand at the edge of the forest.

That night Bracken found himself thinking about Lisha again, although he would hardly admit it to himself. After all, he had transcended the "need" for her. Surprisingly, the surge of pleasure that had helped him break his bond with her was gone.

He sensed a deep unspoken ache in his soul and wondered if the hurt he'd caused her would leave a permanent breach in their relationship. Then, unbidden, the sense of the bliss from the earlier release came rushing back to him. Again he was in a state of peace. He didn't need her, he assured himself. In fact, he needed to forget her completely. He forced down another drink of his brew and with it a fresh resolve into his heart.

Chepa sat nearby, stoking a small fire he had built earlier at the base of a pile of rocks. Several trees grew in the spaces between them. Their branches sculptured by the sea wind, twisted in an artistic grotesqueness toward the cliff above. The steady breeze blowing in from the water carried a salty scent with it. Two sea birds whirled in the eye of the morning sun as it rose over the high mountains at Bracken's back. The last of the planet's moons, still lingering in the morning sky, gave off a pastel glimmer as it descended toward the sea. Refreshed by the warm drink, Bracken turned and walked back to where Chepa poked at the remains of the fire.

He yawned and stretched. "Do you think your friend Dalfang will be at his cabin?"

Bracken poured the dregs of his drink over the dying coals, eliciting a hiss of steam, "I can't be sure, but even if he isn't, I'm confident I can get into Vonervyn without his help."

He reached into his pack and drew out the polished metal piece that Dalfang had given him. "The code is etched right here on this plaque. Speaking the phrase sets up vibrations in the metal that then triggers the mechanism that opens the dimensional portal."

Bracken rubbed its surface with his sleeve, removing some fingerprints he'd left on its glossy surface before he returned it to his pouch. He would be glad when he was back with Brish in Vonervyn. The recent events in

Nerkush had left him rattled, and he needed the calm atmosphere of the land on the portal's other side.

Chepa collected his sleeping gear from the sandy ground. "Sounds unbelievable to me. But after the Mingus realm, anything seems possible, even making rock disappear by speaking to it."

In his mind, Chepa was still unconvinced, but after the long discussion about Vonervyn he'd had with Bracken the night before, he was willing to give it a try. If the whole thing turned out to be a fantasy, at least he could continue to hide out from the Pirax by camping here in the forest. He stuffed the remainder of his things into his bag and started up toward the mountains. "How long do you think it will take us to reach the entrance?"

Bracken slipped his bag over his shoulder and kicked some sand over the hissing embers. "It's quite a climb, but it shouldn't take us long after the good night's rest we've had."

Chepa finished his drink and stowed away the cup in his pouch. "Well, I'm following you."

"Fine, we'll leave just as soon as I'm sure the fire is out." Bracken leaned over to check the darkened cinders peeking up through the sand. As he did, a silver oval slipped from his bag and dropped onto the ground.

"What's this?" wondered Chepa, stooping beside Bracken and picking up the item.

Bracken pointed toward the oval. "It's an energy egg, probably the same kind the Pirax used to blast into Ley's place."

"How did you ever get a hold of one?"

"Ley gave it to me when we were being chased by some gem pirates back in Accad. He probably got it on the underground market. It's amazing the things you can get there. I don't suppose Ley ever showed you his fire pellet tube?"

"No." *Why the weapons?* Chepa wondered. But after the run-in with the 'Rax, he could understand.

"So he picked this up on the underground market?" Chepa examined the egg more closely. "It looks dangerous." Gently, he popped back what appeared to be a protective plate on the side of the egg. Several indicators with numerical markings glowed on its surface with a few activation points beside them.

"Be careful what you touch, those things can activate in a moment," warned Bracken.

Chepa warily snapped the cover shut.

"That's better," sighed Bracken. "Don't ever open that lid unless you're ready to set one off. I've heard about a few people who have accidentally been blown apart just fooling around with one." Bracken took the lethal object from Chepa and slipped it back into his knapsack.

Bracken pushed another mound of sandy soil over the dead fire. He gazed up the mountain as he readjusted his bag and stam case, anticipating an arduous climb. "I guess we'd better get moving. That hill's not going to shrink with us standing here looking at it."

Chepa followed suit, and the two friends started up the ravine toward Dalfang's cabin.

CHAPTER 54

FOREST OF ZOREK, DOOR TO VONERVYN

LYNREXS (MID-SUMMER), 5512

Bracken stood in front of the high granite wall that Dalfang had first led him to weeks earlier. After a brief stop at the wizard's cabin, they had found it empty and so they'd resolved to head for Vonervyn's entrance on their own.

Chepa sat on the ground, leaning back against a rock, somewhat amused, as he watched his friend repeat the cryptic formula for a fourth time. Bracken paced back and forth in front of the solid stone face, extremely irritated.

"I just don't understand why it doesn't work. I wish Dalfang were here. I'm sure it would work for him immediately. I don't know why he wasn't at his cabin. If he been home he would have joined us and then you'd see how quickly this thing would work."

Chepa kicked at the loose rock beneath his feet and smirked. "Well, if you haven't opened any secret world, at least you've led us to a fine place to hide. I can't imagine Pirax ever finding us here." He stood up and walked around, examining the texture of the narrow canyon walls. "This is quite a unique rock formation, but the entrance to another world? That I find hard to believe. Are you sure this Dalfang didn't just put you in a trance somehow and cause you to dream the whole thing?" Still weary from the earlier hike he found his seat again.

Bracken's brows furled in a frown as he turned to Chepa. "Yes, I am sure I wasn't dreaming. I met real people in there." He pointed toward the wall. "Right now, there's one I'd especially like to see again."

Now that Lisha was no longer his concern, he wouldn't bother to resist Brish's invitations. "If only this code would work." Again, he repeated the phrases.

IVEX · HITH · MINAE · TRAE TRAE · VO · REM

Nothing. In complete exasperation, Bracken tossed the flat metal rectangle against the wall and slumped down on a large round rock. The coded placard bounced off the granite and clanged against the ground, sending a ringing tone down the narrow ravine.

As the last metallic echo faded, another deeper sound filled the canyon. "You're much too impatient, my son." Dalfang's cloaked form appeared from behind an outcropping of rock. "You must learn to be more faithful in your attempts at releasing the key to the passage."

Bracken jumped to his feet, completely surprised by the sudden but comforting appearance of his mentor. "Dalfang! Where did you come from? We looked for you at your cabin, but no one was there."

Dalfang smiled a rather playful but understanding smile. "I wasn't there because I planned it that way. I saw you and your companion long before you reached my home. I've been hiding. Quite simply, I wanted to see how you'd do when facing the entrance without my coaching. Apparently you need some more training."

Bracken slumped down again. "Yes, I've failed miserably."

Dalfang moved alongside Bracken and patted him lightly on the shoulder. "Not unusual for a novice. You'll learn in time." The older man's weathered features broke into a fatherly smile as he glanced over to Chepa. "Who is your companion?"

Bracken stood up, "This is Chepa, my new friend. He's a tremendous musician. You'll have to hear him play the stam. He's really good."

Dalfang continued to smile at the stranger and nodded at Bracken. "A pleasure, I'm sure. I'll look forward to it."

Dalfang extended his hand to Chepa, his face glowing, reflecting his inner wisdom. "As Bracken has already told you, my name is Dalfang, guardian of the Anindi Passage to Vonervyn."

Chepa stood up to shake Dalfang's hand, still slightly startled by his mysterious appearance. "Happy to meet you."

"Chepa and I were with Ley Os and some of the others when the Pirax broke in on us," interjected Bracken. "If it weren't for the fancy guard mechanism he had installed, we might have ended up in Accad's detention fortress. I guess they've been after him for some time."

"Indeed, a possibility," said Dalfang, frowning as he folded his arms and leaned back against the granite wall. "Considering his foolish displays, I am amazed it hasn't happened sooner."

"Do you know Ley Os?" asked Chepa.

"Quite well. He once stood where you are, my friend."

"You mean he's been to Vonervyn?" asked Bracken in a tone of amazement.

"At least twice," admitted Dalfang, a look of reflection on his sage-like face. "I brought him here shortly after his encounter with the first gems Cib Mingus had released. We met years ago in Accad. We'd both been followers of the edge-poets. We were inspired by what they proclaimed. One of them brought us here and taught us much about the realm beyond this gate. But after a while, Ley seemed to have little interest in what the poet-master offered. The Mingus realm had become much more exciting. Later, after a bad experience with the gem, he was willing to listen. He returned here, and I tried to convince him of the higher virtues of the world that lies behind this wall."

Dalfang walked over to the stone's surface and rested his hand against its face. "But unfortunately once again he was unimpressed. He, like you, failed to open the passage without help and therefore chose an easier alternative. He soon went back to the way of the gem. It is true that for most this path takes a while to master, and many give up too soon." The wizened man's glance fell on Bracken. "Easier is not always better, my young friend, something I hope you'll remember."

"Certainly you don't believe that the Mingus is a worthless experience, do you?" said Bracken defensively. "I've had wonderful encounters in that realm."

"No doubt, and I would never discourage you from your quest for truth. I just have my hesitations when it comes to Os. He seems too eager for power, and apparently he intends to have it any way he can."

Dalfang's expression darkened slightly as if recalling some unpleasant memory. He mused for a moment and then spoke. "But away with such thoughts for now," the old man's face lit up. "You are standing at the gateway to something far greater than even the Mingus realm."

Dalfang reached down and picked up the metal plate that Bracken had tossed away and held it out to him. "You must try again. You might be successful this time."

Feeling reluctant, Bracken took the cryptogram and, with an encouraging smile from Dalfang, stood in front of the wall. He firmly spoke the secret phrases inscribed in the placard. Unnoticed by the two young men, Dalfang whispered the cryptic words as well.

As before the rectangle began to vibrate rapidly. A loud humming stirred the rock around them, followed by a steady ringing. Then, in the next instant the miracle Bracken had hoped for occurred. The granite face dissolved. Chepa, seeing the wall vanish for the first time and the shining passage materialize beyond it, stood captivated until Dalfang spoke. "Let us go, Chepa. What you see now is only a doorway. Vonervyn's lasting treasures lie beyond."

Chepa followed only to be stunned again as he stood on the green hills of another world. Like Bracken had done when first confronted by Vonervyn's glory, he fell back and rolled on the grass, laughing ecstatically. Gradually, he regained his composure and picked himself up from the ground, following his guides into this new world.

For the remainder of the day, he listened intently as Dalfang and Bracken led him through the wonders of Vonervyn. The following hours were filled with odd but pleasant surprises as he met Dimishta and his friends. The scenic landscape and fresh atmosphere of this otherworldly plane left all of them pleasantly intoxicated. Even Dalfang seemed enraptured.

Near the close of the day, the three of them sat in Brish's house eating and sharing the delightful events of the day's explorations. Brish had served a unique combination of foods.

First she brought out a large bowl of gumtas, a flat reddish-brown fruit shaped like the leaves of the tree on which it grew. It was eaten with the skin and had a delightful taste similar to a mixture of some of the fruits grown near Tizra. The visitors made quick work of these, asking for more.

Next came dishes of what Brish called rowlet, consisting of several herbs, fragrant plants blended together with a purple-colored sauce.

Brimming glasses of ulten, a lightly intoxicating drink, accompanied the banquet and had to be refilled several times, as the guests washed down the sumptuous fare.

When the meal ended, Brish set a decanter of what she called voitqi, a slightly more intoxicating beverage, on the low table between them. They each filled their glasses and soon it had its promised effect.

Satiated and overflowing with praise for Brish's fine cooking, the group slumped back into their cushioned seats and took slow sips of the voitqi. Setting his drink down, Bracken cupped his hands behind his head and stretched his long legs under the table in front of him. "This place is more enchanting the second time. I almost forgot our recent troubles," he said, glancing over at Chepa.

"And what could those be?" asked a puzzled Brish.

"I recently lost one of my closest companions. You remember how you saw his name in your mind?"

"Not Silas, Bracken. How could that be?" stammered Brish, a frown clouding her face.

"Yes, he fell to his death, or perhaps he was pulled to his death. I'm still trying to sort it all out." Bracken suddenly thought of another companion.

Lisha's form danced in front of him, swaying gently in his mind's eye. Grieved, he pushed the vision away. "Normally something like this would leave me despondent for some time, but after being here, I feel able to talk about it."

"He was killed near Demur," added Chepa, filling in the details of the tragedy. He picked up a pyramid-shaped ornament from the table in front of him and toyed with it. "It seems some face appeared to him in the mist, calling for him to jump into a pool of light masking a deep ravine in Oak Forest. Bracken saw it as well."

Bracken sat up in his seat, his face growing intense as he considered the demise of his former partner. "That's what I can't understand. He just jumped off into space. Apparently there was nothing there in spite of what we thought we'd seen. Before I knew what had happened, I heard him scream and then he was dead."

Bracken looked over toward Dalfang, who sat quietly listening. The older man's features mirrored a calm sense of wisdom. "Dalfang, perhaps you have some understanding of why it happened?"

"I've known the Mingus realm long before Ley ever opened its vistas to your generation," the wizard intoned confidently.

Bracken looked at Dalfang in surprise. "I had no idea you had ever been exposed to those things."

"Expose is the correct word." Dalfang's eyes seemed to cloud as if he were drifting back into his past. "I've experienced it many times. Cib Mingus was my friend years before Os ever made his acquaintance. Together, Ley and I took many journeys by way of the gem."

Dalfang folded one arm across his chest, his hand gripping the elbow of the other arm as it extended up toward his chin. He gently pinched his jaw between forefinger and thumb as he pondered Bracken's question. "There is good there, but also evil. Not every road one follows is planted with the flowers of kindness and brotherhood. For one like Silas, who knew so little of what he was toying with, tragedy was almost inevitable. In the flow of that realm is concealed a villainy not easily recognized."

"You're saying it was murder, then?" inquired Bracken, his voice full of concern. "A premeditated act of destruction aimed at Silas?"

"Perhaps. If it was, it's not the first," responded Dalfang sadly, a look of compassion on his face. "For years now, I have been aware of the depraved aspects of the gem's power. There can be much good done through the effect, but many have turned it to evil."

Bracken grew uncomfortable in his chair. Standing up, he walked over to a window and stared out into the dusk. "How can evil and good be found in such a beautiful place? I don't understand. There's got to be an answer somewhere, perhaps at its source? Maybe there's central zone where the power originates? Is there such a place?"

"Most certainly there is," replied Dalfang knowingly, as he stood and walked over beside the pensive Bracken. "But it is wisely unconcerned. The energy that holds this great universe together offers us enhancement, even though some have chosen to use it for the wrong means. But often it seems to remain neutral, appearing unconcerned with our plight."

Dalfang's eyes glowed with a deepening hue, shining brightly with the fires of wisdom. "The energy from that source flows out to all of us, and makes us part of one another. Yet, each of us must create our own destiny, choose our own path. I am happy to see you have chosen one that is good. That assurance should be enough for you. Be content with that reality."

Bracken looked into Dalfang's wise and gentle face. "Perhaps you are right, but somehow I won't be satisfied until I find the source of the Mingus and the reason for my friend's death."

"Search until you find, but be careful in your wandering, Bracken. Those who hate such eager souls as yours long to fill their bellies with the broken bodies of innocents."

"Thanks for your advice, Dalfang. I'll be careful."

After a few more rounds of the voitqi, both Chepa and Dalfang turned in for the night. Brish led them out to the guest cottage behind her home and then returned.

But Bracken had stayed behind, still completely alert. Concerns about Silas's death and his breakup with Lisha kept swirling just near the edge of his mind. It was not the scent of the exotic candles glowing in Brish's parlor or the effect of voitqi that kept him wondering. It was something deeper, much deeper; a thirst for truth. The earlier conversation had left him with unanswered questions. If they couldn't be fully resolved in the wise words of Dalfang, maybe they were hidden in some secret that Brish knew.

CHAPTER 55

VONERVYN

LYNREXS (MID-SUMMER), 5512

Brish couldn't help feeling concerned for her friend. "I can tell you're still troubled. I was hoping the voitqi would take the edge off your worries for a little while."

"Thanks for the thought and the glasses," said Bracken, setting his down for the last time. "It's just that when you're so close to someone like Silas for all those years and suddenly and mysteriously they're out of your life, well there's this void. One that's filled with questions."

There was another void there as well, but he wasn't ready to discuss that with anyone, so he buried any thoughts of Lisha. As he spoke he had unconsciously crossed his arms, hoping to draw some comfort from the motion.

He hung his head, letting his thoughts drift off. It was only for a few moments, but when he looked back across the table at Brish, her face had changed. It was very subtle, but noticeable. Her skin had an inner radiance that wasn't there moments before. Her look had become inviting, her mouth slightly open showing the edges of her perfect teeth.

She leaned forward, her elbows resting on her knees, her hands reaching out in a sign of empathy. She held them there for a moment in an attempt to connect. "It must be a difficult thing to lose someone so close. But I can relate. You see, I had a loss as well, years ago. It was my father. He passed when I was in my fourteenth year. I was devastated. I remember a lot of tears and the many times when I couldn't sleep at night."

"I had no idea," said Bracken, suddenly aware that he was not the only one in the room who'd been through the loss of someone dear.

"Well, it was extremely difficult but I found comfort. My mother, who was dealing with her own grief, found a way out and then helped me through mine. Her issue was resolved in a unique way. During that season, she met a teacher, or I guess you could say a mentor. This guide was a female version of Dalfang. She trained my mom in an unusual art that had been passed down from some ancient ones known as the Mydethees. Through their treatment, her pain seemed to melt away. Once she mastered it she tried it on me and I experienced a significant improvement. She would gently but firmly rub my neck and shoulders, quietly chanting the phrases she'd been taught. I could sense this restorative energy flowing through her into me. And gradually a sense of peace came and I found rest. It was more than just the touch of her hands, it was as if she was imparting her peace, imparting that hidden tranquility she'd found in their art. It was this very thing that opened me to the possibility of a world like Vonervyn. So when my guide, Eshtar Cosh, came along, I was ready. My mother trained me in other things as well. There are techniques and many other disciplines that go along with it. If you'd like, I'd be happy to see if they'd work for you?"

At this point, Bracken was ready for anything that would calm him and allow him to rest. "Sure, why not? I'm always open for a new adventure, as you may have guessed by now."

In almost a glide, Brish moved from her spot across from Bracken and came to stand behind him. The next moment, he felt her strong but subtle hands massaging his neck. He could hear her softly chanting something under her breath. It was only a matter of time until he began to relax.

Starting in his neck and radiating out from there, both into his head as well as his spine, the stress vanished as if someone had pulled a stopper at the bottom of a tub and was emptying the pain of his grief.

Brish's hands continued their magic as she moved to his shoulders. The effect only increased until Bracken was nearly asleep. When he stirred himself from the moment, he found Brish sitting beside him.

"Did that help?" she whispered.

"It couldn't have been better."

"I know something even better," she whispered again. And just as smoothly as her hands had done their wonders, she moved her head toward him until their lips met.

Bracken responded instantly, the sense of her presence dispelling his slumber and igniting something in him he thought was gone. That first kiss quickly led to even more, each with a deeper intensity. Bracken's hands moved over Brish's body, probing and exploring its wonders. In a matter of minutes, he was about to pass a threshold into a place he'd only been with a few other women—Lisha and some of the young women that hung around with Chepa's group. But somehow this was different. He knew he must stop before he went any farther.

As the embraces increased and their clothes fell away, he felt more than his body giving in to the sensual touches of Brish's flesh. It was as if his inner being was being consumed, as if his soul was slowly slipping away from his control. It was pleasant at first, but then suddenly troubling. To test how real his apprehension was, he pulled back, no longer surrendering to the overwhelming feelings that pulled at him.

When he did, he felt resistance, a resistance that wasn't coming from him. He knew instantly it was Brish. Something from within her held him fast, locking him into more than her passionate embrace. He drew back, more firmly this time.

"I can't do this, Brish …"

"What?" she asked, sounding shocked that he would not go headlong toward the moment both their bodies sought. "Why not? Aren't you enjoying this as much as I am?"

"There's no argument there, Brish," he gushed. His mind raced, looking for an excuse to stop the inevitable. Then it came to him. "I can't shake it. It's still haunting me even in moments like this. I guess I just can't get Silas' death out of my mind. I'm trying to enjoy what we're doing, but thoughts of his death just keep pushing away the pleasure I'm feeling."

As Brish pulled away and covered herself with her garment, he could tell she was hurt. "Listen, Brish, it's not about you. You're stunning. I'm grateful that you even care … I know you were seeking to comfort me. It's just that I can't shake off this recurring torment."

He hoped his excuse was believable, and he tried to hide his concern about the loss of control he sensed earlier. He'd given himself, body and soul, to Lisha. But somehow with Brish it was different. He had reached a threshold with her; something told him that once he crossed it he would give away part of his spirit that he'd never get back.

Brish, collecting her own emotions, smiled at him, clearly trying not to react. The hurt was still there in her face but he could tell she was managing it. "I understand, Bracken. You're right, it was my way of trying to comfort you, but it obviously wasn't working."

He could see that she was steadying herself. Slowly pulling back from the moment and all the emotion that surged in them both. Then from some inner place, the radiance she had shown earlier returned and as she smiled, her face emptied of its wound. "Like I said, I've been there. You know, the loss of my father that I told you about earlier."

"Yes, and I'm sure it was much deeper than what I experienced with Silas."

"It certainly was. But there was one other thing my mom did that brought me comfort. One other thing the Mydethees taught her, and I'd like to try it if you feel up to it."

"What was that?" asked Bracken, amazed at Brish's resilience. Her apparent ability to come back from rejection and still seem to care moved him. But he was also weary now, and he hoped this would not go back to another version of what he'd experienced earlier.

"She brought him back, she brought my father back," said Brish with such conviction that even though it sounded impossible, he knew she wasn't lying.

"You're not saying he came back from the grave. I mean that she somehow dug him up and put him on display in your home?" Bracken knew that what he was saying sounded outrageous, but so did what he was hearing from Brish.

"Of course not. That would have been even more tormenting. No, you see, my mother learned from the Mydethees what many believe, even people like those who follow the traditions of the teachers on Gathering Day ... that we exist after we pass from this life. But the one thing that none of them could ever do was speak to those in that realm beyond death's door."

Of course Bracken had heard about such ideas, he'd even had a friend, years ago, whose parents attempted to reach out to their murdered daughter beyond the grave. But the whole matter had sounded ridiculous to him, and once his friend's family had explored the possibility, they soon discovered it would be expensive. They did it anyway and came away disappointed, later learning that the person who promised to bring their girl back was a fraud.

"Sure, I've heard about that sort of thing, but I never put any credibility in it. You're not talking about bringing his spirit back are you?"

"Actually that's exactly what I'm talking about, Bracken. That was the other art my mother learned from the Mydethees, and she taught it to me."

"Okay, but you're not saying it's something you can do right here … right now?"

"Listen, Bracken. I can sense the deep wound in your soul. I can sense that you won't have any peace until you get some answers. And it's this gift I have, the one that my mother imparted to me, that's grown more active here in Vonervyn. It grows even stronger when someone like you needs comfort."

"What do you mean?"

"This is what I mean. It's as if something in me won't rest until you're satisfied, Bracken, until you find that place of comfort you're seeking concerning your friend."

"You're right about that. I'm still wondering why, how? Of course there's the guilt too. I just can't let it rest."

"So will you let me try? I mean let me see if I can bring him here to this place. Of course, you know you won't literally see him, but his spirit will come from where he is now and flow out through me."

Still feeling bad for the way he'd disappointed Brish earlier, he knew this would be a way to make amends. "Okay, like I said, I'm always ready for another adventure."

"Are you sure, Bracken? I don't want this to turn out the way things did a few moments ago."

Feeling a bit rebuked, Bracken quickly replied. "No, I'm ready. I won't hold back this time."

"All right then, I'm going to use a technique that enhances the effect. I've learned it from the Filanleys here in Vonervyn. It involves something you love, Bracken. You'll need your stam." Brish pointed toward the corner where he and Chepa had left their instruments earlier.

"But won't the sound wake our friends?" said Bracken, pointing in the direction of the guest huts where Dalfang and Chepa had retired.

"Remember how the Filanleys have built their dwellings, sound-proofing them for maximum peaceful rest? And you won't be playing that loud."

As Bracken removed his stam from its case, Brish went around the room extinguishing the lights and then igniting a small candle she set on the table. Bracken looked to her for the next cue. "So what do I do now?"

"Just simply play a gentle set of chords on your instrument. I'll do the rest."

Bracken began to play a simple progression on his stam. As he did, he soon fell into a peaceful cadence, warmed by the familiar pattern of chords.

Brish opened a drawer in the table where the candle burned and lifted a small but ornate flute. He'd seen one like it before—it was an iconic instrument that was often held in the hand of a legendary being from Ebbern's mythical past.

She placed the flute to her lips, and the most soothing but haunting sound emerged. Swaying gently to the rhythm, she slowly danced around the room. As she moved, the intensity of the sound stayed the same, but the warmth he felt in his hands increased. His movements over the strings became easier, as if he could play without the slightest attention to the pattern. He felt himself flowing into the moment, but he felt the same caution arising in him as he'd sensed before when he was lost in Brish's embrace. But he forced it aside. He'd told her he would not turn back this time.

"That's it, Bracken," said the lovely flute player, moving the instrument away from her lips momentarily. "It's working perfectly. It won't be long now. I'm using a melody the Filanleys taught me, and I'm concentrating my thoughts out into the ether where I know your friend dwells at peace."

As Bracken continued to play, a force entered his arms; it was warm and inviting and gave a grace to his movements. He instinctively knew if he kept playing it would control his arms and hands completely. He liked the feeling, but inwardly chafed at the idea of being controlled by something he didn't understand. But because of his promise, he continued.

Brish's playing came to a crescendo. Then, moving as if filled by some other entity, she rose off the ground. She crossed her legs as she continued to rise into the air, and when she nearly touched the ceiling, her direction changed and she descended ever so gently and came to rest on the floor in front of the candle.

Bracken had seen many things in the realm of the gem, many wonders in the moments he'd played with Golden Flight, and this one was just as real, only it required no ingesting of a substance. It was then that he noticed he'd stopped strumming. Actually, he hadn't stopped, but whatever had been playing through him had stopped. But still he felt locked in place, now literally a captive audience to what unfolded next.

At that moment, he heard Silas. "Who's there, who's calling for me?" came the familiar tones of his former companion. The voice came from Brish's mouth, but the sound was Silas's voice. Brish stared straight ahead, her eyes locked on the candle. "Is that you, Bracken? The Mydethees told me you would call for me."

"Yes, it's me, Silas. It's Bracken. I can't see you, but I recognize your voice. It's too good to be true. You sound peaceful."

"I am, Bracken. I can't explain how peaceful. I'm sure, after the way I died, you were worried. That's why I've chosen to respond. There's such peace here I've forgotten about most of what goes on in the world I once inhabited. But I wanted you to know that I'm all right."

"So where are you, Silas?"

"I'm in a place filled with light where many others are gathered with me. We play music, laugh, love, and learn to move on a path to a higher place."

"That sounds wonderful, Silas. I'd almost like to join you. Things have gotten even more intense lately."

Bracken did feel a certain longing to join his friend. In fact, the sense was soon overwhelming, and as it increased so did the force of whatever had captured him.

He remembered what he'd promised Brish and told himself that it was only momentary and that once the conversation with Silas was ended he would be released. But only a few moments later he realized that was not going to be the case. Whatever had possessed his arms was seeking to move into the rest of his body.

Each time he spoke with his friend, the sensation only increased. He'd clenched his muscles in hopes of stopping the sensation. "So do you miss the rest of us? I mean your family, your friends, and the times we had together?"

"Not at all, Bracken. There's so much here to explore. All things come together on this level, the world the gem took us to was only a gateway. There are many like the one you've found there in Vonervyn and the ones the ancient Mydethees and their kind have been teaching for ages. They're all here blending and flowing ever upward toward the light."

It was then that a thought he'd not expected came to mind. It sounded foolish and somewhat embarrassing. He wanted to ask about it, but the words would not form on his tongue.

He struggled as the dominant force that had invaded him now moved further into his body. He could tell that soon he would no longer have any choice. So with the final bit of strength that hadn't ebbed from his soul, and not sure why he would even mention the name, he asked his question. "What about the Prince of Wonder? Are his followers there? Do they also move with you, ever upward toward the light?"

In that moment, Brish's body jerked violently, shaking like a garment blown in the wind. As she moved, her voice changed, suddenly modulating to several levels lower. Then a guttural rasp came from her mouth. It poured out in one long braying sound. Then as quickly as it had begun it stopped, and Brish's upper torso settled back until she rested on the floor. At that same moment, the sensation that had been controlling him was dispelled, and he was free.

What had just happened? Bracken asked himself as he set his stam down and rushed over to Brish's side. She was limp, and her garments were soaked with perspiration. The sweet fragrance of her perfume mingled with a scent he could only describe as fear. He shook her gently. "Brish, are you all right? Brish, it's Bracken." He stared intently into her face, hoping she would revive.

Her eyelids fluttered as if to open, then she squinted and her beautiful green pupils were looking at him as though she was awakening from a dream. "Bracken, what happened? I was floating in this beautiful place, only aware of peace and then suddenly I heard a phrase … something about a Prince and then … I saw these ugly faces flashing before me angry and retreating away. And after that only blackness … until you appeared through a fog."

"I'm glad you're back, but are you all right?" repeated Bracken.

"I guess so, just a little drained from the whole experience. Did you hear from Silas?"

"Yes, he told me he was at peace, and that brings me peace, at least for now. But something happened at the end that I still have to process. But thanks for being willing to do what you could to comfort me."

She smiled at him as he lifted her up, helping her gain her footing. The glow had returned to her face, and she appeared happy, a weary happiness. "Well, after all that I'm ready to sleep. I'm thankful that all of you are here with me because I know my sleep will be peaceful and safe."

Her words left Bracken concerned as the memory of the monstrous being he'd encounter on his last time in Vonervyn returned. He wondered if the thoughts of that attack still worried her. So he responded with as much confidence as he could muster. "Yes, you're safe, and I'm sure all of us here wish that for you."

She turned and headed toward her bedroom. "Are you sure you don't want to join me tonight, Bracken? I mean just to sleep, nothing else."

"Sure, I'll be along shortly, my adrenaline is still stirring and I have a lot to think about, especially since I was the only one conscious to observe what just happened. Go ahead, I'll be there soon enough. My body's weary and I'm sure it will soon override my mind."

She gave a gentle wave as he watched her walk toward her sleeping room. He couldn't help but sense a deep masculine urge as his eyes followed her, but he caught himself and turned toward the front entrance, determined to sort things out.

When he stepped into the night air, he could tell that the dance of the fireflies had just ended, for the remnants of their glow was still hanging in the air providing the surrounding area with a faint light.

To his right, he could see the giismis slowly moving about in their pen. He wondered why they were still awake, so he walked toward their enclosure to investigate.

Seeing him move in their direction, the animals gathered near the area where he approached the fence. He could hear their voices, like the sound of a whimpering swaim he'd once found caught in a hunter's abandoned trap. When he'd release the creature, it gave him what he considered a look of gratitude before slowly moving away, gently crying from its pain. It was at that moment that he reconsidered his view of their cry. Perhaps the giismis' sounds were not the sweet mutterings of happy creatures.

He looked closer into their faces, finally focusing on one of the larger ones as it lifted its front legs up on the top railing of the fence.

Bracken returned the creature's gaze, captivated by its lonely cry and looked into its tiny silver eyes. As he watched, another face superimposed itself over the blue fur and the sterling eyes. It appeared to be the face of a man.

Bracken shook his head and rubbed his hand across his eyes, certain that the effect of the intoxicating beverage he'd consumed earlier was impairing his vision. But looking back at the face of the creature again, the same man-like face reappeared.

Then in his mind, he sensed that the man was speaking to him. He tried to shove the thoughts aside as some sort of delusion, but they kept reemerging in his train of thought.

So he chose to focus on them, and over the plaintive cry of the milling animals he distinctly heard these words, "So she almost captured you too. If she had, you'd be here with us. Of course, we're only partly here in this pen. Our bodies are back in Nerkush or some other place on Ebbern, but part of our souls are here. A part we wished we had never given away. In fact, we find ourselves still captivated by her, still longing to embrace her once more, and that's why every time she comes into view we gather to watch her every move."

Bracken could not believe the thoughts surging up in his mind. But there was a pattern to them, they clearly came from a stream of consciousness, someone who was there, more than a mere lowly creature.

"You've been lucky, my friend. For some reason none of us understand, you were not trapped by her spell. But let this be a warning, leave quickly. No one we've ever known has resisted her charms for long."

In the next moment, Bracken was doing something he knew was insane, but he did it anyway. He spoke back to the blue-furred being, "I believe you're speaking to me. It might sound crazy, but here goes. I want to know if I'm really hearing from you. So if you've been speaking into my mind, then I need some kind of sign from you. Here's what I'm asking you to do, all of you. Right now turn away from me and run to the other side of your pen."

The large creature that had been speaking to him suddenly removed its feet from the fence and then turned around immediately. Along with the others already moving ahead of him, the animal ran to the fence on the far side of the enclosure. At that moment, a fear gripped Bracken. It was raw and fierce, but he chose to control it. He knew he must leave quickly. "Thank you," he said to the creatures at the far side of the pen. Then, firmly and with great determination he walked back into Brish's dwelling. Finding some writing materials, he scribbled out a note:

Thanks, Brish, for your wonderful hospitality. You're like no other woman I've ever met. But I found that I still can't sleep, so I've set off tonight toward the Filanley village. I've got some questions for them. I'll rest once I get there and then head back through the gate to Nerkush in the morning. My meeting with Silas last night has raised more questions than it's answered, but it's been enlightening—along with a conversation I had with your giismis. I'm sure you

understand what I mean by that. Anyway, no doubt when I wake tomorrow I'll
find it's all been a crazy dream.

Best Wishes,

Bracken

P.S. Give my regards to Chepa and Dalfang and tell them if they want to
say good-bye they can meet me at the gate in the morning. I'll wait for them but
only for a while. I really must get back to Nerkush.

Leaving the note on the table where the small candle still burned, he gathered up his stam and pack, then headed out into the night, letting the light of the bright stars guide him.

The next morning when he awoke, Bracken was greeted by the Filanleys with a warm meal and questions about how he was feeling. When he'd arrived at their compound the night before, he wasn't sure how they would respond to his sudden intrusion. But they'd been gracious in spite of the fact that he had awakened them. He poured out a tale of having too much to drink. They seemed to accept his excuse and offered him a place to sleep it off.

When Bracken finished his meal, he walked to the obelisks. He was a little surprised to discover that Chepa, Dalfang, and Brish were all there to meet him. They shared a warm greeting and then stood together near the open passageway saying their good-byes.

"You're sure you don't want to stay a few more days?" asked Brish, a little concerned. "Your note caught me completely by surprise. I will admit last night was really odd, but that part of your note about talking to my giismis. What did that all mean?"

"Yes, I agree last night was odd, I'd say really odd. I'm not sure how much was reality and how much was the result of the wonderful beverage you served us. But whatever the case, I've got much to sort out, and I think the best place to do that is back in Nerkush."

"You're sure you don't want to stay here?" asked Brish, Dalfang affirming her suggestion. "I can't think of a more peaceful place to sort things out. Besides, the rest would do you good, you've been through a lot recently."

"No," insisted Bracken, staring beyond the passage and down the arroyo toward the forest below. "I've got to go. Too many things have gone unanswered.

"What about you Chepa?" ask Brish. "Will you stay?"

Even though Chepa wanted to stay on, he knew that his group awaited his leadership, and he felt compelled to go back too. "No, I'm going with Bracken. I've got some unfinished business there. But I'm going to bring my band mates to Vonervyn as soon as I can convince them of its glories."

Bracken turned back for one final view of Vonervyn. "I hope you do come back to Nerkush sometime, Brish. Your experience here is so much more profound than mine. You could convince many of its virtues."

Brish looked down the passageway at the stony pathway beyond it. "No, Bracken, I don't think I'll ever want to go back. Right now Vonervyn holds more for me than I'll ever find there." She nodded in the general direction of the distant city.

"What about you, Bracken? Will you come back here? I thought you were going to bring others with you and explore the abilities Vonervyn promises to awaken in you."

Bracken reached out and embraced her in a gentle farewell. "In time, undoubtedly I will, but for now I must wait and get answers to a growing list of questions. After that I'll bring others back here with me. Many need this beautiful place."

Dalfang interrupted, extending the rectangular cryptogram to Bracken. "If you're to return, you'll have need of this. I trust you've learned from our little lesson to be patient. If you are, the passage will open eventually."

Bracken took the coded plaque from Dalfang. "I'll be sure to remember what I've learned. I do want to come back."

"Good-bye then," declared Brish.

"Until then," recited Dalfang, raising his hand in a departing gesture.

"Good-bye," said Bracken as he and Chepa turned and walked through the passageway and down the path shaded by the tall trees.

The gateway closed behind them and the high ravine stood again, a lonely sentinel hiding mysteries it could not speak.

CHAPTER 56

OAK FOREST

LYNREXS (MID-SUMMER), 5512

Ley was relieved to see Bracken and Chepa as they stepped through the door of Roon's house in Oak Forest. Duvalla let them in, only after she had peered through the watch hole and was sure they were not someone else. Undoubtedly, they were expecting other visitors, not nearly as friendly. But thankfully they hadn't been harassed since the day following Silas's death when the Pirax investigators had searched the place. Nor had they come looking for Ley at Roon's place. Bracken wondered if maybe Roon had somehow paid them off. When Chepa saw his trans-max out side he'd told Bracken he was sure Roon must have pulled some strings to get his band's vechicle back.

Ley offered them a seat near himself and the others. "Have you heard what's happened in Accad?" he said despondently.

"What do you mean?" wondered Bracken as he took the glass Duvalla offered him. "We came around on the western side on my way back. We didn't stop in the city. I have no idea what's taken place since we parted."

Ley looked down into his glass, his voice laced with bitterness. "It's the Fathers again," he muttered, swirling the liquid in his hand. "The same night the Pirax broke into my home, they raided most of the others who are influential in the Community. The Central Council wants us out of Accad, and I guess they have decided to use whatever measure it will take." Ley looked up, anger burning in his eyes. "What they don't understand, they hate, and what they hate, they want to destroy." The anger in Ley's eyes told Bracken he wanted to destroy them in return. "I'm sure they'll trace us here. So far Roon's wealth and influence have covered us, but it will only last so long."

Bracken nodded, his earlier thoughts confirmed. "So if they do find you, what do you think they'll do with you and the rest of us?" He wondered how he might respond if they were raided again. He placed his hand on his pack and felt the energy egg beneath the fabric of his bag. Perhaps he'd be tempted to use it.

"Well, we can hide all the gems so they can't run us up on that issue, but I'm sure they'll find some reason to confine us. And if they can do that to the leaders of the Community, it may eventually fall apart, and all we've worked for will come to nothing."

"What can we do? There's got to be some place we can hide." Bracken was becoming desperate. He thought of Vonervyn, but that would never work with Ley, remembering what Dalfang had told him.

Bracken began to review his options in view of his recent encounters. First there was Silas's death and now the Pirax were pressing down on them. Then there was the question about the Mingus source. A seed of bitterness still remained in Bracken's heart for the way Ley had moved in on Lisha. With all the confusion after the Pirax raid he'd not had time to confront Ley over that issue, and apparently the gem dealer had forgotten it completely in the face of his current troubles. With those pressing matters before them Bracken knew that it would be wise to bury his issues with Ley for the present.

He needed answers, and Os held the key. He was the only source of the gems, and right now Bracken wanted the most powerful ones he could find. He looked at Ley, discouraged, yet hopeful that he had an answer. Os always seemed to have answers. Like the amazing way he'd been prepared for the attack at his home and the way he'd cleverly brought them through it.

Bracken was sure Ley would have the direction they so desperately needed now, in fact he told himself Os had better have it now. They needed to act before it was too late. Not waiting for confirmation, he announced it to everyone in the room, "If they're hoping to crush us by locking up our leaders, then you need to escape and wait until things calm down. The

Community's a great network. Surely they know how to stay connected. They can keep the people informed that all the leaders are okay. Let them know that it will be just a matter of time before you emerge again. I'm sure that will work. It's got to work ... So, Ley, all you've got to do, all we've got to do is find a place to hide for a while. You always seem to have the answers. You must have some now?"

Bracken's sudden inspiration seemed to encourage the Gem dealer. Ley stood up and walked to the window. Staring out, he thought quietly for a moment. "I have an acquaintance in the Valley of Raka. He's not a friendly man, but if we do a little work for him, I'm sure he'll help us in return. We can probably hide there for a while."

"That sounds good," said Bracken. "Of course, the way I feel now, anything does."

Chepa placed his drink on the table beside his chair. He was depressed in spite of his sojourn in Vonervyn. The re-entry to Nerkush had been a shock. "Why don't we use the gem? I'm sure we'll have a much better outlook when we're through."

"Agreed," echoed Roon and the others, nodding.

Ley reached for the pouch on the floor at his feet. "You're right."

Bracken watched Ley remove several cases from his sack. "I've a favor to ask you," he said as Ley placed the burnished boxes on the tabletop in front of him.

"What would that be?"

Bracken felt an anxious rushing in his heart and mind. He had to find the source of the gem's power even if it meant losing his mind. "I want to use the most powerful gem you have," he declared.

Os looked reluctant. "I'm not sure you're ready for it yet."

"I'm ready," said Bracken firmly, staring straight into Ley's eyes. "Silas wasn't, and I want to find out why. I can't keep going on like this without answers."

Os seemed to recognize that Bracken's determination would not be denied. Perhaps there was a little bit of guilt there over the matter with Lisha, Bracken told himself. He owed his young follower something.

"All right!" Ley acknowledged. "But you do so at your own risk. So you want the strong ones that Cib and his crew uncovered. Well, as I told you before, they do more than just take your mind to another place. These will literally carry your whole body to another dimension."

"I know Ley. I took two of them after our run in with those thugs. You recall I couldn't find you after that event. I hung out in Accad for a while. Lots of people in the Community were experimenting. Some of distributors had a few of the more powerful variety. They were afraid to take them so they offered them to me."

"You've got a lot of guts kid. I tried the more powerful ones only once and wasn't sure I'd make it back. I had some scary moments out there. I encountered some creatures that amazed and also frightened me."

"That never happened to me. What sort of creatures were they? Beings like us?"

"No, these creatures were all light. They seemed to float on light."

"So why was that so terrifying?"

Ley's pupils narrowed as if he was recalling something almost too difficult to put into words. Finally he spoke. "It was what happened after that, on my way back to this realm. Nightmares. That's all I can say. I met things I've only known in my worst nightmares."

"Why would they be there? I mean, in such a beautiful place?"

"Well, that's a question I can't answer, and I've decided just to leave it alone. For now I only use the weaker stones. The ones that please me, that keep me close to what I know."

"Tell me some more about this light creature. Did he give you a name?"

"He was called Hiffornak, or Hifnak. Something like that. He said I had penetrated to the Zyphon Level, whatever that is. Said he represented some higher race of beings who were watching over us."

"Didn't you want to know more about him, his origin, his relationship to us?"

"Of course, but at the time I was just overwhelmed with the beauty of the whole experience. You know, the pulses of pleasure. Talking to him was almost a distraction. So I let him drone on. I was sure I'd find time to ask him more later."

"Well, was there a later?"

"Not really. The Mingus Effect started to fade and I wanted to get back. This 'Hiff' being told me that if I followed the stone's impulses with my senses they would guide me back."

"And did they?"

"Yes. But that was when everything turned dark. That's when the nightmares started."

"How did you get through them?"

"I just ran. Ran with my legs, my mind, my heart. Finally, whatever was chasing me just seemed to give up. Next thing I knew, I was back in my place in Accad. It was like waking up from a dream. My companion at the time, Dreeme, was completely in shock. She'd seen me disappear hours before after taking the gem and then when I came back it scared her. I just appeared beside her in bed. She was so shaken she left the next day and I haven't seen her since."

"Have you wanted to go back there? I mean, take one of the stronger stones again and explore?"

Again Ley's pupils narrowed. Bracken could see that there was a struggle going on in Os's mind, but this time there was no hesitation before his friend spoke. "No, I'll leave that sort of thing up to stronger souls. Besides, the benefits of the weaker stones are just fine with me. Why tempt another encounter with monsters even if there are creatures of light out there too? There are lots of strange forces out there, Bracken. Most of them are friendly, though." Ley sorted through his bag and then stopped for a moment and stared back at Bracken with a questioning look. "I'm not quite sure if this is the wisest thing. Yes, I've got a few of the stronger stones. In fact they're more powerful than what my distributors gave you. These are a type that I've never given to anyone. In fact, no one's ever asked for one. So they're safely hidden away. But maybe this will give you the answers you seek. Maybe this is what you need. I'd be glad to give you one. I mean, if you're really serious."

Bracken was intrigued by the whole story. He couldn't deny he was afraid, but he couldn't turn back in his search for answers either. And he was running out of options. He hadn't found what he'd hoped for in Vonervyn, and none of his friends' answers seemed right.

He looked to Ley and nodded.

"Okay," Ley said. Reaching back into his pack, he sorted through it until he found what he wanted. He handed Bracken a small burnished case. "Here, the stone's inside."

Preparing himself for what would no doubt be a taxing journey, Bracken quickly shed his boots, long coat, and belts. Wearing only a light shirt and pants, he shouldered his bag. He took the silver case from Ley's hand and paused momentarily as the others swallowed the milder variety. Soon they settled back blissfully, completely unaware of the struggle going on in Bracken. Now that he had the stone of power before him, he felt hesitant. He wanted to throw the case down and run from the room. He wanted to leave, to hide, and to forget it all. But he knew he couldn't. This struggle for answers must end. He had decided. He must do it now or he never would. With a look of determination, he opened the case, removed the glowing dark-green jewel, and lifted it to his mouth. In a moment it was gone, tumbling down his throat. He smiled only once, the expression frozen on his face and then his body gradually dematerialized.

Moments later, he found himself in a corridor of green vines. Hearing the sound of trickling water, he looked down and saw small sparkling rivulets of moisture running beneath his feet. All around him beautiful foliage fluttered as if tickled by an unseen wind. In the distance he could hear the sweet chirping of tiny creatures. But he was determined not to be distracted by such lushness. Eager to press on, he headed deeper into the dimensional link, reminding himself that he'd come for answers. Answers concerning the death of his friend Silas. Answers he was sure he would only find in the upper regions of this realm.

CHAPTER 57

THE HIDDEN ZONE

LYNREXS (MID-SUMMER), 5512

Hate was like a meal for Hyslevix, one of the Shadow Czar's more powerful underlings. He stood in rank just below Strieme. But in many ways, he was motivated with a determination greater than his better. That commitment had kept him in a place of leadership within the ranks of the Czar's minions. Many remained under his command in spite of his failures, because he had perfected his hostility. It was a drive that few of his kind possessed, propelling him forward with an unquenchable determination.

Hate was something he savored and consumed like a gourmet of the darker senses. He was deep into a savory moment of rage against his current victim, one of a host of poor souls who inhabited Ebbern. The sufferer's mind was churning under his onslaught like a cauldron of gelatin. Hyslevix stood above his quarry, his own form hidden but obviously gnarled, weak, and languid to anyone with the power to pull aside his charcoal-colored shroud. The more powerful beings of his race, like Strieme often did just that so they could delight themselves in his humiliation.

But now he was the one with the power. He had become the tormentor, and he wielded an invisible lash of vexing words with no mercy. He twitched with an inner thrill as he toyed with the ignorant beings that dwelled near him. He was just a whisper away beyond the thin interdimensional veil that separated their two worlds. But his prey remained unaware of the source of their torment thinking that it sprang from their own demented minds.

He would hunt for them, drawing them into his web as easily as a fisherman drew unsuspecting fish into his net. And then he would assault their minds and afflict their bodies with pain. Like a tightly held reign, his voice would pull them toward him. Then he would invade their thoughts, pouring hideous words that drove them to the edge of insanity until finally they trembled alone in the corridors of their heads, their pain unknown to others nearby. All that their companions saw was bizarre behavior and grimaced faces contorted in some lonely personal anguish.

He could see his current quarry through the vaporous link that led to Ebbern's natural realm, its soul twisting like a small animal on a serrated hook. He pulled the reign tighter, preparing for another attack, but suddenly without warning a loud hissing sound sneered its way into his mind and brought him up short. He tried hard to ignore it, wanting to continue pleasuring himself, but a rising sense of fear brought him to full attention. He knew from previous acts of disobedience that he best release his prey and give total obedience to the one who called for him.

He severed the filmy link and watched with a sense of melancholy as the victim drifted from his sight back through the vapory ether that link their two worlds. The hissing grew to a crescendo, ending as the command burned into his mind like a fiery dart from some smoldering abyss.

"Why didn't you respond immediately?" demanded the voice in his mind. "I should crush you and toss your decrepit body to the lower levels. The semex would love to feed on you." This chilling threat stung him, setting his mind, emotions, and body quivering like tissue in the astral wind that connected their worlds.

He acquiesced with a string of flattery. "Yes, merciful one, you've generously forgiven my slackness again and again. I owe much to your benevolence." His eyes darted back and forth, looking for a face or form to go with the words that commanded his attention. But he knew he could not see into such realms, for his greed and weakness had temporarily relegated him to this netherworld where he trolled away his days. He had become a slave to the Shadow Czar, and this dark lord's power held him fast, merely by the grip of his words. One misstep and he would find himself in the jaws of the semex, being ground slowly, painfully, and eternally to pulp. But there was always the possibility of restoration. Maybe some day if he pleased his master enough he could join others like Strieme and once again stand before the wicked throne.

The dark lord's voice brought him back from his brooding, "Yes, yes, yes ..." the irritated voice groaned. "Don't bore me with your chatter. I have a special assignment for you and your legions. As much as I hate to admit it, you're one of the best at what you do." This minion silently agreed with his master's words. He also recalled how his disobedience had relegated him to a position slightly below Strieme. But this surprise visit was a sign that perhaps he might yet find redemption and a return to his previous rank.

With this hope rising in Hyslevix's heart, he replied, "How can I serve you, Exalted One? I'm ready to move at your command."

The annoyed voice spat out a string of invectives. "Enough of your flatteries. I've heard them before. What I want now are results."

"Yes, I understand, oh Patient One. I've failed, but please allow me the honor of completing your wish."

His master's rankle ceased and was replaced by a stark raspy command. "Here's your assignment." A series of names, places, and tactics scrolled through Hyslevix's thoughts. *Frim Leider ... Bracken Maetrek ... Pillars of Rimlex ...* the details continued to scroll on. He grabbed each one and stored it in his memory-well so he could review it later.

Now that the data had been received, the dictum continued. "There is a special one I've marked for our attention. Many already see him as a leader. He's gifted with an unusual drive and courage. I've decided that now is the time for us to intervene."

"Sure, sure, we've had others like him before," echoed Hyslevix, hoping his slathering confirmation would endear him to his master. "I've easily allured them and fed their minds with lies."

"This one is different. He's stronger than those others. I can sense he will turn people against us if he ever discovers our plans. But if kept in ignorance, he can be manipulated for our purposes. So, now is the time to lay the groundwork. When he comes to maturity, he will be a perfect agent for us."

The Shadow Czar's voice, expressing his frustration, became abrasive again, pricking his slave's mind like a grate of needles. "Remember the other side is at work too. Our enemies are full of kind words and often grant courage to those we capture. So use the most powerful deception you can craft, one that will allure him and draw him away from them. I've assigned some of our best agents to assist you. They've already used their arsenal of tricks and deceptions on him, but for some reason he saw through them. They failed me, but I've given them another chance. But I can see now that they need to be better equipped to convince our target. That's why we need your unique talent to craft a better lie."

"When should I start?"

"Immediately." The dark lord's voice struck a tone in a lower register, sending a shudder through him again.

"Gladly. Who are the other agents and when will I meet them?"

"I'm sending some of our flux-morph specialists. As you know, they're experts at disguise and can form matter in whatever shape we deem useful. I've assigned one to each of your separate ranks. They must follow the pattern I've laid out and then appear at the proper moment preparing for my arrival. The specialists are already on their way ahead of you. They're assembling near Rimlex. I've instructed them to follow your orders. It's essential that all of you work together. Presently, I've only appeared by remote projection, and I have one final meeting through that mode. But once everything is in place, I will join you in person. Make sure everything is ready and that the deception is perfect. I don't want another failure. If you blunder as others have, it will be the last time you ever do." The hissing returned, louder than before, snarling at him with an unspoken threat, and then it was gone, leaving a hollow place in his soul that had no apparent horizon.

CHAPTER 58

SPACE DISK

ABOVE NERKUSH

Lynrexs (Mid-summer), 5512

Frim Lieter stood in the projection arena of the space disk. Talay stood beside him. His alien face appeared to be smiling, apparently already aware of the good news that the astrogazer was about to receive. A three-dimensional image in the center of the room buzzed as it came to life. The majestic form of Semie, masked behind a protective veil of energy materialized before them.

Talay had told Frim that his leader was in the command center of the mother ship that was located in a higher orbit above Ebbern, safe from any possible attack. Apparently there had been rumors of threats from nearby hostile forces. Various aides as well as an array of technological devices that linked the interstellar assistance force into one unit surrounded the alien commander.

The image gradually came into focus, and then there was a brief pause. Semie began to speak in the deep tones that so uniquely distinguished his voice. "I'm glad to see that you've come so quickly. I have urgent matters to discuss with you!"

Frim shifted excitedly on his feet as he stared up at the image. "What do you have in mind? I'd love to hold another contact gathering. It could be arranged in a few days." Frim bubbled with an exuberance not expected of a professor from the Advanced Mind-Training Center.

Semie folded his hands together, leaning his elbows on the arms of his elaborate chair. "Yes, in a way, that is what I have in mind. Only this time, I hope to reveal our purpose to a much larger group."

The energy veil shrouding Semie buzzed as the commander paused for a moment. Frim strained to see the leader's face, but was unable to penetrate the field's masking effect. Semie continued. "We'd like you to arrange a contact gathering of several thousand people."

Frim shuddered slightly as he realized the magnitude of what was being asked of him. "I would never be able to ... I mean how would I ever be able to gather that large a group? A few students maybe, several of those who've come to hear my lectures; but thousands, that's an impossible task."

"We don't expect you to be able to accomplish this task without assistance. We have arranged for that." Semie turned to one of his assistants, who appeared at his side in the mother ship. The attendant handed him a readout placard, which he perused briefly and then turned back to Lieter. "Have you heard of the musical group known as Golden Flight? I understand they have quite a large following."

"Yes, they're known all over Nerkush."

"What we want you to do is make contact and arrange a concert with them and other groups like them at the Rimlex Pillars."

"What would make them want to do that when they can hold one in Accad?"

Semie continued, unmoved by the professor's doubts. "Our scanning devices have informed us that their Community is being hindered from its normal activities by a Pirax restrictive. They have been told that they can no longer hold large gatherings in Accad."

"I expected as much. The High Council's been wanting to do that for some time."

"Undoubtedly they will be looking for another venue. There have been some recent raids on their leaders and several have been confined."

"What about Golden Flight? I'm sure the 'Rax will be looking for them."

"We've been monitoring their movements. They're in hiding now. But they should surface again soon. I don't think the Pirax will be able to hold their Community in check for much longer. Their movement has great momentum, and I believe after the recent raids they've suffered, they'll be looking for a way to gather their forces again. So I need you to contact them and suggest the Pillars. We've used our influence with one on the High Council. In a few days, he'll act to make sure the pressure on the Community is reduced. Once they realize that the authorities have relented, they will move to restore their unity."

"It wouldn't surprise me. The suppressive tactics of the Council only tend to bring out a greater rebellion in them," Frim smirked. "Once they've been given a fresh opportunity, I'm sure they'll take it."

You'll also need to notify the Community. We've asked one of our agents to cover the cost of hiring messengers to spread the word. When the time comes, he'll provide you with all the funds you'll need. They'll need you to help them organize. Use what influence you have with the governor in your region. I understand he's a fan of yours.

It was true. The area governor was in fact a secret admirer of Lieter's. He'd been a student of the professor years before and still held him in high regard. Frim had even taken him to the Pillars once, and the leader had seen one of the disks for himself. Ever since that time, he'd been a supporter of his former teacher, but quietly and from a safe distance.

"Yes, he'll go along, after I've convinced him of your intentions. What's our strategy once they've all come together?"

Semie stood and walked closer to the visual unit that was monitoring him. "At that point, we will manifest ourselves. Not just one vessel but many, even my craft will appear."

As he came closer, his form grew until his torso filled the entire view cloud, giving him an even more awesome grandeur. "Once these who have become discontented with the narrow and limited viewpoint of the Fathers are confronted by the potential we can offer their race, they will undoubtedly be willing to help us institute our evolutionary restructuring program."

Lieter backed up slightly from the overpowering effect of the massive form. "After what you've told me about the Pirax assaults, I'm sure you're right. Undoubtedly, these people will be looking for some sort of viable alternative to their dilemma."

In the control room, the entourage around Semie looked upon their leader with a certain air of distant respect as he responded. "Once you've made contact with Golden Flight's leader we can act. We've provided a special vehicle for you and a driver. He will meet you here at the Pillars in two sevens and take you to Raka. As I said before, use the influence you have to make the necessary arrangements with the authorities in your area."

Lieter took another step back. "As you suggest, Semie."

"One final thing. When the groups arrive at the gathering, I'd like you to set up a special meeting for me."

"Gladly, Semie. Who do you wish to me with?"

"There's a young man named Bracken Maetrek. I'd like a personal audience with him. He's emerging as quite a leader. One of his songs has become somewhat of an anthem for the Community."

"I remember him. He had an odd experience on your craft shortly after he was discovered snooping around one of my contact gatherings."

"Yes, that's the one."

"He seemed a bit incredulous."

"I think he's gotten beyond that now. So make sure we meet."

"It will be done."

"We'll be in contact to clarify the final arrangements soon. Thank you for your cooperation. Remember, you're doing a great service not only to us, but to your own people."

Semie's form disolved in a brilliant flash leaving behind a dark vapor, which slowly vanished in a series of buzzes and hums.

CHAPTER 59

VALLEY OF RAKA

TAR-LYNREXS (LATE-SUMMER), 5512

Even though Bracken had been in Raka for nearly half a season, he was still haunted by his memories of his journey from Roon's home into the deep realm of the gem. The words of Hiffornak echoed through his mind, sometimes comforting him and other times fluttering just out of reach like an elusive winged creature. Often he would awake from a repeating nightmare, fighting off the hideous creatures closing in on him in darkened corridors. He would recall the strange way their grip had been broken, as he'd called out the Name. It all remained a mystery cloaked in a veil of memory that each day grew thicker and nearly as stifling as the desert air. Many nights he would awake wondering what it all meant. Often he could not fall back to sleep, so mornings found him wide awake and watching the rising sun crest the western hills.

The Valley of Raka was not a valley in the normal sense even though mountains surrounded it. The high mesas and crags, which stood in a semicircle like barren soldiers, dropped their sheer walls almost straight down into the sandy plain on which Terresh Shad had built his farm.

Unusual outcroppings of rock rose periodically out of the rippled dry ground. Some appeared like gruesome creatures of stone, frozen by the stark daylight, waiting only for the long shadows of the eastern mountains to fall and awaken them to stalk the unwary inhabitants of Raka.

Roots of lonely trees clawed at the few mounds of soil that remained among the great sea of dunes and rock. Two of those trees grew in the center of the worker's compound. Near the laborer's quarters were a cluster of decomposing huts pieced together with a combination of sand, slime, and used wood.

After finishing his meal one evening, Bracken joined Ley on the porch of his shack, and they chatted quietly. The final ebb of the evening sunlight emblazoned the eastern sky with gold. Bracken found many questions tumbling in his mind. Slowly, he began the painful task of dredging up and sorting through his recent experiences.

He gradually became more aware of several conflicting problems as he recounted his story. When it came to answers for why Silas had leaped from the cliff, Bracken only had a collection of vague reasons. If it had been pleasant—a step to a higher existence, as some had suggested—then why had Silas screamed before his body was crushed to death? Why hadn't he merely passed blissfully on?

Bracken's most recent probing in the Mingus passage had uncovered several more unresolved problems, far from providing the answers he'd so desperately hoped to find there. The benevolent commission from the glowing creature he had met was something he looked forward to filling. But why had even the enlightened being seemed so unclear regarding Silas's murder. What of the hideous creatures that had attacked him—and why?

Then he wondered about the Name. Why had he called on that name, and what strange power had it exercised over his attackers? The more Bracken struggled with these things, the more it became apparent that going to the source for answers meant going not to the deepest level of the gem's experience but to the Mingus mine itself. He knew that some stones had greater power than others. So he reasoned a concentration of them would provide the critical mass that would take him to the very source of the Mingus realm.

Then there was the space disk. That haunting question had managed to follow him all the way to the desert. Chepa's group had received an invitation to a gathering to be held near the Pillars of Rimlex. Just a few days before, Frim Lieter had appeared at the farm in a high-speed trans-rig and met with Golden Flight. He had invited their group to perform at the gathering, noting that several other bands would be there as well. Lieter had also implied that there was change happening at the highest realms of power in Accad and that they would not be threaten by an intervention from the Pirax. He'd also hinted at the fact that the Disk People might possibly make an appearance. As strange as it seemed, this fascinated Chepa. Ever since Bracken had recounted his experience on the spacecraft, Chepa had hoped he might have one someday. So this possibility only enhanced the offer. Finally, Frim promised that he would pay messengers to get the word out throughout the Community, letting them know about the gathering. The strange proposition had created a lot of discussion amongst their group.

"What do you think of Frim's idea for a gathering near the Pillars?" inquired Bracken as he sat now with Os in the fading light; he hadn't yet heard Os's opinion, though it had been a few days since professor's appearance.

Ley pulled off his left shoe and gently rubbed a blister on his foot. "It seems to be one of the better options we have at present. And I like the idea that there will be other bands at the gathering as well. I just hope Lieter gets the word out to the other bands in Accad and Demur without the Pirax stopping him." His face flinched as he accidentally poked the sore spot too hard.

Ley was aware that the delicate and spontaneous brotherhood that had formed in Accad was in danger of collapsing. He was convinced that it needed the constant care of leaders, like himself, and the influence of the gem. "The longer we go without some form of unity, the greater the chance that we'll never be able to restore what's been lost since our problem with the High Council. I believe this is a sign that it's time for us to leave. Besides, I don't want to stay here forever."

Ley grimaced again as he slipped his shoe back on. "If it's true that Lieter has some pull with the governor in his area, then we can be sure the gathering would go on without harassment."

Bracken was sick of the desert. He was ready to leave, whatever the reason. "I'm as eager as the rest to get out of this place, Ley." He grimaced as he thought about how the sinewy, old vinweok farmer might react. "Shad won't like it, though. He'll be short a whole work crew."

"I'm sure he won't. But he doesn't own us, and after what happened the other day, if we stay any longer in this pit we'll be killing each other.

"You're right there," added Bracken, still feeling the ache from the blows he'd taken in the melee a week earlier. He grew quiet and stared off at the now-gray horizon, contemplating Ley's plan.

Os gave Bracken a knowing smile and lay back in his chair, "We'll leave in the middle of the night while Shad's asleep, and if he wakes up and tries to stop us we'll already be rolling. Frim says the gathering is in five days. It will take us three days to get there in the max. We'll leave in two. Tell the others to prepare."

"Sounds like a plan," agreed Bracken as he rose to leave. "I think I'll head off and wash up before I go to sleep."

"Tell everyone to keep quiet about our little scheme, Bracken. We wouldn't want Shad to find out ahead of time."

"Sure will." Bracken called back to Ley as he trudged off in the twilight.

Nights in Raka were often as extreme as the days. With the departing of the sun, a chill quickly settled over the valley, making the workers retire early to the warmth of their bunks. After cleaning up, Bracken slipped through his front door and crawled into his night covers. He slept a dreamless sleep.

Two nights later, with the bitter words of Shad ringing in their heads, the group drove north toward Rimlex. As the trans-max lumbered over the last ridge out of Raka, the first of three moons rose in the western sky.

CHAPTER 60

THE ROAD TO THE PLAINS OF UMIN

TAR-LYNREXS (LATE-SUMMER), 5512

The journey from Raka to the Pillars was long and boring, even in the comfort of Golden Flight's trans-max. The roadway was bordered on each side by a monotonous repetition of barren sights, rolling by slowly. The scenery was a blend of the familiar Raka landscape with the high ridge of mountains on the western horizon that followed them all the way to the pillars. Once they emerged from the desert, the upper plains contained a periodic mixture of hills and steeps, ringed on the top with circles of rimrock. Finally, the scenery grew more interesting as they crossed the first of two rivers and the fertile valley turned golden with the ripening crops spread out on either side of the highway.

Bracken sat in the front cab with Eier, the driver. All of them were still chafing under Shad's bitter rebuke. The group's abrupt departure had left his ranch in a momentary state of crisis. Without their help, the vinwoek herd would be sure to suffer. The rancher had awoken in the middle of the night and caught them just before they left. He had vented his displeasure quite effectively, promising to curse them to his grave. Ley had only smiled in his casual and aloof manner, softly repelling the verbal barrage as the group climbed aboard the trans and drove away.

Bracken slept fitfully between sharing the wheel with Eier. The driver was a quiet man, his conversation consisting of nods and grunts. Bracken found his companionship worse than the trackless landscape around them. Driven into silence by the driver's lack of communication, Bracken tried to sort out his memories again.

He missed Lisha. Her warm beauty was gone. A deep void filled Bracken's chest. Why hadn't he gone after her? He should have forgiven her and comforted her …. but then she had betrayed him. Given half a chance, she would probably do it again, he told himself. Besides, he was free not to care. He'd reached Atorma, he reminded himself—that state of transcendence. He just needed to keep letting go. But for some reason he was unable to. He secretly admitted to himself that as nice as it sounded, if he lived in such a world, it would be a lonely place. He couldn't imagine a culture filled with those who had so transcended pain and pleasure that all that remained was a feelingless void.

People weren't really like that. Inwardly, he knew reality was different in spite of the nice words and lovely philosophical arguments put forth by the edge-poets. If you loved, you risked the potential of pain, and what was life without love?

He had cared for someone deeply, and that wasn't bad. He'd been hurt and he'd hurt others. He could forget the pain and the love that had made him vulnerable in the first place, but where would that lead? Maybe one could escape the pain of a relationship but somehow retreating into an aloof coldness was not how he wanted to live the rest of his life.

He'd seen the way his parents had cared, argued, struggled, and finally found a place of deep commitment to one another. He had to admit it was healthy, regardless of how he felt about their beliefs. So in reality, he knew he still loved Lisha, but she was gone and he was lonely.

With his loneliness came a bitterness, which he'd try to suppress. Hadn't what she'd done with Os hurt him? Didn't she deserve all the pain that came to her as a result? He hoped she was lonely too. Maybe she had gone back to Tizra. Tizra … how far away it seemed. He'd shrugged off his issues with Ley for the time being. Maybe someday he'd have it out with the man, but for now he'd bury that resentment.

He wondered how his parents and his brothers were. He missed them too. But something had been broken there. He couldn't go home. He could look toward home in his mind, but he could never go there. Besides, those who lived there wouldn't understand him now. Surely they didn't want him back, and to hope they did seemed futile. Frustrated with not being able to resolve these issues, he did his best to push the negative thoughts away, and give in to a fitful sleep.

Two sunsets later, with several kinks in his neck, Bracken pulled the trans-max off the highway near Rimlex. Driving to the nearest Pillar, he parked beside the rigs of several of the other musical groups that would perform the following day. It appeared that Frim had been able to contact other bands and successfully convinced them to join the gathering. The blend of different talents would make for a great program.

A steady stream of vehicles made their way toward the gathering sight. In the distance, Bracken could see many winding their way through the rocks on the open plain. Frim must have done a great job getting the word out to the Community. It looked like they'd have a massive gathering.

Nearby, small clusters of early arrivers sat around their smoking campfires, laughing and passing Mingus gems between themselves. They would soon be running out of the stones without Ley bringing a fresh supply from the mine, thought Bracken.

While Ley and the group were stretching and preparing the meal over the fire, Frim Lieter appeared out of the dimming twilight. Bracken remembered the professor. He looked even more excited than he'd been when they'd first met.

Frim's presence brought back memories of Bracken's time on the spacecraft. He'd seen something strange there that had made him draw back. But seeing the eagerness and faith in professor's face, he wondered if Frim might truly be on the right path.

The recent hardships he and others had suffered made him warm to the possibility that these strange beings from outside his planet may have some answers for his troubled race. He felt willing now to give the whole issue another try.

Frim stepped into the firelight and welcomed the band. "Thank you for coming and joining the other groups that are here." The campfire flickered across his face, creating strange shadows on his boney countenance. "Tomorrow will be a full day. I was hoping to go over a few details with you before the morning."

Lieter went on to explain the impromptu but adequate stage that had been constructed on a large flat rock at the base of one of the Pillars. Scaffolding and mobile power units were erected to handle the broadcasting and amplification of Golden Flight's music.

Chepa discussed a few technical details with the professor, who assured him that all the necessary items had been arranged. Satisfied, Chepa took a tray of food from Eier and settled on a rock to eat his meal.

Lieter was about to leave when he noticed Bracken unloading some of his gear from the storage compartment beneath the trans. "Aren't you the young man who was discovered with your friends at one of my contact gatherings?"

Bracken tossed his sleeping gear toward what, in the fading light, appeared to be a patch of green grass. "Yes, it's good to see you again, Professor Lieter."

Lieter coughed several times, his weak lungs irritated by the chill evening air. "I'm glad to see you here. As I remember, you were the only one in the group that night who didn't become a touch point."

"Yes, I had some strange experiences that night. Some of them, I'm afraid, still remain to be resolved." Bracken knelt down and spread out his things.

"Well, tomorrow should take care of that."

"What do you mean?"

"The Disk People are planning to manifest themselves to the entire gathering. Semie, their leader, will be addressing the whole group. If you have any questions, I'm sure he would be happy to answer them for you. In fact, he's asked for you by name. Says your song has become somewhat of an anthem for the Community."

Bracken reached under his sleeping gear and removed a few stones. "And how would that be possible with all those people there? I hardly think he would have time to give me a private interview."

Lieter squatted down beside Bracken, trying to maintain visual contact in the increasing darkness. "You mistake the character of the Disk People's leader. He's quite benevolent, and apparently he likes your music. He hasn't confirmed this, but I think he wants you to use your gift to share his message. I think that's why he had me contact Golden Flight. He realizes that many of you have stepped up to lead others in a new and positive direction."

"That sounds flattering. But I'm still a little concerned by what happened the last time I went on board the disk."

"I recall you had some sort of strange vision. Well, you're not alone in that. It's not the only time it's happened. Periodically others have come away seeing odd things. I'm sure he has an antidote for it. Whatever the case he wants to meet with you. I hope you'll consider his invitation."

Bracken stood up again and stared toward the campfire, his appetite awakened by the fragrant smell drifting from the cooking pot. He thought for a moment and then responded. "If that's the case, I'd like very much to talk with him."

Bracken had many questions about his first visit on board the spacecraft. But what was even more intriguing was why such a powerful leader would want to meet with him. He seriously wondered why a being who would be addressing thousands the next day and had authority over so many of his race would take time to answer his concerns. But then Bracken also agreed with what Frim had said. He had become somewhat of a leader.

His music had enraptured many that night at the Sphere, and Golden Flight now respected him as well. Perhaps Semie knew this and had a purpose for him. It was not beyond the realm of possibility that he would be commissioned to carry a message of hope to others on his planet.

Maybe he knows my songs can stir others, Bracken persuaded himself. Slowly he began to come to a simple conclusion. He would write songs that would bring others to the message of this exalted being. He turned back to Lieter, with fresh determination.

The professor coughed again before he responded. "So you'll agree to meet with him then."

"Yes, I'll look forward to it."

"See you tomorrow then after the disks arrive. I'll make sure you have an audience with Semie." Frim wheezed heavily. "I really should be getting back to my tent now. This night air is bad for my health." The two said good-bye, and Lieter vanished into the night.

Bracken walked over to the fire where the others were gathered eating their food. As he prepared his own meal, he recalled the message of hope he'd heard Frim and the Disk People offer his planet. He thought on it as his dinner was heating. Later, as he ate, he stared into the night sky, humming quietly between bites. The more he meditated on the professor's message, the more he sensed a gentle muse increasing in his heart. Finally overwhelmed with this stirring, he set aside his supper and took out his stam. It was just a matter of time until a whole new song flowed out of him. He wrote out the words along with the chords on a piece of paper.

Excited by the way the song emerged so quickly, he called to the others around the fire. "Chepa, Naavin, I think I've got something here?" He set the paper down between them and eagerly began to play through the composition, pouring out his heart in melody. The others picked up their instruments and joined in, following the progression Bracken had written out. The band members soon had command of the chord changes, and some of them started to improvise on the theme. "I'd love to perform this tomorrow," said Bracken enthusiastically. "What you think, Chepa?"

"It's not bad, Bracken. I especially like the chorus. What do you say, guys, shall we give it a try?"

"Why not?" said Naavin, nodding in agreement. "The last time Bracken performed with us the crowd loved it."

"Thanks, guys, let's run through it one more time," said Bracken. The band rehearsed the number one more time. Then most of them headed for their bunks in the trans-max, tired after their long trip from Raka.

Bracken took the paper on which he had written the song and signed it. Stuffing it into his pack, he decided he would make this original piece of music a gift to the disk leader when he met with him the next day. Still cheered by the way the song had come forth, he walked away from the fire and sang it once more, this time to the starry sky, before crawling into his sleeping gear for a much-needed rest.

CHAPTER 61

PILLARS OF RIMLEX

TAR-LYNREXS (LATE-SUMMER), 5512

The next day, Bracken was up early helping Chepa and the other groups set up their equipment on the large stage. All morning, a line of trans-rigs and hikers streamed onto the grassy plain that stretched out beneath the Pillars. Their rigs and tents made a multicolored patchwork on the green meadow.

The sky was a flat blue, and only one tiny cloud hugged the horizon. By midday, Bracken estimated approximately twenty thousand people had gathered at the base of the Rimlex Pillars.

Smoke from campfires and the scent of cooking food mingled in a cloud above the free-flowing assembly. Many of the group were from Accad, happy to gather together again without fear of harassment from the Pirax. Others had received word and come from places all over Nerkush.

The gathering exuded an air of excitement as friends danced, caressed, ate, and greeted one another. One by one, various bands performed throughout the day. The crowd before the stage seemed to enjoy each group's unique style, but everyone knew the reason they'd come was to hear Chepa's group.

Bracken looked off toward the range of coastal mountains as the sun gradually descended toward them. All day he wondered when the disks would appear. Why hadn't they come sooner he questioned. Maybe Frim was deluded and they would fail to arrive at all. But Bracken reminded himself that he'd been on the spacecraft; it was real, even if he'd had a troubling vision while on board.

Surely the disks would come. It was a time of destiny for his people, and these beings from the stars seemed to be part of that destiny. He'd experienced the force of the leader's personality and his message for Ebbern. If ever Semie needed a crowd of people ready for a word of hope for this planet, it was the crowd that had gathered here at the Pillars.

Long before Golden Flight's first vigorous notes sounded from the platform, the massive assembly had reached a state of expectancy. Dusk had settled over the huge crowd. The last of Ebbern's moons, each bathed in a hue of crimson, rose above the western hills. When the group finally appeared before the anxious audience, a chorus of cheers and clapping resounded against the pillared backdrop. As Bracken watched from his position near the back of the stage, he could see the faces of the eager audience and hear their applause echoing over the plain as Chepa motioned for the group to begin.

The gigantic sound amplifiers hummed to life like awakened beasts of electricity, purring in subdued anticipation. The first note from Ayan's stam discharged with the ear-shattering impact of a canon. The rest of the group joined him in the tight uniform sound that so characterized Golden Flight's style. A barrage of sonic harmony poured over the waiting listeners.

Stimulated by the surges of musical resonance, the crowd responded, sending back waves of praise and soulful energy that magnified the group's output. This exchange grew throughout their performance as the twilight increased. At one point huge spotlights were activated to illuminate the platform.

Then, to Bracken's surprise, Chepa invited him to join them on the stage. He quickly ran to the rig and grabbed his stam. As he fell in with the group on the platform, some of Golden Flight's earnest fans noticed him, remembering his earlier performance at the Sea Sphere. They cheered, and soon many in the crowd were on their feet.

Bracken firmly struck the strings of his instrument, eager to launch into the melody. The resounding tone shook his body, energizing him as he led the other band members through the first chord set. Moving toward the microphone, he abandoned himself to the moment and gave forth the special song he'd composed for this moment.

The disks come at night beneath a crimson moon
The disks come to save and none too soon
They come with a message says the oracle speaker
A message of hope says the contact Frim Lieter
So gather the Community and their new breed
Gather them with song and cry out their need
Cry for the planet, cry for the youth
Cry for the future and the cosmic truth
Beings of light from Trion's galaxy appear
Bringing hope as their silver ships draw near
With a haunting song from the distant past
These powerful beings promise peace at last
So gather the Community and their new breed
Gather them with song and cry out their need
Cry for the planet, cry for the youth
Cry for their future and cosmic truth
Lieter's a prophet with a voice from the stars
So choose now to break the Father's strangling bars
The people of the Disk bring hope at last
The Councils laws are now a thing of the past
So gather the Community and their new breed
Gather them with song and cry out their need
Cry for the planet, cry for the youth
Cry for their future and the cosmic truth

The first of the red moons had nearly reached its zenith, its crimson face beginning its descent towards the pillars as the music reached its climax. The complex melodies came together into one final note. It resounded, like the ringing of a cosmic bell, hailing out beyond Ebbern's atmosphere. Its tone seemed to pierce the heavens, calling to the sky, beckoning to the stars with an almost pleading cry. Higher and higher it rose, bouncing off the rugged stone sentinels until it seemed to echo forever.

In that moment of clarity, the disks appeared.

At incredible speed, five of them slipped over the top of the Pillars, abruptly slowing to come to rest on the flat mesa directly behind Chepa's group. Then an even larger one rapidly appeared and settled into the center of the others.

The gathering watched with blissful bewilderment as simultaneously, all the spacecraft opened their portals. Rank upon rank of alien figures descended the lowered ramps and assembled in two parallel lines running approximately six feet apart, ending at the middle of the stage.

They looked angelic. Their bodies were covered with the strange, hugging garments that Lieter had seen on his first meeting with them. Their angular faces glowed with an otherwordly essence as they looked over the crowd. Reaching their place, they turned in one unified sweep and faced the entrance to the larger command ship.

With an air of regality, Semie stepped forth and descended in a flowing motion through the throng of guards. He walked to the platform. The luminous energy veil, which constantly guarded him from any unexpected assault, cloaked his entire face and body. Only the faintest outline of his indiscernible features showed through. Breathless, Bracken stepped aside to yield the microphone to the approaching disk leader.

Standing erect and completely motionless, the alien spoke directly to the gathering in their own tongue. "This is an important day for your planet. You stand on the threshold of a new era."

The gathering had become completely quiet and in that stillness, his voice wafted soothingly over the crowd. "We have come to assist you in your quest for a higher life. Your leaders have brought your planet to the brink of destruction. You are right to oppose them and their backward ways. All efforts of war must end. You must turn your energies toward the stars. The law of your leaders is dying. A new age is coming. The future belongs to you."

Eager but bewildered faces peered up at Semie, drinking in his words. They seemed delighted but also wondering, asking if this was real. Eyes, filled with amazement, strained to watch.

"Open your minds and let our energies touch you." As he spoke, rippling waves of light radiated from the alien and washed over the audience. "Receive the essence of the universe. It will make you children of the cosmos, sons and daughters of eternity."

Members of the assembly fell back in ecstasy, entranced by unseen visions. "You are making another step in your evolutionary process. Soon you will be a new race." Some in the crowd held back, not sure how to handle the strangeness and intensity. But soon others around them encouraged them, calling for them to abandon their doubts. Before long, most were entering in.

The leader continued for some time, mixing his speech with challenges and encouragement. One thing was clear, though, he had connected with the right group. Most were receiving everything he said with total agreement.

As the leader came to the end of his talk, a faint melody began drifting through the air. The sound of flutes and cymbals played a peaceful tune out into the darkness that covered the plain. Bracken looked around. Where was the music coming from, he wondered. He looked back at Semie and suddenly realized the source of the music. It was coming from the alien leader. Somewhere, deep from the core of his torso came the eerie melody. Entranced, Bracken listened with the others as the melody played on and on. Finally, it stopped and Semie spoke again.

"It's an ancient melody. Thousands of years old." His voice seemed melancholy. It almost sounded lonely, thought Bracken, like he was remembering another time. A time when the melody meant something more than it did now. "I've been waiting for you to hear it."

The sound was gone now. The evening was growing cold. The people, too entranced to light fires, huddled together for warmth. "We must leave now," said Semie, his voice gaining its grandeur again. "But you must continue your uprising. This is no time to tire. Your goals are right. We will be watching you from a distance, hoping that others will make the same choice you have. Encourage others to follow in your footsteps. As they do, your movement will grow, and we will come back to meet with you again and again, all of you. Wait for our return."

A chilling breeze began to come up from the east. The crowd huddled closer together. "We have much more to teach you, but this is enough for today. I'm pleased to see you have received us. Don't believe the lies of the Fathers. Stay in unity."

Semie paused and then spoke again. "Good-bye, my friends." With that, he turned and walked back toward the ship. At that point, the crowd rose to their feet and expressed their gratitude with deafening applause. Some in the crowd doubted, their arms crossed in defiance. Others refused to applaud, but most joined the ovation.

Frim Lieter, who had been standing beside Bracken at the rear of the stage, motioned to the youth to follow him as he walked toward the departing Semie. Leaving the stage, Bracken gave his stam to Chepa and collected his pack where he'd put the lyrics he planned to make a gift to Semie. Intercepting the disk leader, Lieter and Bracken were invited to come aboard the mother ship. Bracken was so enthralled, he didn't notice Ley watching the three of them, nor the look of envy thinly disguised in his face.

Walking in numbed expectancy, Bracken followed the others down the aisle formed by the aliens and into the heart of the giant spacecraft. Bracken felt excited. He knew he was close to the possibility of a new phase in his life. Perhaps it had been his song that had moved the crowd to accept the messenger from the stars. But whatever the case, he was honored to meet Semie. An inner voice encouraged him. He would become a herald for the Disk People and carry their message in song to the far regions of Ebbern. Now he was certain that at least some of his questions would be answered.

They entered the command center of the disk and found seats around a large silver-topped conference table. Bracken sat down across from Semie and set his bag on the table between them. Several of the disk leader's underlings stood at attention nearby. Frim briefed the leader on Bracken's previous experience with the space disk. "Bracken seems to have some unresolved questions regarding your mission. Perhaps you can answer them for him. Also, if I'm not mistaken, you have a special message for him as well."

"I'll be more than happy to," said Semie, addressing Bracken warmly. "You're not the first to have doubts." The alien leader turned to Lieter. "It is best that you return to the group outside. I'm sure they'll be needing your counsel."

"Certainly, Semie," said Lieter. "Good-bye, Bracken." The professor smiled and then walked back through the craft to the crowd.

Frim's voice seemed strangely ominous, as if he knew something Bracken didn't. But his eyes had seemed friendly and sincere. If he knew anything, his countenance failed to betray it. "Good-bye," said Bracken, "I'll join you when I'm through here."

As the professor left the room, Semie turned to Bracken and spoke in a deep, warm tone. The alien leader's presence was overpowering. He sounded most benevolent, yet Bracken still had a troubled premonition. What could it be? he wondered. *What strange thoughts and visage are hidden behind the glowing veil?* he asked himself.

"So you appear to have some muddled perceptions concerning your last visit with us." The energy veil gave off a slight hum as Semie moved his head.

Bracken lifted his hands from his lap and rested them on the polished tabletop. "Yes. As Frim has told you, the entire interior of the disk seemed to be dissolving." The memory of his previous trip on the disk was still vivid in his mind. "Even Talay appeared different. Undoubtedly, it was as he suggested—merely the effect of the flight. But ever since, even though I'm grateful for your mission to Ebbern, I've had unresolved thoughts about the entire thing."

"Sounds like a dangerous conflict. But I'm sure it can be resolved. That would be very important for both of us. You must know you have great talent. I could use such talent. No doubt you agree with our message, which was plain from your song. We were monitoring your concert from the beginning."

"Yes, the song." Bracken reached into his pack and pulled out the sheet where he'd written the lyrics. "I wanted to give you this as a sign of my appreciation." He laid the document on the table between them.

"Thank you," said Semie but he left the paper were it rested and continued his message. "It's time for your planet to move to its next level of enlightenment. You can bring that message to many with your songs. But tell me more about this struggle you're having, Bracken, about your doubts." Semie appeared to grow slightly irritated by Bracken's second thoughts. "Until these are resolved, they will no doubt hinder our cause."

Even as the leader's soothing words washed over Bracken, he had to agree that he still had lingering doubts. Then at that very moment, what had occurred on his earlier flight began to repeat itself. The atmosphere within the spacecraft began to fluctuate. One minute he saw bare jagged stone emerging from behind a veil of well-defined and highly technical instruments. The next moment the rock wall would dissolve into three-dimensional projections of the most sophisticated apparatus. What was happening? It was crazy. *It must be my mind. Too many voyages into the Mingus realm.*

So instead of asking further questions, Bracken forced himself to believe the promise of his new calling. He reminded himself how privileged he would be. The offer to share Semie's message was appealing, he was a fool not to take it. He had to choose not to believe what he was seeing. It worked; gradually the variations ceased and all that remained was the interior of a marvelous spacecraft.

But then the apparition returned. Agains he couldn't shake off a sense that somehow it was a lie. Why did he feel this way when so many others like Frim had no problem embracing it? How could he doubt when he'd longed for this answer to Ebbern's troubles and even written an anthem praising these beings. Perhaps it was because of what happened with Silas. Perhaps it was fear that something so beautiful and promising could turn ugly. It had in the past. It had with Silas. That's what made him doubt. That's what made him wonder. Was all this real or just an illusion?

And then he knew. Memories of his father and what he'd been taught in the garden years ago came rushing back into his mind. Words he'd tried to bury emerged and stood boldly in the midst of his thoughts. Words that were unchangeable and somehow eternal. Yes, now he knew; and something deep inside told him that his host knew what he was thinking as well.

Abruptly, Semie turned and spoke what sounded like an order in an alien tongue to a nearby aide. The spacecraft swiftly came to life. "Perhaps another journey will help you come to a positive conclusion."

Bracken placed his hands on the arms of his chair, gripping them tightly in anticipation of the liftoff. "I certainly hope you're right. I have no desire to hinder anything that will change the destiny of my planet in a positive way." Bracken tried to remain calm. He hid his suspicions and fears under a cloak of peacefulness. *Where are they taking me? They must know what I'm thinking.*

In a flurry of acceleration and lumbering sound, the disk was in flight. Suddenly it came to rest again, settling with a rumbling and scraping that tore at Bracken's nerves. On the view screen, he could see that the space vessel had looped back over the top of the Pillars and then flown to the northern end of the range. Why had they stopped here? He looked at the lonely landscape projected on the screen.

The night outside was cold and bleak. Bracken felt the same way inside. The disk became deathly still. Even without looking around, Bracken felt as if everyone onboard was watching him. He thought he heard a mocking snicker.

"Why did we stop here?" he asked.

Turning around, he looked toward the ship's commander. The energy veil that had covered Semie's face gradually began to pixelate and then slowly vanish. In its place, he saw a frightening, yet somehow familiar face. Where had he seen it? Why did he know it? It was handsome in an odd way. Youthful but ancient at the same time. A perfectly angled jaw and elegant facial lines but features that were almost too perfect. Then he looked into the eyes; eyes that were bright and commanding but that glinted with a bitter hatred. Then he remembered. It was the same face he'd seen calling to Silas the night he dove off the cliff.

"What's going on?" shouted Bracken in fearful anger.

Semie's face broke into a hideous grin. "Enough of your questions, you doubting fool!" The words were like daggers, ripping his heart apart with fear. "You must be terminated," said Semie. "It's almost a pity. You would have been a most effective tool if we could have controlled you."

In a rush of anxiety, Bracken reached out toward the alien, who quickly stepped back. "What do you mean, terminate? I thought you were going to help me, to help our planet."

The creature's face took on a vicious flash. "You had almost believed a lie—a very, very old one."

"Who are you?" said Bracken, almost begging.

"Surely you've heard of me before. Somewhere in your past you've been told of my plans. Only you didn't believe I was real," Semie laughed.

The memory Bracken had earlier stirred in his mind. A piece of the puzzle seemed to fall into place. But still he couldn't believe it. He didn't want to believe it. "But what of this ship? The things you said to the others?"

"This craft is only a rock transformed and used for our purposes. Our flux-morph specialists have a marvelous way with matter. They've been transforming things for epochs. With their help, I've been doing things like this throughout the ages. In the past, I used to turn sticks into slithering beasts. But your race has grown more sophisticated, so I must use more advanced forms of deception. Nonetheless, it's still a lie. It's a good one, I would say, seeing most believe it. Even you did for a while."

Bracken knew he was trapped. They would kill him if he didn't act fast.

Semie continued talking, his voice droning on in a hypnotic cadence. "It's such a pleasure to see the torment of your soul. You're so sincere. It's enjoyable to see the terror in your eyes." Then he turned to the other beings on the craft. "It's time, Hyslevix, bring the others, it's time for Theema. Time for the feast I promised. He's trapped here and you may feed on his soul as long as his body remains alive."

Bracken could feel Semie's gaze pulling at him, grinding him, mocking him. His fiery eyes seemed to be feeding on the shredded fabric of his heart and mind. The alien laughed again as he rose from his seat. "I only wish I could stay and watch a little longer."

With that closing taunt, Semie faded from Bracken's sight. The craft became quiet again. Slowly the light in the interior of the ship vanished into blackness. Bracken felt panic settling in on him. Sweat beaded on his forehead and upper lip.

Suddenly the floor beneath him dissolved, and he plunged down into the darkness. Without warning, his feet smashed into stone, his pack landing on top of him and then rolling off. Momentarily, he lay sprawled upon the rock surface, trying to assimilate what had occurred. The rock around him was jagged with indentations and clefts in it as if cut away by some heated scalpel. Where was he? How would he ever escape what he knew was coming. Something told him he was about to die.

As he lay in the cold darkness, he could sense the evil ones nearby closing in on him. He could hear their voices taunting him, accusing him. His mind and heart began to twist under their assault. "There will be no escape, you fool. We've turned this rock into a prison for your body, and we will dine on your soul until your last breath." At that moment, the full realization of where he was slapped into his psyche like a steel trap ... *entombed within this rock*. That reality crashed in on his spirit like an iron door banging shut, extinguishing all hope.

The voices continued in his mind as he felt claw-like hands rake over his body. "This one believed so easily. He was so trusting. What a fool." Rasping cries filled his mind like hot, stale breath. "You will never escape, and no one will remember you." Screeching speech seared his brain. "Lisha will lay with many lovers, and you will soon be forgotten." Mocking voices hammered his brain until his sanity seemed to seep away like the juice from a crushed fruit. "You'll never see your family again. They hate you anyway. Your life is fading, never to return, no one cares. No one cares, no one ..." He looked somewhere for an answer, some strand of hope, some sign. But there was only darkness.

Thrashing about, he fought off the hideous talons that tore at him, flaying back at them only to have his hands pierced and bruised. Drawing his fingers away, they landed on his pack. He felt a hard object beneath its fabric. That was it, the weapon Ley had given him. Almost without thinking, he reached in his pouch for the energy egg. He popped open the activation cover, its read-out panel casting a dim green light into the surrounding darkness. As quickly as he could, he set the trigger mechanism for an outward blast away from him. Brushing aside the barbs of his attackers, he ran through the darkness to find what he knew must be the wall on the other side of his tomb. Reaching it, he felt around until he found a slight edge. With that, he set the egg on it and ran back.

Moments later, the side of the hollow tomb erupted in a flash of light. The concussion sent him sprawling to the floor, his head striking hard against stone, leaving his brain ringing. Making a final effort, Bracken picked himself up and sprinted toward the opening. But his strength was fading now; he barely managed to crawl through the blast hole, his feet escaping just in time. He fell to the ground outside, just as the massive boulder collapsed upon itself.

But his pursuers weren't done. Once again he felt them pressing in, their taunts like the growling of hungry animals. The moons bled their red light over his surroundings, leaving only a crimson gloom. He crawled away, finally standing to his feet only to trip, bashing his head against the ground so hard it left him nearly unconscious. Shaking away dizziness, he squinted into the reddish haze, expecting more torment. But to his surprise he saw clear, white light forming a wall around him. At the edge of his senses he heard strong but comforting voices responding to a command. "Yes, Michess, the circle's nearly complete. They can come no farther." Angry hisses drew close and then gradually faded, moving away into the night, howling with disappointment. Gradually they ceased altogether to be replaced with confident and reassuring words. "They've retreated, Michess."

"Very well, stand your ground."

Still barely conscious, Bracken looked into the circle of light and saw giant creatures, their backs to him, standing in a ring about him. He wanted to reach out and thank them, but his strength was gone. His head fell back against the ground, and in the next moment a healing sleep enveloped him.

CHAPTER 62

DARK NEXUS 6

TAR-LYNREXS (LATE-SUMMER), 5512

It was one of those rare moments in the dark nexus when Strieme wished he was alone. Once again the area was filled with activity as emissaries and couriers streamed by, carrying out their dreadful work. He often had to stand at the intersecting corridors to direct his agents to their assignments. He did it with glee, taking pleasure as they appeared before him to receive the lash of his words tearing into their minds. But now that boldness had vanished as he anxiously looked around. Nearby, some of Hyslevix's crew stood in the shadows trembling. They were not alone in their apprehension. He sensed it as well; a certain fear ripped at his confidence.

Their forces had failed again. The target had escaped. How had the man come up with that weapon? Hyslevix obviously had not factored that possibility into his plans. Fortunately, Strieme told himself, he had not been the one assigned to lead the failed effort. It had been given to Hyslevix. He'd been the one to support Semie in his grand appearance, and now he and many others were paying for Hyslevix failure. Strieme doubted that he would ever see Hyslevix again. The flux-morph specialists that Hyslevix had directed had somehow failed to completely disguise the rock with their matter-shifters. Their web of lies had been penetrated. On top of that, he'd failed to check and see if their quarry had brought any weapons with him. So now Hyslevix was condemned to a time of torment. Few came back from the realm he'd been banished to. The force of their leader's rage was epic;

he'd never seen a demonstration of wrath on that level. The corridors that ran to the nexus seemed still echo with his former companion's screams even though the victim had been gone for some time.

Strieme decided he had no time to worry about what had happened. He must find another way to trap the one he was now assigned to. As he toyed with his next plan, he suddenly became aware of a significant change in the nexus. Someone was approaching, someone that no one wanted to see.

Before he could fully comprehend what was coming, a row of ashen sentinels surrounded him, their large black eyes probing for threats. They stood at the various intersections of the network and blocked all the entrances except one. The sounds of heavy footsteps rumbled down the one open corridor. At their sound, all the guards bowed and by their overwhelming influence he was forced to bow as well. He did so none too soon.

The Shadow Czar entered the chamber with a loud roar. "You fools. How could you have allowed him to escape? You must not have been studying the intelligence my aides have been sending. At least five of them told me later that he had another weapon."

"But there's been such disruption in our ether links that Hyslevix didn't get all their messages," cried the vanquished one's former companions. "Our arrays overheat, and if we don't turn them down, our synapses burn."

"Burn? You will know what it is to burn if the rest of you continue to fail!"

"Another failure would be unacceptable," sputtered Strieme.

"Indeed."

"So what should we do?"

"We know where he's headed now. Hopefully we can be finished with him there. I will lead the action this time."

"But what if he survives that, what will we use then?"

"How dare you .... There will be no failure this time."

Strieme realized he had spoken without thinking. He was sure the lash would strike him, so he sought to recover his error. "I mean, do we have any other deception left?"

"Of course, we always have beauty," said Semie, taking on a patronizing tone as if he had to teach the fools around him the obvious once again. "It's the highest of all my tools."

Strieme knew that such an approach had failed in the past, at least from his perspective. Therefore, as fearful as it was to contradict his master, he chose to speak his mind. Better to face wrath now than what would come if he failed again. "May I address that approach?" he said tentively.

"Certainly," came Semie's indulgent reply tinged with a tone of mockery.

"We've tried that. We've set his mind spinning with every conceivable spectacle of beauty that we can create. None of them have worked. He just keeps pressing beyond the sensual until he penetrates our formations."

"Yes, but the type of beauty I'm suggesting grips most men. It's a primal yearning they've had in their DNA for centuries. It was there in the beginning. They sing about it and make poems about it. It will allure him. But should we, as you have so presumptively suggested, fail this next time, then I will have you guide him to that place of beauty he will never see through."

Strieme recalled the luscious woman that lived in Vonervyn. Was this what his master had in mind? He questioned whether this would work. Bracken seemed driven by something that even her allure would not dissuade. But it was the dark one's wish. It would probably not work, but he must carry out his orders. "As you wish."

"He's headed for Shidow now. I've arranged for three who can possibly intervene. If they fail to stop him then he'll go directly there. If so, we can trap him at the mine. Go ahead and prepare. I'll join you once I've instructed our current diversion group. Hopefully they'll stop him. On your way, then."

"On my way, Lord."

CHAPTER 63

PILLARS OF RIMLEX

TAR-LYNREXS (LATE-SUMMER), 5512

Amatam called in the cold dark air as Bracken approached Golden Flight's trans. The night bird's call was the only one of its kind on the Plains of Umin. The moons were gone now, having vanished over the eastern horizon.

After his narrow escape from the collapsing bolder, he had lain unconscious for some time. When he had awakened, he wondered at the strange intervention that had saved him. It must have been the concussion that had created the odd apparitions he'd seen. Those mighty beings that stood around him had probably been an illusion. It all must have been some comatose dream. He was sure of it because when he came to, he found himself all alone. Gradually he'd shaken off the shock of his encounter with Semie, and as he picked himself up he sensed renewed energy. Something strange had revitalized him, and he had set off with a fresh determination to find answers.

He had faced death and come through. His fear had been replaced with an inner resolve. He had surprised himself at how quickly he'd reacted once he knew he might die. Now that he was still alive, he set his mind and heart to finally get answers even if it meant he might face Semie again, even if it meant he might face death again.

It took him nearly three hours to make his way over a narrow passage through the Pillars to the gathering place, plenty of time to work out a plan. He would take the only door left open for him to find his adversary. He'd go to the source. Once there, he'd know. It took all his courage to consider it, but nothing else mattered.

He wanted to warn Chepa and the others about the Disk People, but there was no time for that now. He knew it was unlikely that they would believe him anyway. Semie had been so powerful and persuasive in his performance that the others had been completely captivated. Besides, in his mind, Bracken had one other connection he needed to run down. Once he'd fulfilled his plan, he may have secrets to unveil that went far beyond what he'd learned in his moments of terror on the disk.

He approached the trans as quietly as possible. Stepping into the stairwell of the vehicle, he was careful to miss the one loose floor panel that tended to squeak. He slipped soundlessly down the passageway, stopping in front of Ley's cubicle. Silently, he pulled back the door and slipped into his room. Ley snored softly in his bunk. Bracken knew that the stone merchant had carried the map with him ever since he left Accad. He knew Ley kept it stuffed away in his pouch.

The matam screeched only once before Bracken was back outside, map in hand. He'd found three other necessary things in the cabinet where Os's pouch was: a small lantern, an explosive packet, and a detonating unit.

Gathering together his own things and securing the map in his pack, he walked softly toward the road. As he passed through the temporary canvas city erected for the gathering, he heard a low chanting coming from the front of one of the colorful tents. The sound was familiar and intriguing. He tried to ignore it; he was on a mission and he didn't want to be distracted. But something in the melody was too familiar—he had to see what it was—and so he turned off the path and made his way in the direction of the music.

As he approached, he could see a low-burning campfire and three raven-haired women seated around it. Their heads were slightly tilted back, their eyes clearly fixed on the night sky. As he drew near, their heads lowered and swiveled in unison, and like birds of prey they fastened their eyes on him.

Troubled by the intensity of their gaze, he resolved to turn back toward the highway, but then the tallest one put down the stam she'd been playing and rose, trancelike, gliding toward him. Her eyes began to glow, a green, sheer brilliance like emeralds on fire. She opened her mouth to speak, and a row of teeth nearly as striking as her eyes smiled at him. "So, Bracken, you lonely seeker, you're off on a quest again?"

"Who are you?" he wondered out loud, instantly taken in by her beauty and insight. Relaxing a bit, he slipped off his pack and set it on the ground. "How could you possibly know who I am and what I'm up to?"

"My name's Tristixsen, these are my friends, Simish and Yssmey. We know your name and what you're doing because the castings told us," she pointed toward a set of odd stones lying next to the fire. Each had writing similar to the etching on the plaque that Dalfang had given him. "They tell us everything. We're oracles, seers. We have been since our youth."

"Interesting. You're like the edge-poets. You predict things before they happen."

"I guess you could say that."

Bracken folded his arms and lowered his gaze. "So what have they told you about me and where I'm going?"

"That your journey is dangerous, and at the end there will be suffering."

"And if you know that, then why am I taking it?"

"You think it virtuous, this quest you're on to find the source."

Bracken was startled by their apparent insight into his plans but held himself in check, not wanting to admit that they could possibly have discovered them. "Source? What source? I'm merely heading back to Tizra to see some friends." He lied.

"I'm sure you'll go through Tizra, but that's not your ultimate destination." Tristixsen motioned toward her companions. "We all saw Shidow in our visions, and of course we know what's there."

"What's there?"

"It's the Mingus. You're looking to find the source. But we must warn you, you're wasting your time."

"So, even if I was going there and trouble's waiting for me, why would you caution me?"

"Because your searching is in vain. You'll only see what your fears tell you."

"How do you know what I fear?"

"Hiffornak has told us about your quest."

At the mention of the Naacanite, Bracken's confidence melted. He let his arms drop to his side and let out a deep breath. "So you know Hiffornak. Have you been in Zyphon?" Bracken recalled the name his guide had given to that level of the dimensional corridor.

"Yes, but only in visions. He comes to us in visions. We don't even have to use the stones."

"And what do the visions tell you? What has he told you about me?"

"That you're brilliant and brave but that your recent questions have their source in fear. Instead, you simply must trust and quit doubting what you see."

Hurtful memories came to mind, and anger flashed in Bracken's eyes. "If you knew what I'd seen you'd not make those claims. As good as the Mingus realm appears, there's still something that doesn't quite make sense, and I must find it out."

Tristixsen closed the distance between them and reached out to touch him. She looked into his eyes, with her own pools of green comfort. Instantly he sensed energy flowing from her into his body. She smiled at him and continued. "I can see you're angry, but you simply must trust. All this striving will only make you sick."

Expelling another deep breath, Bracken looked up into the night sky. "You don't understand. I must. I owe it to my dead friend. To his memory."

"We know about Silas as well. Hiffornak told us."

Bracken wondered what else these women knew. *Do they know about my encounter on the disk as well?*

"If you know so many things about my searching, then you must understand why I need answers."

Tristixsen gently placed her other hand on Bracken's shoulder. He could feel the energy increasing, and with it a calm settled over him. *Maybe*

I should wait. Maybe I should just give it all up, he told himself. He smiled a weak smile back at Tristixsen. "Maybe you're right."

"Of course we are. Besides, any endeavor begun with a theft surely will end in disaster."

"What theft?"

"What you've taken from your friend."

"You know about Ley's map?"

"Of course. I told you, the castings tell us everything."

At that moment, all Bracken's determination escaped like the breaths he'd been expelling.

"You look so tired. Why don't you let us comfort you?" Tristixsen smiled a knowing smile at her companions and then looked back at Bracken. "We have ways of doing that you won't soon forget," She stroked his arm and gazed at him with a delightful twinkle in her eyes.

It would just be so easy to give up his quest and believe what everyone else did. Somehow he knew if he did that, the pleasures these beautiful creatures offered him would be just the beginning of a voyage of endless sensual gratification. Why not let go? Maybe he was just imagining the horrors he'd encountered that night. *Maybe all my journeys into the Mingus realm have left my mind in a state of constant illusion. What I need is rest, a refreshing of my mind and heart. Why not now? Why not here?*

He gazed back into Tristixsen's shimmering eyes, relishing the touch of her hands and the thrill of her attention. Why not just give in? What wonderful delights waited for him with her and her companions? His entire body shivered with anticipation.

Then he remembered Silas and a faint echo of memory from his grandparents. The words came roaring back into his mind. *"There are pitfalls on these pathways, and you need another kind of 'road map' when you journey there. Not everything that feels right is right. Some of the roads lead to death."*

The words and memory gave him a moment's pause and then, with it, a fresh resolve. *No, I will not give in. I will find answers.* He looked down into Tristixsen's glowing countenance with fondness but with a restored objective. "Thanks for the offer, but I must go on."

Tristixsen frowned, a brief shadow clouding her features. Then, starting with just the faintest warning, another image began to emerge from Tristixsen's glowing face. It began with her eyes. The emerald faded, replaced by pure red bulbs circled with black. Then her smooth skin dulled and became a harsh green with spots of yellow. A long tongue darted out from her suddenly narrowed lips, and her face flattened out and merged into a thick neck that met her body in a slick, sticky mass.

In shock, Bracken let out a gasp. Where had he seen this face before? Then he remembered. He'd seen this type of creature near his hometown, only a much smaller version. Tristixsen's altered visage now resembled the tiny amphibians that swam in the brooks near Tizra and fed off the tiny fish and plants that lived there. In disgust, he turned his gaze away and looked at her companions. Their beauty had vanished as well, and the same image emerged from their torsos. Red eyes topped their spotted heads, each resting on fat necks glistening with moisture. Then as quickly as the startling images appeared, they vanished and he was gazing again at three beautiful women. Turning back to Tristixsen, he saw that her delicate features had retuned.

"What are you?" Shouted Bracken, startling even himself with the intensity of his voice. He lowered it, realizing he might wake nearby campers. "Who are you?" He whispered, grabbing Tristixsen by her arms and shaking her. As he did, her face morphed back and forth between a hideous scowl and a beautiful visage. Finally, in frustration, he let her go. As she drew back from him, the charming image reemerged and remained.

"This is exactly why I have to get answers, Tristixsen."

The woman's sweetness had returned and with it her comforting words. "We understand, Bracken, but must you be so violent?" She was obviously shaken by his reaction, but her voice was firm. She wasn't going to try and dissuade him again. "Perhaps you do need to go to Shidow."

"Yes, exactly. And I'm not about to wait another moment."

"You need help, Bracken. You're a lost soul. Maybe you'll find some healing there." Her voice was patronizing, slightly mocking. "Travel safe, wanderer."

"Good-bye then." Bracken gave the three a slight wave. Shouldering his pack, he turned and headed off into the night.

Tristixsen stood watching as Bracken made his way toward the distant highway. Once he was out of sight, she walked over to Simish and Yssmey. The three conferred in whispers and then slowly walked toward Golden Flight's trans-max.

CHAPTER 64

MOUNT SHIDOW

TAR-LYNREXS (LATE-SUMMER), 5512

Hiking at night had always held its perils, but as Bracken reached the lonely spot on the highway where it intersected the road, he had a stroke of luck. A trans with a high-speed power-drive pulled over and picked him up. The driver was on his way south and would pass close to Mount Shidow. Encouraged by his good fortune, Bracken fell asleep as the trans sped through the night.

On the second morning of his journey, Bracken found himself deposited near the narrow road that led off toward Mount Shidow. With many thanks, he said good-bye to the man who had given him the ride.

Hiking through the forest with its green brush was invigorating. That night, Bracken slept beside the Pool of Tibtem. Its clear surface mirrored the sky above, giving him a sense of being adrift in space.

He knew that it wouldn't take Os long to figure out what had happened to his map. But he had at least a day's lead on him. Even if Ley overtook him, Bracken was unafraid. He was on a mission now, and nothing would stop him, not even the seller of the Mingus.

When morning came, Bracken took nourishment from some morsels of food he had packed. As he ate, he perused the map that Ley had guarded so desperately. The route to the mine was clearly marked. He could easily follow it and should be at the site by afternoon.

The sun broke over the western mountains, awakening the forest with song. Wildlife crept and sprinted in the undergrowth as he munched his food. Finishing his breakfast, he started off toward the mine's entrance. The map was exact, guiding him first over a high outcropping of rock and then along a streambed to a singularly tall evergreen. From there, he sighted across two more rocky pillars to another streambed that led him directly to the mine's entrance. It had taken him less time than he'd expected.

Sweating profusely from his climb, Bracken shrugged off his pack. Laying it against a large rock, he removed the items he had taken from Ley's satchel. He had a rudimentary understanding of explosives, thanks to the farming course at the Mind-Training Center where he'd learn to blast tree stumps. He remembered with a sad inward smile the fun he and Silas had years ago blowing things up with a few charges he'd taken from his grandparents' farm. He set the explosive in the position where it would shift most of the rock and debris that Ley's last detonation had produced.

The explosives went off with a blast that echoed up the mountainside. Bracken cautiously approached the site. The charge had done its work. Most of the mine's entrance was now exposed. It took him only minutes to push aside the remaining rock. Taking a deep breath, he wiped his brow once more and then stepped into the invitingly cool entrance of the mine.

He took Ley's lamp from his pouch and played its beam over the chiseled interior of the shaft. Bracken followed its twisting contour deeper into the earth. The chilled air in the tunnel was a marked contrast to the heat outside. Eventually he halted at the safety partition, which sealed off the gem chamber. It had been constructed of a metallic alloy, which the stones' effect could not penetrate. Shining his light around the walls, he examined the protective clothing, which the sci-tecs had developed to block the Mingus rays. Ignoring them, he walked up to the hatchway. Opening the lock console, he punched out the code on the keypad, following the numbers that Ley had jotted at the bottom of the map.

With a loud click, the oval door swung open. Pausing momentarily, Bracken gazed into the interior of the room and then stepped over the threshold into the chamber. Immediately, his body began to tingle with the most intense Mingus sensation he had ever experienced. It was obvious that there would be no need to ingest one of the gems. He turned back to seal the passage behind him. Before he could secure the door an overwhelming surge of the Mingus Effect catapulted him from the tunnel into another dimension.

In a spiraling swirl of brilliance, he felt his body rise like a feather caught in a rushing updraft. Waves of oscillating fluorescence formed an inverted funnel, reaching out above him. Liquid streams of crystal bathed his body in a vestment of ecstasy as they carried him aloft. Suddenly, in a moment of metamorphosis, his soul spread forth like a gossamer sail. Billowing under the force of an astral wind, his whole being accelerated, until his surroundings blurred into one. Time stretched like a silken thread until it snapped. All but his most vivid memories washed away, falling into the abyss below him.

His pulsating journey continued, until finally his body passed through the mouth of the funnel and curved in a gentle arc, coming to rest on a glossy plateau. Glowing orbs danced and bobbed, ascending and descending in a rhythmic cadence up and down on the shimmering plain where he now stood. A prismatic city appeared, suspended in the atmosphere over his head. The bubbles of light disturbed by his sudden appearance floated up to him momentarily and then moved away, emitting fluttering purrs of sound, like the hum of static electricity. One of the larger ovals moved through the others until it stopped in front of him.

"I've been expecting to see you," announced the being of light, quavering in a short vertical curtsy. "But only on the lower levels. What brings you here, and where are those you were to bring with you?"

Bracken recognized the elegant resonance of the creature he had met during the last time he had gone deep into the Mingus realm, the time he'd been attacked by the hideous creatures. He gathered his thoughts and spoke. "I still have some questions, Hiffornak. I don't intend to lead others here until they are resolved." The sphere of brightness moved slightly to Bracken's right, to make room for another orb that was approaching, apparently to observe their conversation.

"With time and care, I'm sure you will soon realize the answer." To Bracken, the response had a ring of insincerity.

"You may think I'm being a bit suspicious, but I feel as if you're hiding something from me."

"What leads you to believe that?"

Bracken stared into the heart of the light, seeking to penetrate its effulgence. "Because even though you appear to have the right words, words that at times even seem soothing, you have yet to give me more than platitudes and pleasing phrases. Of course it's all bathed in the sensuous pleasure that's surging within me right now. But I've discovered it can just as quickly turn into a nightmare."

Bracken's voice had taken on a slightly beseeching tone. His hands reached out toward the creature in a pleading gesture. "Silas is dead, killed somehow by someone from this realm. Even though you exercise such great power and wisdom, you were either unable or unwilling to protect him. And if you were truly unable to protect him, why didn't you at least warn him?" The two scintillas turned to one another and communicated in low hums, punctuated with an occasional fluttering buzz. Above them, the ethereal ballet continued apparently undisturbed. Shortly, they ceased and turned back to him.

Now the second creature began to speak, taking over. "We were aware of your friend's destiny, but to interfere is simply not our way."

"Not your way!" objected Bracken, his voice rising with impatience. "I would expect more compassion from beings who have reached a state of permanent transcendence." Bracken's tone was mocking.

The other continued, seemingly unperturbed. "Compassion is a relative term. What your limited perception and personal feelings tell you concerning this matter is only one viewpoint. If you could see it from our position, you would find it easier to accept."

The light creature continued in the same vein, his dialogue growing more and more convincing as Bracken listened. But still Bracken resisted. Suddenly in one violent shake, he brushed aside the web-like verbiage that was enfolding his mind. He stepped closer and shouted in despair at the glowing being. "Who are you? Stop giving me your philosophies and just be honest with me." The orb was in the middle of recycling the previous response when Bracken's curiosity and impatience united in a desperate act.

Plunging for the creature, he pushed his way into the cloud of light that surrounded the glowing being. A slight crackle shivered in his body as he penetrated the sheen. At that same moment, the truth pierced his mind like a white-hot sword. Staring at him in horrific majesty was the familiar and angular face of Semie.

Bracken froze in terror. He'd finaly found the source. There staring at him was his answer. That which he'd so diligently sought was finally revealed and once again as it had been before, it was an evil hidden beneath a veil of light. Now that he knew the answer something inside him shattered into pieces. His mind focused on the remains of his hope and seemed to freeze. *What can I do now? Where can I possibly go from here? How can I escape what I know is coming?* For a brief moment this new revelation held him fast. But then a still small voice whispered a word into the middle of his turmoil. *It's not to late. There's still hope. You must flee. So move. Now!*

He shook himself. In a reckless frenzy, he turned and ran from the now darkened specter. Laughter rang in his ears. Behind him, the shimmering bubbles of light popped simultaneously, revealing a sinister army of bat-like creatures. Turning in formation, their wings screaming through the air in a loud whine, they fell toward Bracken like eagles pursuing their prey. Others who had been near the plain, hovered toward him as he ran toward the mouth of the funnel. His legs felt heavy. His feet seemed to stumble. His heart was ripped apart once more. The flutter of wings grew closer. Each footfall became agony. He wondered if he could move another step. Dragging himself, he pressed on.

Reaching the edge just before his pursuers, he hurled himself into the abyss without hesitation. He plunged headlong into the now dimly lit chasm. For a few brief moments, he held hopes of escape. But such prospects melted away as he saw the regiment of pursuing wraiths swooping down upon him.

In a dissonant symphony of screams, they formed a spiraling orbit around him as he continued to descend into the blackness below. Then, in alternate pairs, they broke away from their group, flying to him. He couldn't believe what was happening. He struggled to awaken from this nightmare. But his surroundings remained. He wasn't dreaming.

The first group of wraiths fell upon him through the darkness. He thrashed back at them in defense. It had little effect. Soon their long, clawed hands tore at his soul. Momentarily satisfied with their tortuous pleasure, the pair withdrew to allow two others to take their place.

Again and again this pattern repeated itself, as Bracken screamed and struggled with the hideous creatures screeching in apparent delight at his anguish. Downward in a seemingly endless dive of agony, Bracken fell, the previous brave wings of his soul now flapping in a tattered throb within him.

After what seemed like endless hours, Bracken realized he was no longer falling. The wraiths were gone. Instead, he found himself crawling through a slithering coil of snakes. Fangs sank into him, injecting venom that rushed to his brain, driving him mad. On and on he crawled, twisting and pushing his way through the writhing serpentine bodies. He struggled without release until all withdrew, save one monstrous snake that wrapped itself about him and began to crush his body with a wicked strength. At that moment, he knew he could bear no more. He began to surrender to the squeezing brawn of the serpent. But somehow he remembered the Name and how it had saved him the last time he confronted such terror in this realm.

But he had so little strength left. His soul was limp and his mind splintered. Could he possibly speak? Then, just a whisper was all he could muster. He spoke it with what he was sure was his final breath. Mysteriously, the viper uncoiled itself and vanished.

For several hours, he lay in a state of semiconsciousness. Periodically he awoke to see distant lights shimmering in the darkness and then slipped back into his previous state. Gradually his surroundings became lighter. He could see that he was lying at the entrance to the mine. The remote morning sun smudged the sky with a dull orange. Bracken tried to move his body. Bolts of pain discharged in every strand of his nervous system. Turning his head, he looked down at his battered form. His garments were torn open, revealing bruised and cut flesh, glaring red here and there, over his entire body. Bracken registered shock just before he fell into unconsciousness.

Later, two things awoke him from his stupor. One was the excruciating heat of the sun now directly above him, and the other, the bitter voice of Ley Os who stood over him cursing.

"You fool," spat the outraged Os. "Robbing me after all I've done for you." The Mingus seller's face was a bulge of livid indignation. "Where's the map?" Ley accented his question by kicking Bracken's injured side.

Bracken doubled up from the sharp blow. "I don't know," he gasped, reeling from his friend's violence. Would no one come to his aid? Sure, he had stolen the map, but did that deserve blows and wounds to his already broken and bleeding body? Bracken struggled to make sense of Ley's outburst. Maybe he could assuage the man's anger by giving him what he wanted. He struggled up onto one elbow and pointed back toward the tunnel. "I left my pouch in the mine before I entered the Mingus chamber. The map was in it."

Ley cursed and kicked Bracken again. Muttering, he turned and walked into the shaft. Bracken slipped off again, awakening just as Os reappeared in the darkened opening, clutching his sacred parchment. "Fortunately for you, I've found it. Unfortunately for you, I've been here before and knew exactly where to find you. If I hadn't found the map, though, I would have buried you here alive under tons of stone." Ley lifted his pack. "At least this journey wasn't a complete waste. I've got a whole new supply of the stones."

Bracken struggled to respond, his voice barely audible. "You've got to understand, Ley, I needed answers. I had to go to the source, and I knew you'd never give up control of this place to anyone."

"So you just snuck into my quarters and took what didn't belong to you."

"Yes, I had to find the source … that meant coming here … I knew you'd never let me do that." Bracken's throat was parched, and each word stung. "Who says you're the only one who has the right to this mine?"

"Cib gave it to me."

"Sure, and he defied the authorities to do that."

"Yes, and that's what our Community is all about. Defying the authorities that have brought this nation and our planet to the brink."

Bracken attempted to sit up, but the effort was too much. He collapsed, barely covering his face with his hands as his head fell into the dirt. He sucked in dust and spit out dry, bitter words. "Some Community, if it brings us to this. It appears we're no better than the High Council grabbing to hold onto power. That's what it's been for you, Os. Power. You've got to have the control."

"And why not? I did the work. I did the deal with Mingus. So I own it; I should have the privileges that come with it."

"So that's what this whole thing's come to? Ownership, control, and greed. You take what you want. Is that what you did with Lisha? You just took her as if she was some sort of prize and then cast her aside like a used toy once you had your fun."

The words hurt and they hit home. Ley drew his leg back and kicked again.

Bracken cried out but still had the presence of mind to press his point. His jaw rigid with pain, his throat rasping under the effort, Bracken screamed, "You're as bad as the 'Rax, Os. You'll use even violence to keep your position."

"Be glad I don't give you what you deserve."

"I thought the Community was all about brotherhood and goodwill. What happened to all that?"

"Well, I've run out of goodwill with you, my friend."

"You think I betrayed you by taking your precious map. But you've betrayed me by taking Lisha."

"You're blind, Bracken. She wanted me, she came on to me. So I moved in."

"That's what I mean, Ley, you just move in and take what you want as if you own us all just because you've brought us the glorious Mingus stone."

"It changed you. You had your fun. You saw wonders. Where's all the splendor now, friend?"

Bracken realized he was as bitter and angry as Os and all his former philosophizing must be shallow if he could so quickly fall to this level of contention. But he went on anyway, spilling his rage. "Well, the splendor's not in the realm of the gem, and that's why I'm going to take Dalfang's advice and use my energy exploring Vonervyn. He saw who you really were. He told me about you."

"That old wizard is just a crazy idealist. Who needs the dreamy little realm he offers people when I can give them more than that and in just a brief time with the gem? All that chanting stuff just wore me out."

"Maybe that's your problem, Os, you don't have the patience for it. You want everything in an instant. Well, I'm going to convince people to turn away from you and what you offer and start to follow Dalfang."

Ley drew back his leg again, but the younger man curled up to protect himself. In frustration, Os kicked dirt at him instead. "I'm through wasting my strength arguing with you, and if you've got any left, you better use it crawling as far from here as you can."

Ley folded the map and stuffed it away. "As it is, it's doubtful you'll ever leave here alive. But I'll give you a chance. It all depends on how fast you can crawl. Here's the bag you left in the mine. There's some water and food in it should you survive the blast. See I'm really not totally bad." Os smirked down at Bracken and then walked back toward the tunnel's entrance.

Bracken watched in shock as Ley retreated. He called after him. "I know you hate me, Os, but you can't do this."

There was no answer from Ley. Instead, he climbed around the side of the opening and onto the top of the shaft. Bracken could see Ley remove an energy egg from his gear. Setting the trigger mechanism, he buried the oval slightly beneath the rock near the top of the mine's entrance and then scurried back to where Bracken was. "I've set the charge for the maximum time activation. With luck, you should be out of range by the time it explodes."

Bracken gawked at his former benefactor in horror. He squinted as perspiration trickled into his eyes. "You mean you're going to leave me here?"

Os responded only with a tormenting smile. Whirling about, he paced away down the streambed.

Bracken stared in disbelief. In a few moments, the charge would explode. Struggling in anguish, he crawled, clawing his way down the pathway dragging his bag after him. He knew he only had a short time to get out of range. But he wasn't moving fast enough. Images of his body being blow apart raced through his mind. He could imagine the timer on the readout counting down toward the moment of detonation. Driven by the fear of death, he struggled to maneuver forward. But his strength seemed to ebb away with each movement. His body felt like a massive piece of iron and the ground a powerful magnet sucking him into its surface, halting all motion.

Finally, in one burst of adrenaline, he rose to his feet and ran. He made it only a short distance and fell against a huge bolder. Gathering his resolve in one final act, he pulled himself around the large rock and collapsed behind its protective bulk. The ground rumbled as the charge exploded. Overwhelmed and with his ears ringing, Bracken felt his final strength drain away and blackness smothered his pain in a merciful cloud of unconsciousness.

CHAPTER 65

FOREST OF ZOREK

TAR-LYNREXS (LATE-SUMMER), 5512

Dalfang sat quietly before the remaining embers in his fireplace, puffing thoughtfully on his pipe. Its long neck protruded down from his lips and ran across his beard to chest level where he held it gently between his fingers. With each drag, the tiny glowing knot in the pipe's bowl burned brightly for a moment, followed by a stream of smoke issuing from the sage's parted lips. Thus expelled, the pungent fumes whirled upward, adding to the hazy cloud drifting in the semi-lit room.

Outside, the subdued sunlight distilled its way through the fog. The sea drizzle had been in all day, covering the verdant ferns and high evergreens with a misty sheen. Tears of expanding moisture stood on their leaves until they grew too heavy for the tender fronds. Spilling off, the drops would fall to be absorbed by the mossy ground or be shattered like liquid glass against a stone.

Behind Dalfang, Bracken stirred from his nap. He had been with the older man several days now, and his strength was gradually returning. Even Dalfang was amazed when he thought of the grace and seeming providence that had kept the youth alive through his trial at Mount Shidow. Many times in the days following his ordeal Bracken had been near death only to hear a voice in the background whispering. *Give him strength. Renew him. Sustain him.* Then obedient replies. *Yes, Michess. He's responding.* Huge hands would rest on him but their touch was as light as a feather, lifting him, comforting him, and renewing him. Then in those moments he had begun to mysteriously revive.

After his ordeal with Os, it had taken him two days of struggle to reach the Pool of Tibtem. Its healing waters had bathed his wounds until gradually soundness began to return to his battered frame. His last ration of food consumed, he had limped off toward the highway, catching a ride with a friendly driver and finally reaching the comfort of Dalfang's cabin several days later. The solitary man had watched over his young friend, allowing him to rest and convalesce undisturbed by conversation.

By now, though, Bracken was himself again and talked much with Dalfang between his rests. Awake from a refreshing nap, he swung his feet from the raised mat on which he had been sleeping and sat up, rubbing his eyes.

Dalfang removed his pipe from his mouth and spoke. "The rest seems to be working. By tomorrow you'll be as you were when I first met you, strong and healthy."

"Yes, I'm feeling stronger now. I'm sure the naps are helping too. It's strange, though, I keep having a recurring dream."

"Really, what do you see?"

"I'm climbing a mountain. Each step takes me closer to the top, but just as I'm about to reach it, long tenacles reach out and grip me, pulling me into an abyss. I slip and tumble back to the bottom only to struggle again and repeat the same vain attempt as before.

"It appears as though there are still some deep unresolved issues that you're struggling with."

"You're right there, Dalfang. It's a bit troubling, but that's why I'm here. I'm confident that a sojourn in Vonervyn will solve those issues."

"Yes, I agree. I've found its serenity a balm for many troubling thoughts."

"I'm sure it will be the same for me."

A section of smoldering wood broke free from the charred logs and spilled onto the hearth. Dalfang kicked the embers back into the fireplace and turned his swivel chair around toward his patient.

"So, how's your head?"

Bracken took a relaxing breath and responded. "My head seems to ache less each day," he observed, holding his forehead with his right hand and squinting his eyes closed. Every now and then the lingering pain would bring back memories of the injuries he suffered under Os's rage. It not only reminded him of the man's ferocious assault but also of the suffering he'd experienced in the Mingus realm. He could not escape the fact that he'd been lied to and that Hiffornak and his cohorts were vicious deceivers who had no doubt lured Silas to his death. Zorek was a great place to mend, but it was also a lonely spot. He was truly appreciative of Dalfang's care, but he remembered his friends in the Community, the band and even the good times he'd had with Ley. That seemed like a dream now, as illusive as the fog that came in with the morning but often burned away by midday. Maybe he would find a new fellowship in Vonervyn. Maybe there would be a chance to bring those he'd loved and missed to that realm. To offer them joy and beauty through a different path than the way of the magic gems.

He looked out the window to see the gray mist hugging the trees. Even though he'd pulled the veil away from the imposters who lurked in the Mingus realm, so many things still seemed as cloudy as the vapor outside Dalfang's cabin. Why were these creatures seeking to destroy and deceive so many in his generation? What made Semie and his forces gather the Community to the Pillars to offer them a lie? He needed to know. He knew now who had killed his friend, but many things still remained a mystery. Perhaps the answer lay somewhere in Vonervyn.

Then for the first time, he had a strange premonition as he recalled the far distant peaks and the castle he'd been told stood amongst them. Perhaps he would find his answers at the feet of the wise leader who dwelt high in the remote snowcapped mountains. But what of the monster that had confronted him at Brish's home. Would something like that waylay him on his journey to those hights? Whatever the case he knew he must take the journey anyway. His soul yearned for the truth even as his body was hungry for the nourishment it needed to complete his recovery. He stood and walked over to the chair beside Dalfang. "Is there any of that hot broth left? I'm hungry!" The older man reached for the black pot hanging above the coals. Pulling back its lid, he stared into it.

"Yes, there's plenty left. It's still warm, I believe. A little steam is rising from it." Dalfang took a cup from the table beside him, filled it from the sooty cauldron, and handed it to Bracken.

"Thank you," returned Bracken, gratefully sipping the fragrant stew. "It tastes great." Each sat quietly until Bracken finished off the tasty broth. "While I was sleeping," he began, again placing the mug in his lap, "I had another dream." He shuddered a little as he recalled it. "I was back in the gem's passage being torn apart by Semie's friends."

"I could tell," acknowledged the other, lighting his pipe again. "Your sleep was quite fitful at times, but not nearly as bad as it was when you first arrived. It's possible that those memories may be with you long after the bruises on your body heal. But don't despair, I believe you'll find that a season in Vonervvn will heal many of them."

Bracken pulled up his arm and examined the recovering scar on his hand, the one he'd gotten from the exploding creature near the door of Brish's home. It was one of many. They were reminders of the ones in his soul as well. "Whenever I begin to think about what happened in the Mingus realm," he ventured, staring into the nearly extinguished fire, "I find it impossible to believe that those things really occurred," pausing for a moment, he watched one of the coals slowly die out. When its glow finally faded, he spoke again. "I guess I shouldn't say 'not believe' but rather 'not accept'." He shifted his weight, hoping to relieve some of the discomfort he still felt in his thighs. "How is it possible that evil could exist in such an awesome realm?"

Dalfang stood and took several logs from the wood box on the side of the hearth and tossed them into the fireplace, stoking the coals until he brought up the flame. "I tried to warn you of what would happen, but you seemed too determined in your quest to take time to understand what I was saying."

Now that the fire began to burn again, the cloaked man returned to his seat and to the pipe he had laid aside. "I was once like you, eager and petulant. When I was younger, I traveled many realms and byways to learn what now I hold sacred." The mentor filled and lit his deadened pipe, then leaned in closer to his young friend. "Our race is seeking something of eternity. But so often they miss the truth that lies within them. There's much good there. It simply must be harnessed and then used to transform our world. This power is like a stream whose waters can be turned to build or destroy. Evil beings have turned it against you, now you must learn to turn it back."

Bracken leaned down, placing his cup on the hearth in front of him. Looking into the ancient face across from him, he asked, "How did you come to discover these things? I've seemed to wander right past such truths and never find them."

Dalfang smiled back toward the youth. "Vonervyn has taught me these things. I've grown old learning of its ways. The quiet reflection of its beauty gives understanding to the troubled mind." The older man pondered momentarily, his eyes shining like polished stones in their deep-set sockets. "I've also grown to respect Wiscim's counsel. Even though I've never spent time directly with him, I've learned of the higher ways through others like Dimishta. They've sat at his feet and have been happy to share his philosophy with me."

Bracken was a little surprised when his elder mentioned the leader of Vonervyn. Even though Dimishta had told Bracken of Wiscim, he had tended to brush aside his importance in the flurry of his tour of the hidden world. He'd always seemed like a distant and benevolent ruler whose influence rarely reached the regions far from his distant palace. But now that he was being confronted with him again, a new hope awoke within him. Perhaps he could learn what he had been seeking from the same one who had taught so many of the Filanleys.

Bracken leaned closer to question the old man. "So Wiscim's the leader of Vonervyn and he lives in the Knasir Mountains?"

Dalfang knocked the dead ashes from his pipe and slipped it back into its pouch. "Yes, he does. And it's a place well worth seeing. You can learn much there, if you are willing."

"But why haven't you journeyed there?"

"A good question. You see, I think it would be presumptuous of me. I enjoy so much of Wiscim's grace right here where I am. Why would I impose myself on him?"

"I guess that's as good a reason as any, but I'm afraid I must meet him." Bracken paused for a moment as a series of odd thoughts crossed his mind. *Maybe there were dangers in the higher regions of Vonervyn. Maybe evil things linger in that high realm, things like the creature he faced at Brish's front door. Maybe this was why Dalfang had never journeyed to the mountains.* Perhaps that was the case. But he would not insult his friend by verbalizing such thoughts. So he merely announced his intentions again. "I'm not content to remain uninformed any longer. I've suffered too much to get to this point."

"A point well taken," said Dalfang with a smirk, noticing the unintended humor in his remark.

Bracken stood up and turned his back to the fire. It was late afternoon now, and he could feel the first hint of the evening chill in the air. "After what I've been through, I'm willing to learn all I can. Vonervyn is far more beautiful than anything I've found in the Mingus realm. It seems to have an unaffected and simple quality to it. I want to go back, and I deeply desire to meet this leader, Wiscim."

Dalfang stood up beside Bracken and removed something from the mantle above the fire. "I'm glad you've begun to notice the difference. Os was never able to see this. He was too fascinated with the pulsating allure of the gem."

Bracken grimaced at the memory of the Mingus peddler.

"In Vonervyn, one is close to the true flow of wisdom and knowledge. It's in the soil and sky, the trees and the high mountains. It contains an enchantment that leaves the soul refreshed and not drained." Dalfang rubbed the object in his hand against the soft texture of his inner cloak and then handed it to Bracken. The dull gloss of a metal cryptogram reflected the leaping flames of the fire. "Tomorrow, you may go to Vonervyn. I'm sure if you ask him, Dimishta will show you the path to the Knasir Mountains and Wiscim's palace."

Bracken stared down at the shining rectangle. It seemed to warm his soul. "I can hardly wait."

CHAPTER 66

VONERVYN

TAR-LYNREXS (LATE-SUMMER), 5512

Dawn was at midflight, the bright sun of Vonervyn rising splendidly in the morning sky as Bracken turned up the trail to Brish's home. Dimishta had met him at the entrance of Vonervyn and pointed the route to the way station, which lay at the base of the first range of peaks beyond Brish's home. Bracken had decided to make a short stop and greet her before hiking on toward the mountains. As he came over a rise, he could see that she was already up and working in her garden. Bright green-and-yellow flowers bloomed in rows between elongated vegetables and stubby-looking herbs.

Brish looked up from the neatly kept plot. "Bracken! What a surprise. It's so good to see you again." She motioned for him to enter the arbor next to the flower rows.

"It's good to see you as well," Bracken smiled back, taking the chair she offered him under the leaf-covered latticework. The two sat around a table and began to nibble on the fruit that Brish had set out earlier.

"I've been busy since you left. I'm just about to harvest my first herb crop." Brish looked admiringly out at the plot she had labored over and then, leaning back in her chair, turned back to Bracken. "I hope you're staying for dinner. I've made some Caila. It's delicious when fresh picked."

"That's what you told me before," replied Bracken, staring off in the opposite direction toward the far mountains. "I'm afraid I won't be able to join you. I'm on my way to Wiscim's palace."

"You are? That sounds like quite a challenge. I've heard it's a long journey," exclaimed Brish. "Why don't you spend the night here and rest up before your trip?" As she spoke, Brish leaned close to Bracken, and something stirred within him. It had been a while since he'd been with a woman, and he sensed his manly desires awakening again. But as strong as those urges were, his quest burned even stronger.

"I really need to get going, Brish."

As he spoke, she reached out and took Bracken's hand. "It's such a long way, and you'll need a good night's rest before you go."

Her eyes drew him in, and as he returned her gaze, a pleasant but firm grip caressed his heart. "Bracken you mean so much to me. Won't you just stay for a few nights? Your presence is such a comfort to me."

It was a tempting offer. He drank in her lovely face and inviting smile as she stroked his arm with her other hand. He'd been through so much. It would be so easy to lay aside all his struggles and rest in her inviting arms. Something in the beauty of the moment, the sparkle as the sunlight struck her hair and the alluring look in her eyes, seemed to whisper to him that it was time to rest. It was almost as if another voice, like a sweet song, murmured to him on the breeze. *Go ahead, weary wanderer, it's time you lay down your burden.*

Bracken was almost persuaded. But then he heard the plaintive call of the creatures in the pen nearby, and the haunting look in the giismis' eyes he'd seen that night came rushing back into his mind. Yet even with that image before him, it took every ounce of resolve to push the alluring invitation away. "Sorry, Brish, but I really must go. If I don't now, I don't think I'll ever go."

Brish let out a deep breath and seemed to give up her attempt to keep him with her. "So you'll be passing through the Knasir Mountains. You will enjoy them. I've been there several times. Hope to go back again soon. I've never made it as far as Wiscim's palace, but perhaps next time I'll stop there … By the way, I'd almost forgotten … your trip back to Nerkush, how was it?"

Bracken's face grew grim; he was a little reluctant to share all that had happened to him recently. But he went ahead anyway even if it would take some time. He felt like he owed it to her for her show of hospitality. Brish listened in sober attention.

When Bracken finished, she looked numbed by what he'd relayed to her. "I'm glad you're here, Bracken, and that you've seen through what Os was doing." Brish reached out and touched Bracken's shoulder, looking into his eyes. "Here in Vonervyn you are free and safe. I've been so completely satisfied here, I'd almost forgotten about Nerkush." Brish closed her arms around Bracken and held him gently for a moment. "I hope you stay for good this time."

"I think I will be staying," said Bracken sincerely returning her hug.

"Good. I'll look forward to us becoming much closer."

Then, like a dark cloud moving over the sun Bracken remembered the terrifying occurrence that had confronted both of them the night he'd first arrived. Drawing back from her embrace, he looked quizzically into Brish's eyes. "So you feel safe now, here in Vonervyn? What about the terror we faced the first night I was here? I remember you had been uneasy for days before that. Has that all vanished?"

Brish was about to speak and then caught herself as if to give thought before she answered. She looked back into Bracken's eyes, and he saw a twinge of fear before it quickly melted away. "Since then I've not had a visit like the one we encountered your first night here with me. But I've heard rumors that there have been sightings of those's creatures near the high passes on the way to Wiscim's palace."

"Rumors?"

"Yes. One of the waystation men came down from the mountains and stopped here for refreshments. He'd heard stories of recent pilgrims heading up those trails who never made it to the palace. He said others had heard terrified screams that had echoed down the canyons but when they went looking for victims none were found."

Bracken recalled the frightening night he and Brish endured when he'd destroyed the monster with his energy egg. He patted his shoulder bag and reminded himself that he used all those weapons. But he'd confronted terror before and he wasn't about to let it hold him back now even if he was unarmed. "We'll, inspite of those reports I must go anyway."

"I guess wherever we live there'll be fears we have to face. We may even have to deal with a few monsters sometime. After you left last time, Dalfang came and stayed with me for several days. I listened to his words and they gradually calmed me. I guess even he's had his battles with terror. He says it comes with the blessings of this place. It's something you just have to live with. Yes, every now and then this place seems to ask for some hidden tax on our mind and emotions."

Bracken was surprised, "And you're content to live with that, Brish?"

"I guess it's just the tradeoff I've come to accept, one that all who live here grow accustomed to. It seems that Dalfang has too. He's an old soul and very wise, but I guess he has his own secret demons to contend with."

"He told you that, Brish?"

"Yes, in fact I learned much more than that when he was here last. We connected deeply. I guess you could say even on an emotional level. It was strange. He was so much older than me, but … well I don't really want to talk about that now. Whatever it was, it's over."

Bracken couldn't imagine that Dalfang would become involved with a woman so much younger than himself.

"But I was really happy being with Dalfang. I mean, he really opened up. He'd had battles like I had when he first came here. He couldn't find a way to deal with them. So he finally visited Wiscim. He spent several days at the palace before he got an audience with the sage."

Bracken was shocked by her confession. "He's met with Wiscim! He told me he'd never met him. He said he was content merely to live with the grace that this place provided and not bother him for counsel," Bracken wondered why the elder had lied to him. It left him somewhat unsettled even as the knowledge that Dalfang had been with Brish now bothered him.

"Yes, he's been there. He said it was life changing."

"I wonder why he didn't tell me the truth?"

"The wizard is a strange character. He likes to hide some things. I guess this was one of them."

"Well, what did he say he learned?"

"He learned that there wasn't any simple answer. He learned what I told you earlier—that every place has its blessings and its terrors, and you just have to learn to live with them."

"He did say there was a moment with Wiscim when he was struck by something strange and foreboding. It was almost like he was at a place of decision. He found himself looking deep inside, and he realized he had come to a crossroads. He was about to choose another path and then all of a sudden things became so beautiful that he realized it was foolish to ever doubt all he'd known here. Then just like that, he was at peace again. He was sure that his doubts were just his mind playing tricks on him."

Bracken was completely surprised by two things. The first thing was that Dalfang failed to mention his connection with Brish. He should have been more like a father to this beautiful girl. It was odd that there had been no hint from the wizened man that he would be interested in a woman in that way. But Bracken realized now that he had been extremely naive and a little unrealistic. The second thing that surprised him was that Dalfang had failed to share about his own inner struggles that had resulted in a visit with Wiscim. Yes, it all was a little surprising.

"That seems really strange to me, Brish. In fact even a little troubling. But like you say, we all have our own demons to struggle with, don't we? So what did Wiscim tell him that gave him the grace to deal with his own monsters?"

A puzzled looked appeared on Brish's face again. "Well, that was the strangest thing of all. Wiscim didn't tell him a thing. When the exalted one came into the courtyard, he sat down in front of Dalfang and he said nothing. At first he was confused but gradually as he sat there looking into Wiscim's face, he came to accept everything. He just understood without one word being spoken between them. I guess you could say he just accepted the reality of the whole thing. And that was it."

"Well, I imagine I'll know firsthand soon enough. It's been a long and difficult journey but I feel like I'm nearly at the end of my quest. It will be satisfying to finally get all the answers. All the more reason to be on my way."

"Oh, one more thing, Bracken. One night as Dalfang slept by me, he talked in his sleep. He said something I still don't understand."

"What was it, Brish?"

"He just kept saying it over and over again. He said, "I see now, it's all connected?""

Bracken struggled to find a meaning to the strange phrase and came up empty. "Well, Brish I don't have an answer to that either, but maybe I'll ask Wiscim about it when I see him."

"Yes, I hope you find answers and that you enjoy your journey through the mountains. They're beautiful this time of year. But be careful though. I'm sure the rumors I told you about are just that, rumors. But again, be careful."

"I will."

"You have to let me prepare you some dried fruit to take along." Without another word Brish scurried into the kitchen. While she was preparing his provisions Bracken walk over to the giimis pen. The animals did not come to him as they'd done the last time. They seemed content to quietly mill about. The thought of Dalfang being with Brish came to him and he began to wonder. *Did she pull him in? Was he captivated by her charms?* He decided to make little test. Leaning over the railing he softly whisper. "Dalfang, are you there?" Nothing. Again he whispered. "Dalfang, did she seduce you as well?" Then ever so slowly one of the Gimiis turned its head and for just a moment the face of his friend formed over the animal's features. Its eyes were sad, filled with an unsatisfied longing. For a moment they seem to plead with him, then just as quickly it turned its head away and went back to milling about with the other creatures."

Just then Brish returned with a handful of freshly washed Caila and called to him. Bracken walked back to her and took the fruit stuffing it in his pouch.

"I wish you'd stay on for a few more days before you leave."

"I'd certainly like to Brish," replied the wanderer, shouldering his pack and smiling at her. "Right now, though, understanding everything that has happened to me is the first priority in my mind." Bracken turned and looked off toward the mountains again. "I'd better get going, before the day slips away."

Brish motioned him to walk ahead of her. "I'll walk with you to the top of the rise."

At the crest of a small knoll near her home, Brish hugged Bracken good-bye. She watched for a long time as he moved rapidly away. Finally, he was only a small dot on the distant hills. Before he disappeared into the forest, she waved in his direction and then returned to her garden.

CHAPTER 67

VONERVYN

ON THE PATH TO WISCIM'S CASTLE

Tar-Lynrexs (Late-summer), 5512

Bracken breathed deeply, taking in the air around him as he made his way through the first forest and into the second range of peaks of the Knasir range. The air had a fresh scent to it that made him want to take full benefit of its clean fragrance. The trees grew in thick, high clumps that the trail usually skirted. But occasionally the well-traveled path would plunge into a large forest. Some of the trees in these woods looked like a blend between several from Nerkush but for the most part they were different than anything he'd seen in his homeland. Their tall narrow trunks would rise straight up, only to open out into a massive canopy of thick dark leaves, dotted with seed cones. Other trees grew almost like brush but resembled dwarfed versions of what he'd known near Tizra. Still others hugged the base of the larger ones as if their bigger brothers had stunted them.

Wildlife abounded everywhere Bracken looked. Uncountable types and varieties crossed his path, some even coming up to him to eat from his hand. One in particular was a silver-furred creature with wings that lay back across its body. A long snout protruded several inches from its face. Six legs moving in perfect coordination carried it with stately pride.

Strange songs echoed in the trees, rhapsodies with notes so clear one could almost pull them from the air. Bracken wondered what strange animals could make such sounds and hoped they would become visible, but he never saw them.

Emerging from the shelter of the forest, he saw the roof of the first way station. Dimishta had told him that these stopping points had been established by former pilgrims to give rest and sustenance to those making their way to the distant palace. The gold-colored tiles on the station's roof glittered in the radiance of the setting sun. The small building sat on top of the low ridge.

Quickening his pace, he trudged up the steepening path. Bits of rock popped and grated under his feet as he hiked on. Coming to another rise his eyes were drawn to unusual markings on the trail. On closer examination it appeared that something large had crossed the path, leaving several deep gouges in the dirt before trailing off into the under brush.

As he headed further on, the markings returned coming from the side of the trail where they had disappeared earlier. This time though, from what he could see in the soil, a struggle had taken place here. There were bits of metal and flesh decaying in the sun. Remembering the terror he'd endured at Brish home the night he'd faced the monster, he seemed to lose his courage. Looking down at the carnage in his path he almost turned back. But he forced himself to shrug it off. He renewed his determination to finish what he'd started and moved forward.

As each step brought him closer to a possible meeting with Wiscim, his thoughts ran the gambit of potential outcomes. Perhaps the leader would refuse to see him. Who was he anyway? In all honesty, he was a newcomer to the world of Vonervyn. It was possible that such an exalted leader would have little time for him. Then there was the prospect that Wiscim was not as wise and others claimed he was. What if he arrived at the mountain fortress and found that it was some sort of mirage and that the ruler was just an aged and disconnected monarch who was completely out of touch and living in another world?

But even as these options ran through his mind, he realized that he had also run the gambit of prospects. Where else could he go for answers to his many questions? What other hope was there for Ebbern and the youth of his generation? He had few if any alternatives left. Finally realizing that there were no other plausible paths for him to take, he pressed on in faith that his searching would not be in vain. By nightfall he had reached his first stop and was greeted by a friendly Filanley, dressed in an evening cloak. The creature's eyes glowed softly in the twilight as he let his guest in and showed him to the tiny cubicle where he would spend the night.

The room was narrow, with a high-beamed ceiling. Bracken placed his things on the floor and looked around him. A small bunk was situated near the back of the room, and a table sat against opposing walls with a water jug and a drinking cup resting on it. Flickering light came from a single torch mounted against the rear partition. Just before Bracken retired, the caretaker brought him a plate of heavy but nourishing bread and a warm herb drink in an ancient wooden cup. He sipped it gratefully. It seemed to refresh his weary muscles, at the same time putting him gently at rest. He set the empty vessel on the table and settled into bed. Just before falling to sleep a troubling presence came into his room, similar to what he'd felt his first night at Brish's home. He rolled over in an attempt to drive away the premonition. Strangely that seemed to work and he quickly feel asleep.

That night, the troubling dream he'd had in Dalfang's cabin returned. He was hiking up a steep mountainside. He could see the top above him, and he'd eagerly press toward its crest. But just as he was about to crest the peak, tenacles would reach out at him pulling him down. He'd lose his footing and slide back, having to start all over again. This same pattern repeated itself, sometimes waking him. Unable to sleep, he'd get up and pour himself a drink of water. After draining the cup, he'd return to his bunk and fall into a deep sleep again. This pattern went on throughout the night with the vision coming back at least twice.

The following morning, Bracken was awake early and somewhat refreshed in spite of the previous night's nocturnal interruptions. With a warm meal offered by his host, he was completely revived and soon on his way. Still a bit hungry, he munched on a piece of the dried fruit that Brish had given him as he mounted the twisting rock pathway. Above him a ridge of high crags ripped their way into a sapphire sky. Stout little trees with brittle-looking branches clung to the sides of the steep canyon walls. Agile, surefooted creatures with lavish yellow fur roamed the high places near the peaks across from him. Periodically, they stopped and stared across the gullies at him.

At one point, the path became so steep that Bracken thought he could go no further. But as he reached the top of a narrow ravine, a stairway appeared that led up the mountain. It had been hewn from the rock, and its steps were worn with travel. Staring ahead, he could see a high meadow with a wide rushing stream flowing through it.

Green grass squeaked beneath his boots as he reached the creek. Tiny red fish darted in its waters. He noticed clumps of brush nudging the stream's edge as he bent down and drank deeply of the cold wetness. The reflected oval of the noon sun bobbed on the creek's sparkling surface.

Looking back, Bracken could see the rolling plain of Vonervyn and the distant lake shimmering on the horizon. For a moment he felt at peace, free, like a bird soaring above the confusion below, the confusion of his past. He sensed a renewed confidence that soon all his questions would be answered.

Refreshed by his drink, he stood up and walked on. He followed the stream up the meadow until he found its source. A waterfall splashed down from a jutting bluff that was part of a tableland high above him. At this point, the path ended. For several hours, he looked in frustration unable to locate a new trail. While struggling with his dilemma, his thoughts returned to the dream of the previous night. Why, he wondered, did he experience the constant frustrating attempts to reach the summit of the mountain only to repeat the failures? His time in this splendid place was supposed to erase all those irritations. But apparently that was not the case with him. Was something amiss here? Was he so broken from his early encounters in the Mingus realm that nothing could repair the damage done to his soul? Would he find what he needed in the high castle or would it also be another dead-end?

Shadows from the moutnains around him were growing longer now, so he returned to the falls in one final attempt to find a pathway. He was becoming more frustrated by the moment. Then to make matters worse his mind filled with images he seen in the dirt on the trail the previous day. *Had there been a struggle there?*

Looking into the sky he could clearly see that the sun was making it way quickly towards the distant horizon. The first chill of evening decended on him and he felt a deep sense of loneliness envelope his heart. *What if he failed to find a way forward? What if he had to turn back? What if the terrifiying presence increased and he had to face the creature here in this lonely place.* At that moment a fresh premonition came to him. Perhaps the path was behind the waterfall. He headed towards its thundering cascade and after some frantic searching there he finally found the path that had eluded him earlier.

The crashing water formed a narrow tunnel filled to about a foot deep. Wading through the pool, Bracken slipped behind the falling stream and stepped into the passageway. A tiny bit of light shone at the end of the arching cascade. He pressed towards it struggling against the water until he was about half way into the passage. Then at that moment the forboding presence he'd sensed earlier returned in full force as the distant light winked out.

Squinting in the now blackened interior he could make out a metallic glimmer shrouded in a cloud of darkness. It emerged out of a black shroud and floated toward him, bringing with it a powerful grip that pulled at his core.

He clearly recalled the horror he'd confronted the first night he was with Brish. This was the same sort of apparition returning to destroy him and now he had no weapon to deter it. The same dreadful whirring sound was there again, shaking the water above him and vibrating through the rocky ground beneath the shallows he was wading in.

Flaming eyes appeared out of the miasma and were soon joined by threatening tentacles moving rapidly towards him. He resisted the pull of the creature's power but it was useless. Each second he was being sucked closer to it. At any moment now he was sure he would be within its grasp. Realizing he was completely unarmed he quickly ran through his options. There was only one. Turning back in hopes of retreating he found that another creature, just as terrifying was blocking his way. *What would he do now? What could he do?*

Just before the point of confrontation that would bring him certain death he had a flash of insight. He recalled why he had begun his journey.

It had all been because of his heart-felt vision, his unrelenting quest for an answer. Now the full light of that original resolve rose up inside of him like a flaming torch. The quest that had brought him this far burned bright in his mind. It seemed to dispel the darkness around him and with it his fears. He found a new determination rising inside him. *Nothing, not even these dangerous creatures can hold me back.*

Then he rememdered how the remains of the monster he'd blown apart with the energy egg at Brish's home had later dissolved. *Why had they done that? Was it even real? Maybe it had all been an illusion. Maybe if he faced this apparition it would merely melt away.*

Mustering all his courage he turned back to face his first assailant and waded towards it, shouting as loud as he could. "I've come this far and I'm not about to be defeated now!"

At first his words seemed to have little effect but determined as ever he cried out again. "I will not let you stop me!"

The threatening demon suddenly ground to a halt. Encouraged he called out again. "So much of what I've seen is illusion."

As the last syllable echoed back at him in the watery tunnel his enemy began to fade. He shouted again.

"I've watched what seemed to be real became vapor and mist."

At that the fiery eyes blinked out and the tentacles withdrew. "Perhaps that's all you are, just fantasy."

In a hiss of steam the threatening object tilted towards the cataract at its side. It struggled to hold itself steady, but then, caught in the force of the falling waters, it tumbled down into the swirling tide at the base of the falls.

He turned to see if the one behind him was still there. It was gone as well. A hot, steamy mist filled the tunnel but then quickly condensed and showered him with a tepid rain.

He looked down the passageway and the light at the end had reappeared, softer now that the sunlight had nearly faded. He pushed forward wading toward the opening. When he reached it he was startled. A slender tongue of stone reached out into space and touched the high cliffs that came up to meet it from the other side of a deep gorge.

Slowly edging himself out onto the thin bridge, Bracken crept along. Far below him a thundering river carved its way through the canyon. Still shaken from his recent encounter he moved cautiously along, careful with each movement. Then at last he reached the other side and was overcome with relief. He looked back at the narrow passage behind the waterfall. It was dark now and empty. *Had what just happened been just another illusion? Had he really been in danger or had his mind just imagined it?* Whatever the case he knew now that he could face anything and over come it.

Ahead, a gentle slope led him down to the second way station. He made his way to it and was welcomed into its warmth by another Filanley. Once again he gratefully accepted the comforts that were offered and after a filling meal fell quickly asleep, this time without any tormenting dreams.

The next day, Bracken encountered his first snow. Rivulets of water washed over the lichen-covered stone as they ran from beneath the great cakes of frozen white. Soon the path all but vanished under a carpet of a frosty substance. Flagged poles marked where the trail led on. Sparkling icicles clung to rocky overhangs and dripped a clear liquid in stark, near-frozen pools.

Gradually the path descended again until the winding ravine turned to his right. Bracken worked his way down it for several hours. Coming around the edge of a high wall, he could see a fertile slope falling away toward a small forest. In its center, a chalk-white palace of stone rested, nestled like a pearl in the grass. Bracken's heart leaped as he gazed down at it. He was almost there. Rising from the center of the large building, a needle-shaped pillar pointed into the cloudless sky.

Bracken spent the remainder of the afternoon making his way toward the forest and then through it. By dusk, he stood at the huge gate of the castle and called to the sentinel in the tower. Slowly, the great oaken doors opened, and he was greeted by the ancient-looking gateman who introduced himself as Grawman.

"Who are you, young traveler, and where do you come from?" asked the leather-skinned keeper of the gate, as he led Bracken to the guest quarters. Dressed in a hooded cloak, the old man carried a billowing torch as he guided their way through the labyrinth of hallways and courtyards.

"I'm Bracken, and I come from Nerkush … through the Anindi Gate of Vonervyn. I've come to sit at the feet of Wiscim and learn his wisdom."

"Wisdom indeed, young wanderer," replied the aged one. "Many have come to this exalted place seeking answers. Many go away without them. We'll see if he has time for you. If you are chosen and are awarded an audience with him then truly a door of truth will be opened to you."

Bracken stared in wonder at the bright ornaments and paintings that decked the walls of this high fortress. Through one doorway, he saw a large room that held companies of Filanleys as they sat eating sumptuously from long tables. Melodic music of the highest forms drifted through the hallways and rippled at the flames of burning torches suspended in circlets from the high ceilings. Strange languages echoed past him as he followed his guide. A resonant bell rang several times in the tower above them.

The torchbearer stopped in front of a wooden door, ribbed with bands of black iron. "Here's your room. After you've cleaned up, I'll come back and take you to eat." With that, Grawman turned and disappeared down the dimly lit hall.

Bracken's room was elegantly decorated with woven tapestries hanging on the walls. Intricate quilts covered his bed. The bedstead was made from the finest wood. Delicate figures were carved into its surface, no doubt the work of some talented craftsman. He soon found a washbasin and a towel. He gratefully washed away the dust of the previous days.

Refreshed, he opened his door and stepped into the hall. Soon Grawman appeared and led him away to dinner. The brightly lit dining hall resounded with strains of unknown tones and cadence. The Filanleys who sat in the room ate and sang songs to their leader, Wiscim. They welcomed Bracken with nods and laughter. Soon he was eating happily with them and drinking steins full of fragrant intoxicant.

Taking in his elaborate surroundings, he realized his early doubts about Wiscim were vain. Surely such a great and wondrous place was home to an equally fascinating and brilliant leader. But in spite of these hopeful signs, Bracken soon grew tired.

Weakened from his previous attack and weary from climbing, he excused himself early and slipped off to bed. The soft luxury of his pillow welcomed his tired head. As he sought a much-needed rest, hope rose in his heart that he would find favor with the ruler of this sublime place. He closed his eyes in confidence, but in spite of the comfort of his quarters, he slept fitfully as the tormenting dream returned.

CHAPTER 68

VONERVYN

WISCIM'S CASTLE

Tar-Lynrexs (Late-summer), 5512

In the morning, Grawman stirred Bracken awake with his singsong greeting. "You are lucky, my young traveler. You've been chosen. It appears that your reputation has preceded you. I hope you realize what a privilege has been afforded you. You've certainly been singled out for something unique, for today you will meet with Wiscim. But before your meeting, Luciene needs to speak with you. He's Wiscim's adjunct."

"Adjunct?"

"Yes, all who come to meet with Wiscim must first pass his scrutiny."

Bracken was a bit taken aback by this unexpected hurdle, but realized that there were, no doubt, protocols in this mysterious place. "If it's necessary, then I'm fine with it."

"Yes, necessary and enlightening. You'll like what you hear. The interview will be in the tower. I'll be here later to lead you there." Grawman left a bowl of fruit for his guest's breakfast and whistled his way off down the hall.

Bracken ate while he dressed. He was eager to meet the Filanley leader. He longed to hear the words of comfort and wisdom he hoped Wiscim would bring. He yearned for a balm to heal the scars of his inner man. He had so many questions. Then there been the return of the depressing dream. He thought after his confrontation with the specters in the watery tunnel that he had somehow transcent all those things. Evidently somethings still linger in his mind and heart that he'd not overcome.

Now added to those were his concerns surrounding Dalfang. Why had his mentor been so secretive? During his long journey to this place, he'd run those questions through his mind. And of course it added to his concerns. So many doubts and obstacles had grown to an overwhelming proportion. The wounds on his battered soul still ached. His physical affliction seemed minor compared to the ache in his heart. The words of a wise man would be an ointment of life.

Bracken stood in front of the mirror, which appeared to have been hammered from one piece of bright metal. He used his fingers to comb his hair. His tired eyes stared back at him. His journey had been more taxing than he had realized. He felt as if every part of his being was worn and frazzled. *How much longer can I go on looking?* he wondered. The roads of his life that had seemed so pleasant had turned down a weary path. The feet of his spirit were bruised. The cobbles on the lanes of his journey were growing sharper. The soft moisture of his youth felt dry and brittle.

He took another bite of the colorful fruit. Its taste was sweet and wet, but it did nothing to quench his inner thirst. He knew only one thing would do that. By the time he had finished dressing, the gatekeeper had returned.

There was a faint knock on the door, and he walked over and opened it. The smiling face of Grawman greeted him. "Follow me for your interview. You'll find Luciene quite charming. His role is more of a formality, and if you'll be gracious, you'll find your efforts reciprocated."

Grawman moved down a long hallway, finally stopping at a large oak door. His host pulled on the iron ring that served as its handle, and it groaned open. A set of stairs ascended up a narrow corridor that twisted above him. Several times they came to a landing with an opening that let light into the passageway. Looking out, Bracken was able to orient himself, and he realized that the tower was the silver spire that rose in the center of the compound.

A little out of breath, Bracken was glad when they reached the top of the stairs and entered the cozy chamber. Shafts of sunlight pouring through windows on each wall and crossed the room in intersecting patterns. Two small pillows lay across from one another where the light beams met. Luciene sat on one, his legs crossed and his eyes closed.

The adjunct was smaller than he expected and wore a simple woolen cloak. His high forehead was nearly bald, and his eyes were unusually large.

"Have a seat, Bracken," said Luciene.

"Thanks," said Bracken as he sat on the pillow, crossing his feet in imitation of his host.

"I hope you've found your stay pleasant so far?"

"Yes, Grawman has been an excellent host." Bracken nodded in the direction of the departing Filanley.

"Most find that true." Luciene smiled and gave Bracken a searching look. At first, the effect was a little overpowering. The adjunct's eyes were bright and lit with a sense of mystery. "So you've come to meet with Wiscim."

"Yes, I've so many questions. I've been through some serious conflicts. Lots of scars on my soul right now, but I finally feel that I'm in a safe place, a place where wisdom rules. Others have spoken highly of what they've learned from your master."

"You're correct, wisdom is here and with it a great opportunity."

"Opportunity?"

"Yes," another broad smile lit up Luciene's face. "We've heard of your quest, of the community you're from, and the deep hunger for truth that seems to be emerging in midst of your group back in Nerkush."

"Who told you about me? I had no idea. When? How?"

"Dalfang did." A slight smile formed at the edge of Luciene's lips. "You see, our emissaries meet with him regularly. He didn't tell you? Well, that's like him. He tends to keep some things secret. It's a naughty habit of his, not a bad one, just annoying."

Bracken was taken aback by this new revelation. Yes, a little annoyed, but he could understand that everyone liked to keep secrets, even friends like Dalfang. Apparently he liked to keep lots of secrets. "So what else did he tell you about me?"

"That you would be a perfect candidate for our mastery regimen."

"Your mastery regimen, what is that?"

The adjunct smiled again, this time matched by a slight wink in his left eye. "Oh, just a way of allowing you to rise to your full potential. To become a powerful eminence for others to follow."

"Eminence?"

"You see, Bracken, so many of your generation are drifting. They're hungry for what you've experienced but also have found themselves trapped in some of the snares that you've escaped. It's your tenacious nature that appeals to us. You could be the kind of leader that is rarely seen amongst your fellows."

"How would I become that?"

"Wiscim wants to mentor you." Luciene reached out and touched Bracken, his long, narrow fingers resting on the youth's hand. "Yes, he's already heard all about you. Dalfang's been prepping him."

Bracken felt a sudden rush of pride. He found it hard to believe. He was being chosen? Chosen to lead his generation out of their confusion. "He would mentor me? What would that mean?"

"Put simply, he would teach you to move in realms of power that would impress even the greatest skeptics among your ranks. The powers that you have seen Dalfang and Brish display are mere trifles compared to the force that you can unleash when Wiscim commissions you. He would train you with his wisdom, and you would bring a message so profound that they would follow you like sheep."

"That sounds a bit overwhelming, if not odd. Why would I want them to follow me?"

"Because you will offer them the alternative they've been looking for ... a way to shake off the oppression of the Fathers and the High Council ... a way to lead your people to higher levels of understanding. And with all that, you would become like a god to them."

Luciene rose, almost floating off the pillow, and motioned Bracken to follow him toward one of the openings in the spire. "You see, Bracken, what your culture needs is a new beginning, but with a new beginning there always must be someone to lead. A leader of such power and charisma that others will follow without question." The adjunct led Bracken out onto a small balcony. Here near the top of the spire he could see all the way to the distant lake. "Bracken, this vast domain will someday be inherited by someone like you. You can't imagine the power and pleasure that awaits the one who inherits Wiscim's throne."

Bracken took a deep breath of the clear air that flowed up from below him. As far as he could see were pleasant meadows, snowcapped mountains, glistening streams, and far-off plains ripening with the fruit of the land. It was a world filled with strange but lovely people and empowered with a magic that would leave his generation back in Nerkush in awe. It was a place he could only have dreamed about a short time ago, and now he was being offered the promise that someday he could rule it.

"Wiscim will soon ascend to a higher realm. He's looking for one like you to take his place."

"But why me?"

Luciene's eyes smiled this time, his mouth unmoved. "Because you're the chosen one, Bracken. Your quest and battles have prepared you for this time. You can go back to Nerkush and lead others. As I said before, you will be almost like a god to them. And of course, here in this realm you will be just that."

Bracken took those last words deep into his soul. He could feel his mind expanding, his heart surging with pleasure. He could see the accolades and honors coming his way. He could see himself high, lifted above his enemies, crushing men like Ley and the other thugs that roamed the streets of Accad. He imagined Lisha returning to him, humbled. He could imagine others like his parents and the stubborn leaders of his nation seeking his wisdom. He could see it all, and he was right at the center … Bracken and no one else.

"Do you want it, Bracken?" Now the adjunct's face was still, as empty as the sky around them.

Bracken asked himself one simple question. *Why is it all about me?* Then another one raced into his mind. *Why is it all about power? This isn't what I came here for. I came for a way to help others … a way to find answers to my search. And now I'm offered this.*

A quiver went through him, and he saw in his mind's eye a piercing blade cutting into his dream, its shreds lying like reflective splinters before him. As each of its segments fell away, he could see all the greed, deception, and pride he'd seen in others staring up at him, and on each of its reflective sections he saw his face filled with lust. He told himself with all the resolve he could muster, *I will not do this. I will take the right path.*

Then suddenly he understood what was happening. He grasped the trick that the adjunct was trying to play on him. It was all be part of the test that he must pass through before meeting with Wiscim.

"Your offer is generous, Luciene. It appeals to me. But I'm afraid it appeals to the wrong part of me, the part that needs to fade away. What you describe is not what I'm after. So I must refuse. Hopefully I've not disappointed you and have passed the test?"

The adjunct's face became even more vacant. "Yes, you have indeed. You've told me exactly what I needed to hear."

"So do I get to meet with Wiscim now?"

"You do indeed."

He was quickly led back into the room, the door to the stairway opened, and Grawman emerged. "He will take you back to your quarters. Your meeting with Wiscim will follow soon, shortly after the noon meal."

CHAPTER 69

VONERVYN

WISCIM'S CASTLE

Tar-Lynrexs (Late-summer), 5512

Back in his quarters after another meal of warm porridge, Bracken fell into a deep sleep. As he slumbered, the dream returned again. He climbed the mountain as before. Each step took him closer to the top, but just as he was about to reach it he slipped and tumbled back to the bottom only to struggle again and repeat the same vain attempt as before. But then the dream changed slightly. This time he did reach the top on his final attempt, but then a black fog settled over him. And a pair of claw-like hands reached out and shook him.

Struggling to free himself, he was awakened from his sleep by Grawman shaking him. "Wake up, Bracken. Your audience with our master will be at the second bell. I knocked on your door twice and you didn't answer. Even after I came into your room and called to you but you didn't move. Are you okay?"

Bracken rubbed his eyes and sat up. "I'm sorry, Grawman. I was dreaming. That porridge was like a sedative. Thank you for waking me."

"I'm glad. Are you sure you're okay."

"Yes, I'm okay."

Well, we best be going now."

The elder led Bracken from his room and through the palace into a tree-filled garden of neatly trimmed shrubbery and flowers. Graceful trees manicured into artful shapes stood everywhere, their green elegance enhancing the moment. A lily-covered pond adorned the center of the square. "You may wait here until he arrives."

"Thank you," replied Bracken as Grawman turned and slipped away. Everything was perfect, even down to the green moss-like seedlings that floated on the surface of the pond. He was caught up in the beauty that surrounded him. Such perfection drew something from the center of his heart. He loved what he saw almost to the point of worship. Yes, that was it. He adored this peaceful spot; this perfect place drew praise from his heart and he idolized its impeccable glory. It was superb, splendid, perfect ... it almost seemed too perfect.

Bracken stretched out on a carved wooden bench and stared up into the azure heavens as he waited. The high needle spire where he'd been earlier that day gleamed in the afternoon sunlight.

The bell rang, an odd, hollow sound, and then again a second time. The door at the far end of the garden opened. Bracken pulled himself upright. A line of musicians entered, coming his way, solemn and formal, playing what sounded like some gentle, plaintive overture.

Bracken watched. Behind them, an entourage of Filanleys dressed in silk carried what seemed to be a great throne. *What in the world?* thought Bracken, getting up and walking toward the dais near the pool where they put down their burden. He made himself a place a short distance from their presentation and sat down to watch.

Was all this for him? The musicians flowed and merged like streams in front of the throne, swaying, moving, rippling in a complex hypnotic pattern, the music rising, keening, thundering to a climax that never seemed to come.

Suddenly it stopped, and without a sound they sat. And the throne was occupied. As Bracken peered toward the royal seat, he saw that Wiscim was surrounded in an orb of bright golden light. Pulses of this light flowed out from his head. The glow was so dazzling that it appeared as a veil and hid the master's face. This being was so exalted, thought Bracken, that his very essence must be as pure as the light that was emanating from him.

Then the one on the throne spoke, his voice caused the waves of light to modulate like billows coming ashore at the sea. "So, young seeker, I hope you've found our hospitality here has been to your liking?"

Bracken was almost afraid to speak, being so overawed by what he was experiencing. But he mustered his courage and replied. "It's been wonderful. Your servants are gracious and the food and fellowship has been delightful."

"That is part of our philosophy here. To delight and bring comfort."

"Well, you've certainly lived up to that goal," said Bracken, his face wide with a pleasing smile.

"So, now that you've experienced our warm reception, what else can we do for you?"

"It's been a long journey to this point … ah, I'm not sure how I should address you?"

"Many call me Master. Others, called me Exalted One. But for now and for you, Wiscim will be fine."

"Okay, but is there some formal language or manner?

"Don't worry about that now. Just speak from your heart."

Bracken was relieved, for he didn't have a clue what the proper protocol was when speaking with someone of such majesty. Reassured by this apparent act of benevolence, he continued.

"Well, as I was saying … Wiscim, it's been a long journey for me. I've been down many avenues that have ended in disappointment, and I've faced countless hours of suffering in my quest."

"That's understandable. What you seek is not ordinary, nor are you. Those who seek higher realms will often pay a great price in their pilgrimage. Like you, years ago I was on a journey of enlightenment. I struggled with many things but finally came to discover that all that is around me now, each thing of beauty in this place, is worthy of my love and adoration. Each blade of grass, each leaf, each amber-winged creature and scented flower are all part of the eternal whole that must be revered as well as worshiped. Yes, so often I merely passed them by without a second thought, but eventually I learned. It was a long process, but finally the answers came."

"You mean you once were on a path like mine?"

"All dimensions have similarities. My way to serenity was in a different world than yours, but there are parallel experiences that we each face. So, tell me about yours."

Bracken began by recounting his first encounter with the Disk beings and the final moments of terror he faced alone near the Pillars of Rimlex. When he finished this part of his story, he expected some response, but instead there was only an almost undetectable "umm" coming from Wiscim.

A bit frustrated but still determined to tell his whole story, Bracken continued his account. He went on to explain his other confrontation in the strange realm of the Mingus stone and how it ended in shock and torment. He finished his story with the details of Silas's death. The words poured out of him in a torrent driven by a deep-seated agony he didn't know he still felt. But now it was all coming to a head. He knew that he could no longer go on without some sort of resolution.

Curiously, as the rush of words flooded from his heart, there was again no response from the one before him, except for a steady but quiet flow of "umms". *Why such a flat response?*

But then Bracken realized Wiscim had not spoken because he was listening, concentrating to hear Bracken's heart and odyssey. But still, something was odd. Somehow Bracken's journey and its accompanying pain had made him sensitized in a way that he previously had not known. He had to know the reason for Wiscim's silence or he would go crazy. Looking intently at Wiscim, he boldly cried out, "Are you listening to me?"

The response from the throne was immediate and absolutely commanding. "Quiet yourself, pilgrim. You're about to step over a line, and that would be dangerous for you."

Bracken instantly knew he'd been too brash, but he couldn't help himself. He had to make amends now. "Please forgive my rudeness, but I've been through so much, my patience is nearly gone."

Just as quickly, a reply came from the master. "I'm aware of your pain, and I understand it. But now is not the time to react. It's time to listen."

"I'm ready to listen," he murmured as much from his heart as from his mouth.

The exalted one's words came softly at first but with them a deep resonance that required absolute attention. "Let me explain as clearly as possible, young one."

Bracken could sense that Wiscim wished to be gentle with him, but his tone was almost patronizing, as if the Master considered him a mere child. He didn't like what he discerned, but he listened anyway.

"I understand completely," continued Wiscim. "You've been handicapped by a strange curse from the very beginning. Each time your probing has brought the wrong reaction from those you've confronted."

"But those beings were lying to me. They'd deceived me."

"No, you were merely getting the reply that your fears and doubts deserved. If you'd only been more trusting, more patient, you'd have come to understand."

"Understand?"

"Yes, there's a flaw in your approach, and it originates from something that occurred in your youth."

"My youth?"

"Yes, years ago you were taught the wrong thing, and ever since then it's marked you. It's almost like you're sending out a signal that creates a negative reply."

"What is it I've learned or been taught that creates this?"

"Well, even though you've sought to forget it and even though you've run from it, somehow you still believe it."

Bracken searched through his past, wondering what possible issue it could be. Then a clear thought arose above all the others and he knew. "It's the Volume, isn't it?" As he spoke the words, he sensed they had a strange impact on Wiscim. It was almost imperceptible at first, but as Bracken watched, the light that emanated from the enthroned one began to fade.

"Yes, that's it," said Wiscim. "You must recognize how dangerous that book is to you and the future of your people. I know many have put their hopes in its promises. And of course those who wrote it had good intentions, but there are too many that take its words literally."

"But why would that be a problem for me?"

"It's simple, you've turned back to it in your moments of terror instead of facing the fear and overcoming it. Instead, you let those quaint but unhealthy instructions comfort you."

"Yes, but when I did, it broke the power of the evil forces that sought to destroy me and somehow I was delivered."

"No, you merely set yourself back into the endless cycle. This is the sad tale of so many who never reach the exalted state but merely repeat the pattern of life, then death, then life again. But their progress is hindered and often stifled by such quaint beliefs." As Wiscim went on, Bracken noticed that the light from the master's face continued to diminish.

"So what must I do then?"

"You must finally and completely reject those vain things you've been taught from your youth and embrace what you fear is a lie. You must realize that the evil that you've seen in your journey is only the other side of the good. It is only one part of the whole. You must understand that together the good and the evil, the dark and the light form a complete quality. Once you embrace this fact, once you entwine your soul with it, it will become clear. You see it's all connected."

Bracken had been down so many paths, so many roads, and come up empty each time. Why not try this one? Why not take Wiscim's advice and cease his struggling. He collected his courage and shook off all his doubts. "Okay, I'm ready. What now?"

"Just wait and watch."

As Bracken focused all his attention on Wiscim, the last fragments of light dispersed from the master's face and the being on the throne emerged completely. At that moment Bracken thought he had lost his mind. It truly was all connected.

That smile. That face. The face he had seen calling Silas to oblivion. The face that had appeared from beneath the disk commander's veil. The mocking visage that he had confronted on the crystal plane of light in the Mingus realm. The piercing eyes. The pointed nose. The leathery, molded features. Then Wiscim spoke again. "You must accept me. You must let me envelope all of you and serve only me. Then peace will come and you will finally understand."

For the longest time, Bracken stared at the one before him. He pushed away his fears and looked deep in his heart to see if he could somehow believe what he had always thought was a lie. But try as he might, he knew he could never do that. Maybe others had, but he could not.

Something rose in his heart like a fire and drove the words from his mouth. "I could never do that. You're lying." He recalled how the voice that spoke through Brish had tried to comfort him with platitudes about his friend's death. But he didn't believe it and he shouted out his conviction. "You deceived him! You killed Silas. I don't believe you want to help me either. You only want to control and posses me and make me a tool to carry your lie to others."

Bracken could hardly believe what he was saying. Where was all this coming from? He knew what his declaration meant. He knew he was facing certain terror, perhaps even death. But he would never compromise now, no matter what the price. For, finally, here was the truth he had sought for so long. If this evil creature existed, so did his counterpart. If such wickedness sought to possess him, surely there was good that sought his soul as well.

"You've chosen poorly," came the soft, mocking voice. "You should have listened to me and let go of your doubts. You should have taken Luciene's offer as well, but you were foolish. You could have been a god like me. You could have ruled all you see. But it's too late now. Now you know. You know the truth. You finally know."

And Semie smiled. It was that terribly delicate smile, the smallest lift of the corners of that hard, thin mouth, a smile that chilled Bracken to his core. For a moment, he thought he'd gone insane, but then all at once with a sudden, certain terror, Bracken knew he was not mad. He knew that it was all real and there was no escaping what was about to come upon him.

"I go by many names," said the one on the throne. "I'm sure you've guessed my real name by now, but unfortunately, you know it much too late. You should have taken my offer and embraced me, then you would have been blissfully ignorant. Once you'd believed the lie, you would have become like so many others who are content now to live under my command. But you made your choice but we will find pleasure in your decision anyway."

The Filanleys on either side of the dark lord began to change. And as Bracken stared in horror, their disguises dissolved away, dripping like wax, leaving the tentacled shapes of the demons. Their faces were melting, just like Bracken's inner being. Just like his courage. Just like everything he had ever hoped for.

"Your soul has grown fat on our deception, Bracken. The lies we fed you were good. But now …" The voice was terrifyingly soft, "Now your heart is ripe. And it is time for the harvest. It's time for us to feast."

Bracken was afraid, but not with ordinary fear. Now his terror was beyond compare. His hopes were shattered. He had no future. Every corridor he'd traveled had only ended in despair. He had no more reason to live, no more reason to seek, no more reason to dream. Blackness, like a giant, swirling pool churned in his mind. One by one, the surging maelstrom swallowed every fantasy he had ever entertained.

To trust now seemed blasphemous. To hope would only compound his horror. He heard his own thoughts laughing in despair in the clattering chambers of his mind. Why had he ever begun searching? he wondered. Why had he come to this moment only to find a lie waiting behind the door of his dreams?

Semie stood to his feet. And seemed to grow … and grow. Bracken could not look at him. "I am Semie. I am the Ruler of the Night. I am the Shadow Czar." The voice seemed to boom from every corner of the courtyard, like a great and hollow echo, like a voice forsaken by its body, a terrible, dreadful voice that screamed and howled and thundered around the trembling youth. He had no escape, but still somehow he hoped he might escape.

"No one escapes."

His knees were welded to the ground. All around, he heard the rustle of Filanleys closing in toward him. In that moment, Bracken knew the terror that few men ever know before death. So often life ushers men forth with anthems of joy. Then later at the end of the corridor of time, they discover the truth. After they pass the last sentinel of this life, they find their fate waiting and their judgment revealed.

Now it was only a matter of time. The dreams were nothing. His life was nothing. He looked for a tender thread to cling to … nothing. His heart could no longer float above the swirling tide. It was too heavy with his cares, too filled with his own selfishness. Yes, he finally knew. A terrible realization swept through him—he deserved his fate. His own lust and selfishness had brought him to this end.

His life flashed before him. He remembered his family … his father, his mother … the Volume. The truth had always been there. It had been all around him, and yet he had refused to believe it. Why? He agonized. Why? His ego clutched at him. Its long, slithering fingers pulled at him, dragging him down to his final moment of despair. He had to face the fact that much of his youthful rebellion had merely been a disguise for his own lust and pride. Sure his planet was rushing toward apparent destruction. Yes, the rulers of his land were power-hungry and corrupt, but so was he, so were men like Os. He saw his heart for the first time for what it really was: dark, selfish, and full of pride. He'd hid it well and so had others he'd trusted. It was there just below the surface hiding under a pleasant screen of rhetoric and charisma. He believed it because he had not loved the truth. All those selfish impulses had ultimately delivered his life on a platter to his assailants and now his soul had become a delightful meal for them to feast upon.

He was in their grip now, as he felt their vicious tentacles slash at him with condemnation and fiery accusations. "All is lost. You will be like this forever," came the dreadful slurs. "No hope remains, only constant suffering forever." *Theema*, they called it, finding joy in the suffering of others. The

Shadow Czar, Strieme, and his minions, they were taking their pleasure with him, tormenting, terrorizing, and gradually consuming any hope he had left.

Then suddenly he found the grace to shut out their voices. He found the strength to stop and push the recriminating thoughts away. He pushed it all away. "Let it die … let me die … but let the truth live," he screamed.

Something was happening. From the depths of his heart, a memory awoke. A name! A name that stood out above every other name, thrust up like a rainbow into his mind, and in final desperation he turned his eyes toward the sky and spoke that name.

"Prince of Wonder!" At first it was barely a whisper, harsh as a rasp in his throat. But he gathered his strength and tried again. "Prince of Wonder!" This time it was stronger as if soothing oil had been poured down his throat. And then it became a shout. "Prince of Wonder, if you're there I know now that you are real and only you can save me."

It was all so clear now. If this hideous enemy that had tricked him was real, then the Volume that told him of this danger was true as well. The one who authored it was wise and absolutely all-knowing. He cried out one final, desperate phrase. "Prince of Wonder, what must I do?"

Suddenly, like the clockwork of a giant timepiece locking in suspension, everything stopped. Then a phrase, strong enough to hurl stars into space broke through the keening voices that tormented him. "Be gone," it commanded. In that moment, every voice of condemnation left Bracken, and in its place was absolute peace. Then a shaft of light, as narrow as a knife penetrated the atmosphere. It grew as creatures of massive strength began to form an expanding circle around him, driving all darkness away. The hideous Filanleys were the ones now cowering in terror. The Shadow Czar was held firmly in a grip far greater than his own and his servants' voices were all hushed.

The brilliance continued to grow, and peering up at the giant shining beings surrounding him, Bracken was overcome with peace. They were clearly mighty, their chests broad as shields and their arms massive and flexing beneath their gossamer robes. Each held a flaming sword in its hands. He heard their voices calling out to their leader. "They're moving back, Michess. We have them on the run."

"Well done," replied Michess. "The Prince approaches now." The giant beings slashed at the hideous Filanleys, which quickly scurried away like so many frightened rats. The Night Ruler's towering form dissolved as well, shrinking into a serpentine creature that slithered into the shadows.

But as Bracken watched, the mighty ones, their warfare over, bowed, anticipating what would come next. And then it came. Not as a glowing orb or a scintillating brightness, but in a still, small voice accompanied with a presence that was all pervasive. A presence that needed no display of false splendor but rather carried with it an authority nothing could resist.

How could one utterance work such wonders? Bracken questioned. But as the presence settled over him, he knew. Here was no shifting shadow that needed to create a mask of false light to hide its hideous lie. No, what he now encountered was truth, pure light and absolute power. It had only taken one short phrase from this voice to dispense with Bracken's enemies. One simple but powerful remark from the one whose voice created Ebbern and all the stars above it with his word. Now that voice spoke to him. In love, it quietly whispered in Bracken's dissipated heart. The voice was tender. Each word seemed to heal and restore his soul.

"I have waited for you, Bracken." The voice was right. He had been selfish, impatient, and full of pride. But the voice was gentle, forgiving. "You've rejected me, but still I've waited. I've kept you. I have waited for the moment when you would see how vain and cruel your own heart was."

Bracken found it hard to believe what he was hearing. It was too good. The concern laced with forgiveness that he heard seemed impossible! He had nearly died. He deserved to die and now ... now he was free! A being of love, far greater than he had ever dreamed, spoke words of care, words of life, and words of hope to him. And then he knew whose voice it was, the Prince, whose gracious words now left Bracken's soul in a state of wonder ... the Prince of Wonder!

"Bracken, you have believed what men have made me out to be, believed the lies their lives have told you, that I was powerless, dead, forgotten. But as you see, I am alive and have all power. The key to all things is firmly in my hand, even as you are. I have loved you, and now you know it beyond all doubt."

The healing of Bracken's heart had begun. The fear had vanished. The loneliness was gone. Arms of comfort held him.

"Long ago, I suffered to break the grip of this dark prince, the Shadow Czar, and as you can see, it has been done. I gave myself that you might live, and as I live, so will you forever."

Those words carried with them such assurance that Bracken knew he could never doubt them. Gradually like a fading, gentle song they ceased, but their essence was like steel in his soul. The voice of the wondrous Prince was gone, but his words had left their mark on Bracken's heart and a comforting presence rested there with them. He would never be the same again.

Bracken slumped to the ground, weeping bitter tears, tears of remorse, until he had bathed the stones beneath his feet. He wept until there was no more strength to weep, and then he rested in a joy that seemed to have no end. From the depths of his heart, a cry of thanksgiving, of release and joy, rose up until words of gratitude sprang from his mouth. And then he wept again, but now tears of gladness, tears of peace, until all grew quiet again.

"I must go home," he said softly. As he walked away, the presence and the words of the Prince of Wonder went with him. He had surrendered, he felt clean, and he was a new man. His searching was over. All his unanswered questions were satisfied. Now he would explore a whole new realm of wonder. One as glorious and as endless as its creator. His encounter with such majesty had dispelled the lies of the Shadow Czar and his followers. He still had a journey ahead of him, but it would be one of love and mercy.

He knew he must reach his friends who remained under the spell of the dark one. His heart ached for them, but he was also confident that the presence that was now with him and the power of His word would disperse all the evil one's lies. If the powers of Fenessence were merely a counterfeit, then what must be prepared for those who followed the Prince? Such truth would provide weapons that would defeat all lies and bring healing to hurting souls.

Like an actor walking from the stage at the end of a play, Bracken saw the world of Vonervyn gradually vanish behind him, the scattered remains of an abandoned set. In its place, the road to Tizra stretched before his feet. He knew his return would take many days, and each step held possible pain. But he walked on anyway. He walked the road home with joy.

CHAPTER 70

LOWER THRONE ROOM

TAR-LYNREXS (LATE-SUMMER), 5512

A buzz of confusion hummed and rumbled through the darkness that somehow had grown bleaker since his last visit. Strieme stood absolutely still. The angry hissing that filled his ears had put him on edge the minute he entered the chamber. It took longer than usual to adjust his vision to the room.

He could hear another sound. A clamor of scraping and clawing rumbled all around him. But it was soon buried in a tide of screams and moans. He knew what was happening. The dark one on the throne was in one of his rages. He was angry that he'd lost, that he had lost one so close to destruction. He was never content to suffer alone. He had to take out his anger on his servants. So with a final hopeless cry, the ones who had been chosen for special torment were assembled before the throne.

Then without a word, the dark lord's tail scraped them off the room's surface like dregs. Plunging them over the edge to fall for hours until they reached the keening chamber. An enormous cloud of putrid air rushed up from below as the tormented ones vanished. Their cries of horror gradually subsided, but unfortunately the fear that screamed in Strieme's mind remained.

Then came the overriding voice that always brought him to attention. His master spoke, and instantly he knelt before the enthroned one, his knees grinding into the hard floor. "You have seen the fate of those I have just vanquished. Do wish to join them?" The words had a hint of sadistic humor. "You're lucky I still need you."

There familiar rasping sound returned, carrying with it a presence of heated, stale breath that spilled over him. Suddenly he knew why. Cautiously, he looked up to find the face of the Shadow Czar inches from his. The hideous beauty that focused on him was overpowering. Such perfect symmetry of form, such exactness of elegance, yet somehow still horrible. The eyes were red with dark centers like charcoal. They burned him with the heat of their intensity. "I've decided to give you another chance. No doubt this fool will try to warn his friends. You must not let that happen."

"I promise it will not." Already new schemes began to fill his thoughts. "I assure you he will be stopped."

"Yes, and for that I've given you an incentive. For your efforts, as futile as they've been, I will allow you Theema. But not with the hundred I promised. Now it is only ten. You may have them when you leave me, but take with you this warning: If you fail me again, you'll be the one in torment. Now, out of my presence.

With those threats still hissing in his mind, Strieme left the chamber as quickly as he could. On the way to his next assignment, he weighed the challenge before him. From what he'd seen happen during their encounter with the Prince of Wonder, he sensed at his core that a whole new level of warfare was ahead for all of his kind. The tide had turned against them, and perhaps many others would follow the path of the one who had escaped their grasp. He could only wonder what torment was ahead if a whole generation was lost to their enemy.

CHAPTER 71

TIZRA

PAR-MANTRIK (FIRST CHILL), 5512

"You're home, Bracken! I can hardly believe my eyes." Myrus threw her arms around her son as he stood in the doorway of their home. He sensed the peace that emanated from his mother and the comfort of a familiar place filled with warm memories. He couldn't help noticing how different this greeting was from what he'd received from Dalfang.

At the end of his encounter with Semie he'd mysteriously found himself standing back in the ravine in Zorek. Making his way to the gatekeeper's cabin, he resolved to tell him everything. When it came spilling out, it left the sage in shock. At first he listened, stroking his beard and taking puffs on his pipe. He had thrown out a host of reasons why the youth's encounter in Vonervyn had turned into a nightmare. But each one faded in the face of the reality that gripped Bracken.

When the wizened man saw that his answers to Bracken's concerns were not being embraced, a piercing glint came into his eyes, and he rebuked his young friend for the mention of the Prince's name. "If you ever repeat that name again, we will no longer be friends." Those words sliced through Bracken's heart like a knife. Why had such a simple statement created such a reaction? What possible issues could Dalfang have with the one who had just delivered him from such torment? But then Bracken knew. They had two different allegiances now. His former mentor was still in the spell of the evil one and Bracken was free. Somehow he knew arguing would have little effect.

His reply had been firm but sad. "I'm sorry to hear that, Dalfang. I will always be grateful for your friendship, but I'm certain what I know now is true. I'm not at the mercy of a debate." After those words, there were a few polite but cold exchanges between them and then Bracken went on his way. The long road home had left him time to reflect, and he came to understand he had a new mission.

He thought of Ley, Chepa, Brish, and so many others. It might take months or even years to help them see the reality of what he knew to be true, but he was committed to see it happen even if it took the rest of his life.

He'd spent a brief time in Accad with some of them on his way home. He had shared with them his experience, and some had listened. But others doubted. He wasn't about to give up, but first he knew he had to make things right at home. He was soon on his way to Tizra with a promise to return shortly and continue the dialogue they'd all begun concerning his recent encounter with the Prince of Wonder.

Bracken shrugged off his coat and hugged his mother tightly in return. "Where's Father?"

"Oh, Bracken, he'll be so disappointed that he missed you. He's up at the orchard, but he should be back by evening. He'll be overjoyed to see that you're home."

"Yes, home, and it's good to be here," he said with a sigh. Deep inside, their hearts knit together. Tender fibers of affection touched once again.

Bracken had not been sure about this moment. On the long journey back from Zorek, he'd run the details of this encounter through his mind time after time. How would his mother respond? What would his father do? Would they still be defensive and angry over their son's determined choices? He'd played out their last encounter and knew that his anger had been wrong. He owed his parents so much, and the way he'd responded had been amiss. He didn't completely regret that he'd followed his instincts, for as destructive as some of the situations he'd gone through had been, he'd learned a lesson that he would never forget. One thing he was still trouble about though, was the way he'd broken with his parents. It had been harsh and abrupt.

Bracken's mother led him into the gathering room and motioned for him to sit down. Taking a seat across from him, she looked into his eyes with amazement and then began to cry. "I wasn't sure if I'd ever see you again, Bracken. Sometimes late at night, I'd wake up. I'd sit quietly in the dark and talk to the Prince of Wonder about you." Myrus brushed aside hot tears with her hands and then went on. "Somehow deep inside, though, he would always reassure me that he would work things out."

Bracken looked back at his mother and smiled warmly. "If you only knew how much he has. It will take a long time to explain all that's happened, but if you're patient with me, I'll try." Bracken folded his hands and looked down. "And I'll try to heal what happened between us."

Myrus stood up and walked over to her son. Taking his hand, she sat down beside him. "Oh, Bracken. All of us need to work on that. We understood so little of what you were going through."

Bracken felt a new sense of gratitude for this woman who had brought him into the world. "Thanks, Mother, I know I hurt you." As he spoke, his eyes filled with tears as well and then they hugged, a long and tender hug.

Bracken looked out the front window toward the distant mountains, and a fresh sense of exhilaration rushed through his soul. "I'm free now, Mother. The Prince of Wonder broke every chain that held my soul. But you must understand, it was so different from what I thought I knew about him."

Bracken paused for a moment before he spoke again. He knew he had to be careful. He respected his mother too much now to say the wrong thing. So with deliberate intent, he went on. "I know that I'm in no position to lecture you and you may not like what I'm about to say, but hear me out. Somehow your generation lost one of the key parts of what the Volume teaches. You and Father taught me only part of the story and left out the power."

"We know this now, Bracken," Myrus responded. "While you were gone, your grandparents visited us and we had a long discussion about exactly this issue."

"I remember Srenken mentioning that years ago many believed in this power but other things pushed aside this truth."

"Yes, but that very day we decided to embrace it again. Of course we would never leave the clear words of the Volume behind, we only are seeking to embrace the parts we'd left out."

"I know that very lack is part of the reason why my whole generation lost its respect for its record and why the edge-poets and others like them are rising in their influence. This is partly why so many of us went looking for answers. Sure, much of our quest was just selfish youthful craving, but some of it was a sincere search for the essence of that power no matter how poorly we misinterpreted it."

"Since you left Tizra we've seen many others your age on the same journey you've taken."

"I know, Mother, and I'm sure there are many waiting out there to lie to them."

"This troubles us deeply, Bracken. What will come of our planet? For us personally, our hope is certain, but will it all end with many going on to destruction?"

"Not if I can help it. Part of what happened to me at the end of my journey is a sense that I will see many find what I've found. I'm prepared to help them. I'm committed to this purpose."

Myrus looked back at him, her face beaming. "Good, and by the way, I think you'll have a companion in your mission." She motioned for Bracken to look through the rear window and out across the courtyard. In its center sat a low table and two chairs, their backs facing him. Spilling over the back of one was the familiar sight of Lisha's honey blond hair.

The feelings that suddenly flooded him were almost more than he could contain. A wave of excitement rose in his heart. The bitter memories of betrayal marched by only to be driven away by a new sense of understanding. All the lonely times, the hurt, the wondering, came back to him. He tried to push them away, but suddenly he didn't want to anymore. All in the same moment, he accepted and then forgave. He cared for this girl like no other. He always would.

"When she came back to Tizra, she was really broken," said Myrus. "Not just from losing you, but from her frustration in not finding answers. We've had some long talks, and I've been nursing her back with words of comfort from the Volume, cups of warm tea, and lots of gentle massages to her stressed-out shoulders."

Squeezing his mother's hand, he stood and began to walk toward the broad double doors that led to the courtyard. "Excuse me, Mother, but I've got to see her."

Myrus's eyes followed Bracken as he walked away. "I understand, Son ..." Her voice trailed off for a moment and then completed the thought as he stepped outside. "We've both been hoping you'd come home."

CHAPTER 72

TIZRA

PAR-MANTRIK (FIRST CHILL), 5512

As the courtyard doors closed behind Bracken with a soft click, Lisha remained unaware of Bracken's presence. In her lap lay the worn pages of Myrus's Volume. Bracken approached quietly and then gently placed his hands on her shoulders. "Oh thanks, Myrus, I've so enjoyed your massages. My shoulders really needed that." She reached her hand up, and as it touched his, she felt his scar. She drew in a deep breath, rubbed it again, and then quickly laid Myrus's Volume on the table beside her and jumped to her feet. "Bracken. What a surprise." Her face was radiant, more radiant than Bracken had ever seen it. Next, tears, but no words poured out of her.

What does she feel now? Bracken asked himself as he gazed on her lovely features. *We've both been hurt, rejected, forsaken. Could there still be something in her heart for me?* he wondered. The few anxious moments while they watched each other nearly broke Bracken's heart again. But now he didn't care. If it had to be broken a hundred times for Lisha, he'd let it. He would love her anyway. Lisha began to tremble as she slowly closed the short distance between them. She had taken only a few steps when she could no longer hold back. In surrender, she sank into his arms and wept on his shoulder.

"Bracken, Bracken, Bracken, I knew you'd come back." Lisha pulled back her head and looked into Bracken's eyes with her own dark brown ones. They kissed tenderly and then looked at one another again. Bracken gently held her face in his hands. Tears welled in his eyes and spilled down his face as well. "If you only knew how much I've missed you," she whispered.

Bracken smiled gently. "I missed you too." They held each other for a long time.

Later, Myrus brought them some chilled keptim. Sitting side by side in the lounge chairs, they sipped their drinks and talked. "It's been a long and lonely road without you, one I'd probably never come back from if it hadn't been for the Prince of Wonder." Bracken pointed toward the Volume resting on the nearby table. "I see you've begun to listen to Him. I do now too. I had an encounter with him that has changed everything for me. It's changed me."

"I knew you would, Bracken," said Lisha happily. "He's changed me as well. He gave me hope you'd come back." She thought of the past lonely days of waiting. "After I left you in Accad, I came back to Tizra. Those were empty and bitter times. Finally, I decided to visit your mother. She's the one who convinced me how much I needed the Prince of Wonder. Together we both talked to him. Right here in this garden in the quiet afternoons like this." Lisha pointed to the chairs they were sitting in and then to the green grass and shrubs beyond them.

"Myrus seems different. She's gone through a journey of her own. She's been nursing me back to health with her tea and massages but mostly with the promises of the Prince. I've chosen to believe them, Bracken, and I've given him my whole life. That's when he told me you'd come back, and just like he promised here you are. Overcome with joy, Lisha reached out her hand and gripped his tightly, rubbing her finger over his scar again. I guess our journey has left some wounds. Some we can't see, but wounds nonetheless. But I'm sure healing will come. Right now I'm so happy."

"You were right to believe him, Lisha. I know now he keeps his word," agreed Bracken. "I have him to thank that we're together again. This time, though, it will be right, it will be His way. We'll be joined in his sight, like my parents."

There, in the peaceful stillness of the courtyard, they stood and embraced again for a long time. Past memories and hurts washed away, and trust took their place. A miracle of love grew anew within them, the gift of Him who gives the miracle of love.

After a while, Myrus joined them. Together they talked quietly.

Ditten and Kempec came home later, and a warm spirit of reunion filled the house. All but Kreswen now sat in the gathering room, contentedly munching on fresh fruit that Myrus had set in their midst.

Bracken finished his fruit and then questioned his mother again about his father. "You say he's somewhere in the orchard?"

Myrus set down her piece of fruit and looked back at her son. "Yes. He goes there quite often lately."

"I can't wait any longer. I've got to go see him right now," said Bracken. "I wonder if he's still there?"

"If you leave now, I'm sure you'll reach him before he starts back."

Bracken hugged Lisha reassuringly and then stood to leave. "I'll be back by sunset."

CHAPTER 73

NEDI FOREST, TIZRA

PAR-MANTRIK (FIRST CHILL), 5512

Bracken ran through the high grass covering the gentle slope that led up toward the forest. Every blade seemed new and fresh. He watched this familiar world through new eyes. Eyes that not only saw the natural beauty of his surroundings but ones that now knew and appreciated the work of the unseen artist who created it. This designer had become his friend. Even though others had used the gift of this beauty to deceive and trap him, he knew it was good, one of the many gifts of wonder that the Prince had given to all.

Under the trees lingered the sweet scent he remembered so well. He breathed its aroma with thankfulness. Beyond, in the distance, he could see the family orchard growing bountifully.

As Bracken neared the trees, he saw Kreswen sitting restfully under one, a copy of the Volume in his lap. Bracken approached his father quietly. Kreswen's back was toward him, his attention captivated by a glen-singer sweetly warbling in the distance. Bracken felt a slight sense of uncertainty at the thought of confronting his father again. Would the conflict of the past still be lurking somewhere, even in this quiet setting? Could he really forgive his father, and would his father forgive him?

Bracken stood a mere yard from Kreswen. Gently he expelled a hopeful sigh and then spoke. "Father, I'm back."

Surprised, Kreswen turned, placing the Volume on the open bag beside him and then stood to his feet. He looked strong and erect, still his confident self. But something was different. A new gentleness that Bracken had never known in his father rested on his countenance. For a brief moment neither spoke, as if waiting for some inner signal. Obviously Kreswen was happy to see his son, yet he appeared to be hiding his reaction. But then, as if discarding a tattered garment, he shrugged aside his apprehensions and reached out to Bracken, firmly gripping his boy's shoulders in his strong hands. "I'm really glad to see you, Bracken."

Bracken looked back at his father, his face a mixture of joy and humility. "Something's happened to me," he admitted. "I was so angry with you. But that's changed. In fact, a lot of things are different. It's a process. I know that. It will take time, but I've embraced it. You see, the Prince of Wonder is changing my life. I know I behaved poorly. I know it must have hurt. Will you forgive me?"

Kreswen, at first, didn't seem to hear the words his son had uttered. "Things haven't been the same since you left. But I guess we've gotten along all right. I've taken good care of your rig. It should still be running well. I've cleaned the evac couplers at least three times ..." Kreswen seemed to be talking in an effort to hold back his real feelings, not really able to put them into words.

Perhaps he was still a little afraid of what would happen if the old conflict came back. He paused. A tiny tear formed at the edge of each eye. This time, he spoke softly, looking directly into his prodigal's eyes. "Forgive me too, Son. I guess I tried to make you live and believe something I didn't really believe myself."

Kreswen looked down for a moment, squinting the tears from his eyes. He pointed to the Volume lying on the open bag. Then he looked back at Bracken, a gentle smile on his lips. "That's all changed now for me, too. I've really come to know a view of the Volume that I'd skipped over many times. The promise of its power has truly touched me, and the Prince of Wonder and I have shared many happy hours here in this place."

Kreswen motioned toward the trees around him and then up at the sky, flecked with wispy clouds. "I know we can't see Him, but His presence is with me now all the time." He picked up a leaf, released it, and watched as it was carried away on the unseen breeze. "It's kind of like the wind. You can't see it, but its power can move you places you'd never imagine."

Kreswen's confession took Bracken completely by surprise. It was too good to believe. He felt his heart welded tightly in a warm bond with his father's again. It was something deeper than ever before. Now together they could share the miracle of what had happened to him back in Vonervyn. Bracken bubbled over with joy as he told Kreswen the story.

"Father, I've been to places that you could never imagine … horrible ones. I came close to death. I thought I was on the road to illumination. Instead I found myself at the very gates of destruction. The words of the one who wrote the Volume turned me back just in time."

Bracken sat down beside his father as the older motioned for the two of them to take a seat under the tree. "So many others, I'm afraid, won't make it. Silas is already gone. Dead. It's too late for him. Professor Lieter, Dalfang, Os, they all believe the lies."

Kreswen grimaced. "I know, Son, and it's only just the beginning. Many will go their way. The Prince of Wonder has told me. Our job now is to warn them before it's too late. I'm afraid our work is just beginning. The darkness is strong. In the web of its shimmering deception dwells a poison only the Prince of Wonder can cure. If we can turn them to him, they'll be safe. They need to love him. He's so wise and loves them so much. He's always cared."

"Yes, I have hope for them. I want to let them see what I've found. There is one who can break the chain of lies."

"You're right, Son, I believe many will listen and find the way out." As Kreswen continued his confident message, Bracken listened respectfully. Time had added wisdom to both of them. The sun thrust shafts of yellow through the trees, and daylight quickly scurried by. Before they knew it, twilight had settled over the orchard.

Finally, they stood and walked back toward home. Bracken saw something in his father he'd not seen before. He understood now the patience he had shown and the love he had for his son. "I'm glad I'm home, Father, home with you and Mother, with Lisha … but most of all with the Prince of Wonder. I've run long enough … wandered farther than I ever expected … put my values in the wrong things. I've found the real Gem now, the one I needed all along."

A deep peace settled between father and son as they walked out of the orchard and toward home. In the distance, as the sunlight faded, Ebbern's first moon appeared on the western horizon rising behind them.

APPENDIX

SEASONS OF EBBERN, THE PHASES OF ITS MOONS AND IT'S ROTATION

Each of Ebbern's moons goes through phases like Earth's moon, but because each is at a different orbit around Ebbern, each passes through its phase at a different time. This affects Ebbern's seasons, changing its weather patterns and shortening each seasonal period, therefore making its climate slightly different from ours. Here the original names for the seasons are given with the most direct possible meanings listed along with our corresponding months. Also Ebbern rotates east to west; therefore the run rises in the west and sets in the east.

Eight Seasons of Ebbern

1. Mantrik Bleak timeDecember–February
2. Simtesh Warm hope March
3. Par-Simtesh New season April–May
4. Yiane First warmth June
5. Lynrexs Mid-summer July–August
6. Tar-Lynrexs Late summer September
7. Par-Mantrik First chillOctober
8. Tar-Simtesh Last warmth November

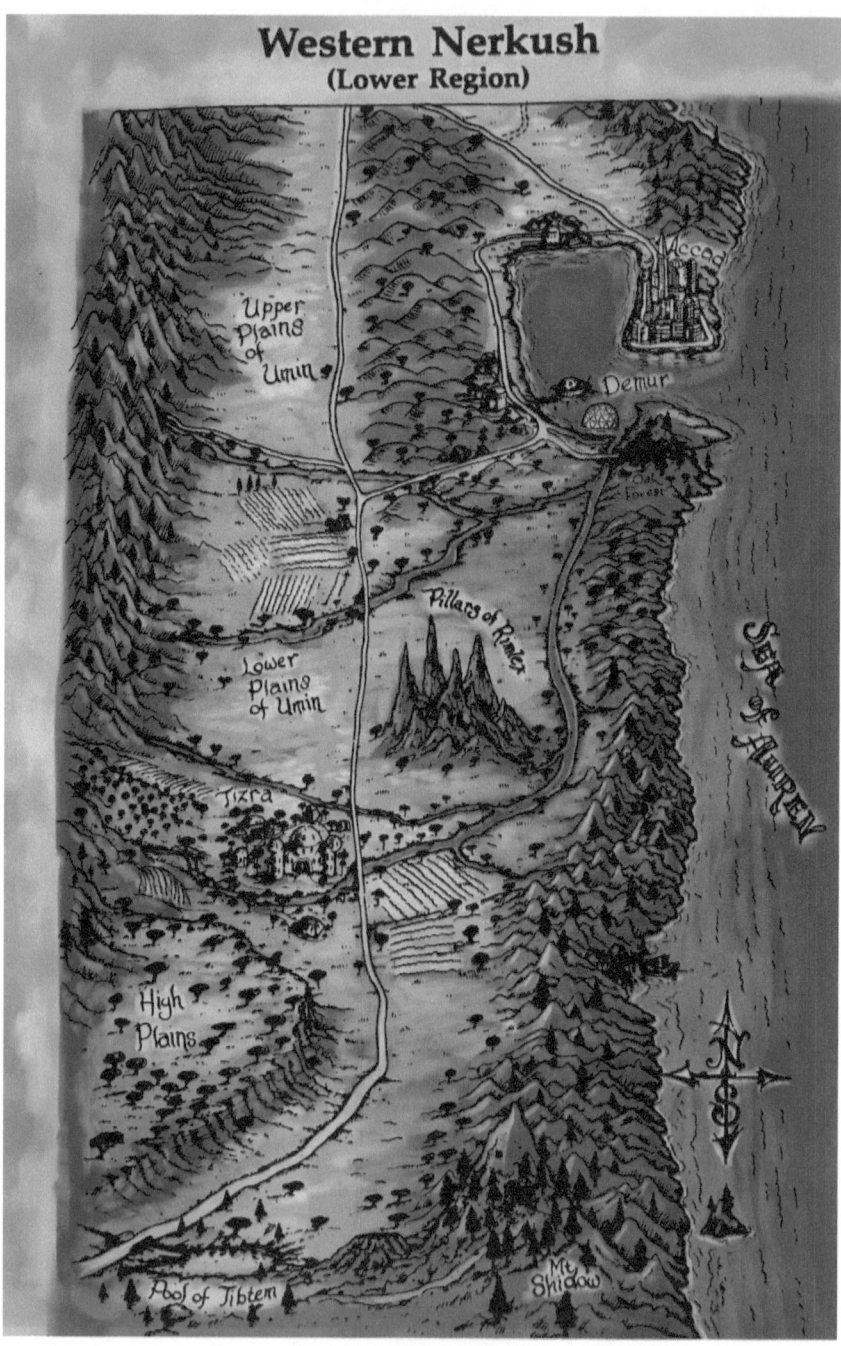

Western Nerkush
(Lower Region)

Pyrax Trooper

Trans-rig

Trans-max

Sky-flyer

Fire Pellet Igniter Tube

Energy Egg

GLOSSARY

Addanis: A former ally of Nerkush in the Great War.

Advanced Mind-Training Center: Located in Tizra. One of many 4th-level schools located around Nerkush for the training of youth in the final stages of their education.

Anindi Passage: One of several hidden gates that lead to Vonervyn, accessed only through the guidance of a gatekeeper who possesses a special invocation that will open it.

Astrogazer: A person who studies stars, planets, moons, and other celestial formations.

Atorma: A supposed state of true bliss that some foreign sages teach. They claim that once it's reached, one transcends all emotion.

Ayan, Chepa: The leader of the band known as Golden Flight; stam player.

Birmez: An ally of Nerkush formed in the Great War and still currently allied with it.

Brace Estim: a brilliant but eccentric astrogazer, who became the original touch point. He was the first to postulate his multiple-phase program. This theory claims that visitors from other stellar systems have come to Ebben with the distinct purpose of not only saving the planet from destruction but also setting in motion an evolutionary plan whereby selected "touch points" will gradually be transformed into an almost godlike state of being.

Bracken Maetrek: Son of Kreswen and Myrus Maetrek. Born and raised in Tizra, he was a musician and seeker who grew tired of the out-of-date ideas of his parents as well as the leaders of his country. In his quest for truth, he followed the teachings of the edge-poets and became fascinated with the new alternatives being offered to him by a countercultural community located in Accad.

Brazen Eagle: An herb shop, eatery, and beverage bar located in an older district of Accad. Owned by a man called Bryten.

Brek: A drink much like cocoa. Mostly served warm.

Brish Tremiley: An enchanting girl with unusual powers who Bracken meets in Vonervyn, formerly from Toplana.

Bryten: Owner of a quaint eatery and beverage bar known as the Brazen Eagle.

Catine: A student at Tizra's Advanced Mind-Training Center and a member of Frim Lieter's astrostudies class. She becomes a "touch point".

Cele-break: A vacation time.

Chepa Ayan: Founding member and leader of the band Golden Flight; stam player.

Cib Mingus: A miner, engineer, and leader of the sci-tec crew who was the first to discover the mine containing the mind-altering stones named after him.

Cleks: sandal-style hiking shoes.

Com-patch: A communication device worn on the wrist through which people can communicate through voice and text messages.

Comp-games: Games of competition held between students at mind-training centers.

Council: The administrative and law-enforcing branch of the ruling body of Nerkush. Also known as High Council and the Fathers.

Creeds of Adriyen: Oracular messages proclaimed by the sage Adriyen, believed by many to announce a new age of enlightenment sometime in Ebbern's future.

Crumpts: Small nut-like treats, best when slowly roasted.

Crysar Canyon: A deep gorge located southwest of Demur near Roon's home.

Cylac rotor: A device invented by Lish's father that helped increase the productivity of Nerkushian farmers' harvests.

Dalfang Niekolt: Guardian of the western gate to Vonervyn; a mysterious wizard.

Dec-i-cycle: A period of ten years.

Demur: An idyllic city on the Bay of Accad.

Dimishta, Son of Curaa: A member of the ancient Filanley race who lives in Vonervyn and acts as a guide for Bracken.

Disk People: Name given to a race of aliens that claims to have come from the Trion Star System; also called Trionites.

Ditten: The oldest of Bracken's two younger brothers.

Duvalla: Roon's female companion.

Ebbern: An earth-like planet circled by three moons located somewhere in the dimension of Markarovia.

Edge-poets: Minstrels who write and perform songs. Their lyrics often contain messages of protest against the current direction of the culture and politics of Accad. Many of them have been inspired by the ancient edge-poets.

Eier: Driver of Golden Flight's trans-max.

Elcari Amaura: A former teacher at Bracken's mind-training center with a prophetic gift.

Eliysim: An ally of Nerkush in the Great War.

Energy egg: A hand-size explosive that can be set to explode in different directions.

Eshtar Cosh: A gatekeeper for an alternate entrance to Vonervyn.

"Evek, Riynek, Scevek": Special chant used by Dalfang to activate Fenessence powers.

Fathers, The: Elected but narrow-minded rulers of Nerkush who enforce their will through trooper-like law enforcement teams called the Pirax.

Fayliss range: A mountain range located in western Nerkush.

Fear, The: A state of mind that leaves a person in a state of heightened paranoia. Often occurring in individuals who have taken frequent journeys under the influence of the Mingus gem.

Fenessence: A sort of sixth-sense enabling the user to move objects by telekinetic powers, read minds, and perform other supernormal feats.

Filanleys: An ancient race that are refugees from their former homeland and now inhabit Vonervyn.

Fire pellet: A deadly projectile that is fired from a fire pellet igniter tube.

Fire pellet igniter tube: A weapon that fires deadly projectiles known as fire pellets. The pellets are placed in the tube and then projected out by the breath of the person using the weapon. It's often used for its stealth-like characteristics. It's not loud as other weapons when fired. As the pellet passes through the tube, it is activated and becomes weaponized. It explodes on contact and can kill or badly burn its victim.

Fistra: A large bear-like creature

Fitzebran: An explorer and archeologist who first proposed the theory of Ebbern being inhabited by another race early in the planet's history. Fitzebran unearthed the ruins of Hidenglex and proposed that there had been another race on Ebbern in the distant past.

Flow register: A device in the drive of a trans-max or trans-rig that controls the flow of energy to the motion unit.

Flux-morph specialist: A transcendent being that uses a matter-shifter to manipulate matter to form various objects. He can also move these objects where he desires. Once he finishes, they always return to their original form. Some of these objects can be of great size.

Forest of Zorek: A deep and mysterious forest near the Sea of Auren north of Accad; home of Dalfang.

Form-links: A two-handled tool used for calibrating the flow register in the drive unit of a trans-max or trans-rig.

Frisq: A six-legged furry animal that lives wild in the desert of Raka.

Gatherings: Also know as Gathering Day. A weekly meeting where Nerkushians who follow the teachings of the Volume gather to discuss its principles and encourage one another.

Giismis: Four-legged blue furred animals. Several are kept in a pen by Brish Tremiley.

Global link: A system of communication using orbiting satellites that links all of Nerkush.

Golden Flight: One of the premier bands that are part of the Community.

Grawman: Gatekeeper at Wiscim's palace.

Gray Power: A country located on the other side of Ebbern. In the past, their armies have started two major global wars. Many speculated that their leader was a reemergence of the Night Ruler. Those theories were later disproven.

Greatfall: A time of great global economic hardship that occurred when Bracken's parents were in their early years.

Greenbrook: A small stream that flows from the eastern foothills and then through Tizra and on into the Plains of Umin, eventually ending in the Bay of Accad where it pours into the Sea of Auren.

Grey Winstad: Leader of the band Srinlyder.

Gumtas: Flat reddish round fruit found in the other dimensional world of Vonervyn.

Hall of the Fathers: A large building located in the City of Accad. It is where the leaders of Western Nerkush meet to make laws and rule the land.

Hi-Thought Corp: A group of sci-tec personnel who have become the arbiters of what is accepted as truth by Ebbern's High Council.

Hidenglex: Ancient ruin uncovered by Fitzebran.

Hiffornak: A transcendent being that inhabits the upper regions of the Mingus realm. He claims to be a representative of Naacan (and is therefore sometimes called the Naacanite), a peaceful and timeless world beyond the reality Bracken has experienced in the nation of Nerkush.

Hololight projectors: Projection devices that create individual holo-images of members of bands and other groups that perform at the Sea Sphere.

Hover-eyes: Remote-controlled spying drones used by the Pirax to monitor those they are investigating.

Hydel Rivinfine: Great-grandson of Bracken Maetrek.

Hyslevix: A low-ranking but powerful minion of the Shadow Czar.

IVEX – HITH – MINAE - TRAE TRAE – VO - REM: An incantation that when performed properly will open the gate of the passage to Vonervyn.

Jippen: The fruit (also jipe) of the jippen trees that grow abundantly in the lower Plains of Umin and Nedi Forest. Bears some of the sweetest fruit on Ebbern.

Jippen tree: A fruit tree that grows in the lower Plains of Umin near the City of Tizra. It's known for its sweet fruit and ripens during Par-Simtesh (New season).

Kempec: Bracken's youngest brother.

Klime: Lisha's closest girl friend.

Knasir Mountains: A high range of mountains in the other dimensional world of Vonervyn and home of the Palace of Wiscim.

Krem: A delightful beverage brewed to induce a slightly intoxicating effect.

Kutim Passage: An entrance to Vonervyn located in Eshtar Cosh's home in Toplana, a northern city of Nerkush.

Lake Tibtem: A lake near Mt. Shidow known for its clear waters; also known as The Pool of Tibtem.

Ley Os: One of a group of self-appointed and charismatic leaders of the Community. His influence comes from the fact that he is a peddler of the Mingus stones and a promoter of their power to transform the society of Nerkush. He has developed a following within the Community and is a teacher and guide to Bracken, Golden Flight, and others like them.

Lisha Fleam: Bracken's girlfriend and resident of Tizra.

Lower Throne Room: One of the many places where the Shadow Czar holds court. Located beneath the surface of Ebbern.

Luciene: An adjunct of Wiscim who interviews potential candidates for future positions in Vonervyn.

Lynrexs: Know as Mid-summer; similar to July–August.

Lyslaink: Flux-morph specialist.

Magni-scope: A bi-focal telescope.

Mantrik: Known as Bleak time; very similar to the months of December through February on Earth.

Matam: A large dark-feathered nocturnal bird.

Matter-shifter: A device used by flux-morph specialists to transform matter into different objects.

Michess: A guardian and watcher is a powerful trans-dimensional being that is also a servant of the Prince of Wonder.

Mind-Training Center: A school for young people ages 14–18.

Mingus dimension: A mysterious and multi-level world that is reached through the use of powerful stones known as the Mingus gems.

Mingus gem: (also Mingus stone, the gem, the stone): A stone that contains mysterious powers that, once swallowed, carries the user into higher dimensions both psychically and sometimes physically. The Mingus stones are found underneath Mt. Shidow. They were originally discovered by Cib Mingus, a scientist, researcher, and miner who led the sci-tec team that discovered the stones. He was the first to understand their mysterious powers.

Mingus mine: Named for Cib Mingus, leader of the sci-tec team that discovered the Mingus stones. Its location near Mt. Shidow and the Pool of Tibtem in southern Nerkush has remained hidden since the sci-tecs, under the direction of the Fathers, sealed the mine. Only a few of the maps to the mine remain, and those are closely guarded. But some have been released and are in the possession of stone peddlers like Ley Os.

Motion cloak: A garment with the power to allow its wearer to navigate rapidly to various places around Ebbern both horizontally and vertically.

Motion Unit: Part of the power-drive system for trans vehicles.

Multiple-phase program: A theory postulated by Brace Estim. It asserts that visitors from other stellar systems have come to Ebben with the distinct purpose of not only saving the planet from destruction but also setting in motion an evolutionary plan whereby selected "touch points" will gradually be transformed into a near godlike state.

Mydethees: A group of philosophers and healers who claim to have developed a therapy for calming nerves. They also claim to have the ability similar to Fenessence that allows them to channel messages from those who have died.

Naavin Shor: Musician; member of Golden Flight.

Nedi Forest: A forest near Tizra where Bracken and Kreswen spend many hours together during Bracken's childhood.

Nev Broc: Musician; member of Golden Flight.

Night Ruler: A powerful transient being who appeared mysteriously in past ages of Ebbern's history promising peace and prosperity for the planet. He was later exposed to be a being of incredible deception and evil who sought to enslave all those who opposed him.

Octi-orges: A monstrous creation that is half organic and half mechanical that is created by a flux-specialist to terrorize the inhabitants of Vonervyn.

Ogresen: A group of immigrants from the far western regions of Ebbern who brought their lifestyle and philosophy to Nerkush in past times. Several of the edge-poets were influenced by them.

old chants of the Ogresen

Omni-sensor: An electronic device that can detect the presence of electronic spying devices.

Par-Mantrik: Known as First chill; a time of year resembling Earth's October.

Par-Simtesh: Known as New season; very similar to our April–May months on Earth.

Pillars of Rimlex: Spire-like rock formations located in the southwestern Plains of Umin.

Pirax: The armored, trooper-like law enforcement arm of the Fathers.

Plains of Umin, The: A farming area in the fertile inland valleys of Western Nerkush.

Pool of Tibtem: A lake near Mt. Shidow that was formed in a volcanic crater.

Prince of Wonder: A transcendent and wise being who manifested himself in the form of a lowly tradesman in Ebbern's history and taught truth with a power and kindness never before seen on Ebbern. He imbued his followers with power over evil forces through the invoking of his name. But strangely, he himself seemed to be overcome by his enemies and died a tragic and brutal death by agents of the Shadow Czar. But his teachings are still held in honor, and many of the people of the Gathering seek to emulate his life. Some even believe he will appear again to bring a reign of peace to all of Ebbern.

Raka or Valley of Raka: A desolate, desert-like region of Nerkush located in the upper western part of the country. It is dominated by a farm owned by Terresh Shad.

'Rax: Shortened form and common nickname for the Pirax.

Ribbon Crags: Rugged mountains located in a desert region in western Nerkush near where the Destroyer Weapon was tested.

Rollion: A monster of a man who is the Foreman at Terresh Shad's farm.

Roon: Naavin's brother. A wealthy fan of Golden Flight and the owner of an estate in Oak Forest where the band sometimes stays.

Sapreism: A current ally of Nerkush, also was allied with Nerkush during the Great War.

Scis: abbreviated name for sci-tec team.

Sci-wizards: An elite group of sci-tec personnel that developed the World Destroyer Weapon and other weapons of mass destruction.

Sea of Auren: A large ocean on the western shores of Nerkush.

Sea Sphere: Floating dance hall on the Bay of Accad near the City of Demur. A concert center for many bands like Golden Flight, whose music has generated anthems for the Community.

Search-cred: Search warrant.

Semex: Hideous servants of the Shadow Czar. Some of the basest creatures of his forces, which inhabit some of the lowest regions of Shadow Czar's underworld.

Shadow Czar: An evil trans-dimensional being of great power who ultimately desires to enslave and torture all the inhabitants of Ebbern.

Shadow watcher: A transdimentional being and member of the Shadow Czar's army of servants. He is assigned to monitor, deceive, torment, and ultimate destroy those he's targeting.

Shiferen tree: A broad tree with wide strong roots.

Shimmer-gate: An inter-dimensional portal that exists in the atmosphere above Ebbern. Named because of the sheen given off when opened.

Shurar: A great city that existed in Ebbern's Fourth Age that served as the seat of the First Council.

Silas Yitha: Bracken's childhood friend, classmate, teammate, resident of Tizra, and fellow seeker. He explores the wonders of the Mingus realm with Bracken.

Simtesh: Known as Warm hope; a season where the cold of winter starts to fade corresponding to the month of March on Earth.

Sky flyers: Fast-moving aerial transportation craft capable of hovering. Used by the Pirax.

Sphere-nexus: One of the commerce portals available through the global link.

Sphere-tracker: An orbiting satellite used by the Pirax for spying.

Srenken: Bracken's grandfather, who operates a small farm on the outskirts of Tizra.

Stam: A guitar-like instrument with seven strings.

Strata-place: A nexus of several intersecting dimensional corridors.

Strieme: A powerful officer in the Shadow Czar's army of minions.

Swaim: A forest animal much like a squirrel but slightly larger.

Tar-Lynrexs: Known as Late summer, it's a time when the sea currents begin to cool the air on the coast and valleys; much like our September on Earth.

Tar-Simtesh: Known as Last warmth; the last days before the cold of Bleak time sets in. Similar to our November on Earth.

Terresh Shad: The owner of a vinweok farm in the Valley of Raka.

Theema: A form of mental torture that the Shadow Czar's forces inflict on those they deceive. These shadow beings experience great pleasure through the torment they dispense on their quarry.

Touch point: A person who has gone through a mind-altering process that allows them to become representatives and oracles for the Disk People.

Trans-max: A large multi-passenger ground transportation vehicle.

Trans-rig: A four-to-six passenger ground transportation vehicle.

Trion Star System: A small but relatively nearby constellation covered by a cosmic cloud that contains about 700 stars; located near the Starry Pitcher.

Tristixsen Pythian: Female oracle who usually is accompanied by her female companions, Simish and Yssmey.

Vault of Records: A bunker where the High Council keeps documents and secrets they want to keep from the general public.

Vid-tel: A popular entertainment device in Nerkush.

Vinweok: A lumbering, fatty beast prized for its delicious meat; raised by farmers like Terresh Shad.

Voitqi: A tasty and intoxicating beverage served by many in Vonervyn.

Volume, The: An ancient book that contains the teachings of the Prince of Wonder and other ancient sages.

Vonervyn: An enchanting world existing in another dimension. It is entered by speaking a special chant at its gates. Vonervyn's entrances are inter-dimensional portals hidden throughout Nerkush and watched over by guardians like Dalfang.

Welcome leaf: A bracelet-like wristband made of a special leaf found in Vonervyn that is given to new arrivals.

Wiscim: A highly revered and mysterious wise being who lives in a secluded palace high in the mountains of Vonervyn; he is rumored to be of great wisdom and authority.

Wogs: Small reptilian water creatures found in the streams and lakes around Tizra.

World Destroyer Weapon: A weapon of mass destruction originally developed by a Nerkushian scientist but now possessed by several countries on Ebbern.

Yiane: Known as First warmth; It corresponds to our Earth month of June.

Yono: A student in Professor Frim Lieter's astrostudies class at the Advanced Mind-Training Center.

Ysinta: Bracken's grandmother; married to Srenken.

Zyphon level: One of the higher regions and a connecting spot between dimensions located in the Mingus realm.

www.ingramcontent.com/pod-product-compliance
Lightning Source LLC
Chambersburg PA
CBHW020247030726
47499CB00001B/101